DAYS
OF
ABSENCE

Also by Alun Richards

Novels
THE ELEPHANT YOU GAVE ME
THE HOME PATCH
A WOMAN OF EXPERIENCE
HOME TO AN EMPTY HOUSE
ENNAL'S POINT
BARQUE WHISPER

Short Story Collections
DAI COUNTRY
THE FORMER MISS MERTHYR TYDFIL

History
A TOUCH OF GLORY (100 YEARS OF WELSH RUGBY)

Biography
CARWYN — A PERSONAL MEMOIR

As Editor
THE PENGUIN BOOK OF WELSH SHORT STORIES
THE PENGUIN BOOK OF SEA STORIES
AGAINST THE WAVES (SEA STORIES)

Plays
THE BIG BREAKER
THE VICTUALLERS' BALL
THE SNOWDROPPER
THE HORIZONTAL LIFE

Television Plays
GOING LIKE A FOX
O CAPTAIN, MY CAPTAIN
NOTHING TO PAY
HEAR THE TIGER, SEE THE BAY
THE HOT POTATO BOYS
READY FOR THE GLORY
TAFFY CAME TO MY HOUSE
WHO STEALS MY NAME
ALBINOS IN BLACK
THE STRAIGHT AND NARROW
THE PRINCELY GIFT
HARRY LIFTERS

Television Adaptations
THE SCHOOLMASTER (Simenon)
VESSEL OF WRATH (W. Somerset Maugham)
LOVE AND MR LEWISHAM (H. G. Wells)

Television Series
ENNAL'S POINT

ALUN RICHARDS

DAYS

OF
ABSENCE

AUTOBIOGRAPHY
(1929–55)

MICHAEL JOSEPH

LONDON

First published in Great Britain by Michael Joseph Ltd
27 Wrights Lane, Kensington, London W8

© Alun Richards 1986

British Library Cataloguing in Publication Data

Richards, Alun
Days of absence: autobiography (1929–55).
1. Richards, Alun—Biography 2. Authors, Welsh
—20th century—Biography
I. Title
828'.91409   PR6068.I244Z/
ISBN 0–7181–2703–X

Typeset by Wilmaset, Birkenhead, Wirral
Printed in Great Britain by
Billings & Sons Ltd Worcester

for Helen

Who do I fear most?
Those who do not know me
And who speak evil of me.

Plato

List of Illustrations

Acknowledgements

To a professional writer, even a first volume of autobiography is in some ways the beginning of the end. Now is the last chance to put the record straight, sometimes to regret that fact was not better presented as fiction. In my case, the end was very nearly in the beginning as this memoir shows and, in recording it, I am mindful of many debts – to those who kept me alive, no less than to those who kept me sane and whole. These are all named, but others I have not mentioned by their real names for fear of attributing to them guilt by association or, in the case of those who offended me, an apprehension that they might even now rise up and strike once more. (I was never blameless.) Above all, this book is for my wife – an overdue bill of lading, as it were, before our particular voyage commenced.

I would also like to acknowledge an award from the Welsh Arts Council which enabled me to complete this volume.

A.R.

ONE

As a boy I was a creature of disguises, a spy in another man's land. There were facts about myself which I could not bear to face and in order to avoid doing so, I began, at an early age, to spend a good deal of my day in reverie, slipping off into daydreams which provided another world where I would not be found out. My secret, the bitter truth about myself, was never told to me in a single sentence, but rather descended like a cloud which followed me over the years of my childhood, and when I finally realised what it was, it was as if bits and pieces of information at last came awkwardly together like the separate pieces of an old and worn jigsaw. It did not happen suddenly or dramatically, but slowly settled on my conscious-ness, imprinting itself, it seemed then, for ever. I was marked. I was not wanted. I was a nuisance. I was not like other boys. I did not have a father. It was better that I did not ask questions – they were painful to others – but there, those were the bones of it, my mark was that of the fatherless child.

If one is not careful, one speaks now in generalities. Sentences arrive as bland as fudge, all insidious. One tragedy is soon dwarfed by another. Even a one-legged man can be comforted by the sight of those without hands. But generali-ties have little effect on the wart at the end of your own nose. In my five-year-old mind, it was imperative that I should not ask questions. Questions would upset. Best to say nothing. Talk about something else. Lie low.

I don't think anybody actually briefed me with those precise commands but still, I knew them, and followed them dutifully until my adolescence. I learned at an early age to watch, to gauge a mood, to know when it was time for me to speak. I also learned to listen, to eavesdrop, gathering what bits and pieces of information I could. I listened from corners, behind doors, on tramcars, to hushed voices drifting out of the vestry after chapel, to the gossip of neighbours talking in the street. If two people talking on a corner greeted me, I would reply politely, then creep back to hear what they might say when I had gone.

'Whose boy is that?'

'Oh? . . .' This with a marked exclamation of interest, sometimes a clucking 'Pity for him!' in a very Welsh way.

There were other sentences, words:

'A waster, a thorough waster.'

'An animal in his drink.'

'Poor dab.'

This was me, I knew, the dab. The other was Him, my ever-to-be-absent father.

I kept these phrases to me, hugging them in the secret place. I had other problems. You see, I was marked in another way too. I had a birthmark that stretched for almost two inches down the right side of my cheek, an ugly brown thing in the shape of an inverted exclamation mark. A full sideboard was how the barber diplomatically described it, bleeding me every time he ran the clippers over it. To me, it was another punishment for something I had not done. And there was trouble coming, I knew. Soon I was to be known by my enemies as Moley.

Until I went to school, I did not have any enemies that I knew about and, but for the mark upon me, I was cradled in an affluence that was later to make me feel deeply ashamed. In 1934 we had a lavatory and a bath inside the house. I had two pairs of shoes, one for best, as well as for the day. When we sat down for meals, there was a tablecloth on the table, knives and forks, doilies on Sundays, a separate spoon for the jam. The jam pot was not allowed. We could afford crumbs for the birds and we did not soak the tea leaves over and over again. Tramps and vagrants put a mark on the gatepost to indicate that this was a good place to call. We could always afford a crust.

Outside in the back yard, there was a brick extension built under a stable which housed my grandfather's horse. This was called the wash-house and it had a door that would bolt from the inside, a fireplace, and a large galvanised tub in which I would sit, paddling my way down the rivers of my dreams while the horse fretted in its stable above. If the driver forgot to clean the stable, sometimes the drains would become blocked and the smell of warm horse piss would come pungently down from above and then I would be up against it, paddling away with a 'kerchief over my nose. There was also a rickety glass shelter leading from the kitchen door, and when it rained the rain would thunder upon it, drumming down, drips forming on the wooden underside so that when a shower was over, the drips went on long afterwards, staccato reminders of what had come before. I used to listen to them in the silence of my bedroom, or crouched in the tub, my arms resting on the long-handled appliance used to baste the washing. I liked the rain and the sound of water because they were part of my escape. In my mind, I have been an escaper all my life and I have never been happier than when near the sea, if not actually afloat.

Another of my hiding places was a space under the Welsh dresser in the kitchen where there was room to curl up and you could see the light of the fire reflected in a large brass-topped hob that was kept beside the fireplace and on whose cool smooth surface I would rest my forehead if I had a cold. There was also a forest of brass on the mantelpiece, a regimental file of candlesticks and two large brass shellcases brought home from France after the first war and in which my grandmother kept Bills Paid and Bills Unpaid, and since they were curved and highly polished, you could sometimes see people's faces in them when they talked. From my hiding place, I could peer through the fringes of the tablecloth into a world of fire and brass and when I was on my own, I sometimes inspected my own face in the shell case. Unlike a mirror, you could manoeuvre it so that your mole did not show.

It was in this hiding place that I heard my grandmother say that I was filthy when she got me, three days after I was born, brought by car in a basket because they did not have a cradle and I hardly had a stitch to put on. I was, as it happened, a clean little boy and I can remember looking at my hands and fingernails when she said it. Photographs of this period survive

3

but they have nauseated me ever since. There is no indication on my face of what I felt at any time. I was a little podge posing for the photographer, tubby in red woollen jersey and short grey flannel trousers with properly pulled-up stockings held in position by elastic garters bought in the Bon Ton, a draper's shop whose owners came to our chapel. My round solemn face is turned to hide my birthmark and I look the kind of plump little boy who sits unobtrusively in the presence of adults, is well-behaved, does not ask for second helpings or fidget, and does not get on with other boys. I do not recognise myself when I look at it, nor do I recognise my grandmother or mother in other photographs in the sense of what they meant to me. Perhaps it is that we are all creatures of disguises. At any given time, the turmoil of feelings is deeply buried and has no adequate visible expression.

Certainly, my grandmother did not realise how much I knew about myself because of my espionage work and when I think of her in those years, it is usually in the absence of my mother whose difficulties began with her separation from my father three days after I was born. While I am inclined to think now of my arrival as being catastrophic, then I had no inkling. All I knew was that my mother was young and attractive, and so 'smart', people said, 'she'd look wonderful in a dishcloth!' But she was frequently away from home and so the person to whom I was closest, who really brought me up, was my grandmother. My grandfather was still alive in my fifth year and I remember him clearly but it was to my grandmother's apron strings that I was firmly attached, and in many ways I never left them completely since it is her face I remember and her voice I hear whenever I tread the paths to home.

In my fifth year there was a good deal of quarrelling between my mother and my grandmother and very often there would be voices raised and sometimes my mother would run in tears from the table, occasionally out of the house itself; and my grandfather, if present, would say, 'Leave it, mother. Leave it.' But there were some things my grandmother could not leave alone. If the quarrelling was fierce, I would start to cry and that might bring a lull but usually this was followed by more accusations and then I would slip into one of my hiding places and listen to the slamming of doors which at last

4

marked the end of the raised voices. Now I can look back and offer all sorts of explanations of that part of our lives, but then they eluded me and I did, I suppose, what any cub in its lair would do – draw closer to the loudest voice and the strongest figure, and since this was my grandmother's it meant, I see now, that I was drawn irrevocably from my mother's side to my grandmother's lap. My mother, I soon found out, could not cope with things. That she was not allowed to, took me thirty years to realise, but I could do nothing then and the only power I had was as a mute figure who was sometimes bundled between them, once stolen by an uncle to be paraded for an afternoon at a horseshow, then put back in the box so to speak. When my mother went away to work, or was away from home, I watched her go with a feeling of relief. With my grandmother I was comfy. In that warm embrace, all happiness was contained, and if I was separated from the true umbilical cord, it did not matter then. Retreating to the safe houses of my imagination while the quarrelling went on, I would re-emerge to be cosseted and spoiled for a time – a time for confidences when it was that I slowly began to realise, not so much who I was or where I was from, but the facts about my grandmother's life and the town into which I had arrived. In those early years, it was as if I had skipped not one generation but two, for my grandmother was nearly sixty then, had brought up a family of five children and I had come to be the sixth and last, and was moreover, a trapped audience compelled to listen when I was not in hiding.

Although I say that I was relieved when my mother was not home and the quarrelling stopped, matters did not end there and I had, by the age of five, given at least one sign of the mark that was upon me. For once, after a stormy episode when my mother had left abruptly, I slipped secretly out of the house upon a peculiar quest. I cannot be sure exactly what the argument was about, for this time I was banished from the table and they made sure I was upstairs before they resumed it, but I had caught one phrase, 'You're not seeing him again?' And then, one of my grandmother's favourites: 'After *everything* that's happened?'

Somehow I seemed to know that 'everything that's happened' referred to me and the Him that I was soon to banish from my mind, my father. All this I kept to myself, but later I slipped out of the house alone and unseen, drawn for the first time to search for some explanation of the mystery about myself. Why did I not have a father? If he was being seen again, where was he? Perhaps he had a birthmark too, and if he had, could he confirm or deny the gypsy's advice that if I spat upon it with fresh spittle as soon as I awoke, it would go away of its own accord? I had, as my grandmother said, 'spat myself out' since the gypsy told us, but not one ugly hair had disappeared and the lump remained livid and immobile. So I had certain pointed questions to ask.

I was also in some confusion about my mother. She was slim and elegant whereas I had a deep-rooted conviction from local observation that mothers were fat. They were to be seen pinafored and aproned, arms akimbo, half-bathed in suds as they scrubbed steps, hair awry, with laddered stockings and worn slippers, when they were not haranguing tradesmen and not having any nonsense. My mother, as my grandmother had to admit, always looked as if she'd stepped out of a bandbox and there was little opportunity for her to do much at home since my grandmother was a compulsive worker – one of those tireless women who could not bear to let anyone do anything she could do herself, although often at the same time complaining that she had to do too much. She had the penny and the bun, as well as the privilege of complaint which was one of her greatest and most eloquent joys. Like the Greeks, the Welsh enjoy their woes and they nourish them in abundance, often preferring remembering to living. My grandmother, like myself, was never quite free of guilt, even for the smallest of tasks left undone. Even in her seventieth year, when I once returned unexpectedly to find her – equally unexpectedly – sitting down with a woman's magazine, she got quickly and guiltily to her feet and said, 'I've only just sat down this minute!' and then proceeded hotfoot to the coal shed to hammer a sizeable lump of best anthracite before I could stop her. Even in my 'teens with my school colours for rugby football, I was not entirely to be trusted with a coal hammer.

But at five it was all a conundrum. So I felt myself impelled to search. I did not say, 'I am going to look for my father', but yet, one grey day, I knew I was going about that forbidden

6

task and so put on an old pair of summer sandals which I had ceased to wear because it was autumn and the leaves were sticking to the roads – I had an intuition that I might have to be fleet of foot. In full consciousness of wrong-doing, I tiptoed downstairs, avoided the creaking telltale loose board on the landing and flattened myself against the wall of the little passage, avoiding the beady glass eye of the mounted fox which my grandmother's brother had caught some years before he was killed in France. (The brush was on top of a wardrobe upstairs but I was not allowed to play with it because it had some kind of mange and she was always on the point of throwing it out, but never got around to it. Like me, she was a great hoarder.)

Down the stairs I went, along the passage where there was a grandfather clock whose ticking pendulum punctuated my days and nights, past the closed door of the front room which was not used in the week unless there were special visitors and which contained such treasures as an ostrich egg in a Swansea china bowl, two mounted Florida butterflies – gifts from an uncle in Philadelphia – all the coronation mugs since King Edward and Queen Alexandra, and a three-corner china cupboard over which war was later to be declared and litigation threatened. There were also hidden photographs of my grandmother's brothers, including an Uncle Jack who, robbed and rolled on the waterfront at Sydney, enlisted with the Anzacs, was wounded in Gallipoli and thereafter returned home to drink himself into such a state that he would be put in the wash-house – my wash-house! – to sober up before being allowed to make his way to his own home. I was already into these treasures and a great dipper into drawers and cupboards, searching for some clue to my father, but now I went to the latch of the front door. Here I paused, listening to that clock ticking. Then I looked at the door whose upper part was partially leaded with coloured glass panes and so composed that you could only see the shape of whoever was outside but could not recognise them, an affectation that was brought back to conformity by a brass strip along the sanded doorstep below which was scrubbed and polished every day. Now I put my fingers up and gripped the knob of the lock through the sleeve of my jersey, just managed to open it, the door swinging inwards. I know I did not close it since this was evidence later used against me, but while it opened easily enough, it was a heavy door and clunked noisily when closed, and I did not risk that. Then I was off, hurtling down the step past the postage stamp of a lawn, not using our gate but stepping over next-door's wall and through their gateway where the gate was never shut, and then I was gone – out on to the hill and the other world that was waiting for me. Like Ali Baba, I knew where to look for strangers. You went to the market. They had everything there, and what is more, the local tradesmen, of whom my grandfather was one, did not like the itinerant marketeers. They paid no local rates and did not contribute materially to the town. They were hobbledehoys, my grand-mother said, riffraff all, and what is more, respectable people did not go there, or at least, did not like to be seen going there – only the Rodneys from the Rhondda Valley.

Although my grandmother would never admit to it, we actually lived on the extreme tip of the Rhondda Valley as our house, one of two built back-to-back, was sunk into the side of the hill where the valley narrowed and the River Rhondda met the River Taff to form the confluence town of Pontypridd which had grown around the site of an old fording place. That Pontypridd was an old market place did not seem to occur to my grandmother as she and her family had lived and farmed there for years before the coal rush and she had an antipathy to change and a feeling of belonging which gave her a sense of ownership so aristocratic that she made few tentative state-ments at any time. Instead she pronounced, granted audi-ences, expounded, as if it were part of her heritage to do so. She had that confidence in the self which very few people have, an assurance that comes from land and place, a sense of belonging which is essentially the inheritance of country people.

The market place lay some way off, however, and when I left the house surreptitiously by next door's gate, I stepped first of all on to a steeply inclining hill road which bisected a much grander road a few yards away. This I came to know as the kingdom of Tyfica (Tee-Vicar). It should never have been called a road at all as it was more like an avenue, rich in chestnut trees and copper beeches where grand houses, some

8

detached and most removed from the road, lay in splendour above the uneven roofs of the smoky old town below. Here, it was said, lived the people who mattered, who *were* Pontypridd. I knew some of them and later in life marvelled at the splendour of swing chairs in the garden by the imitation wooden pagoda and the studied elegance of creamy long-legged women who smoked Craven 'A' through long enamelled cigarette holders and spoke casually of London as 'Town'. Yet the extraordinary fact of our environment was that a mere hundred yards further up the hill where the mountain rose and the slope steepened, a green patch gave way to a crescent of back-to-back terraced houses with unpaved roads, cobbled paths near a little shop which sold lump chalk for the colliers to mark their trams underground. On sunny days, a bearded old woman half-clad in sacks often sat outside the shop on an orange box. She wore a man's cloth cap, chewed shag tobacco and spat copiously when she was not clacking and muttering to herself. All of us, as it happened, faced the opposite side of the valley where there was a leaden slug of a coal tip and the inescapable metal debris and sharp contours of a mining valley; but up above the tip and the pit wheel, the larger contour of the mountain reached up to the sky. At night, the lights of the terraces stretched out endlessly like a necklace of frail cobwebs circling the town, finally going out street by street as the last footfalls of the drunks and shiftmen echoed up the hill and only the darkest shapes were visible – a wall, a tree, the slim spire of the town clock – all standing as still as grass. For me, it had then, as now, a kind of ghostly beauty and I never thought of it as a ravaged industrial terrain because it was always a place of warm associations.

But I put my back to it all and went on down the hill, past the chapel which we did not attend although it was the nearest, past the corn stores – a haunted house with fat lodger rats – then, avoiding the greasy river, ducked up behind the cells of the police station whose frosted glass and bars sealed them off in entirety and hurried on towards the Arcade which had an Inspector with his official title engraved on his peaked cap. A small, short, hangdog, bloodshot-eyed man, he had been, my grandmother said, a full-blooded Oyez town crier but had come down in the world. I was to offend him later as, following the family tradition, I tried to drive a bowley, a metal hoop, through the Arcade with a stick but was prevented and the bowley was confiscated. I had heard my grandmother describe one of my Uncle Jack's exploits: a horseman of repute, he had once ridden a horse through the Arcade in a wild moment, a feat of some daring since it opened out quite near to the police station. The event was related, not with pride but as evidence of his condition at any given time. And there had been other wild spirits in our family, as I was to discover with the story of yet another uncle – obsessed by tradition – who drove a borrowed sports car through the Arcade making a smart exit past the Police Station. The Arcade, like the market, was always crowded, and it was here that I began to study faces as I always did. For obvious reasons, I had a premonition that my father's face would be flushed and angry and his smell would be ripe with hops, that beery Saturday night smell which came from the shabby cloth-capped men who lined the street corners, endless files of them mufflered and despairing – their hopeless waiting reflected in their faces and in the muttering silence that would become known to me as I wandered amongst them later, still searching as I collected cigarette cards. There were areas of the town where men, always men, congregated in these groups of unemployed, and near my grandfather's shop was the Labour Exchange with more endless queues, so many of them that the solicitors' offices put vicious metal spikes on their window sills to prevent the unemployed sitting down.

But the Arcade was always busy, dog-watched by the Inspector who always had a trowel and sandbox on hand in case nature intruded. Here there were bread and cake and sweet shops, school outfitters with Welsh woollen vests and long combinations lumped beside the cap of dreams which indicated admission to the county school and on whose crest the town's one-span bridge was etched like a small rainbow. I was heading for rougher territory, to the opening of the square where the stallholders had their pitches in the open, and no matter what was being sold – china, mousetraps, goldfish, carpet cleaners or patent medicines – they always seemed to be sold at the top of someone's voice, and at the last minute.

Articles were not so much sold as knocked down to you, cheap at the price, for this was Bargain Country.

I could not at first get near the open stalls and the stallholders I particularly wanted to inspect, so I made my way into the covered market where there was an air of respectability. Here the fruit stalls gave way to the carpet stalls where mats and rugs were piled to the roof. Nearby were religious books, home-made sweets and toffee, and the knick-knack stalls. Finally I arrived at the very centre of this universe where the ripe and homely smell of faggots and mushy peas came from the kitchen of the market café. There were seldom any young men there, I was to find, only the old tired men with wheezing coughs and ashen, blue-pitted, coal-scarred faces, the shape of their skulls sometimes standing clearly out of their skin; men who asked for cough medicines, wore strips of red flannel 'for the chest' and who sometimes sat alone, silently staring into space. I somehow always associated this part of the market with the old and hurried away from it, not realising that this was the only place where you could sit down and those who came here often did so because they had to, ordering only one cup of tea and receiving 'looks' if they stayed too long.

There were all kinds of faces in the market, but this day I studied the men. I was looking for a face like mine, for a mark like mine, but I had no idea how I would look at an advanced age so it was the birthmark I concentrated upon and, since I had seen no photographs of my father (nor have I ever done) I had in mind a kind of stereotype of evil – there is no other word – and somehow this was concentrated upon the mouth. It was half-grinning and half-snarling, the leer of a gargoyle, and the head went savagely back as did the head of a man I had seen once beating a stubborn horse. So I kept my distance from those I examined, and here began the first of a procession of melodramatic incidents in my life – real incidents which defy the art of ordered narrative and often send reason scudding out of the window like frail clouds blown by the winds of reality, my reality, the ever-present sense of things as they are, or seem to me.

I kept my distance from the figures that I passed but watched just the same. Perhaps the first inkling came when I heard his voice. I had gone through one end of the covered market and out the other, past the fish stalls with their tubs of Welsh cockles, the great marble slabs of fish and into the hall of china where the crowds did not gather until closing time because the knocking down of the knock-down prices did not begin until later – and out into the surging crowds again. I heard the voice before I saw the man. It was hoarse and gravelly but it had an overlay, one of those large and confident South Wales voices which was syruped with a faint American inflexion that gave it an added persuasiveness. It was not quite as coarse as the cockney stallholder next door who sold women's silk stockings whose seams he would show you with a flourish, holding them up for all to see.

'Madam, you can look behind you when you're walkin', and you can see for yourself . . . Them seams, straight up the back of yer leg, all the way from toe to heel right up to the Blackwall Tunnel!'

He could be nothing to do with me. No, it was a cajoling voice, this other voice, rich and confidential. It was concerned with what might, or might not be, lingering in your stomach – in particular, your intestinal worms, and in describing them, it gushed fulsomely with an expansive aplomb.

'Let me tell you, Ladies and Gen'lemen, the intestinal worm's no more'n a cousin to his brother in the earth but can't be operated upon 'cos no surgeon's knife can find him and the only way to get at him is by persistence, by feeding him what he don't know he's takin', and buildin' him up until at last you got him and he don't know which way to go, which way to burrow – until all he wants is the light o' day. A miner's worm, he is, a little tunneller, as true as I'm standin' here. Well, see for yourselves . . .'

There was a movement in the crowd and through a space I first saw Broncho, a market salesman who, I later found, belonged to a separate and distinguished group, the quacks. Unlike those who only sold patent medicines, they seldom offered reduced prices and stood gloomily by their stalls, mournful beside their silver-wrapped cough sweets, or the strong, smelly, liniment rubs, applicable, they said, to both animals and humans. Broncho was unexpectedly different in that he presented an act and dressed himself up in a large white stetson hat with real sheepskin chaps and carried a six-gun in a holster with which he sometimes fired blanks to attract the crowds. His speciality was the invention of a purple mixture for the banishment of worms from the intestines and unlike the pill and liniment men, his stall was crowded with huge jars full of methylated spirits in which you could see writhing masses of yellowing worms. Beside the stall, there also stood the thinnest and most unhealthy looking boy of about eleven, his deathly pallor and haunted features making him a picture of abject misery – all evidence of the timely arrival of Broncho with his worm mixture; for, as I later found out, Broncho would state flatly that it had taken him a month of regular dosage to extract the entire contents of one of the specimen jars from this very boy.

'All them worms . . . Look for yourself. Pounds of 'em! Arrived, I did, in the nick of time! You only got to look at him to see how thoroughly drained he is.'

Here he put his tattooed hand – blue lovebirds imprinted on the skin between finger and thumb – on the boy's thin shoulder and asked gravely: 'Well, was you, or was you not at death's door until I come across you? Until your mother come to me and begged me on her bendeds?'

The boy nodded gravely. At death's door was one of my grandmother's phrases and the boy, with that awful chalk pallor and the limpid embarrassed eyes, the dirt ingrained between his fingers and the sores about his ankles, was the living embodiment of ill health. But for a fleeting moment, such was Broncho's eloquence and confidence, you thought, this is what worms can do.

Broncho was not just a quack, he was a consultant quack, and when he shook the specimen bottle, some of the tentacles seemed to stretch out towards you, swirling and beckoning in the blue liquid. You could not but wonder if they were still alive. 'Pounds of stuff I got out of him,' Broncho said impressively. 'Pounds. By the cupful!' He cupped his hands to indicate the amount, using the measurement as a specialist might to indicate the gravity of the situation to a layman.

Then he went on and on. (It was his business to, like mine!)

'What I ask is this,' he said, very reasonable; 'why, when the evidence is in front of them, why, oh why will people not take the simplest elementary precaution and put a bit of liquid

13

liner in the stomach as a preventative? You flush a copper pipe
. . . D'you think your own intestines is not worth a moment's
thought? Pains in the morning, have you? A little flatulence?
Tell you it's wind, do they? Wind! That's all they know . . .'
It was my first acquaintance with *They*, the people who
thought they knew.

Now I have to invent to order the narrative, since I cannot
remember the exact words he used. But the ridiculous details
survive: the fact that he carried the badge of a Deputy Sheriff
of Montana, had a crumbling parchment to prove it, and later
said he had learned medicine man's talk from the Seminole
Indians in Florida – all of it is so unlikely as to suggest a spoof
on my part. But it is not, and you have to see him as I saw him
on that day and later, half-illuminated by the flickering blue
light of a solitary naptha flame in a copper bowl, a relic from
the previous decade, a hoarse-voiced and earnest figure in a
place of shadows and mysteries. If his human worm repellent
– very reasonable at sixpence the bottle – is a hoary joke now,
my feelings then were not, neither were the suppurating sores
on that boy's legs, and the week-old layer of dirt. Thirty years
later I saw the boy's image once more in the face of a shoeshine
boy in Fiji whose ulcerated legs and hangdog look caused me
to empty my pocket of coins. It was a futile gesture, perhaps,
but another indication of the childhood that holds me prisoner
still.

Even now, I have a picture of Broncho as he took off his
stetson, noting at once that the leather sweat band was
removed in order to get it on his head at all. He had a high
forehead and a peculiar way of staring down his nose, an
expression of irritated puzzlement at times which I see now as
quite like my own. I too had a very large head with a double
crown and could never get a school cap to fit me. His eyes were
also like mine – green, hurt and sometimes evasive, and there
was another similarity. Shortly before my fifth birthday, I had
extracted the gunpowder from a firework and exploded it by
striking it with the blunt end of a hatchet causing an
immediate flash and resulting in what was to be a permanent
bloodshot corner of my right eye. These blotches Broncho had
in profusion. It is true, I had no idea of his age, but he was
fatherly looking, enough for me. He was also tattooed and

14

those tattoos spelt sailor, wanderer, absentee, another item on the ledger which I had begun even then. The fact was that he had all the credentials of an absent and never-discussed father, and while I could not quite see him sitting down at the table with my mother or any of my family, everything about him spelt movement and disappearance. There is another thing. Although the idea of any physical coupling with my slender mother was quite impossible, this was something I knew nothing about. So complete was my innocence of such matters, it would not even have entered my head. Indeed, I was nine before I saw any sign of physical affection between a man and a woman, and that unexpectedly in the doorway of Woolworth's when a young man, obviously arriving late, suddenly clasped a young woman. She reached up and kissed him, tears of happiness in her eyes and they stood together embracing for a moment, her fingers clasping and unclasping at the back of his neck. Standing across the street, I noted this extraordinary action with complete surprise, almost a sense of shock, just as – about a year later, once again in the market – I was witness to Broncho's disgrace as, tired at the fag end of the day, he paid off another boy even more anaemic than the first and then, partially concealing himself (but not from me!), he poured the remainder of his elixir down the drain in order to lighten the bottles. These he then bundled into a battered old suitcase, eventually wandering off moodily into the night, six-gun, stetson and chaps having long disappeared in the hard weeks before. The worm repellent was not a line that lasted, perhaps being too seasonal, as they say in the trade.

Now, looking back, I smile but never laugh at Broncho, or his itinerant registrars who helped him, their grimy fingers shuffling the bottles forward into eager hands when the going was good.

There were for years, whole areas of my life which lay buried and which I pretended had not existed, ghosts from shadowy places who inhabited corners and danced like spectres on occasion, mocking me for that pretence of normality which I so desperately tried to assume. It was not to be found then, not even at sixpence the corked bottle.

TWO

My grandmother had the kind of face which I find almost impossible to describe. If I see her in my mind's eye, she is bent and old, her mouth slightly sardonic after she had suffered the first of several strokes; a short dumpy woman, both hands swollen with rheumatism and legs misshapen with varicose veins, but her face – strong even at the end – was ever animated by the brightness of her eyes. They were sharp, brown and intelligent, sweeping at you under a frizz of grey hair, missing nothing. Around her neck she always wore a black velvet band, sometimes with a diamond clip, sometimes not, but I never remember her without this remnant of Victorian fashion, and hardly a photograph exists without it. I suspect she must have been very vain of her neck and in photographs as a young woman you can see a firm chin, a wide humorous mouth, all the evidence of a strong face, full of character. She was small, neat, and in one profile she wears her hair close-cropped, again with the velvet neckband, and here she is full-cheeked and there is an imp of mischief which belongs to someone else. I don't think she was ever pretty, there is too much chin for that, and even as a young woman it is the kind of face which stands out in a crowd because you sense there is something capable and reliable about it. There is not just the animation of the eyes, a natural shrewdness, but a steadiness too. She had, she used to say wryly, the kind of face that caused people to leave their children with her on trains. And yet, you would not call her plain. There is something too striking there.

The face I knew, however, was marked by life. Experience had riven it until it was homely, and it was at its best seated opposite me by the fireside when we were alone, with perhaps a treat in an unexpected tin box of Allenbury's glistening blackcurrant pastilles, normally reserved to prevent coughs in chapel. These were the happiest moments in whose early years and it was then that I got a sense of the past which never seems to be like anything I have read.

My grandmother's family can be traced to the previous century, hill farmers all in that most beautiful but happily unknown of terrains, the hilly mountainous country between the bottom tip of the Rhondda and Aberdare valleys, just north of Pontypridd, at whose centre is the parish of Llanwynno. Here my most famous relative, the bard Glanffrwd, is buried; a Welsh poet and cleric whose rise from the obscurity of miner to Dean of St Asaph is a period Welsh success story, the stuff of legends. He was born in 1843 in a small thatched cottage in old Ynysybwl, the eldest of seven children, and his forebears were the descendants of lay brothers who lived at Mynachdy, a sheep farm supervised for the benefit of the monks at Margam Abbey. When Henry VIII dissolved the monasteries, the brothers lost their living but settled nearby, and one descendant – Glanffrwd's grandfather – prospered and became the owner of almost all the land he could see between Mountain Ash and Abercynon. His lease on the land was drawn up in the old fashioned Welsh way, 'to last while water flowed in the River Cynon' and for as long as he paid rent at four pounds per annum. However, he sold it for a trifle in a drunken bout with the result that Glanffrwd began life as the son of a woodcutter, only saved from illiteracy by the patience of a deformed schoolmaster. After a spell in the pit in the early years of the coal rush, he became a pupil teacher, then a Nonconformist clergyman, finally entering the Church of England for which he was prepared at Oxford, where he is said to have consorted with Matthew Arnold and other notables. His end came spectacularly. He collapsed on the platform at the National Eisteddfod at Brecon in 1890 while conducting a choir. He was then taken to his brother's home in Pontypridd where he died. My grandmother was in attendance. He was forty-seven.

His wife, a well-known singer (Llinos y dé), was a beauty in more respects than one, according to my grandmother, who would dispense with all this historic preamble with a flicker of the eyelid. The poet Glanffrwd was her father's brother, but the marriage was not approved of in the family, particularly not by

17

my grandmother who, in emergencies, had the job of lighting coal fires in the beauty's bedroom and fastening up the forty-odd buttons of the button boots she insisted on wearing despite a lifelong lack of manual dexterity – onerous tasks which were sometimes palliated by the beauty's fame, for when she was singing, courting couples were said to come from miles around to listen to her. But on the other hand, the old enemy reappeared again, for during Glanffrwd's lifetime she would very often dispense with half a bottle of eau de cologne in the bedroom before a performance. My grandmother actually helped to dress the corpse with the swigging going on next door, if you please. Her own father at this time was a Deputy of the Tŷ Mawr Colliery, given a silver plate by the men on the occasion of his marriage. One of Glanffrwd's sons emigrated to America but the other, like my grandmother's brothers, was to perish either in France or as a result of the First War. Their photographs haunted me as a child and seem now almost as real to me as my own uncles, two of whom were also to be victims of war. To this day, their medals lie in drawers, a Distinguished Service Order, a Military Cross, a Distinguished Flying Cross, all unlooked-at. They perhaps explain why the only time I ever saw real fear cross my grandmother's face was when I also returned home in uniform, but that was at an easier time, and a long way ahead.

In my fifth year, it was all a mystery, but an entrancing one. On the surface of things there was a mask of respectability, composed of selected facts, but not far below there were the scars left by anguish now long-past, heartbreak which yet had not resulted in any basic change of ideas. We were never pacifists and I was never discouraged from children's games of war, unlike some of my contemporaries whose families also suffered drastically, Welsh casualties being greater per head of the population than any other country in the British Isles. So in my child's mind, I led charges over the top and got at the Hun with cold steel, amply provided with props from the commodious cupboards upstairs – a Luger pistol greased in its holster, a bloodstained bayonet, a Sam Browne, a military tunic with the colonel's crown and pips on the sleeves and, of course, the letters home from the Somme.

18

Dear Mother,
The food is as well as can be expected and we are seeing quite a bit of the countryside.

But there was another reality, I knew, and my grandmother saw that I knew it, not consciously perhaps, but she was sometimes overcome by the uncontrollable surge of memory that defeats all propaganda because it is full of sights and sounds and smells – sometimes, of unrelated images like the one she had of the outbreak of that first war of 'the boys marching through the main street of Pontypridd in 1914, a sea of scarlet tunics and polished brass, laughing and joking as the girls followed them to the station.' I, too, was to be a witness of such circumstances in the second war. But we remained patriots all, seeing ourselves in the larger context of the British Isles, regarding ourselves as part of the mainstream, and this never altered.

As it happened, my grandmother never told me of these things as an ordered body of facts, and now when I attempt to bring them together, I can see inconsistencies which passed undetected then – largely because so many of the things she said came as an aside. A death would be announced in the obituary columns of the local newspaper, and my grandmother would say, 'She led our Willie a dance!' She also liked stories with a moral and as she grew older, her mind would slip back to her girlhood and the early days of her marriage, one of the reasons being, I suspect, that the first war brought with it a time that was too awful to recollect. Everything changed after that. Avoiding it as an area of damage, my grandmother turned instead to her origins, indulging a predilection for the bizarre stories of country life. Her favourite concerned her expectations in a will; not all the family land had been sold, and she had an uncle and aunt who farmed quite near us – the aunt had promised my grandmother several fields. As a girl, she would go there to help out, she had nursed the aunt in one period of sickness but the time came when the old lady was dying and, suddenly and abruptly, the door was barred to my grandmother and all communication was forbidden. The little farm became a prison.

19

'She couldn't even get a note out,' my grandmother said emphatically.

She remembered going to the farm, taking a whinberry tart as a gift, but she was greeted by a servant girl who came out into the yard, barring the doorway behind her. The uncle was away and Auntie Leah did not want to be disturbed.

'Too far gone,' the girl said.

My grandmother couldn't understand it. Knowing her as I did, I was surprised she did not thrust her way into the house; but she did not, although she did not leave the whinberry tart either. A week later when the aunt died she discovered the reason for her uncle's absence. He had gone to see a solicitor in faraway and hostile Neath, had brought him back to the house that very night with the result that the will was altered and my grandmother dispossessed.

'A good job I didn't leave the tart,' my grandmother said. This was what she described as a dirty trick, but you never got a dirty trick story without its sequel and I got so as I used to wait for them. It was not just that I knew she would not have told the story unless it was to prove, as ever, that your sins would find you out. It was how and with what severity the fates struck which were the intriguing things.

Her uncle's name was John. He had been no more than a servant man when Leah married him, a kind of hired help who, however, lived in, according to the custom and was in most respects treated as one of the family. Soon, with the expected indecent haste, Uncle John married the girl who had barred my grandmother from the house, and within no time they were putting on the dog, he with fancy waistcoats, she with her hats and button boots. My grandmother, newly married, began to have her own children and, apart from an occasional sighting, had no conversation with her uncle. Three of her five children had been born, and were all under four years old, when a boy from a neighbouring farm called, bearing a note. Her uncle was ill, too ill to leave the farm, and begged her to visit.

In all my grandmother's stories, people begged you to do this or that. Messengers arrived out of the night and left abruptly, doors slamming behind them. Indeed, some of these doors even came off their hinges and she told me that too.

My grandmother wanted more information when she saw the note.

'Where was *she*? – "the servant girl that was"?'

There was no precise information.

'He's on his own,' the boy told her, shifted his feet, then confided he had been called into the farmyard from the bedroom window, but that Uncle John would not let himself be seen, throwing out the note together with a florin.

'He wants to see you right away,' the boy said. The wife, it seemed, had deserted him.

Something in the boy's manner convinced my grandmother of the urgency. All her life, she was consulted about illnesses, had a handwritten notebook full of herbal remedies, and was an experienced – if amateur – nurse. But she was not free to leave immediately unless she took the children with her so, in the end, that was what she did. With grandfather busy in the shop, she saddled the pony and trap herself, gathered up the babies and set off for the farm.

I have pondered that journey. It was not very far, but still difficult with young children. I have also wondered what was in my grandmother's mind and although the obvious thing is that she was expecting a vengeance of some kind to have descended upon the farmhouse, it also strikes me that there was a strong element of curiosity. She had a great interest in people's dying words, and since she had been barred from Auntie Leah's demise, she must have wondered what had been said. At any rate, it was late afternoon when she guided the pony and trap into the farmyard, and she left the children safely in the trap. The blinds were drawn, and there was evidence that the animals had not been properly fed. The place had gone down, she said. So she pressed the bell and for a long time there was no response; but presently she heard a movement upstairs and then there came footsteps descending the stairs, and finally the same shuffling footsteps came hesitantly along the stone flagstones on the other side of the door. In the last few yards she could also detect another sound, of liquid dripping on to stone.

When the bolts were withdrawn and the door opened, a sight so horrible greeted her that she moved to one side so as to obstruct the children's view from the trap. Around his mouth, her uncle held a bloodstained scarf. He was dying of some incurable and advanced cancer of the jaw. The dripping she'd heard was blood. She told me he had sent for her, to apologise, to confess his guilt.

'Jessie, it's done me no good.'

But my grandmother put a harsher construction on the matter. His lies had found him out, she told me. I saw the deadly logic of it, vengeance taking physical shape and striking like a dart at the offending organ, the mouth itself. My grandmother sent for the doctor but it was too late, and when Uncle John died, it was found the whole place was heavily mortgaged and no one benefited in the end. So the fancy waistcoats must have played their part as well.

'Just as well he died,' my grandmother said, 'otherwise it would have been the Workhouse.' Temptation, Drink, Debt, Ruin, the Gutter, the Workhouse, these were the bogies of my fifth year and I considered them all gravely.

I have, as it happened, told that story twice; once to one of my own children who greeted it with shouts of disbelieving laughter, and at another time – bizarre circumstance! – in the dimly lit corner of a nightclub in Nairobi to an African writer who listened avidly. We had defined a category of grandmother stories – to the outside world, tall and far-fetched, as simple as cartoons; but to residers at the inner hearth, the stuff of life. Kikuyu whores with blonde wigs and slit skirts did the twist behind us, slapping their bare feet on the dance floor under psychedelic lights which transformed me, as one of the few white men there, into a garrulous albino private eye as I sat hunched in the corner, a bottle going, as we exchanged one story after another. His grandmother covered up her father's habit of coffin-robbing until she covered it up no more when he fell into one and choked himself to death.

In later life these stories were to cheer me up immensely in the most dire moments, and strangely enough, they did not strike me as being at all odd at the time I was told them. I liked a simple view of things and when, much later, I tried my hand at the odd macabre tale and was sometimes greeted with ridicule, I hugged to myself the private knowledge of events which made the things I had written about front-parlour stuff. I was also to think of the noise on those flagstones years later as I lay helpless in a post-operative ward, temporarily abandoned because of a greater emergency, when a blood transfusion which I was receiving came adrift and I heard the same slow tap-tapping of blood on the hospital floor. I had other memories of that farm. I was once ordered off it in company with other children. We were blackberrying and trespassing.

Some ran, I did not.

'It's rightly my land,' I said exaggerating. 'Rightly' was one of my grandmother's favourite words.

Later, I boldly went to the farm to ask for a glass of water. There was a more amenable woman there then.

'The tap is round the back,' she said. 'Why did you come to the front door?'

I did not answer. To my disappointment, the flagstones had long been covered over and the stairs were not visible. So I never went there again.

The workhouse, where paupers were sent, figured large in my grandmother's stories and while it might be thought that we were quite well off (which we were by the poverty-line standards so close about us), the fear of poverty was never completely absent. It was everywhere visible – in school, on the streets, in the eyes of one of the members of our chapel whose threadbare respectability was just maintained as he wheeled an ancient cycle around the houses of the congregation carrying an old suitcase on the rear carrier from which he sold lumps or sticks of home-made toffee. If we were unlikely prospects for the Workhouse, others were not, and it was this same institution which was the indirect cause of the only occasion when I ever saw tears in my grandfather's eyes. My grandfather was not a Pontypriddian and he was not allowed to forget it by my grandmother who, when not talking about the world's ills, the evils of drink and the ever-present likelihood of degradation, swung to a completely different tack and struck an altogether more aristocratic note for which her well-rooted, if not landed, background had prepared her. Mentally, as it were, she claimed the fields of which she had been disinherited and was quite likely to strike a certain air as a consequence of being the last survivor of one of Pontypridd's oldest families, as she put it. She meant those who were indigenous, natives before the coal rush which had changed the very air she breathed. Others had prospered and moved away but she had not and never did,

23

and she retained that proprietorial interest in her particular patch which was evidenced by the number of people she knew who inevitably stopped to talk to her.

She had met my grandfather at a Sunday School treat, an annual chapel outing to the fields at St Fagans, near Cardiff, where the National Folk Museum now stands. His journey in life had been more dramatic. A blacksmith's son from the Carmarthenshire village of Conwil Elvet, he remembered doffing his cap as a boy of twelve to Lord Dynevor and made his way to Pontypridd by way of Edinburgh where he had been made an Inspector of Shops by Sir Thomas Lipton, the grocery tycoon. ('He is widely travelled,' my grandmother said; 'he has been everywhere, including Edinburgh.') Starting as a shop boy putting down sawdust on the floor, he prospered in the Lipton's organisation until he came to Pontypridd and finally, after meeting my grandmother, opened up a small grocery business on his own in rented premises formerly occupied by the composers of the Welsh National Anthem. At first he did well, and at the time of the Depression was a deacon of his chapel and a member of the Board of Guardians appointed to supervise the running of the Workhouse. One of his duties was to visit this ugly grey Victorian building on Christmas Eve when a children's party was dutifully organised. He was a generous and kindly man, and I have never met anyone who knew him who did not comment on his generosity, but I think now that there were times when life got too much for him. I can remember him coming home from that visit and sinking into a chair, the tears streaming down his face. My grandmother immediately feared the worst, trouble in the shop. There had been endless discussion about the substitution of the horse for a second-hand motor vehicle to make deliveries and then there was stealing by one of the bakery roundsmen from the daily takings ('Trouble with the baker's bag'), and I was in my hiding place when these matters were discussed. But it was some time before my grandfather could articulate his pain. He had arrived too late for the children's party but had been taken by the Workhouse Master to see the children safely abed in their dormitories. Even though it was Christmas, their shoes had to be left outside the doors and it was the sight of those regimented lines of shoes, stretching down the corridor in neat order, size

24

by size, which had unnerved him – the meticulous order of it, the Workhouse Master's pride. My grandfather was not to live to see the premature death of two of his sons, but those shoes upset him more than anything I can remember, more perhaps than my grandmother's constant quarrelling with my mother when she was there. There was seldom silence in the little kitchen. Now there was. Even my grandmother did not speak at first and I can remember him removing his spectacles, pinching his nose and wiping his eyes.

For all that, I doubt if I would have remembered it so clearly were I not, years later, to learn of a similar incident. This time I was in the company of another writer, Goronwy Rees, and puzzling over the works of Theodore Dreiser whose clumsy prose style had caused an American critic to call him the world's worst great writer. Goronwy had met Dreiser on one of his pre-war jaunts and gave me the core of the man. Once, in Paris, at the height of his fame and the darling of the left, Dreiser had been asked to present prizes at an orphanage. It was a duty he could not escape from but, rising to his feet before an array of cups and certificates, he had looked at the scrubbed faces and shaven heads in front of him and suddenly burst into tears, breaking down completely so that he could not speak and did not do so. This was the heart of a man whose compassion overwhelmed him, and such a man was my grandfather, I have no doubt. At home he was not one to say much, but our doors were open to all and all my life I have never forgotten the procession of beggars who came to our door at his insistence. Eventually I was big enough to open the door myself and once when I did so, I nodded gravely and went dutifully back along the passage to the kitchen. 'I'll have to ask,' I said as I was instructed to say. But I returned to find the beggar had gone. Seeing the telephone wires, he probably feared that we might have called the police since begging was an offence, sometimes punishable by imprisonment. I was soon told to run after him with half a loaf and a handful of currants which I scooped myself. My grandmother's influence was such that I knew it was imperative for me to run to catch up with him, and run I did, not of my own volition but at her expectation and, having found him, watched while he tore the crust apart with shaking fingers, his face riven by a grey despairing hopelessness. It was

25

an experience that was to be repeated many times in my life; my first disappointment in Russia was in finding the same despairing faces, the same outstretched hands of children begging; and again in New York, similar sights in Times Square caused me to wonder whether, like my grandmother on trains, there was something about my face which encouraged them.

At home, as a little boy, the endless procession of beggars that went on until the outbreak of war was a sign of the times, like my neighbour at school being forced to attend in his sister's shoes. There were, of course, worse and better things to come, but I am glad that I felt my grandfather's pain at an early age. I was not sheltered in the way that so many are sheltered and on that day – uniquely, in our house – there was a new experience in finding someone speechless.

When my mother came home, it was a time for treats. There were visits with friends of hers, including a couple who lived opposite and had a car. We went to the coast, to Porthcawl and the Kenfig sandhills, or sometimes up to Caerphilly or the Brecon Beacons when we would climb up and out of the valley and my mother would always breathe a sigh of relief. These friends of my mother's, I soon discovered, were lah-di-dah and inevitably spoke with pronounced English accents – a sharp contrast to my grandparents whose first language was Welsh, although they always spoke to me and most of their children in English. Their speech was often peppered with metaphors which had their origin in the original Welsh phrases. Thus someone might squeal in one of my grandmother's stories 'like a pig under the knife', but my mother's friends were out of a different drawer and were as smart as she was. It was in such company that I discovered a different set of manners. Once, at the table of a household of some affluence, I made a horrible mistake and passed a slice of bread with my fingers.

There was a hushed silence. Fortunately my mother was not present as I had gone with a friend, but the head of the household looked at me over his spectacles and said coolly in the clipped, mannered tones of the English upper class which I came to marvel at: 'I cannot accept that.'

I cringed, but managed, 'I'll eat it if you don't want it.'

When I told my grandmother, she informed me that the speaker's father had begun life as a baker's roundsman with a basket and a brown sack to cover his loaves and not two ha'pence to rub together. What is more, one of the daughters would cross town to get a penny off the price of a lettuce so I was not to worry on that score. It was not that my grandmother did not have precise standards, but they were more related to the character than the bread bin.

Away from home my mother was free (except for the encumbrance of myself) and she would light a cigarette with relief and if, in the company of friends, she went into a pub for a drink, leaving me to play with other children, I was bidden to say nothing about it when we went home. I did not do so, but I could never see that my grandmother was so old-fashioned as everybody said, and for a good deal of my childhood I accepted her standards. I could not get away from them and while I see my mother's predicament now, I did not then and was often sullen in her presence. Even when she took me to school, her youth and elegance made me uneasy and for years I have had to overcome an aversion to being seen with smartly dressed women. Once in a bizarre period of utter craziness in my life I was bidden to squire the American actress Katharine Ross to a meal at the London Hilton. I felt my throat dry with embarrassment as I greeted her, as lovely as a ripe Californian peach but 'done up to the eyeballs', as my grandmother would have said. On another occasion Sîan Phillips turned up for a theatre date wearing a large floppy broad-brimmed black hat like a catamaran running free under full sail, but I could have hidden, there and then. Fortunately she took it off during the performance, but I did not then want – nor have I ever wanted – people looking at me. Exceptionally attractive and specially groomed women are an embarrassment; better they be in the old Welsh idiom 'shrewd in the market place, devout in chapel, and frantic in bed'. That I was certainly the envy of other men did not occur to me, I felt the same uneasiness I had felt before, holding my mother's hand as we walked to school. It is not reasonable. It is not defensible. It is laughable, but I have to recognise that it is, and always has been, me.

I see now that I inhabited two worlds as well as the world that my imagination was carving out for me. For when I entered my mother's world, I did so with my grandmother's critical sense and often a knowledge that I should not have had, for she was often indiscreet and let slip things I should not have known. Even the bank-manager neighbour over the road had marriage problems, and despite the respectability of the bank, there was a tug of war going on between the young step-mother and an old and faithful domestic servant whose love for the child – a girl of my own age – was obsessive. The step-mother wanted to get rid of the domestic, the husband was in two minds, the child played one off against the other. Soon the family moved, and I watched them go with a knowledge of what was happening that was beyond my years. I learned that there were other straws blowing in the wind than those which were above ground.

My grandmother also had a nose for trouble, as she said, and so have I, and while it now appears to me that sometimes I have put myself at risk, she never did. The world and its ills and woes came uninvited to that little house but through it all for me there was always sustenance. When my grandfather died of a heart attack in his early sixties, my grandmother broke down for an hour only. They got rid of me on the day of the funeral but when I returned, my grandmother caught me up in her arms and held me to her and I felt her tears cascading on my own cheeks.

'Never mind,' she said to the world at large and me in particular. 'We still have you.'

It was the comfort of my life, my succour, a lifeline to the future, a love that never wavered and without which no rewarding emotional development is possible, the one love in life that is given unreservedly and without self-interest.

Shortly afterwards there was a ring at the front door bell but since there was now no man in the house, I was not allowed to answer the front door in the evenings. My mother's oldest brother was soon to come home to run the business but on this occasion we were alone once again. I can remember peering down the passage to see a man's trilby hat and shoulder silhouetted against the leaded glass panes and straight away I sensed trouble. We did not get many callers at this time of night. He stood motionless, with his hand on the bell, ringing persistently.

I went into the kitchen.

'There's a man there.'

My grandmother looked down the passage as the bell rang again. Then she removed her apron.

'Stay in here.'

I could sense her alarm, felt a quickening of the senses myself.

'Mind,' she said again. 'Stay in here.'

She went out, closing the kitchen door behind her. Since it had net curtains, it was impossible to see down the passageway and, obediently, I did not look but sat on the brass hob by the fireside. The visitor was shown into the front room. There was a conversation but only my grandmother's voice was clearly audible since it was frequently raised. Presently the man left, my grandmother closing the front door and putting the catch on the lock. When she came back into the kitchen she put the kettle on and composed herself. I did not say anything. I knew the stranger had upset her but I did not want to add to her upset, whatever it was.

Presently, she told me. 'That was your father.'

I said nothing. I did not know what to say. It was not that my curiosity had evaporated but now I did not want anything to disturb me, or to upset her. There had been too many other shocks, even some talk of my going away to an aunt when my grandfather died.

'I know what he wants,' she said. 'He wants to live here. Thought there was money left, but there's precious little. I don't know how we're going to manage as it is.'

Again, I said nothing. I was like an animal in its lair that senses movement outside in the stillness, but lies inert, hoping the danger will go away.

'But don't you worry,' she said. 'He won't get the better of me.'

I was relieved but said nothing, asked no questions. I had already begun to cauterise this hurt part of myself and my earlier curiosity had gone. That trilby hat seen through the glass was all I remember of my father. He never came again and the visit was not discussed further.

I was Grandma's child for another decade.

THREE

Once as a young man, when I thought I was dying (and was indeed in a tubercular ward that was to prove terminal for most of its occupants), I often lay in a state of coma and would awake at all hours of the day and night, opening my eyes and seeing – not what was in front of me – but images which my unconscious mind had formed before I awoke. As usual, there was an element of melodrama because I was suffering from – among other things – an eye condition known then as Eale's Disease whose symptoms were vitreous haemorrhages, bloody floaters which appeared to hang inside the eye, forming a reddish tide like a minute seaweed-strewn foreshore which moved gently as I turned my head, the whole miniature landscape encapsulated within the eye. My other eye was heavily dilated with morphine drops so that for a good part of the day I could see only vague shapes which meant that when I first awoke I saw, not what was in front of me, but what my mind had put there. It was often a scene such as you might come across in those toy glass baubles whose swirling artificial snowflakes will – if allowed – slowly settle to reveal a log cabin with a fir tree, perhaps a central figure like Father Christmas leaving home for what is obviously pensionable employment.

I, however, very often saw the face of my grandmother, sometimes accusing me, for in two years of what was described as strict bed rest I had ample opportunity to go back on the life I had led. But I also saw the homely contours of the Pontypridd I had known as a child which emerged like the gaily painted fresco of spires and houses on a Swiss cuckoo clock, principally the uneven sloping roofs, the three crowns of neighbouring hills and mountain, the smoke rising lazily above the chain works and sometimes the rain beating down from Cardiff. The rain always came from Cardiff, my grandmother said as a matter of geographical fact, and it was in that direction that she always looked when she got up and, indeed, during the war when Cardiff was being bombed and we could see the flashing orange lights of ack-ack fire and sometimes a loom of light faraway in the sky as the searchlights came on, we said, 'Cardiff's having it again!' in tones that were dark and treasonable. We implied in the safety of our hills that anything wicked Cardiff received, it somehow deserved.

But the outline to which I awoke was the view from my bedroom window, my back to the Rhondda, seeing the town below me, a higgledy-piggledy collection of awkward jutting buildings, some big, some small, some minute and white-washed like pieces of confectionery, some Victorian in style, some Rhondda baronial with forests of drainpipes and guttering, some straight marzipan Cardiff Rialto, the whole a representation of architectural untidiness that looked as if the entire town had been carelessly dropped from the sky and had come together by accident around the leaden river which trailed like a black slug through the centre. In the sunlight, however, it was a place of drama. For shadows cut across courts and gullies, bisected streets, blacked out whole terraces, the uneven and lumpy terrain offering up sharp contrasts, and I often thought that nowhere in the world could there be a place where the shadows formed such a variety of shapes and where voices were often disembodied, seeming to come from everywhere, even below the ground. Always, there seemed to be the clank of shunting coal trucks, coupling and uncoupling and, at intervals, pit whistles blew while at other times of the day the roads echoed with the clink of steel-tipped colliers' boots, their faces black then as they came up from the pit.

But let anyone say it was ugly and I would bristle. I never saw it except as a whole, a place of many associations. As I looked at the buildings, there were so many of them which I identified with people because my grandmother had a story about each one. This was where so-and-so had lost a tooth falling off a tramcar, that was where Tommy Ping Pong, a public schoolboy gone wrong, first began selling baby tortoises which he would instruct you to keep outside near a light at night and then steal back for re-sale; here my grandfather first felt his hernia come

31

on, near the back of the fairground, and there, near the Penny Bazaar, was where her cousin, Freddie Welsh, the world flyweight champion, lay in bed one night and surprised a burglar, laying him out with one punch. A world in which an unwitting burglar chose the world flyweight champion's house fitted in hugely with my notions of rough justice at the time, but my grandmother's air of familiarity was not just with such notables but with everyone she spoke about. Freddie Welsh, whose real name was Frederick Hall Thomas, like Glanffrwd's son emigrated to America, was commissioned in the US Army, later opened a gymnasium in New Jersey where F. Scott Fitzgerald was proud to have boxed three rounds with him. All my life, Pontypridd's connections seem to cover the world. Lord Nelson, after all, didn't like the look of Merthyr; it was *our* chain works which anchored the SS *Great Western* and the thumping of the great steam hammers which we heard daily was like the beating of the heart of the town. Small towns, I was to find, were discoverable in an intimate way whereas the vast anonymous deserts of suburbia produce only anonymity and a grey sense of unbelonging. When a distant relative described my home town as ugly, I felt my gorge rise.

But it was the shapes that came first to me in my partial blindness: the lovely contour of the town's famous one-span bridge over the River Taff, the slim white towers which formed the impressive gateway of Dr Price's never-to-be-built mansion, the hills and mountains – even the clouds I remembered, drifting away above the ribbons of terraced houses, and the seven trees I could see from the window of the last classroom I attended and from which I was later bodily removed by the headmaster and momentarily expelled. They were a visual sustenance as I lay in bed immobile, very frequently semiconscious as I was at first resistant to streptomycin and experienced daily comas as I was being slowly desensitised. It was the shapes, always the shapes, which would help me to escape from the torpor of disease, and they could be very necessary at times since there were moments when I thought I might never see properly again and once when I awoke unexpectedly, I just made out the outline of the consultant's face peering at me, shaking his head sadly and expelling breath with a disparaging grunt as if to say, 'No chance.'

But I was a reluctant hero in my mind, there being no alternative other than to expire with the minimum of fuss – hardly a family tradition, and so the shapes returned again. One was the gaunt outline of the Calvinistic Methodist chapel which we'd attended – a grim Victorian monstrosity plonked into the centre of the town and directly opposite an equally ornate public lavatory whose main offices were below ground. The roof of the lavatory was topped with thick, bottle-green glass tiles which caused an eerie subterranean light to filter down to the urinal stalls below. Across the road in Penuel Chapel you might be personally threatened with the imminence of hell and damnation in a sculptured world of highly polished African mahogany as you sat among a sea of pews below a raised and carved bardic pulpit like a lift-off platform to the other side, but when you went to pee, you were in a green Atlantis down below. Here, to complete the illusion, there was a continual sound of running water coming from a drinking fountain for animals and humans above. ('In Ponty, we never forgets the horses!' a councillor told me once.) One could have been the world of Flash Gordon, the other was the place where God found you out – and what was more, he found you out in Welsh too, for the important services were all conducted in what Pontypridd's only historian delightfully called, 'the ancient Kymmeric tongue'.

To my grandmother, Penuel Chapel was the hub of the universe, a centre of social intercourse from which she derived much pleasure and she had been, all her life, what she liked to call 'an active member'. Her standards were chapel standards, couched in simple sayings, 'Do as you would be done by', and in so many ways she was the embodiment of the Christian ethic; but I attended only because she wanted me to, often spending a good deal of my time daydreaming in a state of blank incomprehension since most of the services were in the Welsh Language which I never spoke or understood, although I remember hymns to this day.

I see myself now in my best clothes, seated in the corner of the pew with one weather eye lifting for the ever welcome box of Allenbury's blackcurrant pastilles, the other narrowing to look across at the heavily carved woodwork of the Big Seat where the deacons sat directly under the pulpit. Here the Minister often stood on high, sometimes waving his arms like a gaunt bird of prey, intoning, cajoling, haranguing, usually drawing grunted expressions of assent from the congregation. But it was not only above me, it was beyond me. Like an African savage, I waited patiently for the free gold-coloured medal inscribed with the head of the founder, Thomas Charles of Bala, the free Testament and the Sunday School treat to Barry or Porthcawl where elderly men supervised sack races and older boys got off with girls on the ghost train. I learned my verse in Welsh, duly recited it, then hastened to be anonymous once more.

I see now that I was born into the end of one era of Welsh Wales and Welsh Nonconformity. In Penuel Chapel when I was a boy, the age of the congregation was increasing; there were fewer and fewer young people and the Sunday School classes grew smaller and smaller in my lifetime until finally the building was demolished. The chapel and its religion declined because it ceased to appeal while the Welsh Language was like something to be cosseted as if used 'for best' on a Sunday, then put aside for the working week in the houses of all but a few stalwarts whose children – usually sons of the manse – were unexpectedly, and often undeservedly, to prosper in later years. For them, in broadcasting and other circles, the Welsh language became a caste mark, like an old Etonian tie, and people like myself became outsiders, easily excluded for a long while.

But my grandmother had known a flourishing and youthful congregation in the aftermath of the Revival, and Penuel people were for the most part old Pontypridd people who had struggled along against the competition and the invasion of outsiders in the great population explosion after the coal rush. Then the valleys were opened up; the industrial population doubled in a very short space of time, adding nearly a million souls to what had been a rural area. They came, like my grandfather, from the Welsh countryside and from the other side of the Bristol Channel like the parents of so many of my schoolmates who brought with them the names of remote Devon and Cornwall villages whose names were to puzzle me so much when I read them in obituaries. I was impatient with the lack of youth and vigour about my chapel, the plain foolishness of so much Welsh when the streets were alive with the

34

vernacular; impatient at the do's-and-don'ts of simple people, even at their piety in a world which grew more violent every day, and my restlessness drove me into those same streets which seemed to me to be the real world. I had enough places in which to daydream, but my grandmother saw to it that I was the instrument of her chapel duties; for I became her messenger, first accompanying her when she took home-baked cakes and delicacies to invalids and others, all members of the chapel, and later when she was unable to walk, making the visits myself, a shopping basket forever under my arm. This I did all through my childhood, changing to a more masculine briefcase which I inherited when my mother's youngest brother was killed in the second war and, once again, these visits were a happy accident of my life since it meant that I crossed doorsteps I would not otherwise have crossed. They also led to some strange memories when I lay in hospital; for I was in a ward full of colliers, most of whom had silicosis and heart conditions as well as tuberculosis, and the images which returned to me were rich and varied – all to be sifted, even treasured if they hastened the endless slow procession of days.

As a child I had no direct knowledge of the colliery, only my grandmother's stories of her father's involvement, but I used to visit one old collier who had suffered an accident underground which had paralysed his hand. With the little compensation he received, he had opened a backstreet sweet shop, one of those tiny front-room businesses which sold humbugs and cough sweets and simple household requirements and whose trade was virtually confined to the terraced street in which it stood. Here you would sometimes see men who had come directly from the colliery, their white eyeballs and teeth gleaming in their black faces as they performed errands for their wives with simple requests. ('A packet of Reckett's Blue and ten Woods on the book!') The old collier, whose name was Rhys Jones, carried on with the shop after his wife died, struggling to lift the heavy sweet bottles with his withered arm, and every week I would make my journey with a plate of Welsh cakes or *Tiesion Lap* – a delicacy made with sour milk – and then I would listen while he told me stories of his struggles with stubborn horses underground. He never allowed me to see his withered arm which he kept wrapped up in a woman's black silk stocking, but

35

he welcomed my company and even came to depend upon it as I listened gravely to his comments while the war approached.

'Myself,' he would say airily, shaking the screw of caster sugar over the Welsh cakes, 'I think that Stalin is only bouncing!'

I grew used to the sound of his voice and was pleased at his excitement at my visits, for I was one of the few visitors he received and whenever he saw my grandmother, he would extol my virtues – once stating that in his view I was a likely candidate for the Nonconformist Ministry, which showed a shrewd judgment of what would please her. I was a good listener, he said, implying that it was a rare attribute in that calling.

In hospital I also thought about my schooldays and I would try to remember the names of the children who had sat next to me and the games we played in Infants' School. I suppose I was trying to recapture a sense of innocence and now, going back on it from afar, I realise that I am attempting to lay incidents of my life on paper like a card player would lay a hand upon a table – saying, as the autobiographer does with a flourish, 'Here I am. This is what made me and this is what I made of myself.' But I can detect no conscious pattern of events, and if there is any danger, it is the professional writer's curse – the dangerous habit of trying to please. I have always thought that every autobiography should contain something disgraceful, and yet the loyalties which bind you are like tentacles so that it is often painful to go back, each layer of memory having to be lifted and unstuck like an adhesion. The facts are easy but the least important. You ask yourself, how did you really feel? Perhaps the best guide is to watch your own children as they grow up, and then it is often a matter of revealing the contrast – then and now.

At first I see myself as a little cosseted pumpkin again, Grandma's boy still, standing at her side outside chapel, the sort of chummy little boy whose hair adults cannot help ruffling. I remember I had a tam at one time which I could pull down over my mole like a paratrooper's beret, and I stretched it as much as I could to hide the mole; but when I went to school, it was the mole that interested everyone. There was also the embarrassing matter of my clothes since, by the bitter poverty-line standards of the 1930s we were well off and I had new shoes, a clean red jersey and short grey trousers from the town's largest emporium, kept by a wealthy man whose ill-fitting ginger wig was a source of constant fascination since it slipped continuously, revealing a totally bald pate. I was, I see now, the sort of nice little boy whom schoolmistresses were glad to have in their class. This was to change markedly but, on that first day wending my way into the Infants' School yard, the most obvious contrast was the condition of most of my schoolmates; while there were a few as tidy as myself, my difference was immediately noticeable in the newness of everything I wore and this became one of the first of the stigmas to mark me out from my fellows. I did not have boots which most of the other boys had, but shoes, and I did not have handed-down clothes some of which, I soon saw, had the advantage of being able to stretch over your extremities and could be very useful in wiping your nose. At first, there was not a darn in anything I owned.

Many of the boys wore rubber daps or plimsolls, some did not have socks, and now I became acutely aware, not of rickets, nor malformations of the limbs due to malnutrition, but clanking leg irons which were worn by several children in every class; and it soon became apparent that there were those who suffered from epileptic fits which fact was entered upon a card and the susceptible had to be placed in desks near the aisles so that the teacher could get at them quickly if they began to choke. Leg irons on top of fits constituted a special hazard since the braces could become jammed in the metal supports of the desks. Of course I cannot remember exactly and in what order my perceptions came, but within three days I had made a bosom pal and somehow I knew now beyond any doubt that it was my mole which drew him to me, just as his awkward comic gait had struck me from the moment I saw him in the schoolyard. His name was Albert. He came from the gypsy caravans. He had been run over by one of them when a horse bolted and his legs were permanently bowed so that he could not walk in a straight line. Instead he rolled, a comic opera roll like a sailor in a musical comedy – his whole body rolling, shoulders and legs moving from side to side, his head following as if bowled along by the wind. Albert always had a smile on his face, as if by way of apologising for his oddity

37

and his face, an old man's even at five, which was swarthy, dark, gypsyish and – astonishingly – a hint of his hair receding at the temples. I think he had unruly hair and his mother kept it firmly plastered down with grease. He was none too clean, bit his fingernails and was the owner of a multitude of boards and wheels and bits of broken skates which could be assembled rapidly into a wide variety of gutter transport which whizzed him down hills. He would never walk normally, somebody said. But he smiled, smiled, smiled, and went on smiling. He was a clown but with soft appealing eyes like a spaniel's. He would never hit anybody. He never shouted. He could do a kind of cartwheel, throwing himself sideways and landing on his little bent legs like a cartoon man. He could also whistle with two fingers in his mouth, giving out a real piercer. The first time I spoke to him, he put these two fingers to his mouth, wet them, then fingered my birthmark and we touched like dogs. I knew there was gypsy in him but it did not make any difference to my birthmark – he knew me straight away, from the very first playtime. Then we sat together, went home together, and he used to wait for me outside the house. Every day he had something different to show me, a gobstopper in a piece of rag, cigarette cards galore, a spider in a jar, and always bits and pieces of wheels which he hid in various hiding places along the road. I think some his family collected and sold the debris at the back of the market. They were market totters, trading in scraps, and the last of the haul was Albert's. He got what nobody else wanted, the very dregs, but out of it all he created a wonderland of possessions and within a week he was calling for me.

'Is Al' in? C'mon, I got the bogey.'

Once my grandfather saw us on the road.

'Who is this?'

'This is Albert.'

My grandfather gave us money for sweets. We ran up to the shop, purchased an ocean of pear drops, shared them out; riches!

At first, Albert wouldn't come into the house but shouted over the wall.

'Is Al' in?' That was his cry and I loved it.

'Yes,' I said. I was always 'in' to Albert.

38

We stuck together. If somebody asked him to do something in the schoolyard, he'd jerk his head at me. 'I'm with him.'

There was a boy who was such an uncontrollable farter that he was sometimes sent out of class and when he performed, Albert would look at me and roll his eyes. The roll of his eyes alone was soon enough to send me into hysterics so that, out of consideration for me, he stopped doing it.

Then I went out of the house one morning and Albert wasn't there. He wasn't in school either. After a few days someone said, 'They're on the road.' I mooched about the caravan site near Mill Field but never asked any questions. I never saw him again but if I had a sense of loss, I also had a status. I was Albert's pal, someone who had been enjoined. I had somehow lost the prim niceness with which I had begun, and although it was years before I was habitually in what was frequently described as the wrong company, my friendship with Albert had taken its toll on my clothes, my shoes, socks, shins, knees. I looked as worn as he did. But I belonged. I was, I might have said, when I was not having fantasies about my never-mentioned father, 'lovely and normal!'

'Clothes do not grow on trees,' my grandmother said resignedly when she looked at me.

A long time later, our class suffered the impatience of an ageing war widow who went berserk with an ebony ruler, causing an eruption of parental complaints and the intrusion of the headmistress. We felt as if we'd been under shellfire and I who, together with others, had wet myself in fear, remember thinking gravely, 'I'm very glad Albert is out of this.' He was the first pal I ever had, one of the few people in my life who could make me laugh uncontrollably, an experience no one should be without.

In hospital, memories came like interrupted film sequences, drifting hazily into my consciousness. Now as I try to recall my primary school, I do so with gratitude. Overall and general impressions prevail over the particular now, but they did not when I lay on my back, and while I have always been fascinated by the idea that a drowning man sees images of his past life and I have heard a man of seventy calling in his death throes for his mother, one even murmuring the name of a long-dead greyhound, I am not so sure about the precise order of the recall. I suspect that any conception of form is wishful thinking. Even an attempt to impose order at this very moment somehow diminishes the heat of experience. Perhaps one only snatches at the truth. Perhaps it comes by accident, a stray card falling into place in the ever-fading hand of lost happenings.

In those days when you left the Infants School, you went to the Big School, boys and girls separating out. In our case you went upstairs, skipping a floor which was the girls' school, to the toppermost deck of a huge three-decker building which stood, and still stands, in a prominent position overlooking the town. When you went up to Big School, you literally went up and up a steeply sloping asphalt pathway like a runway extending up the side of the hill parallel to the main building above which, higher still, there was a large playground, walled in but the wall surmountable and giving way to woods and open space behind. The school seemed monstrously high, a gargantuan building, and at seven the path and steps adjoining it were like an ascent into the sky itself and seemed never-ending. It was so steep that latecomers had no chance of catching up if they hurried. You could never hurry for if you were not bent double halfway up, you had already collapsed. When you got to the top, you entered a dark lower yard, bordered by the still-towering building and a banned area under a wall known as the shrubbery where misplaced balls could lie until they rotted amongst dank foliage which seldom received the sun. The main playground was higher up still, but this yard was the place for lining up before we went into school, for fire drills, for being 'tooled' by bigger boys anxious to inspect your private parts, and a game known as Bumberino when a file of boys gripped each other, heads bent and feet wide apart to form a caterpillar which ended with a strong boy holding the others firmly against a drain pipe. The caterpillar formed, a jumper would attempt to leap the whole, and sometimes two teams competed with each other and the cry 'strong horses, weak donkeys!' would be heard. This was the formal game, but more often than not, it went off at half-cock: there was no more than one team and the aim seemed to be to manoeuvre the biggest and fattest boys into the line of jumpers so that their descent was like a six-chamber game of Russian roulette when everybody got hurt. Sometimes you would be grabbed to form the caterpillar and automatically expected to take your medicine and be a bumberino. Strangely enough, despite injuries, it was never stopped completely and as juniors it was always our aim to escape into the bigger yards where it was never played because of the lack of supporting drain pipes. It was really a licence to cause pain given to the fat boys, but it became a boast to be able to say, 'I had Fatty Watkins on top of me today.'

It was in the lower yard where the teachers blew their whistles calling us to order, and at first we judged them by the fear they were able to inspire. When the whistle blew, you were expected to freeze on the spot and there were boys who made it their business to wait for the master on duty to appear. The moment he put the whistle to his lips, they would deliberately adopt the most lunatic postures so that they would be embalmed in them as soon as the whistle blew. These expressions and stances they held until the second whistle blew, instructing us to go to our classroom lines. Some boys would be perched like storks on one leg, their mouths yelping derision; others would stuff their fingers up their noses, or somebody else's, the toolers would be about their tooling, and even the bumberinos would be immobile, especially if some weak donkey was in danger of suffocation. You had the cane if you were detected in the slightest movement, with the result that the attitudes of even the most innocent of boys resembled those of a lunatic asylum caught at the pitch of madness. But we froze twice daily, enjoying the licence to pull the most frightening jibs as a matter of pride once we got older. Then the second whistle blew, legs would come down, fingers would be removed from whatever orifice they had found, the bumberinos unscrambled and we would lawfully proceed like sheep to our class lines before the command, 'Monitors!', came when six of the bigger boys would move to yet another set of steps and supervise our progress upwards once more.

It was on the stairs in my very first year that I basked in the glory of unexpected privilege. I had what I have so often lacked in the dark Welsh sense, influence! My cousin David, the son of farming relatives, having failed the eleven-plus examination, was a monitor and since he was easy-going and kindly, especially looked out for me so that I was sometimes privileged to receive an extra bottle of free milk, the distribution of which was one of the monitors' perks. I have seldom been more grateful for a friendly face, not that the school was unduly rough, but his cheerful wink on the stairs set me up for the day. As it happened I did not like milk but I soon sub-contracted the privilege, enjoying my own influence in turn. Like the Rhondda councillor with a full glass who is offered further obeisance and says 'I'm all right for now, but I'll have a large Players' since you're offering!', I had entered the scheme of things, and throughout that year I basked in the shadow of my protector. I liked school. I was happy, and the early voices remain.

'I want a noun! Give me a noun! What is a noun?'

'A naming word, sir.'

'Very good. Give me a noun beginning with B. *Hands!*'

I can see the hands now, a forest of them, for we must have been forty in the class and a boy called Cookie blinked when singled out.

'Bum,' he said informatively without a trace of mischief.

Hysteria again. We had learned to laugh at the misfortune and ignorance of others, and there was nothing funnier than when the teacher's false teeth fell into the tadpole spawn. It wasn't long before I learned that I was expected to pass the eleven-plus examination with three or four others in the class. We were not the ablest, but the most parentally driven. Others were required to leave school at fourteen and work, but they were better off than young people now since they were almost certain of a job. For all the crying waste of that society of the thirties, it did not enfold the young with the hopeless and never-ending blight of present-day unemployment where the haves have become even more impervious to the have-nots.

By this time I had taken the eleven-plus, the second war had broken out and that led to another chapter in another place. In the all-age school, or Lan Wood, as it was then called, I learned the greatest of gifts, to pass unnoticed in the crowd except perhaps for my propensity to accidents for I was cut, bruised, stitched, scoured, disinfected and bandaged more than most, especially flying down the escape ramp but I wore my scars as comforting badges of normality and suffered little. I took pride in never fainting which was quite commonplace then, perhaps because of malnutrition or, equally likely, the massively efficient central-heating system; for on some days the radiators steamed with the burden of drying clothes so that each classroom resembled a laundry. But that was all normal and I regard the school now as a humane place with none of the evils of bullying which many associate with such schools in big cities. It was in all respects a neighbourhood school and if we learned little more than to read and write, it was a sociable place and the masters kindly. We chanted our tables, fed the goldfish, watched mustard seeds germinate on blotting paper, wrote happily and at length about 'A Day in the Life of a Penny' and once we even had a visit from a writer – Jack Jones, massively handsome with his silver hair and resonant voice. He called in to present a pair of gleaming working boots to a virtuoso, a boy who had not been absent or late in the whole of the seven years he spent there. I can remember thinking, he probably had never even coughed aloud either. He was an unknown boy, unseen, never heard to speak, one who had kept well and truly in the background. He might have been a lesson to us all. The prizes came to those who were most easily managed.

So the memory deals the cards – seven years gone and a chapter closed. But my time in hospital preserved the memories and there was one day which came back to me almost in its entirety since it seemed to be more truthfully part of my life than the cosier reminiscenses with which I sometimes indulge myself. In the intervals between bouts of pain, men will recall the joys of their lives, the most recountable incidents and, like all storytellers, will attempt to show themselves in some kind of acceptable light. But as the days go by the tall and the long stories give way to exchanges of a more common kind, incidents at first simple but often more revealing. Almost all Welsh children have a memory of a school trip, usually a visit to some desirable venue which can accommodate large numbers of unruly children. There was a minimum age limit, usually fixed at nine, and for weeks we looked forward to the expected day – particularly those who had never been beyond the boundaries of the town, or at least as far as cold, wicked Cardiff. Sooner or later we would be told the venue and in this case it was

Bristol Zoo, which was a manageable distance in the space of a day.

Once announced, the excitement generated was quite incredible. As the day approached some boys confessed they could not sleep. The whole school was going, the upstairs boys and the downstairs girls, and for a week there were exhortations as to our appearance, the necessity for socks, handkerchiefs if they could be managed, above all cleanliness. The headmaster, a peppery little man who sometimes played soccer in the schoolyard and was a dustbin cricketer of repute, gave us to understand that People Would Be Watching The Lan Wood Boys and, what is more, as a special privilege we had been granted what seemed to be the freedom of the ancient City of Bristol because we would be welcomed and marshalled from the railway station and the police had been told of our impending arrival. I did not know until I got to our own railway station that the privilege had actually been granted to most of the schools of the lower Rhondda as well as Pontypridd, but this was the first of many such speeches I was to hear in my life and, indeed, to compose myself a few years later. But at the time I listened gravely. The headmaster had decided it would not rain so that raincoats would not be carried and since refreshments would be provided, there was also no need for sandwiches. Sandwiches made a mess and the Great Western Railway had inspectors especially briefed to diagnose a Lan Wood mess. There was also the matter of being sick on the train. 'Now I'm warning you well in advance, no one is going to be sick, especially those who fill themselves up with sweets, whose parents have more money than sense. There's no reason why we shouldn't all enjoy ourselves, BUT . . .'

Dutifully, I bore it all in mind. I have since tried to define a day in my life when I began to see through such exhortations, a time when I no longer bluntly accepted everything that was told to me, but it was a long time ahead, and I would not then have disobeyed a single instruction. It was to be a fun day. Bristol, we said, and paused – awed – as we might have said Mecca. And the Zoo! We spent days discussing what animals we might concentrate our attention upon. Intelligence reports from a previous year revealed that there was a hippopotamus which urinated continuously and had won a kind of celebrity for being the most disgusting exhibit, next to the chimpanzees whose red arses and wandering fingers invited hysteria, especially if you stood next to a teacher when they were performing. Perhaps we were joyously anticipating the sight of unrestrained versions of ourselves by courtesy of the City of Bristol. At any rate, we discussed it endlessly, even arranging our seats on the train well in advance.

My grandmother instructed me to wear especially clean underclothes in case of an accident. She was obsessed with the need for cleanliness next to the skin when visiting major English cities. It was a reversal of her normal positive character and showed a curious inferiority which was characteristic of many Welsh people at the time. 'Suppose you were run over?' she would argue; 'you don't want people to know where you're from!'

I had then, and later, a vision of myself as a crumpled figure in some metropolitan gutter with a police officer fingering my immaculate Bon Ton vest and pants.

'He's not from Ponty', you can tell!'

These exhortations were to become more complex when, as a young man, I attended interviews in London – one in Queen Anne Mansions in the Admiralty, inwardly the most unlikely candidate for His Majesty's Commission.

'Speak clearly and stand up straight!' my grandmother instructed me.

What the English thought of us in Bristol or elsewhere, I had no idea and did not care. But on another occasion I experienced a neat reversal of role. Descending in civilian clothes from a bus carrying a naval rugby team to Colchester Garrison, I was accosted by a sentry.

'Who are you, then?'

I told him.

'Tough shit, mate,' he gave a cruel grin; 'the Taffies are here.'

He was right. The Welch Regiment had returned from duty in Berlin and a strengthened Colchester Garrison side beat us by a cricket score.

But Bristol . . . Ah, Bristol.

'Remember where you're from!' my grandmother said once more before reminding me of the presents her own children had brought her back from such outings. I clutched two silver half-crowns in my trouser pocket as I raced to school. The weather, as ordered by the headmaster, was obediently fine.

In the yard, there was a hubbub of excitement. The poorest boys had been found an array of presentable clothes from the headmaster's charity bag, a collection of odds and ends of boots, shoes, jerseys and trousers which he solicited from wealthy friends and kept in the storeroom for rainy days when children were soaked coming to school and such occasions as this. Some children had brought games to play on the train, even tattered comic annuals to read; others, disregarding the instructions about sweets, were well stocked up and there was an air of buzzing expectancy that accompanied all such bonanza days. It was such a treat to be going anywhere.

There was first, however, a slight confusion. On such days, as in fire drills, the teachers marked the registers in the schoolyard and we did not enter the school at all, but a last minute act of generosity by a local fruiterer, known as Tommy Potatoes, in collusion with the headmaster, had resulted in the late arrival of several crates of Fyffe's bananas on the previous evening. Even more welcome was a parcel of slim white drawing pencils, each one stamped with the Fyffe's insignia, a golden banana on a blue oval. They must have arrived just as the school was closing and now, so that they could properly and fairly be distributed, it was decided that we had to enter our classrooms where registration would take place as usual. I suspect that the headmaster realised that there was not enough bananas to go around and so he wanted the distribution to be done in an orderly manner inside the classrooms. It might have been his intention that we ate the bananas before we left, but in any event, we were doubly elated. It was not just that we were to have something for nothing, but the pencils in particular were prized and perhaps something else that might occupy us on the train. It was such a glorious day anyway that anything that was to happen could only be an added bounty.

So we were sent to our classrooms as usual but we were not usual children and the monitors could not control us. We scampered up the steps, bounding, leaping, racing across the assembly hall, jumping into our classroom where our teacher, usually a kindly man, found himself doubly harrassed by our

46

exuberance and by the ominously small bundle of bananas in the wicker basket beside his desk. There were also not more than twenty pencils glistening in a partially opened box.

He told us to keep quiet and to sit still but we could not on such a day and now came the problem of dividing up the gift, a complicated matter which necessitated a pencilled tick opposite your name at the side of the register. There were other such distributions throughout the year and our teacher would keep a record so that he could refer to the haves and have-nots in the past. But now he was all of a hurry as we clambered about him.

'Sit down!' he shouted.

We hardly moved.

'Silence!' he said.

We were too excited.

His problem continued. There were forty of us. There were enough bananas to go round, but not enough pencils and the pencils were the real prize, as he well knew. He made a decision. Finally, he got us to sit down and we folded our arms as instructed.

'Right,' he said. 'Stand up those without fathers!'

I think I could have died then. I certainly wanted to. In all my nine years, I had never experienced such a humiliation. I was exposed, laid bare. This was no piece of information surreptitiously received from muttered voices by me alone. It was a public announcement of what separated me from others. More importantly, the matter had never been mentioned before. It was new information. There was dead silence. Alone, I got to my feet. I felt every eye upon me, my throat dry, my eyes already filling, my heart beating and beating away. And it was to have been such a bonanza of a day.

He realised my embarrassment immediately. He was a good kindly man. His own embarrassment was almost as great as mine for he must have been told of my circumstances. He covered up at once, avoiding my filling eyes.

'Right! Stand up all those whose fathers are unemployed.'

There were twenty on their feet straight away, all eyeing the pencils.

'We'll go backwards down the alphabet, Y, W, V, U, S, T, R . . .'

47

I got my pencil. He made sure of that for I was an R. Then we were out into the yard, made to eat the bananas until the monitors collected the skins, and finally moved in a long crocodile towards the railway station in pairs. My pal did not say anything. He had new shoes borrowed from his brother which was a change from wearing his sister's. They pinched his feet. He was suffering too. I broke the pencil into bits in the lavatory of the train, put the bits down the pan but they floated so I took them out and threw them from the window. I did not think I would ever get over my humiliation. Now everybody knew.

When we returned that night, I sat silent and tired in my seat. We enjoyed the day. We did not let anybody down. In the train, the teachers played solo whist on an upturned suitcase and you could tell they'd had a few since they did not want to be disturbed and the beery smell of hops came from them when they patrolled occasionally down the new corridors. When we went through the Severn Tunnel, I made a long journey down the whole corridor. There were shrieks of laughter coming from the lavatory at the far end of the coach. A half-dozen of the bigger boys had hold of a girl who was not quite all there, as we said. They were holding her forcibly, her knickers were on the floor, and one had his hand over her mouth. I can see her reddened face now, the pain in her eyes, her unruly mop of wild ginger hair. I didn't know what they were doing to her. 'They're tooling her,' somebody said. She was still flushed when she got out at the station but they'd given her knickers back. Another girl, big and freckled with flaming scarlet lips and mouth, had her arm around her and threatened the boys.

'I'll fucking get you tomorrow,' she said.

I brought a china tiger home for my grandmother, and a penguin for my mother. I said nothing to anyone, but I had discovered more about the world.

'He doesn't seem to think a lot of Bristol,' my grandmother said, not without a certain pride.

These were two incidents in my life, my earliest memory of the reality of pain. Now I doubt if I would have remembered the one without the other. A writer's path is made with such connections. Without them, he is only a trader in information, or other people's ideas.

FOUR

A fatherless child is more sensitive to the men he meets in his childhood than other children. In a sense, he is window-shopping for the father he might have had. There is also the matter of authority. Away from the female apron strings, there are strange males to be investigated and sniffed at and, invariably, some who appear large and dominant, often figures of fear who seem to breathe a different air from normal men. In the child's mind, they can be difficult to envisage in domestic situations for they are mostly encountered in institutions, backed and cloaked by public trappings. They exist as triumphant role-players, frequently seem larger than life and, at times, their very presence seems designed to make those with whom they come in contact seem smaller and weaker. These are the rulers of their little kingdoms who do not seem little at the time because there is seldom any immediate escape from them.

Such a man was my headmaster in the County School to which I went once the all-pervading battle of the eleven-plus examination was overcome. Like Pharaoh he ruled all he surveyed, I soon came to feel, but bull rushes were in short supply. Whenever he was around, there were no hiding places. Like other rulers, I heard about him before I saw him. In the hazy summers after the war broke out, I often played with children who had made the all-important transfer to the County School. Since colliers and collier boys invariably came home blackened from the pit, the contrast between the two kinds of education, ours and theirs, was often dramatically illustrated within days of leaving school. A boy who left at fourteen could literally appear the next day with working boots and tin jack, his eyeballs and teeth gleaming brilliant white against his blackened face and helmet. One day, he might be a neatly jerseyed monitor on the school stairs, the next he had joined the working world of men who spat and swore, the steel tips of their pit boots clanking and striking sparks as they walked by their former classmates who passed them self-consciously in blazer and short trousers and the peaked school cap it was then obligatory to wear. Fourteen was the age when normal-sized children passed into long trousers, but many continued to wear short trousers to school long after and so the gulf remained immediately apparent.

Now the boys with whom I played were all destined for higher things, if not the County School, then private school – more exclusive still as they entered the world of 'hols' and tuck boxes and 'fags' which all figured importantly in the 'public' school stories we all read avidly in the comics of the day. It was never expected that I should fail the eleven-plus and I came thirty-first out of about ninety entrants, among the top seed as it were, and those a year older who had gone before soon informed me that I would be in the first stream, paradoxically called the 'B' Stream, and that meant I would have so-and-so for 'Geoga' or 'Chem' and, most important, Pig would keep an eye on me.

Pig was my headmaster's nickname, the most loathsome imaginable, and boys were known to wet themselves in his presence. These and other facts were known to me long before I ever encountered him. He was remarkable in that he memorised every boy's name within seconds of meeting him and his very entry into an assembly hall was enough to stiffen a multitude of five hundred boys into an abashed silence. The silences his presence invoked were legendary. He beat you, harangued you, and found you out. Like Stalin, or Mao Tse-tung, or Field Marshal Kitchener on the famous wartime recruiting poster, his eyes were always on you. He did not leave you alone – ever. And there was The Stick, a substantial bamboo cane which he kept in his room or about his person – down his trouser-leg, sometimes tucked up the sleeve of his gown – and then there were the fearful questions he was likely to shoot at you, muscling you into a crevice as he gave you the third degree on sight. 'Twice the half of two-and-a-half, boy!' He had caned a prefect for being caught by a farmer with his trousers down in the act of sexual intercourse on a mountain

50

path, school cap in his back pocket, each buttock rising and falling, bringing the school further and further into disrepute with each continuing stroke. He had also struck out at a member of the staff for not wearing a gown, later protesting a justifiable mistake. When he walked down the main street of the town in the day, the streets were likely to clear of boys who had the slightest connection with the school. No Western lawman ever walked down a street with more effect. He was not known to have any hobbies or leisure pastimes and nothing human about him had been reported to me, although I knew vaguely that he had a wife and a daughter but these were seldom seen. In addition to his degrees, he had won a boxing blue at Oxford, and the fingernails of his right hand were upturned as a consequence of continually poking and jabbing at offenders with his stiffened palm. He also smoked Gold Flake which was to prove immensely important to me.

Then there was his face.

'You wait until you see him!' my informants told me. 'You won't laugh.'

I never did, as it happened, or at least, not for years. All the information I received then, I believed in its entirety. For every exaggerated claim, there was a basis of truth, and he remained a feared man, much talked about, a man who created waves.

It was like me, I see now, to get off on the wrong foot with him, and the County School. My elevation to the blazer and cap-wearing peerage was much celebrated and very soon after the results were announced, I was taken to the little school outfitters' in the Arcade where the dark maroon blazer and cap with the bridge motif emblazoned upon it were duly tried on, and my grandmother regarded me with pride. I have never since felt with such intensity that I stood at the threshold of a new world, and the fond looks I was given exaggerated my sense of self-importance. I had done something at last. It was natural that having won my spurs I should want to demonstrate myself and wear the blazer at once and, indeed, did so on several occasions. So I was wearing it one evening when I played on the street with several other boys who had already entered the school. It was high summer, the chestnut trees were in bloom, one of those still evenings when you could smell the horse manure wafting up from the Co-operative stables below the railway bridge, and although the light was fading, we took advantage of the shadows as we hid from each other.

I was hot and sticky but kept my blazer on. Earlier we had bought some chips, the remnants of which I now ate from a crumpled newspaper. I think I had opted out of the game, or been caught out, when suddenly the cry came from one of the boys who had strayed furthest away.

'Pig's coming!'

'Where?'

'Down here . . . He's coming this way! He is! Honest!'

There were five or six of us, all boys, playing release mob – a game of seeking and finding, the person 'on it' having a tennis ball which he threw at you if he could find you before you returned to base. But now the street cleared, my playmates were nowhere to be seen, save one, a slightly older boy who cowered behind a wall near me. I looked in terror at my blazer, realising that the wearing of it was premature.

A phrase of my grandmother's came to my mind, one that has often returned.

I was not legally entitled.

Then there were the remnants of the chips in the vinegar-soiled newspaper. They compounded the felony and the charge began to frame itself in my mind, 'Bringing disgrace on the uniform you were not entitled to wear!'

I hastily stuffed the chips down a nearby drain, ramming them well-down and beyond sight.

He was not, as it happened, coming down our particular end of the street, but passing it, and I soon saw him in the gloom as he moved away from me, crossing the street to head for his own home, a thickset, olive-skinned and moon-faced, trilby-hatted figure with the stub end of a cigarette glowing sinisterly between his lips. He wore thick, horn-rimmed spectacles and they glinted as he cast a sidelong glance at the deserted street and passed on, an unusual breadth of shoulder visible under his shabby raincoat, his footsteps stealthy on rubber soles. Soon, he was no more than a retreating shadow.

'He'd have had you!' my hidden companion said when it was safe to do so.

I was sure he would have.

' "Chips as well!" he'd have said!'

52

I'd got rid of those.

He did not live more than six hundred yards away in a semi-detached house set high above the road with a long rising pathway leading to a shrubbery which hid the bottom of the house. Later, I would look up at it half-expecting smoke to rise, or to see the glint of some powerful telescopic lens as it beamed towards me, such was the power of the myth he generated, and myths ruled me until I could think for myself. This was my problem and I soon found I could not concentrate in the classroom and had little interest in what was being taught me.

Very soon, the awful reality of war descended on us. After the initial excitement of marching soldiers and the appearance of my mother's youngest brother in air gunner's uniform, I began to realise that once again we were at the periphery of events which were happening far away from us. I remember the paper boys crying the slogan 'War declared!', and Chamberlain's quavery voice on the radio; then my mother said, 'It's not Hitler. It's the men behind him', taking a very South Walian view and pretending to be in the know. This view was shared by the local newspaper which proclaimed, 'The promises he [Hitler] has broken were enumerated in the pamphlets recently dropped over Germany. We have no quarrel with the German people and wish them well.' My grandmother said nothing, however, and now she would sit silently in the chair for long periods while propaganda took over the radio bulletins and the newspapers, and stories of German depravities became known. There were also the immediate household trappings of war: blackout curtains, sticky tape to cover the windows in case of bomb blast, and, of course, ration books.

My own war, save for some half-hearted attempts to collect salvage with the Scouts, was a very private one and at first I laid low. Teachers who should have retired, plodded on in the absence of younger men and soon there was fire-watching, the Air Training Corps for youthful cadets and the appearance in chapel of older boys, their fingers blotched and swollen with frostbite, survivors of early torpedoings. You could go to war at an early age in the Merchant Navy, the South Wales ports were at hand, parental consent forms were often forged. It wasn't long before the casualties came, one after the other. To give a factual account of these times diminishes them. As they linger

53

in the mind, sentences return, remnants of conversations that stand in the memory like old scars that will not go away, some of them searing conversations in the classroom.

'Why are you crying, Leonard?'

No answer. But there were always informants.

'Please, Sir, his brother went down on the *Prince of Wales*.' Then there was the brother of the boy over the road, the brother of the boy up the road, brothers along this street and that, and the most dreaded sight became the telegram boy with his push-bike and leather pouch. When my own uncle was killed, shot down in a Wellington bomber over Le Havre, family connections with the Post Office meant that the telegram was intercepted, but the news came just the same: *Missing, Presumed Killed*. Again, I saw my grandmother howl, again a parcel arrived marked, *Effects to Next of Kin*. It was only bearable because it was happening to us all as it had happened before, and somehow we survived while others who had lost an only child began visibly to shrink as the weeks went by. My grandmother began to regale me with old exhortations, addressed I suspect as much to herself as to me, saying 'Best foot forward!' and 'Stick at it, John Willy', both sayings from her own childhood which she repeated automatically, no stranger to the numbing chaos of loss and war. But she never lost the will to go on, literally to put one foot after the other. Surrender of any kind would have been unthinkable, even to morbidity and she gave herself more and more to tasks, caring for this one in chapel, visiting another, several times being the first caller in a house where another casualty had been reported. She was more and more welcome as one who had experienced most things. You could tell her nothing about grief and yet she managed a smile, invariably a little gift, or a comforting word. Somehow it is hard to convince young people now of the feeling of impotence which everybody seemed to feel in the first years of the war. Generally there was a total scorn for pacifists, little understanding of any intellectual or religious objection to war. South Wales was ever a rich recruiting ground for poor men's sons anxious for foreign adventure. The feeling persisted, 'Everybody is in it together', and was shrewdly manipulated by newspapers. The exhortation 'to do your bit' was general. There were, of course, attractions – escape from the confines of a small town, the excitement and glamour of uniform, the almost universal distortions of reality in the stories servicemen told to civilians when on leave and, to those who stayed at home, a feeling of missing something vital. And yet, as each casualty was announced by telegram, the sense of loss was total and near at hand: the baker's son, lured to sea by an older friend after a quarrel with his father over a trifle – whether or not he should help out with deliveries after school; the butcher's son, recently proudly qualified as a doctor, dying of wounds in Java; the air gunners, the radio operators, the seamen, the grammar school boys who formed the bulk of air crews who were being decimated with heavy casualties – this was somehow so normal that it became a daily fact of life. If I wept at night for my own kin, part of my grief was my sense of personal loss, but the consequence of all those other deaths seemed to make my elders even more determined to redouble their contribution to the war effort. No matter what happened, you conformed and I had no experience of any kind of rebellion – except perhaps in my grandmother's howl of anguish, repeated across the road by a neighbour when yet another *Regret To Inform You* telegram came. It was as if she had no vocabulary to deal with these events, and no real comprehension of them, only of their effects. It was a gap in her armour, I sensed, and when the time came for her to go to Buckingham Palace to receive a posthumously awarded medal, she became so concerned about what she should wear that I sided with my mother who felt an indifference to the occasion. Uncle Ithel was dead. Nothing would bring him back and I wished my grandmother had been her usual forceful attacking self, but she conformed, and later reported knowledgeably on the King's chalk-white pallor. His hand shook, she said. She hoped it wasn't drink!

In my own case I moved into a world of fantasy in which the figure of my headmaster began to occupy more and more of my thoughts, and beside whom Adolf Hitler became increasingly provincial and remote. I have described my first sight of him as rationally as I can, but reason became a frail friend as it slowly dawned on me that I could not cope with school. Now the consequences of my fantasising came home to me. There was so much which I did not understand. I could not concentrate and I could not take things in. I grew thinner, more haunted, and at first, very wisely tried to hide, finding my level in the back seats of classrooms with others equally anxious to be anonymous. From an early age I found my level with the masturbators and droolers, with those who came late and were often unkempt, dilatory with their homework, yearning like myself to be away. A hero's death with a sad little photograph in the local newspaper was easily achievable, it seemed, and the caption, 'Sadly missed by all his former workmates', which I read so often, was not entirely out of the question. 'Richards, A., Form IIB. Missed by his classmates in the back seats, but not by the staff!'

Now I began to develop frenetic scenarios in my mind, all of which had a sombre aspect. I had to pass my headmaster's house every day and began to judge the precise times when he appeared and learned to avoid him with an expertise that was immediately rewarded, because for a year he was not aware of my existence. Nor, indeed, were the other masters for I cheated and copied most of my homework and remained undetected with hardly a blemish upon me. 'Crime *does* pay,' I said to myself with relish in the first blissful months of keeping out of sight.

I had begun to fly imaginary bombing raids daily in my mind, screaming into the intercom as I held an imaginary joystick in my hand. At other times, I might be a parched lifeboat survivor gasping for water and at any time of the day my facial expressions might resemble those of victims in the furthest reaches of pain. I considered death by burning, drowning, even cannibalism, and in the midst of some incomprehensible lesson I would sometimes look thoughtfully at the exposed thigh of the boy who sat next to me, a strange expression coming on my face and occasionally I would say quite incomprehensibly, 'I'm sorry Bevan, but you've got to go!', then retreat – masticating solemnly – into my mysterious self without explanation. Occasionally, prompted by the example of an older boy next door who had shrewdly decided on a divinity course at an opportune time, I preached to congregations. Once in the physics laboratory when a student teacher lost half the dwindling supply of the school's mercury down the sink, I made up a little sermon and addressed myself frequently in the manner of the old Welsh preachers. 'And the Devil looked out

of the watch tower with a lusty leer upon his dirty chops . . .
"Mercury," he cried. "Whereby is my Mercury?"' At first, I
kept my fantasy life strictly to myself and I became known as
the silent one, an anonymous face at the back of the classroom,
but the war first intervened when my Uncle Ithel was awarded
the DFC shortly before he was killed and, suddenly, the two
most distinguished old boys on the Roll of Honour – a copper
plaque at the back of the assembly hall – were both relatives.
This occurrence, together with the results of the end-of-term
examinations, became known to my headmaster and my life
changed. I was now bottom of the class.

'I was thirty-first when I went into the school and I've kept it
up,' I told my grandmother, already putting a face on things.
There were actually thirty-two boys in the class as we'd had a
late arrival who only sat half the examination papers, but there
was no mistaking my lowly position and poor progress. When
the new term started, I stayed with my form as there were no
demotions that year, but within a few days Pig arrived like a
holocaust. His appearances in the barrack-like extension of the
old buildings called the new school, were less sinister than in
the original building – a place of corridors, stairways and tiny
classrooms with coal fireplaces. In the new school he could be
seen in advance and he would peer into classrooms as he
marched along the corridor, sometimes trailing his stick,
sometimes causing it to tap sinisterly along the corridor tiles.
When he entered the new classrooms, he would do so abruptly
and we stood up as if electrified. In the older buildings, you
could hear his footsteps on the stairs as he bounded up them.
The effect of his entrance was that of some identifiable
controller in a horror film, the grotesque mastermind in a world
of weaklings which he could galvanise into action and bend to
his will. It was invariably melodramatic, noisy and imperious,
often with scant respect paid to the teacher who had charge of
the class. You could feel the muscles of your calves stiffening,
and sense the same stiffening in the boys next to you. Fear
communicated itself mysteriously as it does with rabbits. He
had a habit of bounding in, immediately marching up the aisle
and bending his face to within inches of your own, so close that
you could see up his meaty nostrils, noting your own cowering
reflection in his dusty spectacles as you got the full cheesy waft

57

of him while he asked you some probing question. Woe betide a boy sitting alone in a double seat. This meant someone had to be accounted for. The balding pate would bend towards you, the thin lips parted, then sometimes there was a vicious dig with the prodding finger before the third degree.

'Where's Millwyn Jenkins?'

Somehow you had to find an answer, to say something – anything, just to speak.

'He . . . he . . . he . . .'

'Speak up, boy! Out with it! Sharpen up now!'

'He . . . he . . . He've got a job!'

This was years later, but the horror on his face at this grammatical mistake became as much described as the expression on the Mona Lisa. Now he exploded, gasped, spat, shivered with wrath:

'*He've got a job?* Central Welsh Board School Certificate English Examination within a week. You can do better than that, boy! *Again!*'

This time the victim thought hard, came out with a pearler in the poshest voice he could manage.

'Sorry, Mr Thomas. He have obtained a position.'

But these repeatable jokes were in the years when we got to know him. On this day in 1942 he came bursting in, clutching one of his bulging files, briefly acknowledged the master and swivelled his eyes around us as we stood like thin, under-nourished storks trapped in a pond before him. He had one query and a demand.

'Form 3B?'

'Yessir!' we said shrilly in unison, the obnoxious anxiety to please overwhelming.

'Richards, A.?' he then said, the malevolent eyes searching for me amongst the staring faces which all immediately turned to my hiding place amongst the dreamers tucked away at the rear.

I was already on my feet like the others, but now my legs went and I began to tremble uncontrollably. I had so much to hide. I was so puny by this time, gawky and peaky faced, all elbows and knees, my adolescent spots beginning. I was unable to speak. Fish-like, my mouth opened and closed. In an instant, saliva became a thing of the past. This was what he could do to you – reduce you to a thing! The boy beside me elbowed me out

58

into the aisle, even a movement on his part an act of courage, coupled with the assurance that somebody else was going to get it – a relief I often felt myself. Somehow or other, I went sideways down the aisle like a gawky half-sized beanstalk tottering in the wind.

He glared down at me. His normal expression was ferocious. He seemed continually to be in an appalled state but was even more so in these confrontations which he continually sought. It was as if all of you appalled him, your face, your pimples, your grimy spectacles, your crumpled socks, your scuffed shoes. His very stare seemed to create a visible reduction in everything you were, or owned, as he looked. It was not just a matter of cutting you down to size, but he was X-raying you as well. I was aware that I was still in short trousers and last week's underpants showed. Neither did I know where to put my hands or feet as I drifted before him like a damp cloud. If skeletons had feelings, this was how they must have felt, I thought. I could feel fear rattling in me. It went down to my groin like an electric charge.

'Come here, young man!' he said in his oratorical voice extending the phrase like a singer.

He beckoned me forward.

I stood close to him for a second, close enough to see the homely egg stain on his smudged waistcoat. But then he moved his plump repellent face and followed it with his body, opening the door wider, but cunningly leaving a space between his crooked arm and body for me to pass.

'Come with me!' he crooned. 'Come-come-come!'

Hesitating, I eventually went through the tunnel like a lurching goldfish down the plug hole and without another word to anyone, he followed, closing the door behind him, but not before I heard the class gasp with relief at their own collective escape. Later, I was to feel that such a sacrifice now and again was worth anything to be rid of him. In war there had to be casualties. Be thankful it wasn't you!

Outside the classroom, he was on the move at once in a flurry of feet, files, waistcoat and billowing gown, his feet skidding away.

'Follow me!'

His feet seemed to dance down the corridor, the gown flew out behind him, neck hunched, beak raised, like an overfed bird of prey who has already hypnotised his victim so that I followed powerless as if drawn on a poisoned thread. Further and further down the corridor he strode, hurtling forward, up the steps of the covered way and I suddenly realised that he was heading for the assembly hall. He did not look around once. Reaching the door, he threw it open, once again standing to one side so that I would have to go through the tunnel, brushing against his waistcoat, those eyes flickering down at me. Like all predatory creatures, he seemed to caress you appreciatively with his eyes before moving forward for the actual act of destruction.

A class was taking music at the far end of the hall but he paid no attention to them, or to the master in charge, and soon I saw the reason for the summons. I have said that the names of the war dead were inscribed on a bronze scroll at the rear of the assembly hall. For 1914–18 they were ranged in order of rank, so that my grandmother's brother led the list – Lieut. Colonel W. E. Thomas DSO, MC. But now the scroll had been extended. New names were being added piecemeal, week by week, and these names were burnished in new bronze so that they shone brilliantly in glistening golden letters and among them was my uncle's name – Flying Officer Ithel Jeremy DFC – and somehow the lettering was altogether more bold and pronounced, more real for me because, of course, I could put faces to these new names. In Ithel's case, I had walked so proudly with him down the main street, tried on his leather bombing jacket with its trailing electric flex and felt his hand holding mine as he took me on the dodgem cars at the Easter Fair. He was the father I would liked to have had, youthful and humorous with a ready wink, but incinerated now and committed only to memory save for those dreadful golden letters.

'Here, boy!' Pig said, beckoning me closer.

I did not move. I began for the first time in my life to feel a dull and sullen resentment, a stubbornness that might have been born at that very moment, welling up slowly like fuel gathering imperceptibly at the bottom of a tank inside me. It was not fair that I should be so singled out, not fair according to any accepted case law, in that my spurious homework had not been detected or the evidence laid before me, crime proved.

Neither had I said a word out of place, or ever sought to be anything but inconspicuous, lost in the crowd. I had just been sitting there in my desk minding my own business. It was all I ever wanted in my life – to be left alone to dream.

Something of my resentment must have showed on my face. Surprisingly, I was not in tears and the exertion of the long march had left me calmer. At any rate, the stare which I now fixed upon him was as slow and probing as his own. And equally as insolent. It went up from his shoes, the grubby grey woollen cardigan which he sometimes wore under his waistcoat, over these, past the egg-stain and up to his sallow porker's face, finally to the narrowing impatient eyes as he evidently waited for me to perform some act of obeisance. Exactly what he expected me to do, I cannot think, but I did not do it, did not move at all and he gave a gasp of impatience, seized me by the neck and thrust my face forward towards the scroll so that I could feel the raised bronze letters under my nose. I was pressed so close to them that they must have left a physical impression on my face itself. And the bronze was so cold, cold, cold.

'A family of heroes,' he said in his most scornful and biting voice; 'and what are you?'

My tears had begun by then. I tasted them under the pressure of his hand. But when he released me, I kept my head bent, taking my time before I looked up at him. I was choking with resentment now. In that moment, perhaps, the worm turned for ever after.

'Alive!' I said, choking at the back of my throat. I spat it out. I bored at him with my eyes, thrusting my own eyes at his. I was aware at the same time that we were being watched. The form taking music had the enchanting diversion of the monster and the mouse at the rear end of the hall. I distinctly remember a loose and nervous note from an oboe as there were some of the school orchestra under tuition there as well, but all eyes were turned to look at the two of us as we stared each other out.

I was not then aware that I had him, in a sense, as the saying goes. I did not realise that I had more or less summed up the position so neatly. I *was* alive – just. I had survived Pontypridd's one night of bombing, seen a stick of screaming bombs come down a searchlight, picked shrapnel off the school yard, and had also gravely considered the intelligence that the entire enemy raid was directed at Pig's greenhouse which lay at the exact centre of the bomb craters. I had also heard that the traitor, William Joyce, known as Lord Haw Haw, had once kept a stall in Pontypridd market and had old scores to settle. All these pieces of dubious information remained with me, but were hardly pertinent at that precise time for Pig gasped, stared at me, seemed about to explode but – incredibly – took no further action, and the famous prodding right hand lay sheathed in the folds of his gown.

We must have stood there looking at each other for a full minute. I kept my eyes on his because, somehow or other, I knew that it was the only thing to do. When I said no more, he was confronted with a problem and was dumbfounded, it seemed.

'Ha . . .' he said. 'Hm . . .'

I did not think it then, but now I realise that he must have been aware of some of my feelings and the consequence of his classroom abduction. I am sure he understood that by any standards he had gone a little too far. There was also the unexpected nature of my reply. I have not forgotten how I looked, perhaps more insolent than wretched when under pressure. And I had snapped the word out at him, 'Alive!' More important, I see now, was that I had yet to learn one cardinal fact about him. He had a weakness for a villain, being one himself. So not only had the worm turned at that precise moment, but a career had opened up for me.

He folded his arms, rocked back and forth on his heels, considered me. I realise now that he was putting on his act. This was the formidable presence that quelled the five hundred every day in morning assembly. But I did not alter my gaze.

Presently he spoke. Above his folded arms, the lips moved; now came a grimly insinuating note of threat:

'From now on, I shall be keeping my eyes on you, young man.'

I said nothing.

'Richards, A., Form 3B. Disgraceful end of term report?' he said.

I continued to say nothing. He had rubber-stamped my report with his signature and the comment, *Must try harder*. If I had said one word, I knew he would have struck out, or invoked some punishment. And, besides averting retribution, my silence and glare were having a positive effect of their own: he did not know what to say.

'Cut along,' he said finally. 'To your room!'

So I left, slinking away, just hearing him turn on the audience at the far end of the hall. His voice was full of confident shots once more, as he raised it, imperious and in full command again.

'And what does *this* form think *it is* doing?'

From that moment on, I acquired a certain notoriety as One Who Was Watched From Above.

'What did he say?' they asked in the back row when I got back to the classroom, eager for news of my demolition.

'Nothing much,' I said shrilly, putting a hard face on it and concealing my alarm. I felt that in some way I'd won a victory, although I knew there was a price on victory. But I had already joined the ranks of the army of Them, the put-upon, the hard-done-by, and those pronounced guilty without trial. I had also, I was to find, entered into a much more select group, one marked off from the common run by the headmaster's penchant for a rebel – a pronounced preference of his which overrode all other characteristics and was to last throughout the tumultuous years of our acquaintanceship. Unlike any academic I was ever to meet, or any person in such authority, he regarded the wayward as being exclusive members of his special parish and ministered to them according to their demands. I was now one of them, marked, the villain from a family of heroes and from that moment on I might have had a special patch sewn upon my uniform rather like a jailbird who is considered a top risk escapee. I had ceased to be anonymous. Before long, 3B found it had a liability in my presence for his visits became more and more frequent and now I experienced a second feeling of rejection – this time from those who liked a quiet life and felt my presence to be dangerous. This I came to enjoy and, indeed, suffered a loss of status later on when the sins of others transgressed my own. But by this time, in one subject, at least, I had become what I had earlier despised – a swot.

FIVE

For a year, Pig declared war on me and never left me alone for long. He would sweep along corridors, come bursting out of the shadows and back me into some tight corner whereupon he would pepper me with his sharpen-you-up questions, sometimes laying the tip of his cane upon my exercise books whose neatness, if nothing else, markedly improved. I felt his eyes upon me everywhere as he seemed to hurtle around the school, sometimes in the company of uniformed old boys whom he would dragoon into giving us pep talks. You might be sitting in the classroom listening to some boring account of the Wars of the Roses – we read history in turns from a textbook – and then he would burst in with a hangdog, grinning flight sergeant whom we remembered as an oafish prefect on the stairs.

'Flight Sergeant Jones, David! Just returned from a bombing raid over Bremen! Give him a big hand!'

And we would applaud, relieved of our boredom.

My own war was more private. Now that I had ceased to be anonymous, I decided to take him on. Still obsessed with the idea of being demoted, it was some years before my experience of failure gave me an intense desire to prove I was good at something, no matter how long it might take. At first I hid, then, being detected and singled out for the headmaster's attention, I developed – as it were – in fits and starts, as if like a ball being bounced on a hard surface, my shape altered imperceptibly, responding to the pressures of contact. For years no one took much interest in me except my headmaster, and although I felt at the time that but for him, I would have escaped undetected, now I see things differently.

At thirteen, I looked a miserable specimen. The chubby, jerseyed little boy became an elongated, bespectacled freak who suffered from boils. 'Eggs,' my headmaster said. 'Eggs it is, you can be sure!' He had an answer for everything. There was, early on, another confrontation which added to my reputation as a card which I carried with me into the fourth form. One night I accidentally burned my hand while putting coal on to the fire at home. A small and painful blister developed on the palm of my right hand within seconds. This was on a Saturday night and the remaining two examinations in mathematics were on the following Monday. As I looked at the burn, it occurred to me that a heavily bandaged right hand would prevent me from sitting the examination. I knew that my grandmother would never give me any encouragement to stay away from school, but an injured hand, together with my regretful presence and pathetic attempts to use a protractor, might easily result in my being excused. I saw the scene immediately: the sympathetic teacher, my intense concentration, the reluctant failure, my own dialogue regretful.

'It's no good, sir. I've tried and tried.'

At first I contemplated moving my hand closer to the red-hot coals to increase the size of the burn, but I could not face the pain. Then I remembered a box of wound dressings which my mother, who was then nursing at an Army convalescent hospital, had brought home several days before. When I opened it, I saw that it also contained a tube of Acraflavin and very soon I realised that I would have to construct two dressings: one for immediate use – a mere plaster – and the second, much larger, which I could hide in my schoolbag and slip over the first when I left home on the Monday morning. I would need a dressing so obvious that it would not require a note or any explanation. The dressing would have to look authentic and, for some reason, I decided it would also have to smell like a burn which attention to detail occupied me for several hours. We had at the time a cat called Ginger whose hairs when singed gave out a particularly revolting smell and, mixed with copious amounts of Acraflavin, now formed the base of a kind of glove which I constructed. It enveloped my palm, a creation so large and untidy that it began to look like some bedraggled battlefield dressing, the kind you saw in pictures of the Crimean War. The yellow ointment soaked through the bandages, the cat's hairs stank, and I used so much bandage and plaster that the size of my hand doubled. By Sunday I was already beginning to refer to it as the Sebastopol Glove and on the Monday morning I slipped it on outside the house, noting the weekend's accumulation of grime with satisfaction. It was now moulded into a totally credible shape and as I made my way to school, realising that I would have to pass the headmaster's house, I also adopted a slight limp, hunching my shoulder under my schoolbag, muttering to myself as I went forward.

It was a walk I made every day and about each household that I passed, my grandmother had given me certain information, usually coloured with her own perceptions. There lived a Mr Jones who drank so much that a single scratch from a thorn killed him in an instant, leaving his whiskered widow to sit regretfully in a permanent aroma of polishes, while across the road in a much larger house the stipendiary magistrate, constantly visited by saluting policemen, came and went on foot in a shabby overcoat, often nodding sociably to me – his importance quite lost upon me until, years later, I was to trek up to his book-lined study in search of the character reference so necessary to bolster up my poor academic record. Then I passed a house once owned by a dimly remembered Aunt Polly who also had a parrot of the same name and, finally, came under the lee of my headmaster's house itself. Since it was set high above the road with a long set of winding steps, you could pass close to the gate without being seen above. I always approached it with a sense of apprehension, taking the deliberate risk of slowing down as I passed, my ears straining for any sound of him above, enjoying the tension created, and then hurtling past like a prisoner on the run. On this morning, limping, the bandaged claw outstretched, my face contorted with imagined pain, I played the same game, lingering dangerously by the closed gate, one step – two – and then I was clear! But I was hardly past when I heard a door slam high up in his house above me, and soon I was aware that he was behind me, his soft sinister footfalls audible. I did not dare to run but quickened my pace, stretching my legs so that I was almost goose-stepping, the Sebastopol Glove held far in front of me, my body hiding it. Fortunately, a woman came out of a house behind me and stopped to talk to him and I was clear once more.

Amazingly, none of my classmates suspected me in school. 'What have you done?'

'Oh, had an accident. Coal fell off the fire.'

'Trust you! Lucky sod. Alg' and geom' today.'

I sat manfully with the others in the geometry examination and made an attempt to complete the paper as I had planned, but now the Acraflavin began to seep through the bandage, staining the examination paper and the smell was so overwhelming that it irritated the master in charge, so much so that I feared he would send me out of the classroom to the library where I was certain to be detected since it was situated within a few yards of the headmaster's study and he made it his daily business to check who was in there.

But I insisted on trying to complete the examination paper. When it was seen to be clearly hopeless, the master told me to take out a reading book and duly wrote an explanatory note on the stained paper and I was left alone while the others continued, pens scratching away at the paper for this was the age of the relief nib and the cloth pen-wiper.

Then – of course – the expected happened, and we heard the telltale sound of boys in the next classroom scraping their chairs along the floor as they hurriedly stood up to attention, examination or no examination. The monster was on his rounds, varying his routine between the upper and lower school like a clever turnkey, his presence calculated not just to deter likely offenders, but also to remind supervising teachers that boys could be vile. In the practice of such deterrents, nothing was beneath him and in my travels in later life, I would sometimes come across old boys who had been on his list like myself and their greetings were invariably couched in imitations of his voice and special chastisements. Some of them were policemen and they would recall his peculiar habit of announcing returned ex-servicemen by rank, substituting their own with the inevitable debunking.

'Chief Superintendent Evans, J. 'B' Division. Smoking now, I see, Chief Superintendent? It'll be the young ladies next!'

Into the classroom he came, bald pate gleaming and flowing gown in a flurry. We jumped to our feet.

'Sit! Sit! Sit!' he snapped. I was sure the dressing flashed, illuminating me like a lurid beacon as I moved.

'They know they're not to borrow equipment? Nothing to pass from hand to hand?' he enquired of the master in charge. '*Hend to hend?*' he pronounced in the familiar South Wales posh.

'Yes, Mr Thomas.'

'Everything in order?'

'Yes, Mr Thomas.'

He nodded, almost amiable for a second, then against all expectations, proceeded briskly up the aisle – my aisle – and stopped beside me, peering at the blotched bandages, a look appearing on his face which was a caricature of incredulity. His eyebrows lifted as he snorted unbelievingly. He hooked his thumbs into his waistcoat.

'*What?-What?-What?-What?*'

'Accident, sir.'

'*Accident?*'

My voice now assumed a nervous confidentiality:

'Yes, Mr Thomas. Putting a coal on the fire, Mr Thomas. The er . . . bucket came down on top of it. I mean, the tongs, sir. It came down. Right down. *On it*, sir.'

He stared at me and soon a delighted smile broke across his sallow face. It was like a welcome issued by the porter at Hell's gate to the inner circle of the damned. I knew I was discovered and his smile has lingered in my mind. I once saw a Royal Marine colour sergeant, six and a half feet in height and with the foulest breath in the Corps put his moustachioed face through the doorway of a detention cell – straight into the face of a violent psychopathic prisoner who had broken the jaw of an officer. The colour sergeant had the same kind of smile and when he spoke, his voice had all his world in it, the vocal chords strained by the issuing of a thousand commands to men beyond all repair.

'Hard man, are you, Sunshine?' he said throatily. 'Little bit of a tiger, are you?' The prisoner did not speak and the colour sergeant smiled again. Like my headmaster, he relished the prospect of difficulty and in confrontation he was in his element.

'Putting a coal, *one coal*, on the fire?' said my tormentor; '*cole*?' he pronounced.

'Yessir.'

He chuckled evilly and bent forward.

'Remove it!'

'Pardon, sir?'

'The bandage!'

The examination had, of course, gone by the board. Every eye was upon me, or rather, upon it – the Sebastopol Glove. Once again, I was the centre of events and the atmosphere was charged by the genuine interest of my fellows, one of whom dared to stand up so as to get a better view. He was followed amazingly by others, and they did so unchecked.

I began to dismantle the Sebastopol Glove piece by piece, removing the holding strip of plaster from the wrist, then unwinding the long length of grubby bandage. It came off slowly, damply, the smell increasing and the cat's hairs showing clearly until finally the original small plaster dressing over the blister lay revealed. It seemed to have shrunk in size. I turned my palm over for inspection. There might now, I thought, be an act of clemency since the removal of the final strip of plaster was an act which might be considered too painful but his narrowed eyes gave me my answer. I lifted the edge of the small plaster and there lay my blister genuinely revealed, about an inch in diameter.

I felt I had to say something.

'I didn't know whether or not to burst it, sir?' I said hopefully, as if I could promote some casual conversation.

But my classmates let me down. Those who could see began to laugh, tentatively at first, then with his obvious encouragement much more loudly. The master in charge came up the aisle to inspect it and the laughter continued.

Then a snarl silenced everyone.

'*This thing!*' he said, referring to me. He looked at me for a moment, then turned abruptly and walked out. It was the beginning of my life as a comedian. I waited for days for him to send for me, the usual follow-up, but he did not. Perhaps he forgot about it, perhaps his silence was the real poultice upon the wound of my inadequacy. I never cheated again.

There were other confrontations. I made that walk, hugging

the wall of his house every day for six years, once carrying the school bell which I had purloined to take to the rugby ground at the Cardiff Arms Park when our school half-backs were capped for the Welsh senior team and again, he followed me, the bell chinking under my raincoat but this time I was undetected. On another occasion, he expelled me for refusing to go to a 'voluntary' lecture by a distinguished old boy and when, ignoring the expulsion, I returned to school the following day, he punished me for failing to bring a note to explain my absence! He was at this time, like almost everybody else, a recruiting officer and on Speech Days, although still gowned, he now appeared in the uniform of an RAF flying officer since he was Commanding Officer of the School Air Training Corps. Once, proudly displaying his First World War General Service ribbons, he proclaimed: 'Our old boys are serving in the four corner of the world! In Africah, in In-jah . . .' This was followed by a pause which indicated to me that he had run out of countries, but not to be undone – he was never undone! – he promptly repeated himself with aplomb: 'In er . . . In-jah, Africah!' On another occasion, standing magnificently in the centre of the platform, he got carried away. 'At the present time in two world conflagrations, ninety-seven of our old boys have paid the supreme sacrifice . . .' he began, then, pausing for effect with his customary glare around the hall, he lost his trend, probably thinking of examination results and continued volubly: 'and we have every hope and expectation that the number will reach treble figures by the end of the school year!'

But simply to quote him is to do him an injustice. He was a concerned, engaged, forthright man, never diffident or aloof, often wrong, but always moving forward, making a two-fisted attack on life, unafraid of its abrasions to the end. In some ways, for me at least, he remains enigmatic as a human being and I have recalled him as he appeared to me in those crucial years. There were at this time no effective form masters or house heads, or indeed anyone else who took the slightest interest in your progress through the lower school and we were like coins haphazardly pushed into a machine. Some set the machinery in motion, some did not, and reject coins like myself would otherwise have been left unspent. Old men pressed back into service while their juniors went to war lacked the energy to motivate us, and were further handicapped by the general restlessness in the air. But for my headmaster, I suspect I would have become an even more dire casualty. Later he was to praise me when he could and gradually I came to be chastised with a new preamble, 'A person of your intelligence . . .'; but in those first years, it was as if his physical presence was all that I had to think about. I was a fatherless child. I clutched at whatever root extruded from the undergrowth in which I sought to hide. Of all the men I knew up to that time, he was the most dominant and forceful and the only one interested enough in me and my fellows to pursue us, praise be, with such vigour. This he once did carrying his cane underneath his raincoat, walking a mile to a billiard saloon where the aroma of damp chalk and the shuffling sound of greasy playing cards falling on grimy tables provided us with yet another haven from the reality of school. He drew his cane and struck out from the hip as soon as he entered. And we – a half-dozen of us – dived for cover, scuttling under the snooker tables as his cane flashed, decimating a row of cues which fell as if struck by bullets with a staccato rattling of expensive timber that merged with the roar of his voice, 'Richards! Watkins!' – and a host of other names; 'To my room!'

Thus he intruded, offended, risked making a laughing stock of himself, and often chased us hotfoot, using fear as a weapon in a world which still grew more unpredictable and violent every day. His was a physical presence, but our physical wellbeing was not his concern. I was to remember his concern when I last saw him, a haunted and shrunken man, his greying face weakened by the onset of a throat cancer, he of all people frail and mufflered as our paths crossed once more under the chestnut trees. I had travelled several hundred miles to attend his retirement presentation, but this was some time later. Now he could scarcely speak but he gripped my hand warmly and I think he said, 'Keep them at it!', for I was teaching then myself. I could not reply to him, nor articulate my debt and, watching him thread his way homeward, his unsteady invalid's tread punctuated by the tap-tapping of his walking stick, my eyes filled with tears for the second time in our acquaintanceship. I was afraid no longer, but he left his mark indelibly upon me for later I was to stand on another school platform in morning assembly, one hand holding a vicious metal knuckle-duster, the other the ear of a miscreant, while I too fulminated.

'Make no mistake . . . I am not going to teach in a school where thuggery rules in the playground!'

Later a young supply teacher, a few years my junior as a pupil at my own school, buttonholed me in the staffroom.

'You know who you sound like? Pig! The image!'

It is true. Unless I am careful, on public platforms another monster lurks, loud-voiced and overbearing, looking likely to bustle up the aisle to the smokers' corner at any minute. The eyes are the same, so is the stance, but my voice belongs lower down the social scale, sounding, as a charming Old Etonian once informed me, 'like that of the shop steward British Leyland most want to sack!' I care not. Is there not another voice whispering in my ear? 'By their deeds shall we know them!'

The turning point in my school life came when I began to look ahead beyond my immediate peers to those a little older, some of whom were no more successful than I. Sooner or later an adolescent boy will recognise certain traits or attitudes in others which present themselves as likely future aspects of himself. What others have done, he might do. There will be those he likes and dislikes and also, if he is a realist, he will begin to realise that there is a ceiling to his ambitions. In my case for several years I was spoken to as if I were dull and stupid, and if praise came my way, as it eventually did from my English teachers, I had always to move into the next classroom where I had to revert to this other self for much of the school day. For four years I was a no-hoper, backward, unable to cope, sometimes the butt of sarcastic remarks and I often resorted to playing the fool to entertain my friends, becoming a mimic to this end. Every group creates its own black fool because it needs him to reassure the successful and to comfort the mediocre, and for the outsider, becoming the entertainer is one way of belonging.

Strangely enough, I now feel this is an experience that no one should be entirely without at some time of life. It is a healthy reminder of other people's difficulties when roles are reversed. I have often noted that nothing is more detestable than the way in which so many people, particularly English public schoolboys, develop the autocratic habit of brusque speech known in the services as 'good power of command' but which usually implies that they are not speaking to recognisable human beings of the same species. This was once brought home to me by a story of the African nationalist, Tom M'Boya who, backward at school, could only proceed to a technical college course where he qualified eventually as a sanitary inspector. On the first night of his appointment, proudly wearing his uniform in the splendour of the Nairobi Public Works Department, he was suddenly confronted at his desk by a planter's wife who strode in accompanied by her dogs. He stood up expectantly. It was his first moment of authority. He was in charge. But she looked through him haughtily, his black skin preventing her from seeing him as a person.

'Is there anybody here?' she said.

Like him I was a mentally absent and invisible person for much of my school life and, naturally, when I looked ahead, I looked keenly at those boys who were castigated and treated in much the same way as myself and soon I began to see a haven. Just as in rugby football which I had begun to play, I knew at once that I should be a forward and not a back, so did a place appear where I might be contained in the shape of a form called 5U, or occasionally 5 *Remove*. This group inhabited an old and dingy classroom in the old school block and beckoned me like an exclusive gentleman's club.

Here, tucked away in an ancient room under the stairs, were the savages and rowdies who comprised the most notorious form in the school, some of whose stalwarts dominated the rugby team. They had failed their school certificate and had reassembled to resit it. They were thus bigger than their contemporaries, being a year older, and for the same reason were much interrupted in class to carry out their roles as the school's hewers of wood and drawers of water. Although seldom called by the name *Remove*, it was the name best applied to them, for they were called upon to remove all the furniture in the school when such domestic changes were required. Among them was the Dirty Jobs Squad which might be required in emergencies if the caretaker went sick, or was not to be found

73

when some unfortunate vomited in the corridor. Here too were the valiants who could be called upon to chase wild and uncontrollable dogs, who were the bulwark of the fire-watchers when there was a threat of air raids, burly sand-and-bucket men who quarrelled over the Air Raid Precaution helmets, purloined the leaflets explaining how to deal with incendiary bombs, and often had a lawless authority of their own, sometimes intimidating the prefects who left them well alone. When they removed anything, they did it noisily with scant attention to authority, and since their resit year was the most pleasant they had experienced in the school and they were not intending to spend another year in it, they seemed collectively to adopt attitudes which were quite different from those destined – in the headmaster's words – for 'Higher Things in Education'. There were other important caste marks. Free of the pressures put upon sixth-formers of their own age, they had more time to turn their eyes to the world at large – and also looked different, and this became important.

Although the war had its effect upon us in many ways, nothing was more levelling than the short supply of clothing and, as it went on, the general appearance of people became more alike. In school we were at first obliged to wear ties and blazers, but as the stock of uniforms diminished, there was a less rigorous insistence so that we began to wear clothes which would not have been allowed at other times. Many of the boys wore their blue Air Training Corps uniforms, some attended on certain days in matlo's bellbottoms and jumpers if they were sea cadets and, here and there, items of service dress like khaki or blue pullovers were seen. But for some reason 5U seemed to stand apart and, when I looked at them, it was as if I too had my first intimation of the world at large because there were a number of them who dressed at the height of pre-war fashion, often the handed-down clothes of relatives who had been killed which included fancy fawn waistcoats, lemon pullovers, and in one case – incredibly – a pair of plus fours put in an appearance for a day or two. About them all, it seemed to me, was a raffish air fittingly described by the headmaster who would descend occasionally, prodding his fingers into the elegant waistcoats as he exclaimed, 'Young man about town, eh?'

That was it exactly, and while he sometimes euphemistically called 5U the 'Army Form', as if Sandhurst were beckoning, the fact was that the demand for manpower was such that anything was feasible. It is hard to convince people now of the imperceptible changes which the war caused in schools, particularly in our youthful expectations and the idea of a career which could be mapped out, those pleasant avenues of success divided up into stages by the passing of this examination or that – all was severely shaken by the defeat of the British Army in France. Some, naturally, pretended nothing had changed, but others sensed that a more chaotic wind was blowing. A peculiar kind of local history was being made before our very eyes and it was nothing like the past. Oafs whose bulging thighs protruded from ancient desks that were much too small for them and who were generally regarded at best as 'characters', at worst as 'thicks', suddenly reappeared after a year's absence with subaltern's pips in immaculate khaki uniforms, carrying leather-bound swagger sticks and perhaps the explanatory insignia of the Pioneer Corps, or more exotic still, the familiar Prince of Wales's feathers now representing some Ghurka regiment in the Indian Army. There were others too, the well-known rebels who scorned all uniforms – these appeared in shabby mufti with a silver badge and the letters MN for Merchant Navy. The classic Welsh exhortations from those who regarded scholarship as the principal avenue out of the pit had lost their immediate force and everywhere about us we had evidence of a more quixotic fate which was laden with ironies.

There was one classic story of two friends, neither of them exactly gifted, both rugby players whose school career had paralleled mine in poor performance and general waywardness but who were old enough to leave when the war was at its height. They did not see each other for several years, but chanced to meet on the night of the Old Boys' Dance which was held in the school assembly hall. On this occasion one of the friends came down the covered way immaculate in dress khaki, his one pip, shoulder straps and Sam Browne gleaming as he tapped his swagger cane imperiously against his leg. Beside the entrance a former classmate lurched drunkenly in a shabby suit and jersey, all survivors' clothes from a recent torpedoing, his third. The seaman was coarse-faced and strong with immense arms and fists which had earned him a nickname like Bashie, whereas the second lieutenant was genial and lazy. But another world had intruded and begun to mould him. As he gazed incredulously at his former classmate, he blinked unbelievingly. Feeling a sudden physical need as of old, he then enquired in the peremptory tones of the accent we had come to ridicule, 'I say, Bashie, old man, whereby is the pisshouse now?'

There was this story and that, and the world intruded constantly into the life of the school as we witnessed the return of those a little older than ourselves. One boy of burly physical appearance, old for his age with a fond parent who had connections in the clothing industry so that he was immaculate at all times, decided that he'd had enough even of 5U. Soon he appeared in the handsome uniform of a Merchant Navy cadet with kid gloves and white silk scarf, all embellishments which we admired. Then, as did so many others, he disappeared for a year and we went about our school work or improved our snooker, most of us sexually backward in both theory and practice. Suddenly, our friend reappeared, tanned and seeming broader, smoking Turkish cigarettes, already an habitué of the fastest bars in town, some of which had been placed out of bounds to US forces. He had little to say about the Merchant Navy, although his hands bore the peculiar marks of long and persistent immersion in hot water.

'Where have you been?' we said, eager for details.

'All over,' he replied expansively. It was the golden phrase of the time. It meant, the World. But he had been to Sydney, more cabin boy than cadet. You had to learn to stand with your back to the wall, he said impressively. We nodded wide-eyed, not understanding. In Sydney, he told us, he'd got off her as soon as he could.

'Who?'

'The ship!'

As soon as he docked, he gave the mate the slip and got in tow with a woman they called the Duchess, an ex-beauty queen of remarkable prowess. Staying ashore in her flat overlooking the harbour for a long weekend, she had finally driven him by car to the gangway. There he was spotted by the captain who seized a megaphone to order him to pick up a crate of lettuce and carry it aboard. He had done so at once but upon reaching the deck, such was his physical state, that he promptly collapsed in a dead faint.

'Couldn't even pick up a crate of lettuce!' he told us, shovelling around his duty-free cigarettes.

'How many times a night?'

'Five. And three times without taking it out . . .'

'Bloody hell! All in bed was it?'

'Twice on the stairs, once in the bath.'

'In the bath?'

'*French* . . .'

'Did you have to ask her, Billy?'

'You don't in Australia. They don't give you a chance.'

We sat riveted, open-mouthed. It was the Duchess, of course, a woman who haunted my imagination for years until I began to see her as one of those sinewy, twisting, sexual athletes revealed in lurid poses on cheap editions of the *Kamasutra*, with three or four pairs of arms and legs, the whole attached to the blonde tresses and deadpan face of Veronica Lake, the current screen pin-up who, incredibly, I later accidentally tripped up on the dance floor of a London night-club. Unfortunately – I have worked it out – she was fifty-four at the time, an age I then thought unforgivable. Another shock was that she was as small as a large garden gnome, only the peek-a-boo hairstyle and the immobile, deadpan features remained the same as the face I had planted upon the Duchess. The vision stuck in my mind for years, as did the sentence which galvanised the school.

'Did you hear about our Billy down in Sydney?' we said. 'Couldn't even pick up a lettuce!' And it wasn't long before we added knowledgeably in our piping voices: 'You'll do all right in Sydney!'

Thus are our minds formed and the central focus of my education began to switch to that core of experience which emanated from the snappy dressers and the studied elegance of the lemon-yellow pullovers and white riding macs of 5U, the whole ambience more 'county' than you would have expected. There was, also, rugby football which came to dominate our school life and provided another world which sometimes seemed to exist independent of the school, although the social approval which the school cast upon it was one more way in which South Walian forces moulded our lives in traditional ways. I did not know then that prowess at rugby football would eventually carry with it a kudos which would provide a magic key that opened doors to entire careers for those especially gifted. To me it was at first an extension of the kind of sub-world which existed in that gentleman's club under the stairs and on the periphery of the billiard saloons increasingly populated by county schoolboys and the local YMCA which, at the time, was little more than a services canteen with thriving snooker and card tables, and a complete absence of any kind of authoritarian supervision. Here worthies gathered for a game of solo whist or brag, eventually contract bridge, and there was a strange mixture of town and gown as the hallowed letters YMCA provided a safe haven for modest gambling and only the headmaster ever penetrated it as vigilante. Here we went after school for a quick frame of snooker and mixed at an early age with servicemen on leave and heard the stories which revealed a different world to that described by visiting dignitaries.

'*Brigadier Stubbings*', said the school magazine, '*talked so entertainingly on the Indian Army that the boys privileged to hear him evinced little desire to return to their studies.*'

Studies also went by the board for rugby football. That we knew, since for the whole of my time in the County School we had an unbeaten school first fifteen and the aura which attached itself to the players outshone that of all other groups. When our school half-backs, Glyn and Wynford Davies, were capped – first for the Welsh Secondary Schools team, then for the senior team itself, while still schoolboys – we had a half-holiday, and the headmaster frequently read aloud glowing match reports praising the play of our heroes in the school assembly hall. But this was excellence, a stylish excellence at that. Underneath there were tiers of performance, second fifteens, form teams, club and cadet teams, an infrastructure of groups whose buzzing enthusiasms formed cadres from which the progress to stardom and its concomitant glories began.

In my own case I lacked the physical coordination for excellence, but early on I sensed that there might be a place for me. At first it was simply a matter of group loyalties, us against them – the school form to which I belonged, 4B, having taken it upon itself to respond to a challenge from our inferiors, paradoxically known as 4A. They wanted a match. They could have one.

The game was on a Saturday morning at the edge of the cricket field in the centre of the town's memorial park. We changed in the open, few of us with proper kit. I had been lent rugby boots two sizes too large for me by a boy whose brother had recently been killed in Java. I had PT shorts but no jersey and so wore an old pullover and short socks which stopped at the ankles. Those who had precious jerseys were allowed to play at three-quarter, one of the reasons being that their jerseys stood in less danger of being torn or damaged than if they played at forward. There was not a single spectator. The referee was a senior boy who could be trusted with a school ball. As we gathered behind the sight screens, our shrill voices echoed in the damp air.

'Jonesie's got two pairs of socks!'

'Give us one!'

'Can't. I'm wearing them both.'

'Come on!'

'Can't. I'm playing in the front row.'

There were two boys in this team whom I was to meet later on, in the strangest of circumstances. One was even then over six feet in height, a drifting skeleton with staring myopic eyes and a habit of talking soundlessly to himself. He did not seem to have a will of his own in class and invariably followed others, joining groups automatically where he stood out like a vulnerable lathe. We called him Knocker because he was an obsequious knocker of doors, appearing like a lamplighter in the corridor windows. Now he had brought with him a large pair of foundryman's working boots with steel toe-caps which were laced with strong hessian cord, and, like myself, he was without stockings or jersey and determined to play in his woollen vest which was much too large for him and hung in folds. He looked a sight with pinhead protruding from its drapes and it was as if the huge weighted foundry boots at the end of his stalk-like legs acted as an emplacement for a slender secret weapon – in fact, the great tottering length of him above. But he slipped his spectacles knowledgeably into his shoes for safety and I followed suit.

The other star was a boy who had three Christian names

79

which was regarded by the master filling in the register on our first day at school as both a conceit and a wanton extravagance, since he had difficulty in writing them all down in the appropriate column.

'Name?'

'Evan John Keith!'

The master protested so we immediately called the boy Bugsy, the choice of nickname dictated by an outbreak of nits on the school bus. He was also unusual in that he wore his vaselined hair exceptionally long with the result that it flapped oddly at the back of his neck. But on this morning he was immaculate and properly kitted out with starched flybag shorts with pockets, polished rugby boots, scout stockings and a white tropical shirt of substantial cloth so that there was a touch of class about him and he outshone us all. He also made it plain when we sorted out the positions that if he wasn't allowed to play at wing-forward, he wasn't going to play at all.

We were short of a hooker.

'Rich', will you go?'

'All right,' I said.

'Good boy, Rich'.'

I felt superior to Bugsy already.

Knocker had to be in the second row and when I found his pinhead sandwiched against my thighs as we tried out our positions, I could just see him out of the corner of my eye but the thinness of his bones meant that every time we packed down, he cut into me like a butcher's steel. This was to be his strength and when play began, he became a leaping, elbowing apparition, a creature of sharp edges, elbows and knees, all working like flailing scissors. But as well as cutting into our opponents, he also collapsed our own scrums and took against Bugsy who soon began to talk continuously, giving such gratuitous and meaningless advice as 'Short and take!' and 'Feet! Feet!', which Knocker thought were personal remarks expressly directed at himself. ('Whose feet, please?') So he did the opposite, stretched and writhed, the foundry boots carelessly moving this way and that, the elbows jabbing and prodding, working against all who came near him, friend and foe.

Soon it began to rain continuously and there were further

complications as the weather got worse. These all seemed to centre around Knocker. First, having got the ball he never released it, not once, not even when Bugsy told him to. Then, having caught it he hid it, the rest of us binding and milling around him like infantry looking for cover behind an absurdly slim tank. But the flailing limbs created spaces in front and we invariably drove forward like a wedge in which he was as much germ as weapon, salivating, biting and grunting as he writhed on. 4A panicked, the cowards got out of the way, and only the odd stalwarts stopped him, usually by the inferior tactic of kneeling down in front of him as if in prayer. But this counterplay took time and we had made several dashes of ten or twenty yards before they grew wise.

'Good boy, Knocker!' the cry came from our captain who stood as an interested spectator in the centre of the field. It was a cry much repeated as we drove on and on, even approaching their goal line. Once, having been prayer-matted then bowled over with others, Knocker hid the ball under his copious woollen vest. At another time he tucked it under both arms and found himself attempting a somersault, the wildly raking legs in the foundry boots slashing at the air like some futuristic piece of agricultural machinery, but still creating valuable space. In this period, he seemed to be playing 4A on his own. His face was flushed, he salivated continuously, his myopic eyes peered about him and all the time his lips moved soundlessly as he continued to trail part of his private world about him. At times he was the schoolboy vision of the mad professor, but his effect was that of a street fighter. The men were very rapidly being sorted out from the boys in our opponents' team, for their pack had disintegrated and become a team of wing-forwards who all sought glory hanging about on the edge of the mêlée. They had also begun to quarrel amongst themselves.

'You go opposite him?'

'No, I'm not. You go.'

'I've been.'

'Come on, boys. He's getting through all the time.'

'It's all very well for you to talk out there on the wing. Why are you always throwing the ball to him?'

'I can't get it over his head!'

'Well, shut your mouth then, or come in by here!'

There were also injuries now – injuries, stoppages, evil looks. One boy got Knocker's elbow in his eye. It swelled up at once, blackened as if poisoned by some deadly venom. Then Knocker trod on the foot of some unfortunate who only wore plimsolls and he went off the field sobbing and did not come back for half an hour. And through it all, Knocker blossomed, peering after the casualty modestly. He seemed to be unstoppable by virtue of an eerie form of hypnotism, for we seemed to be living in the lines-out and no matter which team threw the ball in, it inevitably ended up in his hands. It got so that his look was enough, the ball simply would not pass him; and once he had got hold of it, the rest of him moved at once. The ball became like a coin which you put into a slot machine. The moment it touched, the monster moved. Now 4A tried various tactics. They raced to the line-out to get there first in order to avoid him. This failing, they began to trail in the hope that being last was safest, but then Knocker began to move his position so that the line-out went backward and forwards, extending like a snake, then compressing; and all the time, he rose above it, his thin limbs extended and waving like signal flags until he pounced. Now there were hoarse shouts from 4A's captain who played at full-back.

'Come on, boys! Mark him!'

There were mutters in reply, low furtive voices already mutinous. 'Mark him? He's marking me. Come and have a look at my leg.'

Inevitably, we soon got within a few feet of their line when Knocker got felled himself. He was kicked, a half-dozen people fell on top of him, but he scorned attention and once more we lined up. Now we could smell victory. There must be a try coming. Bugsy had now ingratiatingly placed himself near Knocker and kept close to him, sensing glory. Knocker took the ball once more but then there was an accidental tactic, for 4A, led by their captain, immediately piled in like angry wasps, shamed at last into action, but to our amazement Knocker began to run the wrong way with three or four wasps hanging on to his vest. Knocker had become disorientated and so had we all, with the result that both teams hustled him into touch, combined efforts being needed in a unique emergency.

'You've got to turn him,' Bugsy said to the rest of us. 'Keep the wind at the back of you, Knock'.'

Knocker looked sheepish, but Bugsy was right. Again and again, we lined up and now we shouted, 'This way, Knocker! Wind behind you!'

It would have been fitting if Knocker had scored, but he did not. It was Bugsy sneaking in on the massive heels of the foundry boots who saw his chance, picked up and went over like a rabbit, now a dirty mirage in off-white. Up went the referee's finger, a firm blast on the whistle, a try!

We had an impromptu party on the spot, shrieking and gyrating, clapping Bugsy on the back.

'Good boy, Bugs!'

'It was Knocker really,' Bugsy said modestly. Ambitious, he was playing his cards right. He wanted more. The captain told Bugsy to attempt the conversion, but before he went over to take the kick, Bugsy called me to one side. He was very excited but his manner was confidential.

'Rich'?'

'What d'you want?'

He came close to me, sidling up, turning his back to the referee and our captain who stood waiting to hold the ball while 4A huddled disconsolately behind their posts.

'Favour?' Bugsy said out of the side of his mouth. 'Hold on to this for me.'

With the most furtive of expressions, he put his hand deep into the pocket of his flybags and removed a large army clasp knife, complete with marlinspike, and slipped it surreptitiously into my own hand to hold for him while he took the kick. Then he trotted off, his vaselined hair bumping lumpily, all attention upon him.

The kick failed, he returned to me and merely held out his hand. I handed over the knife, no explanation being asked for or given, and the game finished soon afterwards. We drifted about the park, at first together, then in twos and threes – highly elated, so together that we did not want to go home or leave one another.

'How did you get on?'

'We ate 'em!' we said, again and again.

To this day I have never discovered or been able to make up

my mind whether Bugsy regarded the clasp knife as part of his essential rugby equipment, to go with his white flybags and shirt, or whether – more likely – he had found the knife on the field since the Territorial Army used it for exercises. He was never an especial friend but years later, after a long period abroad, I was delighted to see him in the enclosure at Twickenham – the first homely face I was to see that day.

'Bugsy?' I shouted at the top of my voice. I was overjoyed to meet someone from home.

He was elegant in white riding mac, yellow gloves, Old Boy's scarf, the hair more discreetly Brylcreemed and in the company of two high-heeled girls, both elegantly dressed and one on each arm.

He nodded briefly, did not stop and passed on, both he and the girls displeased.

I could almost read his lips.

'At school with me. Never cared much for the fellow.'

So do our paths cross and uncross. After I left school, I saw Knocker only once, this time as a booking-hall clerk in a railway station as he argued with an irate customer, his neck extending through the glass partition like a giraffe's from its stall. He was evidently giving one of his long speeches. I never saw either of them again. But once we walked proudly together as victors.

'Good boy, Rich'.'

'Good boy, Knocker!'

'Good boy, Bugsy!'

That old ambition of mine to join the select ranks of the resit form was to be thwarted. As expected I failed my Central Welsh Board School Certificate, since a combination of five subjects was required, but because I had opted for Spanish and the timetable could not be rearranged to suit me alone, I merely marked time for another year in a form of younger boys. This proved successful, since a number of events now took place which altered my life in subtle ways. Chief among them was my appointment as the headmaster's Gold Flake Boy. A heavy smoker, he was constantly in need of this special brand of cigarette and since my form-room was the nearest to

84

his, he made it a practice to appoint a smoking factotum from this form – an appointment which he frequently coupled with the position of Bell Boy, an equally important task since the ending of lessons in the old school was marked by the ringing of a handbell which he checked at forty-minute intervals, sometimes by the second hand of his own watch. It was, he gave me to understand, a position of immense responsibility and in my case, if appointed, it would be a signal honour.

'You have a watch?'

I had a watch.

'Is it accurate?'

It was accurate.

'I am considering you,' he said, but shook his head gravely, clenching his gown and sucking at his breath as we stood in the gloomy corridor where he had summoned me. 'For, you see, there will be other duties.'

When he was talking to you in the corridor, those who passed did so with bated breath and other boys made as wide an encircling movement as possible. You could feel them wanting to be invisible, at the same time curious, like spectators at a nasty traffic accident. You were sure to be cross-examined later, for each public interrogation was a minor event. ('What did he have you for, then?')

'Other duties . . .' he repeated. He did not reveal their exact nature then, but he finally came to a decision.

'You will be on approbation,' he said.

So I became his Gold Flake Boy and several times a week would be sent on his tobacco errands when I had the power to swear in a deputy to look after the school bell. It was an appointment not without its nepotistical flavour since cigarettes were in short supply and another uncle of mine had returned home to keep my grandfather's shop, but this connection was seldom necessary as he had his own supplier. I was sent on these errands in the middle of the school day and somehow or other I knew I had to return discreetly with my purchases, bringing them quietly into his study. If there were visiting dignitaries present, I would unobtrusively place the cigarettes together with the change in a paper bag near the door, having first secured the nod from him but taking care not to display them. I became a model of discretion like the butler on the Kensitas cigarette packets, adopting a suitably solemn and confidential air. As Gold Flake Boy, I could often choose the lessons I wanted to miss and these occasions did not pass without comment.

'Four Eyes has gone out for the headmaster,' my former cronies said bitterly.

I had a new status. I enjoyed it immensely.

SIX

People often think that education comes to one by virtue of attendance at some place where it may be 'got'. In my own case, I 'got' very little as a consequence of formal lessons and my struggle was simply to survive. At first I went for cover, needing to pass unnoticed and undetected amongst my fellows; later I tried to find some place for myself within the life of the school. The dread of school felt by so many is rooted in fear of exposure and ridicule. Every individual craves some chance of success, a status; if not in academic subjects, then it must be found elsewhere – in sport or in the other activities which go on, often reflecting the enthusiasms of individual teachers whose contributions in this way are immeasurable. If the home circumstances also cause anxiety, the pressures on the child multiply and the need to escape from both sets of circumstances may provide an impetus which leads to all kinds of delinquency.

For me, reading became the only total escape until the war ended and the younger teachers returned, bringing with them enthusiasms which had been lacking for the most part – doubtless the battle to keep the school going at all left little over for extras, but I was not to be aware of that. By the time the war ended, my school life had changed completely. It was not that I grew any more or less intelligent, but that my search for knowledge of lives outside my own led me into the pages of fiction which I devoured omnivorously and uncritically, book after book. Often reading under the bedclothes at night by torchlight, to keep myself supplied I had frequently to make a daily visit to the local library whose shelves I haunted, withdrawing the maximum number of books, sometimes returning them in the same day. I read anything and everything, from Richmal Crompton and the structured world of her 'William' books, and all of Percy F. Westerman's adventures of Cadet Alan Carr, to Maugham and particularly J. B. Priestley whose voice on the radio distinguished him as a man of place, immediately identifiable amongst the bland and mannered tones of others who seemed to have a monopoly of the microphone. I often carried a bookstrap and became conspicuous.

'You can't have read all those?'

'Test me!'

I obtained extra tickets to last me over the weekend and came – fortunately – to be spoilt by the local librarian who smiled benevolently upon me. That was one stroke of luck; another was the return from the army of the senior English master, Ken Railton. It was to him, a diffident and sensitive man whose disapproval of the headmaster's hectoring ways became obvious, I owed my change of heart towards school for under his tutelage I began to succeed – to win, for the first time, modest praise which acted upon me like an elixir. What is more, on one of the headmaster's rounds, I was praised publicly and it was as if the enemy had been sent packing; as if I had passed into other hands and there, in that gloomy and ancient schoolroom which had the Victorian sign 'WORK FOR THE NIGHT IS COMING' slotted upon its walls, I had magically found a way ahead. I began to abuse my position of power as Bell Boy, daily extending the English lesson by delaying the ringing of the bell and now I laboured over homework like a monk scratching at a parchment, becoming in the process another person. Then there was the school play – produced by another returned soldier – in which I was given a part, a school magazine which welcomed my contributions, and the poetry I had begun to write. This, although mawkish and sentimental, also gave me a sense of difference. It was as if a skivvy had come out from under the stairs and joined the family.

It was not an abrupt transition, but the effect of praise was dramatic. There were the usual intrusions and we continued to jump to our feet when the Gauleiter checked up.

'Sit!-Sit!-Sit! Form 5B about its labours, I take it? Hm . . . How d'you find Richards, Mr Railton?'

'Exceptional in every way.'

'Hm . . . Hm . . .' Words actually failed him.

On his face there was only disbelief, but there was now born in the ogre's mind that further phrase with which to chastise me: 'A person of your intelligence . . .' He continued to have good reason because my general examination results remained poor. But I just passed the dreaded School Certificate and the time came to think about a career, a decision which I put off for as long as possible. There was an odd form called 6B (Commercial) which existed for boys who were not taking the Higher Certificate and filled in an extra year by taking commercial subjects like book-keeping and shorthand.

'There may be a place for you in commerce?' the headmaster said expansively as if the City of London awaited me.

But there were typewriters in that classroom and the amiable master in charge had, I was to discover, a private library from which he introduced me to Evelyn Waugh's *Scoop*, an event in my reading life. So to 6B (Comm) I went, free of the pressures of an examination, and there I spent a happy year untainted by the social disapproval which still attached itself to the gentleman's club under the stairs. Miracle of miracles, I was a sixth former.

Eventually, I responded to school by doing the best I could and I was lucky, both in my headmaster and in my English teacher whose very different selves acted upon me like sharply contrasted instructors, always at loggerheads but who, in their joint efforts, contrived to keep the swimmer afloat. In the sixth form the headmaster relaxed, especially after I began to play rugby for the first fifteen and when I won an essay competition in the local newspaper and scored the only try of my career in a key match, I might have been a genuine hero for my virtues were now extolled from the assembly hall platform. There were real heroes, among them Tasker Watkins, later a Lord Justice of Appeal, who won the VC and was the cause of a half holiday. Now it seemed the headmaster never lost an opportunity to praise, and if the praise was too fulsome, the notes stentorian, often the trumpet blasts of a propagandist – it was still praise. As we got older we began to realise his limitations, to see through his bluff; but by then he had become a character, always a caricature of himself, a shared hazard and a decisive and abrasive part of our growing up.

There was another world, however, outside of school and it is from this world that images most often return. There was after all a kind of order in school – common enemies, common delights and routines which faced us all; a togetherness created by age, or simple geography. We were all in that together, like the war itself; but outside, at home, along the street, in the billiard halls we frequented, we each made our own way separately and carved our different niches. At home, my problems remained. My mother's tours of duty at the army convalescent home allowed her to return home several times a month when she often took me to the cinema which had began to absorb me. I knew nothing of her life away from home and although I once visited her at Miskin Manor, which had been converted and was used to rehabilitate the wounded, and rowed her around the lake in a small boat, I never went again. She was too busy. I found her visits home an embarrassment, although she gave me pocket money and such treasures as brass soldier's-cap badges from many regiments and a button stick for cleaning brass which I kept all my life. Her brother Tudor now lived at home and ran my grandfather's grocery shop and I was aware of an antipathy between them, with the result that I clung closer to my grandmother who remained the constant and stable influence. The feeling that I was a nuisance as a small child ended; but as I grew older and began to have friends and a life of my own outside the house, I began to live two lives and I see now that I was already taking steps to escape. I already felt that there was so much which my grandmother did not understand about the world in which I lived, and there was a good deal which I left unreported about my own life and that of my contemporaries. Between a woman in her sixties and an adolescent boy there is a necessary reserve and I had already realised that there must be secrets, and that her feelings must be spared. I could not bear to see pain upon her face, she who had suffered so much. So I, by censorship, by slight embellishments, invented my own doings in a sense – creating a reportage of them that was acceptable to her ears, just as, I found, her own children did. It was as if I was already taking steps to become a popular author while all the time I was noting another kind of reality, keeping it to myself, filing it away, reserving it until I could deal with it. Thus, I came to have another persona. But when I addressed a simple letter of enquiry to the sports pages of the *South Wales Echo* and they printed the answer, together with my name, and my grandmother proudly flourished the newspaper as if I were a distinguished contributor and promptly announced to our neighbour, 'They do not understand him in that school!', I was quite capable of modestly bowing my head, and did.

Like all fatherless children, I had a secret wish for normality. It was never to end. All through adolescence in the houses of my friends, I would study the behaviour of fathers rather as a butterfly hunter examines a species, collating odd items of information for future reference. There were fathers who farted and fathers who shouted and fathers who sulked. There were fathers who swore, gardened, went to the pub or the club and others who never went anywhere. (What's he doing? He's moping!) They seemed, did fathers, to grow on garden allotments where on any given summer evening you might find them sprouting collarless and unshaven in clumps, and I studied them all gravely. I once saw a collier-father bathing in a tin bath, on his naked back the bright raw redness of new blood glistened through a layer of coal dust from a nasty wound. But he laughed at my alarm and when he produced a sixpence to send his son on an errand 'Over the shop for Dada!', I felt another stab of self-pity. At the other end of the social scale was the stipendiary magistrate and his rage when the maid misplaced his normal pint-sized breakfast mug for a mere tea-cup. And then there was our chapel minister who lived nearby – a gaunt, haunted man with sepulchral features who locked the door of his front room on days when he prepared his sermons with the air of one communicating personally with the Almighty; but he was disturbed like any father when his erring son, a pianist of note, absconded on the Irish mail-boat to join Waldini's Accordian Band and had to be brought home shame-faced.

'He has gone! He has gone!' his mother announced dramatically.

We thought she was referring to the old man whose winter

bronchitis was as usual severe. He always looked, as my grandmother put it, like Death itself.

'The Lord sends these things to try us . . .'

'No, he has gone to Ireland to join Waldini.'

I was most envious of those boys whose fathers accompanied them to rugby matches, for the most part amazingly young men. Just as I thought all mothers should be fat, so for a time I imagined fathers all to be old and grizzled. Another friend's father had been gassed in the First World War, then prematurely retired so that he was continually at home, able to take part in games with his son. Then fathers came home from the war in large numbers and I felt even more deprived, but mainly I was curious – of all of them. Again conscious of a missing element in my life, I fantasised and invented stories of a father killed in action; but I told no one, and if anyone asked me any questions, I said he was dead and dismissed it from my mind. I soon came to avoid company where I was likely to be asked such questions and my friends never referred to the matter. I must have communicated my hurt in some way and was spared the pain of answering questions by those closest among my friends, most of whom I kept for the rest of my life.

One of the great happinesses of my childhood was that I was welcome everywhere I went outside the house. At first I moved up and down the social scale without being aware of it, and since my uncle took over my grandfather's shop when the old man died, we continued to live in a condition of modest affluence – although not quite as comfortably as others nearby whose children were sent away to public schools and who returned home, gulping like lost fish. They were accented with polite manners, the boys often shooting from a sitting position on to their feet when confronted by the opposite sex – a habit which profoundly startled me when I first witnessed it. I did not envy them, but noted with satisfaction that they welcomed my company in the holidays as they became increasingly estranged from the streets where I seemed to know everyone. There was this group, and there were others – my schoolmates, including the companions of the difficult years who remained intransigents and continued on what the headmaster called 'the downward slope'. I see now that I had a foot in many camps, moved among them with ease, my bookishness hidden as I joined the card players or squinted under the lights of the snooker tables.

My conception of social class was indeed slow in growing and my grandmother put the definitive seal upon it. We were first and foremost chapel people, and that was that. Free of the petit bourgeois constraints which surrounded her, the only concession to ostentation she ever made was in her sixties when she accepted a fur coat from her surviving son in honour of her visit to Buckingham Palace to receive Ithel's Distinguished Flying Cross. Upon it she often pinned a simple sprig of artificial violets and she never felt quite at home wearing it, although her two daughters always looked at it with envy. After she was dead, it had a life of its own since my mother wore it for years in one shape or another, finally having it considerably shortened until it was little more than a cape.

As far as my own clothes went, clothes rationing prohibited any marked difference in my appearance until my late teens when I began to favour the county-set clothes affected by 5 *Remove* – tweeds and riding macs, the stiff white kind now associated with sex offenders and indecent exposure. Then they seemed to give the highly desirable impression that the horseless had recently stepped off a horse. My grandmother approved of this style for she was from a long line of farmers, although a blue suit for Sundays was for a good while the order of the day. There were, however, special constraints at home. My Uncle Tudor, a bachelor until middle age, like his father had to disguise his breath whenever he took alcohol outside the house since it was never allowed inside it. So I grew up with the firm smell of peppermint until it was replaced by chlorophyl tablets, including large-size animal chlorophyl tablets intended and advertised as very satisfactory for farting bulldogs, which I eventually came to take myself in copious numbers – one tablet for every three pints of ale, I eventually calculated. Even when my uncle became a magistrate, the deception continued and the surface appearance of all our lives was dominated by the fierce Nonconformist spirit of a little woman who would not compromise. Her great fear for me, she often told me, was that I should follow my always absent and seldom discussed father or her brother Jack, the horseman who had 'drunk himself into his grave' – a phrase that made me think of him actually toppling into it. Drink – all of it, anywhere in any company – was a demon and she never let me forget it. The attitude was not uncommon amongst older people who had witnessed the rapid industrialisation of the valleys in our chapel, and the consequent debasing of the rural life it replaced.

My mother was away all through my teens, my uncle was busy – at first resentful at having to give up the freedom of his life as a commercial traveller to settle at home, he had little time for me although it was his efforts which supported us – so that I was left pretty much to myself. My books, my reading, the forays into sport, rugby, table tennis, snooker were tendrils of normality – and I carefully nurtured them, discovering a life for myself, forming habits that would last for ever. Some of these skills, particularly table tennis, were to help me forty years later in Japan since I remembered a highly idiosyncratic service – illegal, perhaps, but it won me games and was the subject of much discussion, all a step towards breaking down barriers. In my childhood there were few barriers.

But if I had other things to occupy me, I was still a misplaced person. Under the tendrils, a disturbed self peered out at the world and my condition was not improved by the sexual stirrings of adolescence. In adult life it is easy to forget the teenager's single-minded obsession with sex, but my own perceptions were stark and stand out in my mind still. When my grandfather was dying, a nurse stayed in the house for several days. We'd had a bathroom built on to the end of the house, access to which was through my bedroom. One night she forgot to lock the bathroom door and I walked in upon her stark naked as she sat smoking on the edge of the bath, powdering herself. The amount of hair upon her body disgusted me and my revulsion must have been obvious for she sought me out later and gave me a number of cigarette cards by way of recompense. I did not see a naked woman again until, intoxicated and inflamed, I burst drunkenly through the bead curtain of a brothel in La Linea in my twenties and for years my sexual knowledge proceeded in lunatic fits and starts, comic in retrospect, painful at the time.

94

I lived a chauvinist life separated from girls for the whole of my formal education and most of my childhood. They might have been a different species but, of course, we talked about them constantly and later investigated. First, however, I fell in love, hopelessly and idiotically and – curious imitation of the pattern of my relationships with Knocker and Bugsy – the subject of my adoration re-entered my life in an oddly unexpected way. Between the jerseyed cherub and the bookish young man in the white riding mac, there was another figure – itchy in a blue serge suit, bespectacled and staring, the omnipresent mole remaining like a dago sideburn. I had, I am told, an unnerving stare. Like Richard Burton I practised it, as if I could will people to crumble in front of me. (But when I tried it out once on him, I lost. I could not keep it up.)

The subject of my adoration has a special significance in my life since, despite my wayward progress through school, there was always a respectable side to me, a part which wanted to behave in ways of which my grandmother would approve and so it was natural that the first girl should be a regular attender at our chapel. She was dark, neat and fresh-complexioned and pretty with high cheekbones and that gypsyish air which Welsh girls sometimes have. Her hair was quite long and naturally curly with jet-black ringlets so that when she shook her head you half expected them to chime. She also spoke Welsh and came from a family who suddenly arrived in our midst like ghosts from our own past. Her father, an inspector for the National Society for the Prevention of Cruelty to Children, known ironically as Powell the Cruelty, brought with him from the unknown territory of North Wales a wife and seven children. All of them spoke Welsh fluently and naturally as their first language and about them there was a healthy robustness that brought an infusion of life into the sparsely attended and decaying chapel. They filled a complete pew, descending in size like minature toby jugs, and all were handsome, fresh-faced and vigorous. The eldest brother, much torpedoed, swaggered home with frost-bitten fingers; the eldest sister was in the Wrens. All had about them an air of the world that contrasted with the cowed air of many of their chapel neighbours. Perhaps because they were poor, they were not quite so ostensibly respectable; the younger brothers wore

95

handed-down clothes and there was a liveliness to them that somehow did not belong in that gleaming mahogany temple of righteousness.

The middle daughter's name was Buddug – the Welsh for Boadicea – and although I even then regarded it as slightly ridiculous, and her friends called her Biddy, I kept that treachery to myself. I had already pressed my attentions upon her. Misusing my position as Gold Flake Boy, I had contrived to wait all morning for her outside the dentist's, just to get a glimpse of her, and perhaps a few hurried words; but she emerged swollen and red-faced and obviously annoyed to dismiss me with hardly a sentence. Both of us were in the chapel Christmas play but I never seemed to be able to get her on her own. Once a group of us decided to explore a loft in another church building and I, ever the perfect gentleman, stood aside to allow her to climb a ladder but she refused pointedly and I suffered again, for I saw that she believed that I wanted to look up her skirts when no such intention was in my mind. Another put-down occurred when an elderly woman died almost in front of us one night in the chapel vestibule. It was a violent death, the woman expiring in a fit, her cheeks blue, eyes staring, vomit cascading on the marble floor. One of the deacons ran for a doctor but the doctor was too late. It was a frightening experience and although later I attempted to put on a George Raft face and some sophistication as if to imply, 'Suckers get it all the time!', the experience disturbed me profoundly, as did the impotence of those who tried to help. It was the first death we had both seen and when I confessed my horror at those choking sobs, she said: 'Oh, you get that with asphyxia.'

I sought her company constantly and did everything I could to impress myself upon her and thought about her continually, but I still could never get her on her own. Finally the chance came when I contrived an expedition to Caerphilly Castle – a place of approved interest since we were both studying history – and she finally agreed, her bright green eyes laughing with amusement. All week I worried about what I should wear, how I should behave, and fatally decided to vaseline my hair which stuck up in sprouting clumps because of my awkward double crown. It was still the mole-time in my life, however, and much as she occupied my thoughts, I doubt if I occupied her. I was conscious of my innocence and longed for the poker face, the marks of age and experience, all evidenced by the American film stars who had begun to influence my fantasies. But now, I thought, I would at last get her on her own and have my chance to shine.

But when I called at her house to collect her, she was in Girl Guides' uniform holding the hand of her snivelling eight-year-old brother. She had to take him. It was a condition of us going together.

'You'll have a *lovely* time!' her mother said in the effusive Welsh way.

As it happened, we had an awful time. It rained. We spent an hour looking for a public lavatory and the brat kept crying all the time. It was the end of my romance with Buddug and shortly afterwards I ceased to attend chapel on any regular basis, doing so only at the behest of my grandmother on special occasions. There was no one reason, just my general dissatisfaction at the elderly ambience, and the echoes of the ancient language. It all belonged irretrievably to the past.

Its values would haunt me, however, and half a lifetime later Buddug's snot-nosed brother Gareth turned up in the disguise of a millionaire paperback publisher sporting a Rolls Royce at the precise time when I was busy complaining that most of the people you met in positions of power in London had been at school with each other.

I reminded him of that day, of Caerphilly Castle in the rain.

'D'you remember when I gave you sixpence to clear off?'

'You're wrong,' he said. 'It was threepence.'

He did not publish my books and loftily informed me that he did not read most of what he published and promptly disappeared once more, one of the few millionaires to apply for an assisted passage to Australia. His sister became an actress, appeared in the first stage version of *Under Milk Wood*, and also disappeared. I never saw either of them again.

Such memories of childhood, I have found, are popular amongst Welsh people who tend in retrospect to idealise the past, often imbuing it with a quality of golden innocence. But in reality, it was never like that. Innocence soon changes as a conception of sin is formed and the simple black and white values of the primitive Nonconformist religions can sometimes bring on the seeds of madness. My infatuation with Buddug was both an end and a beginning and an example of normality. Later, however, knowledgeably avoiding chapel girls, I found another girl – a discovery with dramatic and lunatic consequences. Slipping my hand under her blouse in a youth club party, I found my explorations welcome; but when I returned home two hours later than I had promised, I entered the little kitchen to find it empty. Upon the table was a Glamorgan Constabulary helmet with shining steel spike and gleaming chain mail, a pair of white cotton policeman's gloves beside it. The sound of voices came from the front room at the end of the passage, from the room that was seldom used, except on Sundays or when there were important visitors. There was an unmistakeable smell of burning in the air. For a second as I looked at that huge blue helmet, my heart trembled for I immediately associated its presence with my first sexual adventure, although there was no rational way of connecting the arrival of the police with my wandering hands – my attentions had not exactly been repulsed, and the girl could scarcely have had time to get home. Later, before I was sent to bed in disgrace, I found that I had inadvertently left a candle burning in the loft over the wash-house where my uncle was illegally storing large quantities of greaseproof wrapping paper, then strictly rationed. As a consequence of my negligence, half the stock was destroyed, the fire brigade and the police had been called so that, in a sense, fire and brimstone had attended my first mutually acceptable erection and my guilty mind connected the two events as sin and punishment for a good while. My grandmother often said, 'God will find you out!'

'Two hundred pounds worth of damage!' my uncle said, striking me across the face.

I slunk away to contemplate my navel.

There were other girls but never the release I sought and I slowly began to move in different circles, avoiding the chapel girls and seeking out the more sophisticated company of those who returned from public schools for the holidays; but now and again I returned to the chapel – to keep an eye on it, as it were. It continued to be a microcosm of the old ways. One of the boys older then myself surprised me one day by the fierce dislike he expressed for a local hero whom he thought of as a glory hunter with his decorations. The boy had been a young soldier in the same military action, had been overrun by German infantry and only survived by feigning death amongst a pile of bodies for two days during which he did not dare to move, an experience that affected his whole life; for he became a chronic asthmatic and died prematurely, a shy, retiring person. His view was the kind of contradiction of public acclaim that somehow reaffirmed my own existing suspicions that there was another side to everything.

Never forgetting the moment of terror when I saw that policeman's helmet, I became completely sceptical; but that moment also returned to me, the memory held like a flawed pearl on a string – trapped between its fellows. There were others to come. As a trainee probation officer, I was required to interview a woman whose son had attempted to castrate himself with a cut-throat razor, and had nearly succeeded when interrupted by the milkman. Upon discharge from a surgical ward, he was transferred to a mental hospital where I had to visit him and complete a standard form after consultation with his mother. One of the column entries asked for a statement describing the mother's attitude to the matter in question. I think it said, 'Attitude to the Offence'.

In the dingy almoner's office, a little woman sat opposite me, demure in a purple hat, a fox fur; on her lapel a clutch of artificial flowers of the kind which I always remembered my grandmother wearing. She had come down the valley to the hospital dressed in her Sunday best. For me it was a poignant moment but I adopted a breezy confidentiality as I questioned her.

'Tell me, Mrs Williams, what d'you think *yourself* about what Emlyn's done?'

She smiled, a tight little smile from those purse-like lips, clasping her hands primly about her handbag.

'What our Emlyn have done is wrong,' she said carefully; 'but it was on the right lines.'

I had then, as I had many times, a sense of relief at my own escape from entrapment in the dark rivers of lunacy which lie beneath the surface of many ostensibly respectable lives. This was a bizarre and extreme example of warped puritan belief but there were skeins there, part of a cobweb which connected to my own experience and also the experience of my chapel contemporaries – two of whom later developed sexual peculiarities, encouraged by an overwhelming Methodist conviction of sin that proved ineradicable.

In my own life I was to respond to many situations in life with an absolute conviction of right and wrong which allowed of no compromise and often led me into headlong confrontations, later creating a sense of guilt that at times proved intolerable. We may attack the past, but we can never destroy it, or deny it, and a conviction that simplistic beliefs are no preparation for the complexities of life does not alter what we have experienced either. Perhaps my luck was that I was never wholly contained in any one world and when I began to discover in the pages of Sinclair Lewis and John O'Hara the complexities of the small-town life which I also had led, I found myself nodding in agreement, becoming in the process an outsider myself and subtly withdrawing from the most extreme pressures of the life around me. There was thus always a part of me that did not believe, would not be swallowed wholly, and although in my other everyday pleasures I was ordinary enough, there was another self in the making during all these years of adolescence.

It was at this time in my life that I began to understand how society divides itself up, how the great inequalities of life begin and, in some cases, are structured from the start. At the beginning of the war, however, the narrowness of the wage differential in a small depressed town obscured the most obvious class divisions. While the war was on, most of the people I knew were in some way involved in 'doing their bit', as they said and, as we all knew, the casualties came irrespective of social class so that there was a sense of being 'all in it together' which made it a unique time to be alive. The collier was perhaps the one who suffered the most since the pits had no glamour and conscripts drafted into them often felt unfairly singled out. Most public officials were jingoistic and pontificated frequently in the name of the war effort about men who were caught sleeping underground, or who were detected with cigarettes or matches – age-old colliery offences which now became unpatriotic. Generally everybody believed that there was, as the song said, 'something about a soldier' and the prize of a uniform held sway for a long time.

But gradually, once the fighting moved further away across the continent of Europe and extended to the Far East, old social superiorities reasserted themselves. Rationing was not so strict, produce began to come in illegally from the country, and money reasserted its power. It was as if the common purpose and a public togetherness had been held in suspense while the pressures were on – the very presence of so many soldiers before the invasion of France, negroes from Alabama, or 'Free' Poles marching daily about the streets, encamped in public halls and chapel vestries, acting as a constant reminder of 'something going on over there', words on everybody's lips. It was the great age of the cliché. But once the soldiers had marched away and the pressures eased, normality began to return and a skin that had been drawn tight began to slacken revealing wrinkles and folds where the mixture stayed the same as before.

So when at fifteen I played the drums with a friend on guitar at a concert to mark the retirement of an old drayman who had spent his life in the service of a wholesale baker, it was not thought unusual that the managing director's Roedean-educated sister did a scarf dance by way of entertainment in a working-men's club hired for the occasion. This was somehow also to do with the war effort and that general feeling of togetherness. But within a year or two, the gaps widened. Petrol had become more freely available and once again the Armstrong Sidleys and the Morgan three-wheeler sports cars began to appear. Alongside the widening rifts, though, there flourished the stories of local celebrities and illegal goings-on told with a nod and a wink which we savoured for the tribal feelings they fostered. They were further proof of our difference.

One concerned a prominent butcher who, forceful and domineering, used to visit the local golf club every Thursday afternoon, the time of early shop-closing. Here in the company of his fellows he would play solo whist, at the same time obligingly providing a frying pan of chops and steaks which would be fried on a coke stove. It was a long-standing custom and since the golf club was situated in a remote place, illicit drinking or such rationing offences were unlikely to be detected. But the war had brought with it another problem, the difficulty of finding a suitable steward. A number were tried and found unsatisfactory, so the butcher announced that he would deal with the matter. He would make a search himself. A week or so had gone by when he announced triumphantly:

'Got the very man. From Tonypandy. Ex-Indian Army. Knows his place.'

The candidate appeared, was engaged, and Thursday became Thursday again as the friends gathered as usual, took up their positions at the card table with the comforting knowledge that the lean, white-jacketed figure at the bar was at their service. When a coal fell from the open door of the coke stove, the steward came from behind the bar to retrieve it, but at that precise moment the butcher picked up his cards and examined them – the steward pausing and glancing interestedly over his shoulder.

'Misère,' said the butcher impassively, indicating that he was prepared to lose every trick.

The steward gasped. Perhaps there was a collision of experience, between the ex-Indian Army man who knew his place and the truculent Tonypandy youth. Perhaps it was that the cards spoke more plainly to him than anything else. At any rate, he could not contain himself.

'You silly bugger!' he said. 'You're not going a misère on that hand?'

Such stories delighted us. From an early age we hoarded them. Pontypridd, like Damascus, we were given to understand, was a universe within itself, but it was always dangerous to get ideas above your station. The exception was sport, particularly rugby football where the pursuit of excellence was quite normal. This was where the real status lay so that when a young Geraint Evans came home on leave in the uniform of an RAF corporal – known as we said, 'To have a bit of a voice' – it was his brother-in-law, our international fly-half, who really stole the thunder.

I'd had a taste of thunder myself by then. My grandmother, realising that my birthmark remained an embarrassment, prevailed upon the local doctor to have it removed and when I was sixteen, I went to the cottage hospital where a surgeon operated upon me and I came away with an impressive facial scar. I was moley no longer. It was an event and it was shortly followed by my inclusion in the school rugby team in which I just managed to keep my place. This gave my last years in school that sense of belonging which was so completely missing in the beginning. Suddenly, I was physically different and caught up in the most powerful of local forces. It was not just kudos that the first fifteen conferred, but the key to one of the few Welsh activities in which excellence was everywhere in evidence – and not just excellence but style, that elusive grace and flair of the truly great players which I learned to recognise because there were such a number of them on my own doorstep.

It is a matter easily exaggerated. (But not by me then. I thought of nothing else for two whole winters!) When I was not playing I was watching, hard up against the railings on this ground and that, usually in the company of my team mates with whom I had already played in the mornings. We were not so much supporters as clinicians, for we often left Pontypridd to make our diagnostic forays to Cardiff where the post-war sides contained players whose individual skills, and skills in combination, were never really to be equalled in quite the same way. We went, sporting our colours and often our scars, with the conceits and confidence of Italian *bravos*, swaggering at times for we were the best, we felt, with the results to prove it. We were also players looking at players, therefore it followed that we knew what we were talking about and we conducted inquests in which our elders joined when we returned home, often to the public houses from which, quite soon, we were ourselves recruited to play for senior sides.

Never before or since have I felt such a part of things. Soon my enthusiasms reached a pitch so that, as for many of my contemporaries, the game took the place of theatre, a theatre in which there were heroes and villains, and there were moments when the touchlines were not so much touchlines as footlights. I would study individual players as if they were actors, noting their facial expressions, their stances, their every movement. When there were controversies I took sides, until I saw not players but personas and when the cool insouciant and insolent grace of our own side-stepping fly-half, Glyn Davies, was threatened by the mechanical kicking skills of Cardiff's Billy Cleaver, it was as if a poet was being assassinated by an accountant and I willed bad games upon him, staring venomously through the railings. It was not reasonable, but it was me.

Such passions also produced pictures with the result that certain players of this era remain vividly in my mind, cloaked by images which reflected their style of play. There was a full-back playing for Cardiff named Frank Trott, the image of dependability, the kind of blacksmith full-back who is encouraged to stay behind the anvil until the bull runs amok. I saw him – and I see him now – as the kind of doughty and reliable figure who puts you in mind of a curly haired, barrel-chested British Tommy going on up the line in the driving rain with tin hat, full pack and cape and a shrug of the shoulders as if to say, 'What comes, comes.' There were many players I saw in this way, villains as well as heroes, and for a time nothing would have pleased me more than to have become some kind of sporting journalist, but I would have been very unsatisfactory since I was often so carried away with my enthusiasms for certain players that I almost ignored games just to watch them. It was a harmless passion but it took me into the heart of things local.

When the time came for me to think of some kind of career, I followed the line of least resistance and pleased my grandmother by deciding to apply for a place at a teacher training college. If I had any ambitions as a teacher, it was only to emulate my own English master and I approached the forthcoming selection interview with a confidence that amazes me. Shortly before I had sat in the bar of the public house where the town rugby team gathered strays to play for its second fifteen. Noticing my interest, the landlord pointed out an ancient browning photograph of three world champion boxers, all born and brought up within a five-mile radius.

'Champions of the world, boy!' he told me pointedly; 'not bloody Machynlleth!', attributing all the aspects of parochialism to that remote North Welsh town. This was, of course, the hub of the universe talking and the landlord, like my grandmother, never let you forget it.

I was suitably impressed and when, later in the year, I sat before the Principal of the training college at Caerleon in Monmouthshire to which I had confidently applied, he had two pertinent observations.

'Pontypridd?' he said ruminatively. 'You must have played with the famous half-backs?'

I had, and told him so.

Sport was very much uppermost in his mind, for he then told me that he had boxed with Freddie Welsh as a young soldier in the First War.

'A relative actually,' I said.

These were useful conversational lubricants, but more important was the reference from my headmaster.

'You have a very ordinary School Certificate,' the Principal said, 'but in all my years, I have never seen a reference quite like this.'

Pig, Boss, the Ogre, the Old Man, the nicknames had softened as we grew older, and in my case, on my behalf, he had done his stuff to the end. Now I had fallen into that special group for whom all his superlatives were reserved. If only half of them were true, the Principal observed, accepting me with a smile, I would be an acquisition indeed. As it happened, I was never to fail another examination in my life, and sitting there, I saw that enraged appalled face, the gleaming bald pate, the imperious manner, the prodding forefinger, the hasty flurry of his gown, and I heard that loud domineering attacking voice which scoured corners and had once struck terror into me until I learned to challenge it, and I swallowed hard. Somehow the gratitude we feel for imperfect people is more poignant than that which we reserve for saints. Soon I realised that at last I had a foothold on some kind of career. I was immediately to become a student teacher and while my horizons remained small, my life as a schoolboy had come to an end.

SEVEN

Seven years later, it was my life that nearly came to an end. I became an invalid, a condition for which I had no preparation and less sympathy, and now for a time my days lacked definition – beginnings and ends, even – as I lapsed into lengthy periods of coma. I was home again, home after my wanderings. This was the only hospital that would have me, an old grey stone fever hospital set apart from the town, the last exit for the incurable.

My grandmother was dying, my mother's face drawn with worry when she could get to see me, and for long periods I could not speak, just lay limply in bed, looking blearily at the coke stove in the centre of the ward. Hardly ten minutes went by without some paroxysm of coughing being heard. There were five elderly colliers with silicosis, as well as tuberculosis – our common complaint, as we said. Some of them also had heart conditions and two had to be supported in a virtually upright position day and night since they could not breathe at all if they lay prone. The sputum pots of the old men were emptied two or three times a day so that the refinements of life which we all take for granted were part of a past that was gone, and gone for ever, it sometimes seemed.

In the nights, one of the colliers often cried. You could hear him whimpering in the darkness. The coughing and wheezing were more or less continuous, but when the coughing got really bad, the night sister came in with morphia and very soon screens were put around the bed. Once the screens came, you knew that was the beginning of the end. As well as the colliers, all in their sixties and seventies, there was a bus driver and a young plumber, Rob. Rob couldn't take streptomycin either. There seemed to be some extra complication for all of us and in my case there was the fact that I could barely see, having suffered vitreous haemorrhages in my left eye. Nobody seemed to be able to understand why. There was no visible damage, nothing visible at all save through an ophthalmoscope, and my eye condition – as it was described – had begun sinisterly like a visitation some months before.

I had been working in London when I began to notice a tiny white spot in front of my left eye. It was minute, like a blip on a radar screen, as small as a spider's egg and hanging suspended as if by an invisible thread. At first, I polished my spectacles in the hope that it would go away. But it did not and when I asked anyone to look into my eye, they did so, and then stared at me blankly. Nothing was visible. There was no pain, not even the slight irritation that comes with some speck of dirt under the eyelid. But it was there, my white spot, visible to me and omnipresent, a constant and unwelcome companion.

A few months before, I had been appointed a probation officer in the London Metropolitan Magistrate's Court area. I had been three years in training and now was beginning a career that greatly interested me. Each day I met new people and on a Monday morning I would visit the police court at Clerkenwell to see prisoners who had been arrested over the weekend. It was my task to interview them so that I might detect any whom the stipendiary magistrate might think needed a probation officer's help.

But it soon turned out that I was in need of help myself. One day there was a middle-aged man slumped in a cell, a Canadian arrested for ordering and eating a restaurant meal without having the means to pay and to every one of my questions he responded too glibly, skilfully presenting himself as a genuine case of need so that my suspicions were aroused and I suggested he be remanded for further investigation. This was done, and I received a telephone call informing me that he was in fact a convicted murderer who had spent years in Sing Sing and was wanted by the Irish police, although he had no previous convictions in England. I was about to congratulate myself on seeing through his attempt to deceive me, when my habit of rubbing my eyes became noticeable to my colleagues. Gradually, almost imperceptibly, the habit had become as pronounced as a nervous tic. I had already been to see an optician, but a change of spectacles having produced no result, it was clear something had to be done and I soon found myself in Moorfields, the London eye hospital. Now I was being referred for further investigation myself.

At Moorfields I was asked if I had done any heavy manual work recently.

'Tree-felling, or anything of that sort?'

I had not. There now began the first of many such silent periods spent staring into blackness while a registrar with an ophthalmoscope stared into my eyes. The blip was still there, still like a spider's egg, and still unhatched. At first, no one would answer my questions.

'What is it? What is the matter with me?' I became aggressive and nervous.

I saw two or three doctors. If I saw one, he called another. I became interesting. I looked into the collective medical face. As my questions increased, so for a brief time did their evasiveness. They were not sure. They did not know. If they did know, they were not saying. Like a government department, they wanted more information. I was told to get my chest X-rayed, and that meant another visit to another hospital, taking myself and my blip with me. I had not yet discovered how compartmentalised medicine was, but once my chest had been X-rayed, there was no doubt. I had tuberculosis. When I was told, my immediate reaction was one of relief. It was at least a name, a known disease. In 1954 it was still the white scourge – one of my mother's brothers had died of it – but somehow, I felt I could face it. It was the blip that bothered me, hanging there like a thing from outer space. It would not go away. I could see it even with my eyes closed in the darkness, a tiny elusive spot; and some nights it did not seem to go away even when I was asleep, for it figured in my dreams.

In London, there was an immediate problem with hospital beds, a six-month waiting list for the Brompton Hospital. I had been employed as a fully qualified probation officer for only three months, not long enough to qualify for sick pay. Very soon, I would not be able to pay my rent. So it was the road home, and any hospital I could persuade to take me once there.

Then I woke up one morning with a trail of blood floating inside my eye, deep, bright and red, with an additional dark smudge of matter floating like minute particles of weed, lazily moving to and fro in the current. The blip had gone. It had haemorrhaged and now everything I saw was through this bloodied curtain. I stared and stared. Of course, I rubbed my eyes. Of course, it did not go away. Describing it to anyone produced a universal response. They wanted to move away from me. This happened several times. The sooner I was in hospital, the better. I felt 'not quite right' in the head. I was cruelly reminded of a schizophrenic patient I once heard solemnly describing the nest a jackdaw was building inside her skull. Only now it was not other people suffering, it was me. At last I was told I had Eale's Disease, an obscure allergy to the tubercle.

For years I seemed to have procceded, as the police say, with confidence. Once I got to training college, I found I could cope with the academic work, and as a teacher I could joke with classes in front of me. As a young sub-lieutenant in the Royal Navy, I had held my own in that most cruel and barbarous of conflicts induced by the English class system which had confronted me like a blow in the face. Placed on the spot, I soon invented a phrase that was a statement of fact: I did not mind being dressed as a sub-lieutenant, but I wasn't going to think like one. At university later, another world opened up to me. I made friends with my tutor, and when I left my last final examination, to complete my education I grabbed a sea bag and joined an old tramp steamer carrying coal from Swansea to Antwerp, peeling potatoes for a laugh on a hooligan boat with a hooligan crew – an altogether more enriching experience than showing the Flag from the broad expanse of an aircraft carrier's deck in the Mediterranean holiday ports where the protocol and the number of functions were so great that we had to be detailed to attend them. I was, I like to think, a weathered man. I had been, in the phrase of my youthful heroes, 'all over' and was able to mix as easily in the fo'c'sle of that old Panamanian tramp as with the admiral who sought my company for bridge (I had rediscovered a card sense, another of my billiard-hall attributes). Like many of the men I spent so much time with in ships or institutions, I had learned to listen and could spin a yarn myself, and I had that easy confidence that comes from rubbing shoulders with all and sundry. I was not precious. I had not been sheltered. From the moment I'd left school, I'd had a kind of blue-chip life, but now I entered a world of ill health and its existence confronted me with a sense of total shock. It was as if, I thought, remembering my earlier despair at school, I was like a light-skinned negro passing as white and the time had come for the impersonation to cease. I was back in a corner and it was all a discovery – the lassitude, the night sweats, the general feeling of second-ratedness about every limb you owned – and I suddenly began to put meaning to all those stories of despair I had collected on my travels, as if my mind had hoarded them for a very special purpose. In whatever company I had been, I had always sought to look below the surface of things – all the better to guard myself, as I realise now, against the inevitable blow when it came. There was always a part of me which expected a kick up the pants around every corner. If I had confidence, it was in myself, and not in the fates. The fates, as it happened, were rubbing their hands. This was a period when things got progressively worse.

As usual, little showed on my face. I was wan but unbloodied externally and on the day I came home, I made my last visit to my grandmother, treading up the stairs past the stuffed fox head and the silver collier's lamp which had belonged to her father and along the landing to her bedroom where she lay, paralysed after another stroke.

It was the worst moment of my life. She'd had the photographs of her children put beside my grandfather's on the dressing table and mine was there too, as a little boy in the velvet-collared jacket which showed me smiling at her. It was how she liked to remember me best since I was her sixth child in every sense, and now as I looked at her, her mouth distorted, her thinning hair white against the pillow as she managed a smile for me, it was all I could do to keep my voice steady. It was agreed that I should not tell her of my plight and somehow or other I began to joke. She approved of my new career but confused it with the prison service and we had once been together on a railway station platform when a handcuffed serviceman had been roughly handled by two military policemen, provoking her immediate and voluble wrath; so she told them off forthwith.

I made some joke, to explain my sudden presence, about having come home unexpectedly as an escort. It satisfied her. She could understand but could not speak. I think we both knew that we would never see each other again. Looking out of the window, I could just make out the dim shape of the town clock through eyes already dilated with morphine drops and once again I heard the thump of the steam hammer in the distant chain works. Below on the road I thought I could see the local newspaper reporter swaying as he came up the hill, but I did not mention him. It was a fine warm day and the sun shone, dividing the little room into shadows. When at last I turned to her, I said defiantly, as if someone were arguing, 'Well, you've done everything for me anyhow.'

My tears were strangely absent. I am not a crying person but in my heart there was the terrible knowledge that she would not be alive long enough for me to do anything for her, and knowing my own condition – the blood swilling evilly all the time in my eye, the morphine drops merely dilating the pupils to ease my journey – I was suddenly deeply ashamed of my life. I had nothing to show her, no evidence of any success; the few short stories I had then written, I had been foolish enough to send to the BBC in Wales and they took almost two years to broadcast them. When I left the bedroom, I really felt as if a part of my life had ended in a way that no mature person should confess. There is no other love so uncritical as that which forms our early years and she had so amply filled my childish need of her that no one now could ever take her place.

When I got into the car which was to take me to the hospital, I peered out at the blur of familiar landscapes and I had the bizarre sensation that I was attending my own funeral as people in turn looked curiously in at me.

This was continued when I entered the hospital ward. There was complete silence and the other patients looked at me with blank hostility. Even when I had changed into pyjamas, sent my clothes to be disinfected and levered myself into bed, the patients continued to look away from me, pointedly avoided my eye, and there was not a word spoken for at least ten minutes. There was very definitely an atmosphere and there was no one to explain it to me. Even when I asked a few questions, the politeness of the replies was so formal as to amount to a cold rejection, and this went on all afternoon.

A few days later Emrys, the bus driver in the bed opposite, explained.

'That cow of a staff nurse told us you were a Nonconformist minister and there was to be no swearing or smoking, and everything was to be according to the book from now on. We couldn't even have a drop of grog in!'

'Me, a Nonconformist minister?'

'That's right. We were all itching to know how you got syphilis as well, but we was told not to ask. That's what she told us!'

I could only laugh.

'Lavatory seat,' I said. 'In the places I've been, the bugs have learned to jump.'

I was back once more in the exclusive company of men, and there was to be no privacy, no world other than that of my bed except for the one I created in the often hallucinated dreams which the daily injection of streptomycin induced in me. For three or four days I seemed to be asleep continuously and my mind did not at first adjust to the new routine. Daily, I slipped off into limbo.

Sometimes I would go back over my life, especially at nights when there was a blue light kept on and with my one good eye I could peer around the ward without embarrassment. Directly opposite me was the oldest collier who was propped upright permanently and kept rum illicitly in an HP Sauce bottle; since he often could not sleep, once the night sister had made her rounds he would light up the butt end of a cigarette, give himself a tot and wheeze away the hours. I would see the flame of his match flicker and hold it in my line of vision until the blood began to swirl in my diseased eye and then I would lay back and give my mind over to the past, people drifting into consciousness like ghostly shapes. Sometimes I would be asleep half the day, the nurses having to wake me up for meals, so that the nights were a time for reflection when I would drift into the limbo of memory and surrender myself to voices.

'Why am I here?' I asked myself many times. My

headmaster's voice returned, 'You are heading for serious trouble!' (He was never wrong!)

Then there were others. 'You will go too far . . .'

Sometimes I recalled whole conversations and saw myself as a slim and earnest sub-lieutenant with my feet on the wardroom fender, waylaid by those who sought to impress their ways upon me. The Royal Navy was a world of gloves and visiting cards, of dressing for dinner, of svelte bum-freezers and starched wing collars, the Royal Marine Band quartette playing in the ante-room, bugles at dawn, at dusk, and occasionally the soft-eyed looks of the most incredible girls. And for those a little out of their depth like myself, there was always advice from good chaps who knew the ropes. There were, I was to discover, standards, and it was not done to let the side down; I had always to be mindful of that as, of course, had everyone else. These English voices came back to me as, not yet able to accept the new world which I had been forced to enter, I recreated the old. In my life fantasy has always mingled with reality because sometimes reality is too much to bear.

'Taffy, is it true you're pursuing Monica Thing? She's a cookhouse Wren, you know?'

'I am not saying,' said I. (I began my career as a sub-lieutenant, young, earnest, and anxious to do well.)

'You know what they call her, don't you, old man? The Station bike.'

'Naval establishments on shore are always called ships, that is why the prefix *HMS* is always attached. "Station" is inapprop-riate.'

'Clever bugger!'

'Thank you.'

'You don't want to be *seen* ashore with her, you know. This is a very isolated spot. If you take a bus anywhere, you're bound to be seen.'

'I just thought of going for a walk.'

'A *walk*?'

'Well, first, like . . .'

'Don't let the Wren officers catch you. They'll cut you in the wardroom if you're seen going out with a rating. I mean, don't say I didn't warn you.'

'Thank you.'

'And another thing, you should always wear a hat, you know. In civvies, I mean. A cap won't do. If you haven't got a hat, you can't pay the proper marks of respect to the officer of the watch at the main gate.'

'A cap will do.'

'You can't *raise* a cap. I mean, what if you were caught short when colours were sounded?'

'I'd doff it.'

'Hm . . . If I were you, I'd start thinking about doffing Monica Thing.'

'How did you guess? That's just what I am doing.'

Monica Thing had the body of a chorus girl, the hair of a Fiji Islander and the dreamy blue eyes of a film star locked in permanent dazed close-up. Everything, you felt, was a shock to her. She was, in civilian clothes, a creature of tight straining sweaters, bulging drawstring blouses, slit skirts and the highest of heels – a decorated lady of thighs, handbags and jewellery and the perpetual scent of face powders which she plied about her heavy chin and large beauty spot so often that the cost of an evening with her on your shoulder was quadrupled, since it inevitably meant a visit to the dry cleaners. But to me she had IT in profusion, a glamour that reeked and screamed and swung at you, her physical presence drawing me to her like an ant to honey. She also looked slightly scatty and wild at times, but this was only when her hair was awry. It sometimes seemed to have a vicious life of its own and rebelled against the comb, unlike her full shapely mouth which glowed like painted lips on a Valentine card in the darkness.

'Don't mess me!' she'd say on a bad night, and then she would be at her most statuesque, lolling against the corrugated iron of the WRNS ablutions like a gorgeous cutout fronting a cinema, but a cutout that came alive. For the first and only time, I overcame my aversion to dressed-up women. Quite frankly, it was her breasts.

Then when she spoke, her voice seemed to chime as if a cockney bell were installed at the back of her throat but every sentence she uttered cut me down and she in turn regarded me, not for what I was, but as a representative of some strange image which she had already formed in her mind. I had but to open my mouth and behind me, pit wheels span, Welsh male voice choirs gave forth with rousing choruses and I seemed always to be a part of some fantasy which ran and ran in her private cinema. I was the leader of a hunger march, a rabid left-wing agitator, the hero of *Love On The Dole* or *The Peasants' Revolt*, or merely an extra from the film of *How Green Was My Valley* which made her weep, she said. She had seen it six times and once suggested I should read the book aloud to her. I would have, if I could have found a copy, for I was well-aware of the competition. But I could not. Then when she agreed to go out with me, there was a series of investigative questions.

'Have you ever actually been down a coal mine?'

'No.'

'You're a bit of a swizz then, aren't you?'

'Come here, Monica.'

'No, I won't. Are you a communist? I won't tell.'

'No.'

'Ever been on a hunger march?'

'Not a march exactly. In college once they gave us herrings for breakfast and the roes for tea. There were ex-prisoners of war who couldn't stand the food; we had a strike once, but it didn't do any good.'

'There's one thing anyway, you're in the rugby team.'

I was for a time, and while I was, I prospered and Saturday nights were heaven. But not for long. Playing against the Reserve Fleet, I got badly concussed – so badly that they gave me sick leave and Monica took up with someone else for a month or two. But later, standing idly at the wardroom bar with an amiable surgeon one Saturday lunchtime, my career and my chances were renewed in an unexpected way. We were drinking gin fizzes in an agreeable session and I was defending Dylan Thomas whose reputation as the Jack Dempsey of poetry I thought unfair. It was a conversation that had gone on since the bar opened at midday and it was nearly two o'clock when a Royal Marine messenger appeared.

'Instructor Lieutenant Richards?'

'What can I do for you?'

'They want you over on the playing fields, sir. There's been an accident.'

'Are you sure it's me they want?'

'Yes, sir. They're short in the rugby team.'

I went over to the changing rooms.

The scrum-half had torn his fingernail in a locker door and couldn't play. The teams were already on the field.

'Oh, come on, Taff. You'll do.'

I couldn't think of anybody better and stripped at once. There was always an amiability to this kind of rugby. I was amiable, and willing. No reserve scrum-half ever took the field with such confidence. There was even a cheer. If I passed the ball in a well-oiled haze, it was still with a certain elegance, the flowing wristy movements of a stylish cricketer. No game takes place in Wales without needle, a battle for name and fame, but this kind of services rugby football was for the game itself – a recreation among amiable fellows to pass a blank Saturday afternoon. It also proceeded sluggishly which suited me and when, diving gracefully at the feet of wandering forwards who sauntered through a line-out, I felt a kick in the face that rendered me unconscious, then in the split second before I passed into the darkness, I actually heard a gasp of regret, if not an apology most sincerely meant. But I was outers again.

When I came to, I had been carried to the touchline. A sick-berth attendant was in attendance and Monica was there, the full swell of her large breasts silhouetted in a scarlet jersey. But she was looking at me in horror, her hair on end, her normally vacuous expression now resembling that of a spectator at a street accident. (The colour of the jersey was accidental, not worn specially for me. She'd thought she could do better with a man of action, one of the commissioned gunners whose highly polished gaiters and boots made more satisfactory stamping noises than my stealthy shuffle.)

I got to my feet, shook my head, saw the game was still in progress, prepared to go back on the field.

The sick-berth attendant caught my arm.

'Sir!'

'What's the matter? I'm going back on.'

I felt no pain. If I had been shaken, now I had recovered. I was ice-cool. If ever the rugby unions are to recapture the amateur spirit, the simple delights of recreation, they need look no further than half-a-dozen gin fizzes, a controllable anaesthetic that lasts the full forty minutes.

'Mon',' the sick-berth attendant said. 'Show him.'

I can remember the familiar use of her Christian name. Monica found her handbag. There were no other spectators, a small enough cast for what turned out to be a major drama in my life. From her handbag she produced a small steel mirror. Lying in the sandhills, I had seen her use it to repair her face. She used lipstick like toothpaste, moulded it on and redrew her eyebrows if there was the slightest smudge. Sometimes you had to wait for twenty minutes, as for a rich creamy confection bursting at the edges of the box.

Now she held the mirror up to my face and I noted she wore her *How Green Was My Valley* look. In her mind, the pit whistle had just gone. There was a very definite roof fall in Number Nine Level, and even the canaries had fallen silent below ground.

I peered short-sightedly into the mirror.

At first I thought I had no nose at all but, squinting, I found it had been neatly spread back along my face, almost at a right angle so that the centre of my face was strangely flattened. I couldn't understand how there was so little pain, merely discomfort.

'Lucky it happened here, sir,' the SBA said. He meant on our playing fields, for there was always a medical officer on duty at the base.

He took one arm while Monica took the other. Between them, they led me as I was to the distant sickbay where I was handed over. The sister made a telephone call. I was going to be operated on immediately. I felt no alarm, they prepped me on the trolley, wheeled me along the corridor. The last positive, distinctive and full-blown smell I ever remember came to me as I was wheeled into the operating theatre. It was gin, wafts of it, in large quantities. It came from the surgeon who had been drinking with me for most of the lunch hour and had now been roused from his slumbers. He must have had ten gin fizzes. He grinned broadly. I wanted to ask him if he'd had any lunch, but I was already pentathol-dizzy, slipping away into limbo again.

'Jack Dempsey rides again,' the surgeon said.

117

Two years later I had to have the entire operation repeated, but the Lords High Commissioners of the Admiralty gave me a handsome parchment – a *Certificate of Hurts and Wounds*, whose form had not changed since Nelson's day. It contained a citation: 'Did fracture nasal bone while stopping a forward rush.'

Monica came to see me the next day, but only to say that there was no chance. I must have given her an especially appealing look. But it wasn't my nose, my reduced sensibility to her multiple scents, it was that I was generally a disappointment to her. She gave me her reasons in that chirpy voice. With others it was that they had the one thing on their mind all the time, and although I wasn't quite like them – the others – in that I was 'gentle with it and would talk after', it was, I gathered, that she did not quite know who I was. In her heart she was looking for singing miners, more of the *How Green Was My Valley*. But there was one compliment. After my nose was done, she said that I sounded like Richard Burton on the phone.

I did not give up my pursuit of Monica, however, and the winter went on interminably. The establishment was training boy seamen and they would pound the barrack square when they were not swarming up the transplanted mast of the old HMS *Ganges* or pulling in whaler races on the river, and it remained an isolated place. Then I heard that Monica had taken up amateur dramatics, so I went along to the play-reading in the information room and when the time came to read Emlyn Williams's *Night Must Fall*, I came at last into my own. The central character, a murderer, had a distinctive voice, half Welsh, half Irish – a psychopathic croon, I described it – and it was made for me.

'What d'you think of Taffy in the part?' the producer said.
'Type-casting!'
'He's got the voice. Looks right too.'
'We'll be sorry.'
'What about that girl as the servant?'
'She's common enough.'
'I think we'll give it a whirl.'

I now felt I had wasted my life pretending to be a rugby player, a hearty. It was time I discovered the thrill of being other people in public, and Monica was delighted. It was soon all off with the SBA, all over with the commissioned gunner. 'They're all married,' she said bitterly; 'and out for the one thing,' her favourite phrase. I was not like them strictly speaking, I kidded myself, although she was as enticing as anybody I could then have imagined and everything about her fascinated me – her laborious make-up, her voluminous underclothes, the constant neck-stretching to examine the seams of her stockings, the angle of her bra, the impress of her suspender buttons against the tightest of skirts. Everything had to be examined and checked, including her hair which got in your mouth when you danced with her. These were obvious attractions, but there were also the constant, startling revelations about her life – the men, the boys, the step-father who'd pursued her; their collective deviousness which included car lights failing, cars breaking down, once the attempted use of chloroform stolen from a dentist. The whole world was after her and at her and all her life there seemed to have been a forest of hands stretching out, always to touch her where it was not proper so to do. But now we were starring together and when I kissed her goodnight, shuffling and straining in the darkness behind the WRNS ablutions once more, she put her hands under my raincoat to keep them – and me – warm, an inflammatory process.

If I was over-eager, she would say, 'Later . . .' with a cockney inflection that brought the blood to my head.

'Come on, Mon'? *Now* . . .'

'Lay-tah!'

As predicted, we were seen and the WRNS officers were cold towards me in the wardroom and I should have had a sense of trouble brewing. But soon we were rehearsing in earnest, and now my dreams were of stardom. I taught fractions and decimals by rote to boy seamen by day; by night I immersed myself in Emlyn Williams, and Monica. It was a few weeks before a peculiar problem developed for me alone. Confident – even brilliant – with the script in my hands, the moment I put it down and rehearsed without it, I found myself adding to the speeches. Little inflections here and there became odd half sentences, then whole sentences as I immersed myself in the character. There was a physical complication. In the scene with Monica, I invariably had an erection. With the old lady, played by a dour petty officer Wren who thoroughly disapproved of me, my eyes were often elsewhere as I salivated and drooled, doing my demented bit.

'Cues!' the producer would shout.

'Pardon?'

'Cues. You're getting the cues wrong.'

'What?'

'You've got to end the speech as it says in the script. The same bloody words, otherwise the other actors won't know where to come in.'

I had not had this trouble on the one occasion I had acted before in the school play. Then I was Bradshawe, the lawyer who prosecuted Charles I and he spoke mostly in lengthy monologues. I'd prosecute any monarch!

'You've got to get the cues, Taffy. The voice is A1, the rest's fine; but you're throwing people, you see, old man?'

'Give me a week,' I said.

Now Monica began to cool. Perhaps she could see failure appearing on the horizon like a grey cloud. She was having difficulties remembering lines herself. Then most of the cast were officers and when they spoke to her, it was as to the maid, not the actress. I did not know then the story of the official at the Governor General's residence in Hong Kong who once asked the principal actors of a touring company for cocktails, but excluded those actors who had the misfortune to play domestic servants. The same evil English code applied here and Monica felt threatened.

'I haven't had no real education,' she told me once. Her eyes were wide and troubled.

'Neither have I,' I said. 'Not really.' I thought it more true in my case than hers. At first, I was such an innocent in these matters of social class.

'You liar! You'd talk the hind leg off a donkey when you want something.'

But they were getting her down. Men pursued her constantly, but girls were jealous and she could not stand being treated as if she was as common as dirt.

'We had a car and a lawn,' she told me, holding out her little finger as she flicked the ash from a Craven A. 'We never stayed in boarding houses; hotels, it was. Always . . .'

I think it was the hotels that gave her an idea of glamour. The more you have on display, jewellery or self, the better they treat you.

But the woman petty officer Wren called her by her surname. It made her livid. There is no other group in the world with the in-built capacity and skill for the further reduction of the status of the individual who does not quite belong, than the English middle class – usually emanating from or imitating the Home Counties – of whom even the dullest has the capacity to isolate, distance and hurt. This they do, even to their own intimates who have the misfortune to expose the slightest chink in their armour. It is as if one of the deprivations of a vanished empire is the chronic need to find a substitute for other, weaker peoples, to create an internal foreign policy as it were – a policy once brilliantly described by Lord Salisbury* who identified a prevailing tone, even principles carried out 'with no consideration of the feelings or wounded honour of those to whom they are applied, but rather with an ostentatious insouciance. It is throughout a tone by which the weak are made to feel their weakness, to drink the bitter cups of inferiority to the very dregs.'

I could not help Monica.

In the play rehearsals, I kept getting the cues wrong and she panicked.

'I'm not going to see you for a bit, not socially.'

She meant sexually. I think she had in her mind that I ought to be isolated as boxers are separated before a title fight. So I kept to myself, and over-trained.

Shortly afterwards, I found myself rehearsing on the stage of the information room one afternoon. By now arc lamps had been rigged, shipwrights were busy in the rear making flats and a draft programme had been prepared with my name on it, '*Danny* . . . Instructor Lieutenant A. Richards, RN'. Now the stage was lit, dust hanging in the beams and as I was doing my 'bit of acting', out of the corner of my eye I could see the producer and a group of cronies with their heads together at the back of the hall. Somehow I knew they were talking about me, so I pulled up my socks and crooned away evilly, putting

* After the bombardment of Kagoshima in Japan by the British Fleet in 1863.

plenty of pep into the psychopathology. Then the producer appeared and beckoned me to him. There were only a few days to go, but I was sure I would be adequate and I can remember the feeling of relief when I saw my name on the programme. It was a proof of achievement. I would send it home. Monica was having a costume-fitting, throwing out her bust to such effect that the more spinsterly Wrens moved away with a curl of the lip. I left the stage.

The producer took me on one side.

'It's like this, Taff, this business of cues . . .'

I was fired. The others had taken a break and as they sat around, the silence had become total; but soon little conversations were started up here and there, the shipwrights took advantage of the break to begin their hammering and everybody else was pointedly not looking at me. I got the feeling, later on confirmed, that everybody knew except Monica and although my inclination was to protest, I knew that my inability to memorise parrot-fashion had led me to take my first step in play-writing. In fact, I was rewriting. They were right. But I was a team man. They couldn't possibly find another actor in the few days left. I was still prepared to try.

The producer gave a small, confident, executive's smile.

'Don't worry, Taffy, old man. We've been on the blower to the Admiralty.'

'*The Admiralty?*' I grew scared. It was only an amateur dramatic society. Was I going to be court-martialled?

'No. We've got hold of a Chatham "Danny". Played it a few weeks ago in barracks there. He's being drafted here tomorrow.'

So did His Britannic Majesty's most Royal Navy deal with the likes of me. Now it was not only the WRNS officers who avoided me in the wardroom, but Monica joined them at the back of the ablutions.

'I told you and told you and told you. Everybody told you. What d'you think it's like for me, going on stage with someone I've never held in my arms before?'

It was the end of my career as an actor. The Chatham Danny arrived, an education officer like myself. Everybody responded to him as to a hero, as they had to Admiral Sir

Philip Vian, the captain of HMS *Cossack* who boarded the German merchantman, the *Altmark*, with a cutlass and the cry 'The Navy's here!' He had once spoken, not to me, but of me: 'That officer has bulging pockets!' the least-known of his many famous remarks. Now I was relegated once more, to be met with silence and worse still, the polite kindness of compassionate sympathisers.

I did not attend the performance, remained aloof. Monica was a smash hit, her breasts arousing cheers from the ship's company whenever she revealed them, which she did at every possible opportunity. Then events, as they so often did in my life, began, like cogs in the machinery of fate, to mesh. On Saturday mornings, I had to take my turn giving a weekly current affairs lecture. You either took a brief from a prepared handout, or extemporised from the daily press. The Korean War had broken out. I missed the morning's newspapers and delivered a forty-minute lecture giving cast-iron reasons why the Chinese would never enter the war. The class sat mystified as did one of the senior education officers. At first they thought I had found a brilliant ploy to hold everyone spellbound, but it was not so. I had not done my homework. The Chinese had entered the war the previous day and it was front-page news. I was talking through my ill-prepared hat.

That was one black. Then there was another. The successful cast sportingly invited me to the amateur dramatic society's party in Felixstowe. I went. I made it up with Monica. She was seated, straddled on my lap in a public house near the house where Mrs Simpson had entertained the Prince of Wales. But this prince was out of luck. Monica, as well as being straddled on my lap, was balancing a pint on her head when the same senior officer who had just reminded me of the Chinese advance walked in. It was bad luck. He lived ashore nearby, had run out of tobacco and just happened to call in.

The following day I was carpeted. It was not the thing. There were standards. We were officers after all. Then he told me in confidence that there had been an intimation from the Admiralty. They were worried about our men being indoctrinated in Korea. The Royal Marine Commando was about to sail. They wanted several education officers to join them. The British way of life needed explaining, pointing up in case our men were taken prisoner.

'They don't just want anybody, old man. They want rugger players, that sort of thing.'

There was never a minute's doubt that I would not put my name on the list of volunteers; I felt it was all I could do. In recollection it is very easy to describe the events of the past ironically, to point out absurdities which are palpably obvious now; but at the time, I wanted to be Bulldog Drummond, Raffles and the Unknown Soldier rolled into one. I had let the side down, the top of my head said, so I would have to atone. So, I suspect, did my ancestors go over the top: weapons at the ready, glory, medals and death awaiting them – victims of the game we call Making Good. I, too, was dead serious. I would atone.

I wondered if the Captain would make any comment when I dressed up in my best Number One suit and stood rigidly to attention before him. There were others on draft, but I was received first.

He shook my hand warmly.

'Well done, Collins,' he said. 'You've done a splendid job with the ship's choir and the orchestra. Excellent show.'

I blinked, said nothing and did not bother to ask if Instructor Lieutenant Collins got a rocket for carrying on with Monica in a public place.

I never saw Monica again. Her success had gone to her head, just as her charms had contributed to my downfall. But I thought about her constantly and I never forgot her accent.

'Later!' I would sometimes call in the comas induced by the streptomycin, the colliers told me. 'Lay-tah!' I never mentioned her name, but apparently I kept the inflection and for years I never heard a cockney voice without looking up. One of the nurses must have guessed at the connection for when she wheeled the trolley in and prepared the syringes, she would look at me mischievously, slide her hand along my exposed buttock and ask:

'D'you want your injection now, or later?'

For months I lived on memory, like a horse with a feedbag around its neck, even the worst moments of the past being preferable to that enclosed and contained present in which the coughing never stopped.

'Why me?' I kept asking myself as death beckoned each one of those in the beds around me.

'Oh, Sally! Sally! Sally!' a dying collier cried with his last breath. It was the name of a beloved whippet, a winner of long ago.

'Oh, Mammy – Mammy – Mammy!' another called, a man of seventy who daily sent across the bacon from his breakfast plate since he could not chew.

Now I was to see a desperate man calling for the overworked nurses, and when they did not respond at once, he deliberately overturned a sputum pot on to the floor – the blood-flecked slime of its contents spewing out like the obscene trail of a diseased slug.

Sometimes one man would make an impromptu speech in the middle of the night to no one in particular, or occasionally to me, still smoking in the darkness opposite.

'D'you know, the best fuck I ever had was in Mountain Ash?'

'Is that so?'

'In a shop doorway, just a quickie, like.'

'Naturally.'

'I was driving a coach at the time, dropped the party, and I came across this little piece . . . tiny little thing, but I propped her up on two stacks of bricks.'

'Very interesting. They turned out to be handy, did they? – The bricks?'

'No, I fetched them from a building site round the corner and kicked them away, like. At the right time.'

'Is that so?'

'Aye, but I felt awful after. And for years I'd never take a stopping coach to Mountain Ash. Always got out of the Mountain Ash jobs. Awful thing, isn't it? It was years before I went there again, and then I was looking over my shoulder for someone like me.'

Someone like me, I thought; and then again, why me?

When an aunt told me that my grandmother had died, I cried for the last time in my life. I spoke to no one but I was inconsolable and the question returned, 'Why me?'

I did not think I would have more than a year to ponder it.

The following day, the plumber opened a letter from his wife and gave a sardonic snort.

'Fuck me!'

'What's up?'

'It's the Missus. She's been done for shop-lifting. Marks and Sparks.'

We all laughed, even the dying, wheezing ruefully behind their screens. It was somehow uproarious, a sign of life.

'Silly cow! As if I haven't got enough to put up with in here. It'll be in the paper an' all!'

Horse-racing was the immediate solution to all our woes. Each day the hospital handyman came in to clean out the coke stove, remove the illicit flagons from the lockers of those who could manage a drink and laid on all the bets for us with the local bookmaker. When I felt myself slipping off into a streptomycin coma, I would hastily lay the money and a betting slip on my locker.

'The Reverend's off again. You can see him going. Watch his eyes. Silly bugger!'

'What d'you mean?'

'Look at what he's done today. Arts Degree!'

It was true. I followed that horse throughout the summer and a year later, a survivor of the ward next door which had walking cases was wheeled past me to the operating theatre of another hospital. He was himself slipping into unconsciousness.

'It come up, Al', he said. 'Was you on it?'

I was not, and lost every shilling I bet on it.

But that was later. In the meantime, I had lived an eternity and the question remained unanswered.

'Why me?'

EIGHT

When I awoke in the early morning, I would sometimes be afraid to open my eyes in case my right eye had haemorrhaged as well as the left. Both eyes were dilated with morphine drops, so I could not read. If the other, unaffected, eye haemorrhaged as well, I would be totally contained and blind, I thought – a prospect I could not bring myself to face. And so I would often awake sweating, coming to consciousness with an immediate stiffening of my body as my nervous system remembered its plight. I tried to train myself to open my eyes without moving my head or body but always, as the dawn broke and light filtered into the cramped little side ward and the coughing began, the floaters reappeared uncoiling lazily; and always there was this fear of a new spider's egg hatching in the right eye. But it never came, although every day for eighteen months I dreaded it.

Then again the daily injections of streptomycin continued to send me off into comas so that I was rarely conscious for longer than about three hours at any time, and even then I felt that euphoric lassitude that comes with tuberculosis. And, of course, there were the constant night sweats which I had been getting for a year so that I sometimes awoke with hands clenched and every nerve taut. When I later wrote about it in fictional terms, I tried to introduce some of the frenzy but the mind, censoring in recall, only succeeded in making it amusing, omitting the long low notes of despair that stayed with me – especially in the early morning and those dreadful waking moments. Then as I looked at the sleeping faces of the men around me or at those who lay comatose and still like myself, staring vacantly at the ceiling (or into the past because there was no future and most of them realised it), I was always aware of the greyness of it, of old men and disease, and in moments of self-pity which I had to fight, it sometimes seemed to me that I had had no youth at all. Pain, heartbreak, fear, embarrassment, inadequacy, casualties and empty chairs at the table, were all prevalent although I did not realise how much they protected me from the cosiness that characterised the upbringing of so many of my middle-class contemporaries. Immediately it bore down on me that the colliers were all old men; Rob the plumber was my age, but he too had his coal scars and of them all I had ventured the furthest since I was the only ex-serviceman, the only one not to have left school at fourteen. Yet as I looked back on my life, it seemed to me that the strains of it had led me there as surely as the complications of the coal- and stone-dust diseases had affected the colliers whose sputum in death was flecked with coal dust, just as the marks on their hands and faces were blue-black – the unmistakeable stamp of the colliery which had shaped the lives of so many.

When the colliers spat, they often looked into their sputum pots and reflected on the coal dust which was visible in minute tell-tale threads of black.

'Back to where it came from!' they said, and I grew to hate the metal clink of the sputum-pot lids, a sound that punctuated my days and nights. Later when I wrote my first play for television and insisted on the accuracy of the kind of death I had witnessed, which that splendid actor Rupert Davies recreated with gusto, my television play was rewarded with switch-off figures which must have been a record. But then I could never switch off, and so I lay there re-examining my life, rewarding myself with a catalogue of its ludicrous moments. I soon began to compose sentences about myself, some of them not rational.

It was, I told myself, a bio-gardener who lay there, struck down by the ill winds. It was, and is, my most prized qualification, officially recognised by the University of Wales and recorded on parchment – *Dip: Bio-Gardening*.

When I left school at seventeen, moving to Caerleon Training College in Monmouthshire, I began my long apprenticeship in institutional life and the almost exclusive company of men which lasted until I was twenty-five. I do not recommend it, but it was my experience. It was the age of the ex-serviceman and we were a mere handful of young ex-schoolboys swamped by older men, some of whose bodies were marked by wounds. One had a white necklace of machine-gun bullet scars swathing his back and thigh, a present received as a Gurkha major in Burma – an experience he wrote about for the college magazine as naturally as I tried my hand at schoolboy poetry. The ex-servicemen brought with them the cheerful obscenity and air of the barrack room – their language peppered with ex-service slang – and many of them, the old soldier's habit of laying low and not being noticed. We spoke of going to the village as 'going ashore'; some, in a time of food-rationing and abominable college food which was the worst I have ever eaten in my life, tried hard to cultivate the village girls, hoping to quite literally get their feet 'under the table' – obtain a free meal. The atmosphere of the barrack room was constant and we might have been in a joint services camp when away from the lecturers. The college itself was ill equipped to receive us, at first still maintaining a prefect system, an evening roll call at 11 p.m. and 'Lights Out', with marked warnings about being in bedrooms at the same time as the maids who seemed to have been selected on the grounds of their unattractiveness. One had a moustache, another a pronounced squint and they skittered about us as if they were inmates of the neighbouring lunatic asylum, no doubt having received a similar warning from the huge matron whose Dickensian appearance in blue uniform and starched cap belonged, like the food, to another century.

Immediately there was a choice of courses to be made, the Principal insisting that every student should do a 'practical' course, and those without skills or aptitude for art or woodwork were inevitably drafted to take a subject known as bio-gardening. This was discussed like a new order pinned to the notice boards in the sergeants' mess, the language inevitably coarse.

'What is it?'

'Fucked if I know.'

'What have you got to do?'

'Mug up on the old biol', do a bit on the old gardening plots and generally keep the old nose clean, head down and away you go!'

'I don't fancy it.'

'Can't help that. Every other course is full.'

'But what have you got to do?' It was a perennial question.

I never found out and followed others like a sheep for two whole years until, growing weary, I attempted to shine and very nearly paid an awful penalty. For me being a bio-gardener was to enter the realms of a living fantasy, a circumstance created by the training-college authorities, probably in response to some educational report which decided that gardening was a subject worth teaching in the newly created secondary modern schools. It was a good and sensible idea, but in Caerleon it became my nightmare since the lecturer responsible for teaching me was one of those men of whom we charitably say, 'He is brilliant at his subject, but cannot communicate it.' And for me, he took on all the attributes of the Mad Hatter – a walking caricature of the fool academic whose distracted air, insane rapidity of speech and complete inability to look anyone in the eyes made him a kind of permanently absent presence. Almost completely bald, with wandering eyes that slid evasively over people, ever seeking blank spaces, he was a perpetually embarrassed man whose limp apologetic smile created waves of bewilderment whenever he appeared. You had almost to run to catch up with him and then the watery eyes slid everywhere. He was a man of water who had all the vanishing properties of water, who dripped, flowed, appeared and disappeared like a mirage, but never penetrated. I never succeeded in making any communication with him and if he spoke, it was to the floor, the blotting paper, to the branches of trees, and I might not have existed at all.

In his introductory lecture on the mysteries of bio-gardening, his rate of speech was so fast, it left us speechless. Nobody asked a question. We sat there, twenty or thirty of us, in a state of shock. It might have been forty minutes of gibberish, and still the restless, terrified eyes wandered everywhere. If he was as nervous as a stoat, we were also acutely embarrassed and bewildered. What was bio-gardening? How could we cope?

Perhaps I was more worried than the others. My contemporaries were old soldiers, ex-marines, airmen. They had been around. Some had made enquiries of the second-year students. They'd got the gen, were already clued up, as they said in the slang of all three services. There was no shortage of cheerful advisers.

'It's like this, Al', you've only got to get forty marks. Bone up a bit on the old plant life, reproduction and that, chuck in a bit about fertilisers and show willing always. Main thing is to show a bit of interest.'

'Interest?'

'Any trips, zoological gardens, horticulture and that, slap your name down straight away. He goes a bundle on that. And don't skip lectures. Nod when he nods, don't look him in the eyes, and then, of course, there's plenty of chance to bull up – the Diary and the old Thes'.'

'Thes'?'

'Thesis.'

Every bio-gardener had to keep a gardener's diary, a seasonal production to indicate continued interest which was little more than a compilation of 'Things To Do In The Garden' throughout the year, and which became for me a straight crib from several gardener's books on the subject. And my adviser remained the same man.

'Own handwriting, mind, and chuck in a few pressed flowers, beans and that, just to show a bit of interest. You've got to pull the old finger out, Al'!'

I did, and each term my diary was returned ticked without comment by the Mad Hatter.

The thesis was another matter. It was supposed to be a dissertation on some topic which you were first required to hand in for discussion but which, in my case, went undiscussed once again – the paper as usual returned with a solitary tick. The Mad Hatter's factotum was a second-year student who was called the bio-gardening prefect, and from him and others we learned the rules, ever grateful as they bent their experience to the spotting of examination questions which we permutated, learning off huge chunks of useless bio-gardening information. None of this did any lasting good in that the moment the examinations were over, we forgot all we had ever learnt. The main hurdles were in the second year when the thesis, or written examination, and the inspection of the individual garden plot allocated to each one of us by a visiting university professor was preceded by an oral examination, all of which I greatly feared. But I survived, getting by with the minimum marks, and as the terms went by each Friday's double bio-gardening session passed like a duty visit, the chattering lecturer appearing like a caged invalid who spouted incomprehensibly from the moment the keeper's bell admitted me. I understood nothing, nothing at all, not a single sentence and began to sit once more at the rear of the lecture room. But my life as a bio-gardener was the sole relapse into my wayward school habits, for I soon found I could cope with every other subject and now I was unexpectedly witness of the difficulties of others – of men who after five years of war could not at first sleep at night because they could write essays only with the greatest of difficulty. Others were pitifully self-conscious when faced with a class of schoolchildren and one man, an ex-RASC driver who had been through the Italian campaign, was so nervous of appearing on the assembly hall platform and reading a passage from the Bible – as we all had to do – that he left the course and gave up all idea of teaching. Compared to the lame ducks and late starters I was confident and fluent, and I was even more surprised to find myself regarded as intelligent, and actually had my essays borrowed by men ten years my senior. I had, for the first time in my life, status as an academic – a new experience, and it delighted me. But not as a bio-gardener. As a bio-gardener, I was back in the sub-world of hopeless blank incomprehension in which no light ever penetrated.

In the second year, I inherited the garden plot of another bio-gardening duffer. Rhubarb grew wild, the brick compost heap crumbled, the soil seemed acid, the whole tiny area shabby and derelict beside the prize plots of the diligent. I must have had weekly tasks. I must have planted something, but whatever I did, the appearance of dereliction remained. Once the subject of celery came up on one of the Mad Hatter's rapid perambulations down the centre path where he some-times strode, followed by a small group of students who had succeeded in communicating with him. On these days he occasionally wore a gown under his duffle coat, wellington boots below, so that his appearance grew more and more eccentric. On this day, hearing the word 'celery', my ears pricked up. I recognised it as an exiled student might gratefully come across a single word of his own dialect in a foreign language, and repeated it.

'Celery?' I said. I tried a smile.

The Mad Hatter happened to be standing near my plot, suddenly seized a spade and promptly began to build a celery trench on my rhubarb patch – digging and packing with a frenetic muscular vigour, talking all the while, words spraying out in an incessant flow like pips until he had completed a proper deep trench with firmed sides. At last, there was something tangible available for inspection upon my arid patch. Then, having comandeered compost from other heaps as the final touch, he left without a word or a glance at me and although, later, I planted celery, it never grew. Still, I shored up the trench, patted and protected it and kept it there for the remainder of my stay in college. It crumbled eventually but remained, like a small Egyptian tomb, a sad decaying monument for an unborn child. The comments were kindly.

'You done all right on the old celery, Al'? The trench, anyhow.' It was indeed evidence of something. But the farce continued. And so did the advice.

'For the old Thes', Al, you want to pick a good old waffle subject. Give yourself a bit of room to move.'

Bio-gardening did not lend itself to waffle subjects, but I had a year to cross-examine the second-year students and to shuffle through the lists of previous theses, some of which were annually offered for sale by student speculators who profited by our anxiety, and I finally arrived at what I thought was a brilliant idea. I would offer an imposing title, 'The History of the Potato (and Its Diseases)', a choice of subject that would get me partially away from the 'bio', I thought. I sent in the title via the bio-gardening prefect. It was returned, ticked once more without comment, and I finally came up with some hundred neatly typed pages with traced and coloured drawings to complement the whole. I also had an arty cover designed by a friend at home who was an architectural student, and he illuminated the title with three dimensional letters – a current vogue which was to stand me in good stead in the viva. As well as my dissertation on the history of the potato, rewritten from an encyclopaedia, I duly copied out brief descriptions of disease symptoms from leaflets published by the Ministry of Agriculture so that the result looked weighty enough, although none of it had passed through my head.

It lay on the desk in my room and attracted both visitors and comment.

'The old Thes' looks a treat, Al'. You done right to bull it up.'

'Dark horse, you are!'

'Bloody scraper!'

It gave me a false confidence for a while, but as the day of the oral examination and the outside inspection of the gardening plots drew nearer, I began to worry. Apart from the now-crumbling celery trench, my plot remained rhubarby, with a few beans, a healthy radish or two, some stringy lettuce – the whole resembling a slum garden once more. I looked and looked at it, but it took me weeks to see what was wrong. Strange as it may seem now, although I was engaged in a deception, I did not fully realise it at the time. Since I'd had not one single conversation with my tutor, all my actions were based on the casual advice of my seniors, resulting in a dull copying of the efforts of others – all I could do to show that I belonged to the bio-gardeners. It took some time to dawn upon me that if I was allegedly interested in the history of the potato and its most documented diseases, at least I ought to take some practical interest since it was a practical subject. But I was a bio-gardener on Fridays only and it was not until a week before the visitation of the external examiner that the vital insight came. I should have had potatoes growing in my plot! It was an unforgivable omission, especially as the appearance of my thesis was now so attractive that the art students had asked to copy its style. The parchment cover, the multi-coloured drawings, the alphabetical list of diseases all available for handy reference and all designed by the friend at home, now resembled an already published work. It was, in fact, my first book. But I did not have a single home-grown potato to show. What a fool, I thought. I was not alone in my difficulties. An ex-infantry officer whom I privately called the Colonel, had developed the habit of addressing the Mad Hatter as he might have spoken to a local shopkeeper which caused him to vanish even more quickly and the Colonel was feeling his own frustrations. Like myself, he was not a digger. His own plot was none too clever, as we said. The brick compost heap which he'd tried to repair, had crumbled. Brick dust covered his lettuce while slugs devoured mine. ('What are you doing, Al'? – Renting them space, or what?') The Colonel was not a particular friend. I had unwittingly deceived him too. Since clothes were still rationed, I often wore an old pair of my uncle's RAF officer's trousers which had led the Colonel to believe I was officer material, a cardinal phrase of the time. I had also contradicted him on several occasions over minor matters. I suppose I looked much older than my age. When he found out that I was only eighteen and had come straight from school, he could not forgive himself for his mistake. He had made several. A forceful and direct man, he had drawn attention to himself by standing up in the assembly hall to address the Principal during a food strike when we had all walked out of the dining-room after a particularly atrocious meal had been served. He complained about the stench of the daily polished tables and said it was unhygienic. It was an act of courage, a colonel's way, but the Principal lost his temper and bawled, 'I am the Principal of this College. Write that down in your book, sir!'

The Colonel was forced to sit, out-Colonelled. The food did not improve. The tables continued to show their daily thick rub of odorous polish and the Colonel had violated the barrack-room code. He had got himself noticed, singled out for attention and had done himself no good in the process, drawing comment from all ranks. ('I told you, Al', boy. Keep your head down, lay low. Never let the bastards see what you're thinking. Only way.')

But now, as bio-gardeners, the Colonel and I were in the same boat. Three days to go and our gardening plots a shambles. We had a late-night conference.

'Only one thing to do, Richards.'

'Anything,' I said. 'I've got to get some bloody potatoes.'

'Potatoes,' the Colonel made a note. 'Right. But it'll cost you.'

'How much?'

'A couple of quid,' he said. 'Thirty bob, maybe, especially if we have to work after dark.'

He had a plan. He was not an ex-Colonel for nothing, but the mention of money made me pause. I had ten shillings a week pocket money, allotted to me by my grandmother, and an occasional pound from my mother who was now working as the warden of Land Girl's Hostel in the Vale of Glamorgan. I was very hard up compared to the ex-servicemen, most of whom received five pounds per week from special grants. But I really felt my future depended on a pass in bio-gardening. Thirty bob for a certificate, I thought; what the Principal called imposingly, 'Your licence to teach'. 'You're on,' I said.

There was a lunatic asylum near the college with large grounds. Sometimes at night you could hear weird cries coming from the inmates and once, during an impromptu seance held in the college room next to mine, one of the students felt he was in touch with disturbed spirits nearby, had an asthma attack and collapsed. Seances were then banned on the head prefect's orders. But the Colonel's contacts were more worldly. He had met one of the asylum gardeners in a nearby public house and filed his name for future reference. Now, with three days to go, there was no time to be lost.

So the Colonel, who daily spit-polished his shoes and presented an appearance altogether more distinguished than the rest of us, took his shooting stick and went about his task. It was tricky, and since he had to have a whole new brick compost heap constructed – bricks delivered and laid with new cement, then disguised with black paint purloined from the art department – a commando job was required. I only wanted a dozen or so potato plants installed 'as new', but any help in 'bulling up' the plot generally would be much appreciated, I said. I left it to him, and the work was done stealthily one Sunday evening when the Mad Hatter was known to be absent. I purposely kept away, so did the Colonel having identified the tasks, and when the Monday morning came, I handed him the money and went to inspect. The whole plot was tidied up, the path-edging immaculate and professionally done but, best of all, a small compound of potato haulms flourished near the rear wall – a neat clump that might have graced Kew Gardens. Nearby the Colonel's compost heap was a sight to behold, the mortar black-edged, and the professional skills were everywhere evident in the neatness of the construction. If anybody said anything, he was going to play on his war wounds for he too had been in action and was in receipt of a disability pension. If threatened further, he was going to make it hot for the Principal since he had made extensive enquiries of the wholesaler who supplied our abominable food and darkly hinted that there was something fishy about the expenditure and that he knew enough to make a fuss. I never knew the exact details, but the Colonel was a formidable man of about twenty-nine with a ferocious cold-eyed stare and when he spoke it was in the short clipped sentences known as 'good power of command'. I must have learned it from him for I soon acquired the trick of doing it myself when required, another part of the protective mask I was assuming. In a shoe shop I once heard him say, 'I want a pair of shoes. Have you *good* shoes?' It put the shop assistants in a lather, and I must have had him in mind when I once composed a sentence for dealing with offensive people in gentlemen's clubs. 'Surely, you're not a member? But then nobody would have invited you as a guest – even inadvertently!' England awaited me with its labyrinthine class distinctions and I would have to survive there too.

But the Colonel turned up trumps for me. Or so I thought. My potato clump might have been Captain Bligh's newly stowed breadfruit, so much did I treasure it.

On the Tuesday, we queued up outside the bio-gardening room for the viva. The visiting professor was a woman, a formidable figure whom I was to meet again.

The appearance of the old Thes' set her off.

'Why is the title written without capital letters?'

'To draw attention,' I said.

'Don't you like capital letters?'

'Everything traditional is not necessarily unimprovable.'

'There is no such word as unimprovable.'

'I like things to look neat and elegant.'

'Then you don't like modern art?'

'I like an expression of the self.'

The Mad Hatter was present and did not know where to look. I think he sat on his hands. I was nineteen. Somehow or other, I could stand up for myself. I was not nervous in her presence. I was when queuing up outside, but once committed, I followed what my grandmother had on occasion jokingly described as the family motto, 'Go for the throat!' And all the time my thesis lay like a glossy advertising brochure on the table.

'In what way is this an expression of yourself?'

'It looks like I want it to be. I've thought about it, and when they first brought the potato here, the day before the ship made the English Channel, I expect they dressed the ship overall,' I said. 'They probably wanted to create a good impression too.' I was flannelling on four cylinders.

She smiled. I think she was bored. We did not mention the potato as a plant. We did not mention its diseases. She asked me how I had obtained the Ministry of Agriculture pamphlets which described the diseases and which I had fortunately acknowledged.

'It's the old story,' I said. 'I have a cousin who is in the Ministry.' It was true, and it was his brother who had given me extra milk in primary school. Influence again!

I thought the Mad Hatter would tie his wrists in knots and coil himself under the table, for he was already writhing in his private and unidentified agony. This was not the bio-gardening way. But the professor smiled, engaged him in some unintelligible bio-gardening conversation and I was dismissed.

'How did you get on, Al'?'

'Cakewalk.'

'Piece of piss, was it?'

'The old Thes' did the trick.' I was very grateful to my architect friend and his eternal catchword, 'a good piece of design'. It had occupied most of the interview.

'Told you to bull up, Al'. Bullshit baffles brains!' That was another catch phrase, and I knew it by heart. Now if I could only spot four questions out of seven and spill out enough information in the examination paper, I was through. I would have my 'licence to teach'.

But in the afternoon, we had the inspection of the gardening plots.

'Stand by your plots! If you've got any wellies, give 'em a shine!'

When I got to my plot with the other students, I saw the

Colonel, elegant in his country tweeds and a sporty cap, his shoes brilliant as he stood defiantly by the gleaming compost heap. He was going to brazen it out with that ferocious stare and, indeed, he came smartly to attention and removed the cap with a flourish when the professor came down the centre path. But as soon as I got to my own plot, the most elementary fact of bio-gardening was soon made obvious to me.

This was Wednesday. On Monday, the potato haulms had flourished, elegant and green in the heavily watered soil. But now they were on the wane, limp and bedraggled, sagging like elderly drunks after a football match. The colour had gone out of them as it had out of the soil which had reverted to its grey slum hue, and what had been green and luxuriant haulms in good health, were now reduced to a decrepit invalid state. The potatoes were dying on me. What a bloody day to pick, I thought!

The professor ignored the new compost heap, ignored the Colonel and came unerringly to me, followed by the Mad Hatter at a run, his bony wrists working at his long shirtsleeves as if they were Greek worry beads, eyes on the slide, his embarrassment only partially covered by a slithering smile which made him look even more uncomfortable. He was the kind of man who looked as if he apologised to himself even in his sleep. I felt myself tense as I looked at them both. The Mad Hatter was also required to watch us teach children in the local schools on teaching practice and, worse still, to grade us – to assess our powers of communication, a task for which he was singularly ill equipped. Left alone with a class of unruly boys, they would have removed the roof. What right had he to sit in judgement on me? If I failed, perhaps I should take a leaf out of the Colonel's book, attack him, and bring the system down with me? This was what the Colonel had threatened. But now he stood resplendent but ignored beside those gleaming bricks, passed over.

The professor looked at the wilting potato haulms, picked up a shrinking blackened leaf with the edge of a pencil and gave it a clinical look. There were spots there, spots! The asylum gardener had off-loaded his own casualties on me. Thirty bob's worth, I thought, and all poxed!

The professor said, 'What's wrong with those potatoes?'

I stared at her wildly. I did not know. I had no idea. They were not my potatoes. Through my mind, flickering in a rapid succession of images, came the diagrams of those diseased haulms which I had copied out laboriously, printing their latin names beneath. There was disease after disease and I tried desperately to remember just one. Then I remembered my adviser, a cheerful ex-Marine.

'If they ask anything, don't just bloody stand there! Say something! Take a swing at it!'

One incomprehensible phrase stuck in my mind since the typist had misspelled it.

'*Phytophothora infestans!*' I said. Weighty gibberish, I thought, but it sounded impressive.

The Mad Hatter practically disappeared under his jacket. The professor's mouth hardened into a small disbelieving 'O'. She looked through me.

'No,' she said. 'It's common garden blight!'

Then she swept on to a geranium king who had had special permission to cultivate seeds in his bedroom.

I must have failed, I thought.

'Dropped a right bolluck there, Al'! *Blight*, for Christ's sake! Bloody blight! Didn't you see them spots?'

Not in time, I hadn't.

'Bloody good job you bulled up on the old Thes' then.'

It was true. I got my forty marks, forty-one if the truth be known. I remain a qualified bio-gardener. Nearly twenty years afterwards I had just bought a large house near the sea many miles away, inheriting an immaculate garden (which soon deteriorated), and one day I spied the Mad Hatter walking along the road outside, still wearing a duffle coat, still embarrassed, still striding out with those limpid eyes shimmering as they swept the gutter, the road, the empty spaces. I gasped. I do not think he saw me, but I do not know. I ran into the house and locked the door. I have never known a man whom I understood less and he remained a mystery. Perhaps others saw him differently; perhaps to those who found some contact with him, he was another man. For me he just evaporated each time I saw him and left only trails and, ironically enough, a few days later I was standing on the front lawn of my new home in my best clothes when a peppery old gent leaned over the wall. He made a classic mistake.

'Here!' he said imperiously, and crooked his finger impatiently.

I went to the wall.

'What's the best thing for moss on a lawn?'

It did not take me seconds to realise that he thought he was talking to the gardener.

'Oh, *Phytophothora infestans*,' I said.

'Pardon?'

I took another swing at it.

'Mercurised sand,' I said. 'Rub it in night and morning for about a week.'

He went off impressed and mystified. I remain a qualified bio-gardener, but I have never practised.

I soon lost touch with all my training-college friends. It was an undemanding period. I got my licence to teach. The parchment proved useful. It was my grandmother's ambition for me, a salaried job with enviable holidays and a settled life and, had it not been for conscription and the inevitability of military service, I might have had one. Importantly, training college was the place where I began to read again, following on from my last idyllic year in school. It was there that I discovered a country of the mind, but I seldom engaged in literary discussion. I just read ferociously on my own. There was always so much to escape from, and it was in books that I found my refuge. I became a reader perhaps unconsciously seeking an explanation of myself, some identification, some glimpse of another's pain, the feel of lives elsewhere because my own left so many questions unanswered. I passed all my examinations without exerting myself. I did not engage my feelings. I provided what was wanted. I did not think, nor was I stimulated to think; but I read and read in private, and it was a habit that was to prove my salvation. I see now that my literary ambitions were a form of exhibitionism designed to place me on a par with those who could do all the things I could not and there was, buried within me, a sense of being unwanted – except by my grandmother. But all the insecurity of the lonely child was increasingly disguised as I learned to pass muster, in the company of men at least. And I remained a reader, omnivorous, although unsystematic.

But for months in hospital I could not read and this crutch was removed, a terrible blow. There were, however, little things to hope for – straws at which to clutch, like an increase in weight, or some remote hope of improvement when I was conscious. Once a month, those who could be moved left the little side ward and were taken by ambulance to be X-rayed in another large hospital nearby. Most of the colliers could not be moved, but those who could were automatically placed in another category as if they alone were worth photographing – another unspoken mark of status, life being the ultimate prize.

It was a month before I qualified for the privilege, and for days the conversation in the little side ward was concerned with the likely identity of the ambulance driver. Emrys, our coach driver, had connections in the trade. If the ambulance driver was Dai Twice, an old colleague who had worked suicidal double shifts for years, we might be able to stop off for a pint provided we kept our mouths shut and there was a suitable discreet place for the ambulance to park; and the thought of a pint set us off for the morning. It would be a reunion with the living. In case I had any scruples, there was no need for alarm since the landlord of the likely public house was a relative of our coach driver and the glasses we used would naturally be disinfected after we had used them, although our presence in pyjamas and dressing gowns would not go unnoticed. It was the thought of the treat in store which bucked us up, and the opportunity to break rules in the traditional Welsh way. But when the sister came round with her check list on the day before, she had bad news for the coach driver. Emrys had been taken off the X-ray list. He could not be moved. She made her rounds briskly and cheerfully.

'Mr Richards, Mr Jones – just two in this ward tomorrow.' And then she was off. The import was unmistakeable. It was like a sentence of death. Once you were off the list, it meant that they were not bothering to X-ray you – another slight but stabbing sliver of reality that struck with a deadly chill. Emrys looked at the ceiling, then away, his eyes filling. We dropped the subject. You could hear the seconds ticking away. Everyone knew. It was a step nearer.

142

In my own case there were further complications. The last opthalmic specialist I had seen was in Moorfields Eye Hospital where I was pronounced interesting. 'We don't see more than six cases of this a year, so it's impossible to give an accurate prognosis.' There now appeared to be some difficulty in getting the local opthalmic specialist to come and see me. He would not leave his Cardiff base to come to the little isolation hospital, so I had to be taken to see him. It meant the cancellation of my X-ray trip and the remote chance of a pint, and so I had to wait another week.

For some reason, I built up my hopes. I did not then understand what was the matter with me. I knew the words 'Eale's Disease', but who Eale was, I never found out. I kept thinking of my eye condition as an injury and injuries, I hoped, healed. Like fractious children, you gave them something and they got better. Apart from the morphine drops and the reduced amounts of streptomycin, I had been given nothing, and it was now several months since that first haemorrhage and I felt worse as each day went by. There was the depersonalisation which hospital produces, the sense of handing yourself over to others and the gradual lessening of your identity and status; and then there was the daily toll of worry, the ever-present miniature horror film running every day inside my eye, the brightness of the blood and those sinister floaters, the minute and treacherous undergrowth inside my eye which greeted me every morning. We still believed that tuberculosis was a wasting disease and each day I took two raw eggs in milk, nauseated by the effort of swallowing them which at least enabled me to watch the quivering pointer on the weighing scales at the end of the week with the same keen interest as the others. When I reached twelve stone, I felt it was an achievement, although the general feeling of lassitude grew worse. In another ward a gypsy boy who had been admitted, brought in during the last stages of consumption, escaped one night through a window and went off to die on his own. It somehow seemed a noble, sensible and natural thing to do.

Before the visit to the opthalmic specialist, I thought vaguely in terms of an operation inside my eye. I thought in picture-book terms – the skilled hands of the surgeon, the glare of the lights in the operating theatre, perhaps the muttered command, 'Forceps!' But I would have been satisfied with a sticking-plaster job – if only they would try something! You could put up with being spoken to as an idiot, the habitual practice of most of the doctors I had met if they were not humming and hawing or being noncommital, bolting if there was the slightest danger of you asking a difficult question. I could take that provided there were results. The problem was that I did not understand that my eye condition was an allergy to the tubercle in my lung, and no one enlightened me for months – probably because they did not really know themselves. When the day came, an ambulance was sent for me, but I was to remain in my pyjamas and dressing gown under the supervision of a nurse – my lean self a fragile thing to be shepherded everywhere in an invalid chair. The colliers showed unusual interest.

'All the best, our kid.' In the long months, I had progressed from the Reverend to Our Kid.

'Everything you wishes yourself!' another said.

It might have been an interview for some splendid new career. One even shook my hand as I passed his bed.

'If you get a chance, slip the nurse a quickie in the ambulance,' Rob said. 'Don't hesitate!' But if I had a wet dream, I awoke in terror in case of another haemorrhage. Even the memories of Monica were bad for me.

The nurse was nervous and found me an onerous responsibility. She told me to lie down once I got out of the wheelchair, propped up my head with blankets, did not permit me to smoke and I could not look out of the window although she held my hand and had brought a flask of tea. At the infirmary in Cardiff, a wheelchair was waiting. Once again I was parcelled up and swept along corridors, a known 'TB'. At the opthalmic clinic the specialist, a German-Jewish refugee of the inter-war years, plied his trade behind closed doors, a queue of patients awaiting him, some with obvious injuries. But I was kept well to one side of them. The nursing sister had been in school at the same time as me, and was plainly embarrassed by my presence. I waited an hour, fussed over by my own special nurse who produced a sputum pot for my special needs. I sat there slumped in my chair like the

Hunchback of Notre Dame. People moved around me and the curious stared. No one spoke and my special nurse must have felt her new status for she was several times called to one side and questioned. I had an insane Rabelaisian wish to produce an enormous erection and wave it over the heads of those who stared at me, shaking it at the startled probationer nurses who shouted your surname down corridors. 'Treat me like a hunchback and I will become one, but this is what you will get if you are not careful!' But I contented myself with slumping under the blanket, head to one side, the embodiment of a drooling psycho. (Exposed in pyjamas and dressing gown in a public place, you rapidly lose any identity.) The hour passed like a day. Presently I was summoned, people moving hastily away as I approached, and wheeled into the darkened cavern of the man I later referred to as the Beast. He – the opthalmic specialist – was a large, obese, unattractive and ugly man in his mid-fifties with a pronounced German accent and he appeared to me as a kind of nonperson, as unclear and unknown as some stereotyped German extra in a propaganda film. He asked no questions, uttered no pleasantries, merely grunted, consulted my notes, then roughly parted my legs with his knee as he adjusted the opthalmic disc and came closer to stare into my eye, grunting as he did so.

My eyes watered, flickered, he grunted again, then I realised he was holding his breath. Finally he straightened, turned to my notes, presenting me with his back. It was all I was to see of him.

I found some questions.

'Will it get better?'

'*Nod* possible to say.' His accent was thick.

'Can't you – can't you give me some idea of a prognosis?'

'*Dere* is no brognosis.'

'Well . . .' I gulped. 'If I'm going to go blind, will I have to learn Braille?'

'You vill be told in *goot* time.'

'What about treatment?'

'*Garry* on *vid der* dreatment.'

'Is there any special treatment? – An operation?'

'No.'

145

The nursing sister intruded to tell him something in private. I am sure it was a suggestion that my family might consider private treatment for he said, 'It makes no difference.'

I tried to think of another question.

'*Dreatment* as before,' he said. He scribbled on my notes and went out. That was all. The sister gave the notes to my nurse who was called back in and I was repackaged, bundled up and returned to the little side ward, the floaters now moving wildly in my eye.

'How did you get on, our kid?' they said in the ward. 'Anything doing?'

'Nothing,' I said.

Somehow everybody knew. Bad news was their expertise. It came like winter weather in continual icy blasts. That day somebody had presented a television set to the hospital. It must have been one of the first and that night it was our ward's turn to see it, most of us seeing television for the first time, but only for an hour. Once the handyman had wheeled it in and replugged the cables, there were barely forty minutes left; and then the picture took ages to materialise until a huge contralto was seen in a shimmering dress, her bosom heaving. The sound took longer to materialise than the picture, but finally we identified the words she mouthed and then they echoed in the smoke-filled room. She was singing 'Home Sweet Home'.

The tears began to run down the face of the collier opposite me. He found his HP Sauce bottle, began to swig at his rum. Another man was also crying. I closed my good eye, squinted through the floaters at the performer's huge swollen face as the sound now reached maximum volume and reverberated in the ward. Television was such a rarity and our experience of it almost non-existent so that it was as if we had been suddenly catapulted into the middle of a live concert in the Workman's Hall, all of us landing in the middle of the front row in full and immediate view of the artist – a solemn and serious occasion which no one dared interrupt, not even to cast a side glance at our neighbours. We sat it out, one man even applauded. There was silence as the handyman arrived to dismantle the set, then hushed tones exactly as there had been when my grandmother lowered her voice on the arrival of German bombers overhead in case they might catch her comments.

Somehow television seemed to belong to Victorian drawing-rooms, with Aunt Cissie's Christmas solo ever expected. We did not ask for it again, and regarded it as an embarrassment. Indeed, we seldom bothered even with the radio earphones except when there was horse-racing. It was as if we had quit the outside world for ever and wanted no part of it, including visitors who, as the months went by, seemed increasingly to be removed from us. Life was the coke stove, the racing papers, the horses, the bets, the weekly arrival of the weighing scales, the daily jabs, the latest quote from *Reveille*, the blood in your sputum if you were ailing and ready to move on. One or two men were in plaster corsets which kept them in a permanent stiffened posture to drain their affected lungs and their relief was the brief daily removal of the corset, and mine that I was allowed to walk to the lavatory – the privilege of my hospital career. My cough was dry.

Summer gave way to autumn, then winter began to set in. I began to get acclimatised. I had a punch-up with a boy who would not turn off his radio, a quick single punch to the throat, and was first out of bed to remove the Dunlopillo mattress of a man who had died, choking to death in his own sputum in the night. These mattresses were in short supply and I'd had my good eye on it for weeks, ever since the telltale arrival of the oxygen apparatus. I wanted that mattress and I got it. I was growing harder, and after the solitary punch, one of the nurses whispered a congratulation in the lavatory. It was what she would have liked to have done herself. Then the deaths began, there were newcomers, and unwanted change. We had been a cosy group and had got to know each other well. Now there were new faces to replace the missing.

Then without warning I awoke one morning and found my eye had haemorrhaged again, the amount of blood inside the eye had doubled, and there was another black floater. It was the end of me, I thought, the end of sight and I was still not properly adjusted to the streptomycin. I waited an hour before telling anyone, but there was no doubt. Since there were no resident doctors in the little hospital, I had to wait for the daily visit. The chest physician did not examine my eye. He said quite frankly that he did not understand the condition and there was nothing he could do, but I had better stay on complete bed rest. It was another step down, another loss of status, and the question returned to my mind.

'Why me?'

I did not realise it would take me a lifetime to answer it, and then only haltingly. There were other lives to be considered first.

NINE

Many men were convinced they had only themselves to blame for being in hospital. Long periods of introspection convinced them of it, periods when, like myself, they would go back on the high and low moments of their lives, piecing together the fevered excitements of youth and, inevitably, their indiscretions which were largely sexual and recalled with gusto. It was as if the one natural urge common to all of us still held us enthralled, a remembered evidence of spirit, the animal self long denied.

'Oh, I've been a heller in my time!'

'How d'you mean?'

'Wimmin!'

'Get away?'

'I tell you, I've come down the roofs of houses just in time!'

'The roofs?'

'Just got out of the bedroom before the key went into the front door. Warm as toast, I've been.'

Some men had taken their wives suddenly and violently when black with pit dirt from the colliery; others spoke of men who'd had intercourse by impersonation, creeping into strange beds in the darkness after a shift and they even recalled prosecutions for this practice, and although I queried it – as ever wanting details – my disbelief was contradicted. While not a common practice, it was a practice; and then there were the tales of miraculous encounters, sudden and quick lusts which were always reciprocated.

'Never had a bit on a moving staircase, have you? (While it was movin', I mean?).'

'Never.'

149

'Bloody county schoolboys! Can tell you never got your matric.!'

I would lie there and listen to the most ordinary of men relating in detail some domestic orgy and brace myself to stay awake on the next visiting afternoon in order to see the other, consenting, partner; but more often than not, she would turn out to be a demure, squat, little middle-aged woman with a cheery smile who would make it her business to come over to my bed with a plate of Welsh cakes since I was sometimes short of visitors.

'No, thank you, Mrs Jones.' But I would hear the earlier male voice – 'Wet and ready for me, she was, boys! Against the mangle, I'm telling you. Never had a bit against the mangle, have you?'

'No, I haven't.'

'Call yourself a sailor!'

So our days were spent. By the common standard I had been as warm as toast myself, but any idea of the ordered life had long been denied me whereas most of the colliers had lived their lives in one place. Few had travelled save to London for a football match or a boxing tournament and they were the biggest babies when it came to eating hospital food, or even undressing in public in front of other men which profoundly embarrassed some of them. Theirs was a generation that had never left home. They wore underpants and cardigans in bed, demanded the screens for the slightest thing and would sulk if the Worcester Sauce ran out. They had never eaten institution-alised food, never been away from home for long and each visiting day eyed the shopping baskets of their wives or relatives for delicacies, a leg of chicken, or a home-made whinberry tart. Few spoke of women except as sexual objects, or as capable housewives who kept 'a good table'. 'My old woman', 'my old tart' were common expressions. It was the language of the workplace where to confess an affection was a weakness. But it represented only the surface of things and disguised the real affections which were ever in evidence in the simplest of gestures. It was with the habitual coarseness of everyday speech, however, that I learned a black colliery humour which was to ease my passage in strange company for years, especially when I visited Russia.

(*left and right*) Tom and Jessie Jeremy, my grandfather and grandmother when young. He was not a native of Pontypridd and my grandmother never let him forget it whereas she could trace her antecedents to two lay brothers, tenant farmers, evicted as a consequence of the Dissolution of the Monasteries; (*centre*) my mother on the day before I was born in 1929. Perhaps her eyes relate what was in store for her. She separated from my father three days later, never to be reunited.

(*left*) Myself, aged five; (*centre*) my grandmother as I best remember her. One of her favourite sayings was, 'Best foot forward, John Willie!' John Willie, I always understood to be a soldier; (*right*) with my mother, Megan.

p) The bard Glanffrwd, whose rise from collier to Dean of St Asaph was a period
elsh success story, and his wife, Llinos y dé, a famous singer of the day; (*above*) a
serted colliery winding room, all that remains of the Tŷ Mawr Colliery where my
eat-grandfather and the bard Glanffrwd began their working lives. (*Mike Richards*)

Uniforms and dead heroes haunted my childhood. (*top, left*) Most distinguished
Uncle Willie who joined the Welsh Horse in 1914 as a private. He was killed in the
week of the war, a Lieutenant-Colonel with a DSO and an MC; (*top, right*) uncle J
his brother, joined the Anzacs in Australia, was wounded at Gallipoli, returned h
to die prematurely after the war; (*bottom, left*) my Uncle Ithel who was also decor
and shot down over France in the early years of the second war; (*bottom, right*) u
Cliff, my mother's eldest brother, in the Welch Regiment in 1918. He also
prematurely of tuberculosis.

(*top*) A magazine photograph showing Ithel (extreme left) and some of his crew. It was captioned, 'Three airmen obviously ignoring the superstition of three lights with one match.' A month later all were killed; (*below*) my mother (centre) in the Victory Parade in 1945.

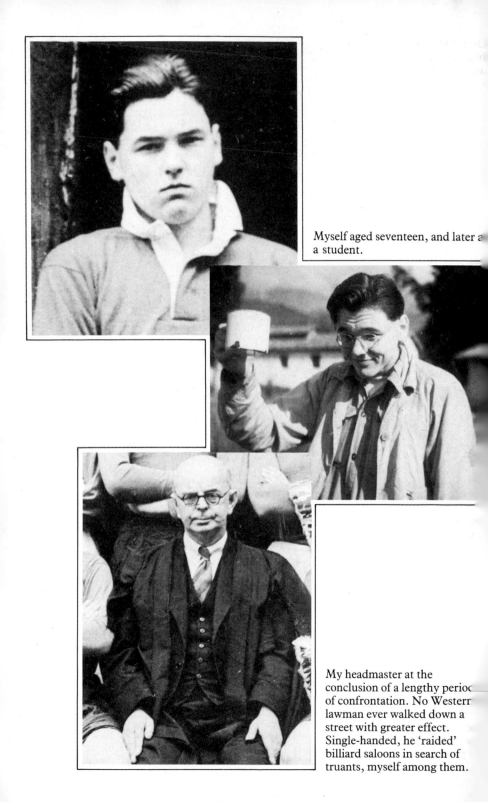

Myself aged seventeen, and later as a student.

My headmaster at the conclusion of a lengthy period of confrontation. No Western lawman ever walked down a street with greater effect. Single-handed, he 'raided' billiard saloons in search of truants, myself among them.

'Orator's Corner' aboard
ship off Ushant. I am,
unusually, on my feet.

her shipmates aboard a
Panamanian tramp steamer.

own period in uniform was less
spectacular; in this snapshot, the
only risk was that of detection for I
had purloined the Captain's 'brass'

Myself at twenty-three. The smile is illusory for my eyes were already dilated w
morphine drops and a week later tuberculosis was diagnosed.

'Did you hear the one about the fella killed underground?'
I had not.
'Crushed unrecognisable, he was. Fall of stone, see. Roof collapse. So the manager turned to his mate and told him to break the news to his wife. "Break it gentle, see?" "Aye, all right!" So . . . Down the terraced street in the early hours of the morning go the booted feet, hammer-hammer at the door. "Break it gentle . . ." Presently the upstairs window goes up and the old lady looks out, "Yes?" "Break it gentle . . ." "Does the Widow Jones live here?" "There's no Widow Jones, but I'm Mrs Jones." "D'you want a bet, Mrs?" '
We laughed and laughed at that one. It was what was happening to us. 'Survival?' We might have asked. 'Did we want a bet?' We did not. 'Tell us another one, Dai!'
As for myself, I'd had years of institutional living, moving from one institution to another – from dormitories to ships, to hostels, to bachelor rooms and now a hospital ward. Wherever I went, I had been hemmed in by the close proximity of other men. But here there were new torments to add to the old: the fevered shouts at night, the moans and groans, the stained sheets and twisted blankets, the clanging doors, and the permanent aroma of strained cabbage, urine and disinfectant which lingered interminably. Then there were the inevitable bathroom crooners in the next block where younger men were mobile. The favourite was a song that seemed to haunt my childhood and youth, and I heard it in a thousand places, sung by lorry drivers, deliverymen, burly prisoners in cells, matloes in singlets and drunks bawling in their cups.

> *South of the Border*
> *Down Me-hico Way . . .*
> *That's where I fell in love . . .*
> *With stars above.*
> *Dah-dah, dah-did-dah dah . . .*

Thirty years later I was constantly asked to sing it in Japanese tatami rooms to orchestral accompaniment, and a part of me has always been south of the border wherever the border happens to be. Mine, and the war-affected generation before mine, were always telling the unseen and unknown Mexicali

Rose 'to stop crying, to dry those big brown eyes and think of me' – which is another way of saying that we grew up in a period of unrelieved chauvinism. Wherever I lived, women lived 'out there', beyond the main guard gate, the gangway, the porter's lodge, the caretaker's cottage, and we might have been dogs on heat awaiting our chance, slipping out at night to make contact only to be greeted on return with an inevitable bawdy enquiry.

'How did you get on? Did you get your end away?'

If I shudder now and regard aspects of my own nature then with regret, at the time I yearned to pass muster, to find my place amongst others – accepting the common mores without thought. I was Grandma's child trying to be a man and sex was a guilt-ridden problem. There were girls who did, girls who didn't. The very words 'opposite sex' spoke volumes. So often they meant 'opposite' people against whom any kind of physical inhumanity could be perpetrated. It was the psychology of the gutter, overlaid in my case by the more pernicious traits of the Methodist Church which I thought I had long abandoned, but which remained. If as a boy I was a creature of disguises, a spy in another man's land, as a young man there was a part of me that remained distinct so that when I failed to come up to the expectations of my superiors as I sometimes did, I had the comfort of a retreat into that other self which was never wholly committed to the business in hand. It was not that I was even then thinking of myself as a writer – aiming, like the young Dylan Thomas, to 'put you all in a book by and by!' – but that I always felt myself to be an oddity and a part of me never joined even when, as later happened, I found myself in what was often referred to as 'the wrong company'. In finding this, I seemed always to excel.

After leaving home, I was soon in a world which I could never discuss with my family. 'You will have,' my grandmother said, 'to stand on your own two feet!' I did so, but all the time I was conscious of my special difference. I never thought of myself as normal or even able, rather – very often – as a permanent imposter. There were always things to hide, mainly the sum total of my inadequacies which were complicated by some lucky and wayward gene which made me resistant to those absurdities which often so characterised those in a position of power over me. If there was an underdog, I always identified with him. Positions of power left me uneasy, but if I was threatened I learned to cope, although the shock of the English class system so codified in the Royal Navy – and particularly by naval officers' wives who often took on attitudes corresponding to the gold stripes on their husband's sleeves – was sometimes a brutal one. Although I realised the privileges of being an officer, I never really enjoyed them.

After leaving the shore-based Boys Training Establishment, I served at sea on an aircraft carrier. My application to accompany the Royal Marine Commando to Korea was fortunately not accepted, and once more I found myself in the exclusive company of men.

The carrier I called HMS *Indescribable*, since that was the name we gave to bewildered dockyard policemen in Gibraltar when we went ashore. She had no aircraft and no aviation spirit which meant that she was always light and under-ballasted and rolled onerously in any swell, the flight deck sometimes acting like a sail in the wind, making her movements awkward and unpredictable. She was used as the flag ship of the training squadron and once carried an admiral who, bored, invited the scallywags of the wardroom to play bridge with him and listened amused while I, resplendent in mess undress, starched shirt and bum-freezer, put up a spirited defence of Aneurin Bevan who was then the subject of universal condemnation, if not hatred, as a consequence of his felt remarks about verminous Tories – some of whom actually formed a club with a vermin insignia which they wore on their lapels. Slightly tipsy, it amused me to point out that Lloyd George had forced the convoy system on a reluctant Admiralty, and then to watch the apoplectic faces of my senior officers, blimps to a man. To be seated at the Admiral's table, a marine servant behind every chair, the entire ship's company sometimes kept waiting if the meal was to be followed by a cinema show in the empty hangar, was one more indication of the stratified society and it made me feel ill at ease. Generally, though, the further up the naval ladder you went, the more senior the officer the more relaxed and amiable the man. It was the passed-over lieutenant commanders, stuck halfway up the ladder, whose animosities and bile produced the worst upsets; especially, I found, if they were originally Welsh – men who, having adopted the alien code, found my intractable presence a perennial question mark. I made them uneasy, scorned their well-meant advice. I was a Taff. It was as good a label as any other and I never minded it.

There were immediate disappointments. Going to sea was one since a warship is so crowded and large, with each task so specialised, that you are seldom able to see the whole picture and, as I soon found, instructor officers were supernumerary in the sea-going operation. The mass of incomprehensible tasks was another. We instructor officers were responsible for keeping the operational plot at sea, maintaining an illuminated table under the bridge which the officer of the watch could occasionally inspect to see an instant picture of the fleet as it manoeuvred. I understood little more than the simple mechanics of keeping the table, marking the accompanying ships and vessels in passage, following instructions by rote and memorising my tasks with the aid of mnemonics like 'Barking Dogs Can't Shout!' – the first letters indicating the order of verbal reports to the bridge when vessels were sighted and their courses plotted in Chinagraph pencil. Thus I would report Bearing, Course, Distance, Speed when vessels were sighted on the radar screen which stood beside the table and from which we were required to chalk up the picture.

In the operations room it was like being closeted beside a large illuminated amusement-arcade table game in the darkness, peering at lines and drawings and attempting to make some sense out of them, with the bridge – from which we heard the real commands – immediately above our heads. To me it was a kind of madhouse without rhyme or reason and I followed the bio-gardener's way once more, concentrating frenetically upon those tasks I could understand. I never actually went on the bridge but slunk to the operations room as stealthily as a bookmaker's runner, trying to avoid being noticed, limiting communication to the minimum. At the beginning of each watch you were required to inspect the operational chart and sign for it, indicating that you accepted it as a true picture from your predecessor and this I did like a librarian stamping a book, praying for the four hours to pass without incident. Any new vessels sighted on the radar screen had promptly to be reported to the bridge, their progress watched and recorded, the blips given names until positively identified. Sometimes there was a rating to assist you whose expertise was inevitably greater than yours, an occasion for delight on my part since I had received not the slightest training that made any single operation comprehensible to me. But the early dog watches were spent alone and then I would stare myopically at the blips on the radar screen, hoping against hope that nothing untoward would happen, grateful when no new vessels appeared and communication with the bridge was nil. I was laying low again, an imposter crouched there in the darkness while the sounds of the sea, the ever present wind and the sometimes deep wallowing of the ship made her rise and fall like an old waterlogged sofa, causing the boy seamen and others to vomit at unexpected moments – some of them being made to carry and use buckets as they went to their classes. Luckily I was and remain unaffected by the sea, but I worried constantly about my simple tasks. Once, ploughing in concert with HMS *Vanguard* up the North Sea to Scapa Flow, the moment I dreaded came: a new blip on the radar screen, clear and unmistakeable just after I had signed for the plot and settled down alone for the night's vigil.

I reported it dutifully, but it was at a time when we were manoeuvring.

'Operations room-bridge?'

'Go ahead . . .'

I reported my discovery, the Barking Dog That Could Not Shout. I gave it a name, Charlie.

'Yes-yes, we've got that.' The officer of the watch was busy and impatient.

But the blip remained and so I dutifully plotted its course at five-minute intervals, reading the bearings from the radar screen, transferring them to the chart, and soon found that Charlie seemed to have a course like a dog's hind leg, wandering all over the chart as we moved, producing an untidy squiggle indicating a course that no reasonable vessel would take. Normally we were supposed to report all changes of course but as they were busy on the bridge and the officer on watch was clearly irritable, I left it, handing over the chart at the end of the watch to my successor who pretended to be extremely knowledgeable. I knew what to do with knowledgeable people. I gave them a problem.

'What's this, then?'

He was a tall thin young man of my own age who wanted nothing more than to stay in the Royal Navy for ever. As a teacher, he disliked the stench of the taught and viewed the prospect of teaching in grubby industrial areas with horror. Consequently he took extra care with his appearance, studied and copied every mannerism of his senior officers, saluting with a precise quivering movement of the outstretched fingers as if on a parade ground and was always moving forward to obey instantly. He had also purchased a pair of the extremely expensive, ankle-length, patent-leather Gieves bootees which shone like glass and were often worn by senior officers, and wherever he went he was at pains to impress. Like me he had signed on for three years to obtain a short-service commission, but whereas I soon regretted it, he congratulated himself every day. He was in his element and I envied him, but of course my own attitudes were forming, some of them becoming known, and not for the first time in my life I was considered dangerous to be seen with. My remarks at the Admiral's table, although greatly amusing the Admiral, were becoming known to others, including my immediate seniors. This was a man to be watched, and for the wrong reasons. There was, as ever, something about me that was 'not quite right', a something that, however indefinable, was nevertheless a definite property and one unlikely to help me in my career. I had it then and indeed I apparently have it now, for only recently, bored in the unexpected company of an American military historian in faraway Japan, I proposed a society for the abolition of footnotes in historical texts. When he realised I was serious, he went pale and his hand shook. He was genuinely upset. 'Think of the reaction of critics?' he said. 'They could ruin your career!' I was once again a man to be avoided.

Perhaps it began with the mysterious vessel I named 'Charlie' whose course, crossing backwards and forwards upon itself, now to the east, now the west, now a touch north, presented a unique problem.

'I can't make it out,' I said.

156

'Have you reported it?'

'Straight away.'

'Did you report the change of course?'

'They didn't want to know,' I said. '"Yes-yes, we've got that," they said.'

One of the problems he had encountered was in being too conscientious. Technically I should have kept on reporting the change of course of Charlie, but it was a fine point and if the officer of the watch knew about it, the matter seemed settled. There was, however, the problem of explaining the phenomenon. I was a known ignoramus, but the relief officer was also puzzled. We poured over the chart. All I wanted was a signature on the log book so that I could slink away, but it was clear my relief wanted explanations for himself. Finally, after much ado with the parallel rulers and an inspection of the sea chart of the area, he decided that what I had encountered was a fishing vessel using drift nets, drifting backwards and forwards upon itself. There was indeed a warning on the chart that fishing vessels were likely to be in the area, so that the explanation seemed perfect.

'I'd never have thought of that!' I said admiringly. I pushed the log book forward for signature, obtained it and sloped off once more, hastening to my cabin in the bowels of the ship. I was free, and that was all that interested me. Here I lived a secret life with my books and a biscuit tin that contained a slab of my grandmother's rich fruit cake which she persisted in sending me together with a weekly copy of the *Pontypridd Observer*. Both sustained me in my difference and years later I was able to remember that some individual – now particularly distinguished – who had been fined ten shillings for 'allowing a dog to foul the footpath', replied when charged, 'I can't help it – meaning the dog, your Worships!'

There was no reading that night, though, and I went straight to sleep. Several hours later, there came a hammering on my cabin door. A Royal Marine messenger stood there, his face impassive but somehow such messengers always knew when you were for it. Sensing your imminent discomfiture, they become more precise and proper – this one saluting with military aplomb.

'Navigating officer wants to see you in the ops room, Sah!'

I dressed hastily. The dawn was breaking, a chilly dawn with grey seas and a whining wind. The navigating officer had spotted my squiggle, given my successor a rocket since he was marginally more experienced than I, and now he drew me to an open space and pointed. There in the distance as the dawn broke was an obscure lighthouse whose imaginary course I had plotted in error, its movements fictional, a compound of our own movements relative to it and, of course, my unsteady hand at work with the rule. There were days when I could not draw a straight line, never mind read a protractor.

'Fishing boat?' he said. 'Where did you dream up that idea?'

I carried the can, drawing an expression of momentary relief across the face of my predecessor, and becoming known as Lighthouse Richards. But it was not my only mistake. Later, closed up at action stations during a NATO exercise with a rating present, I was unfortunate enough to be on watch when the Captain decided suddenly that the radar should be regarded as having been put out of action and that all calculations should be made without its help. He ordered a black cloth hood put over the radar set, stood a sentry beside it to prevent cheating, and made us do the calculations from visual reports on the bridge which were passed down on flimsy pieces of paper by tube. Alas, I had just sent the rating to get some coffee and was stuck on my own, desperately trying to arrange the signals in order of time received which was essential in making any calculation of course and speed. Now, since we were closed up at action stations, the lights went off automatically when the door opened and to my horror it was opened, the pile of unmarked signals blew everywhere, never to be replaced in order and, moreover, the lights did not come on again as the door was not properly closed. I was left in darkness, in a fix once more. I thought the rating had returned and enquired politely.

'D'you think I can see in the bloody dark?'

A throat was quietly cleared in the darkness.

Then the door was properly closed and the lights came on. There stood the immaculate figure of the Captain, a wartime hero and a VC.

He looked at me. I looked at him. It was the only time I ever spoke to him. I saw myself with buttons cut off at the point of a sword, court-martialled and disgraced.

But he grinned. 'Sorry,' he said and went out, narrowly avoiding the radar rating returning with the full coffee cups. A lesser man would have made a parliamentary speech, and many did. Later he often passed along our ranks at Sunday divisions with a grin for me although, standing like a ramrod, I did not dare return it, of course.

My main task was the instruction of boy seamen and ratings, but there was also another onerous duty in decoding the TOP SECRET messages which were thought to be too confidential for the eyes of ratings – something of a joke, because we were so ham-fisted with the decoding machinery that inevitably we depended on the good nature of the Chief Yeoman. Our main excitements were the cruises with the training squadron, to Scapa Flow, Gibraltar and once to France where the runs ashore were much anticipated and talked about. In those voyages I came of age, and was witness of the reality of the kind of life I had so yearned to take part in when I listened to the stories of others.

'Where have you been?'

'All over.'

In the Royal Navy, we said 'Going foreign', and it was a term I'd heard so often on the lips of my contemporaries, and it was implanted in my mind together with a series of images that might have been taken from the illustrated cover of *Treasure Island* – the palm trees waving in the wind, white sand and coral reefs, the sea stretching into a blue infinity. If I wanted anything in my fantasies, it was to break the bead curtain of a Pernambuco bar and hang my sailor's hat upon the wall, perhaps upon its own hook like those staff-room tyrants in the schools of my youth who sometimes taught in the same classrooms using the same text books for forty years. I did not, of course, want the permanence but the adventure of it and the experience of sallying forth unknown; so when *Hands To Stations for Entering Harbour* was piped and we mustered on the flight deck, the ship dressed overall, I felt I was fulfilling part of my destiny. But I trod the road Hornblower never knew about.

I had not, as the colliers said, been a heller in my time – not quite. My whole life was a struggle to attain some kind of norm, struggling in bio-gardening and such kindred subjects, struggling with my radar watch, frantically trying to decode messages from the C-in-C to some Governor General to rearrange golf matches, managing on the whole with ease when it came to teaching the simple educational syllabus to seamen and developing an expertise when it came to getting the senior NCOs and petty officers through the English examination which the General Post Office then required of ex-service entrants wanting to find new careers on demobilisation. I knew what it was like to be terrified and dumb, to be completely in the dark, to lack the confidence even to begin a sentence. I was clear, I set attainable tasks, I was sympathetic and always glad to do something I knew I could do well. I was also ever available and was in return rewarded by the most important hierarchy in the ship – the long-serving senior ratings, the shipwrights and chief stokers – so that my cabin furniture, the specially made bookcases, the reading lamps, the tobacco jar hand-turned and made of handsomely polished Burmese teak which I have to this day, were all a reward for my eternal search for something I could do well. Sometimes there were even compliments which I could not help overhearing, the best references I'd ever had.

'Taffy's the boy to get you in the GPO. You want to see the fucking essay I wrote on fucking spring!'

This was an era when the three-badge stoker mechanic was a legendary figure, like his language.

Some of these men were decorated. All had joined the Navy well before the war and most regretted it, perhaps because they now felt the return to civilian life to be an ordeal for which they were ill-equipped. They often shared their memories with me. One had seen a warship sinking while the Royal Marine Band imperturbably played a waltz until the water reached the deck and they were ordered to lay down their instruments; another told me that in one convoy he had seen 'five ships go down in five minutes', but now the immediate requirement was the facility of writing descriptive essays for which I obligingly provided a framework and exchangeable descriptive sentences and phrases which could be adjusted to a multitude of topics – Spring, Winter, a Summer's Day, or Arctic Night! These were for the bio-gardeners amongst them; but others were able and with them I took extra classes, even attempting to persuade one man to stay in the Royal Navy and apply for a commission, telling his astonished divisional officer that he was far too intelligent to serve in a subordinate position – another remark that created waves. ('Who does the chap think he is?')

I also had some strange encounters. Once, seated alone in the education office high up on the aircraft carrier's 'island', the window open on its leather strap as we made our way south towards the balmy Mediterranean airs, I heard booted feet on the stairway outside, the heavy clumping immediately indicating a Royal Marine. Inboard, the Marines kept their caps on and were required to salute indoors unlike the sailors so that when my caller appeared and did not salute, I stiffened automatically, seeing before me a large man of forty-odd, bemedalled with campaign ribbons and the long-service chevrons of a veteran. But he was wild-eyed and staring, salivating at the lips and unnaturally pale. The failure to salute was a warning, as odd as if he had come in shoeless, a pronounced difference in the everyday routine of things. Marines always saluted. Marines went by the book. Marines were correct in all respects. This man was different. I shifted uneasily. I was alone in the office. There was no one within calling distance. There had been one or two cases I'd heard of involving senseless violence, when men attempting to work their tickets had struck officers for no other purpose than to gain a psychiatric discharge. It was somehow more convincing if you struck someone you did not know and with whom you had no quarrel. This was a big awkward powerful man far gone in the turmoil of some personal tempest.

'Yes?' I said. 'What can I do for you, sir?' It was a shopkeeper's trick, but the look of him frightened me. He struggled for speech, a pink sliver of tongue wetting his lips. He looked capable of anything but he was nervous, something building up inside him, clearly a long-seated and deep resentment. But I had never seen him before.

'What is it?'

He couldn't speak. His fists were clenching and unclenching. There was no way I could get past him to the door. The telephone was on the opposite side of the office. I had already had two official wound certificates, one for 'falling at the feet of forwards', the other for a bad concussion – also a rugby injury. A third for a broken jaw as a consequence of some inexplicable assault would not add to my reputation. 'Did fracture jaw on educational duties', I thought. It was definitely to be avoided.

I tried a command.

'Sit down!'

That seemed to take him by surprise and he found a sentence.

'They're getting at me,' he said.

The absence of the obligatory 'sir' was another surprise. Normally the Marines shouted it loudly, almost like an insult. You might get stroppy sailors, resentful petty officers kept on past the time of their disengagement because of the Korean War emergency, but this was a Marine with at least twenty years in.

'Who?' I said.

It came out like a curse. 'The young lads!'

We'd had an extra contingent of Marines board at Plymouth, and although this man was an old sweat, the new recruits had got to him. It took me an hour to get any sense from him. When the coder came with my coffee, I ordered another cup, causing the coder to raise his eyebrows. 'Coffee for a bootneck?' That would go the rounds of the messdeck. 'Taffy a brown-hatter, is he?'

But it was a tortuous story, a tale of woe that I only dimly understood. Both the Royal Navy and the Royal Marines prided themselves on the educational standards of new recruits, who were all literate. Those who could not read and write went into the Army. But this man, by some quirk of fate, had joined the Army before the war, then after Dunkirk had found himself involved with amphibious landing craft with the Royal Engineers. His unit had been taken over by the Marines and he had become a Marine and for years he had covered up the fact that he could not read or write, learning to deceive, to feign understanding, passing muster with the others and, no doubt, protected by his mates until, with age, he had been given some position of authority and now came a new threat from the young. One bright spark among the new intake had found him out and he was being chivvied all along the messdeck. Matters had reached a pitch that morning and an old shipmate, a stoker, had advised him to come to me and had even found out when I would be alone in the education office. 'You'll do all right with him!' the stoker had said.

Once explained, it was so easy to understand.

'Leave it to me,' I said. I took his name. I would do what I could.

Later that day I had a drink with the Captain of Marines, a senior officer who had been especially amiable to me since we both shared a profound dislike for our executive officer, a commander whose voice and mannerisms haunted me for years.

I broached the subject casually.

'One of your blokes came to see me today.'

He stiffened. I knew at once that I had said the wrong thing. Ignorant as I was of so many codes, I should have realised. This was the Marines.

'Came to see you?' He was first astonished, then appalled.

'Yes,' I said. I explained, but the Marine captain's features were already implacable. No matter how pressing the need, nor even the extraordinary nature of the story – the one illiterate who had escaped the net – the rules were broken. A Royal Marine with a problem should first approach a Royal Marine officer. That was the rule, inviolate. It was now a matter for the Marines. They would deal with it. The subject was closed.

I was twenty-one. There was hardly a more junior officer. The Marine captain was a senior officer, although passed over and shortly to end his service. His word was still absolute. I'd have done better to approach one of the young lieutenants. But I knew better than to protest. I attempted to offer to provide classes, as I had foolishly promised the man, but there was no discussion.

A few weeks later, I asked one of the Marine lieutenants what had happened. There were two thousand men on board and most of them I never saw.

'Oh, him,' the lieutenant said. 'We've got him chained to the keyboard flat.'

This was a deck where all the duplicate keys of the ship were kept in a glass case and once I saw my prospective pupil there, standing stiffly to attention and on guard. His eyes gave no sign of recognition. He had reverted to type, become as faceless as the rest. I mentioned the matter to the senior education officer. He shrugged his shoulders, looked at me peculiarly, then changed the subject and, to my shame, I did not pursue it. My grandmother would have done so, relentlessly. But I did not. I never saw the man again, and no other Marines ever came for instruction while I was on board.

The Captain of Marines, as it happened, I had thought approachable in a case like this, despite the fact that his cabin – like himself – was heavily scented, and he remains the most immaculate man I have ever met, always equable and charming except for that one transgression. He never failed, like myself, to register his disapproval of the Commander whom I first met in a most extraordinary and unwelcome way, an incident that remained in my mind and often returned to me in the nights when the rain beat against the hospital windows, the wind soughed in the trees and the night staff came skittering on duty, their high heels clattering under the covered way while I tucked myself further under the blankets and slipped willingly into the unedited slough of memory. I was three years in the Royal Navy. As much as anything, it helped form my character even if in surprising ways.

One night, after a run ashore, I missed the last liberty boat to the ship from the jetty at Portland only to be told by the civilian night watchman that our Commander had ordered his own boat to be alongside at 1 a.m., and I was welcome to wait in the shelter of the watchman's hut if I wished. The night watchman was from Newport, a supporter of that rugby club, and finding I was Welsh, shared his sandwiches with me and brewed up – one of those chance meetings that have occurred to me many times across the world but never with quite the same consequences.

It was a vile winter's night, a gale getting up, the wind lifting the little corrugated-iron roof of the hut, and out beyond the breakwater I could see white water, a sure sign of worsening weather. The ship lay miles out and the last liberty boat had reported difficulties getting alongside, the watchman said. He wouldn't have been surprised if all liberty boats were cancelled, but the fact that the Commander had ordered his own boat meant that it would have to be a full gale to cause a cancellation, an order that the officer of the watch would be otherwise reluctant to give. So we settled down to wait and the time went quickly. I had met the Commander previously, a brief introduction when I joined the ship shortly before. Then his eyes had flickered over me as he stood on the quarterdeck with his telescope under his arm, cap at the Beatty angle, a handkerchief in his breast pocket, the top button of his tunic undone, his cutaway collar and silk tie an indication of a stylish officer of rank. He was the kind of man whose luxurious silken tones gave him the rich sibilant voice of a character actor and the more I got to know him, the more he seemed to be an actor, a man of poses. He often spoke of 'the Old Navy' when you had to ask the Captain's permission to get married, an act that was likely to blight your career if you proceeded with it before the age of forty. He was, as might be guessed, unmarried himself, a man of cyclonic moods – relaxed and affable on his special stool at the wardroom bar, often the first to arrive and the last to leave, but quite likely to erupt at the slightest provocation when away from it. He would growl 'Slack ship!' at the sight of some misdemeanour and occasionally berated his officers in a loud voice, especially if – like himself – they drank to excess and hovered in the wardroom after breakfast. Then he would clear it, 'I will not have my officers hanging about in the mornings!' A speck of dirt would cause him to say, 'I will not have filth on my ship!' It was always 'my ship'. He was the kind of man you used to see berating Pullman car attendants at the top of his voice, immediately changing gear to be charming to a female companion – a man who slid through synchromeshed emotions like a well-oiled machine. For all this, he was somehow untypical of the Royal Navy, a constant talker, expansive in his gesticulations, too articulate and too demonstrative – what the sailors called a Jack-me-Hearty, all over you one minute, frosty the next. The last Commander, I was told, never smiled, and was dubbed Black Harry; but he was a reassuringly predictable man whose moods were constant. This one was a shirt salesman, as the Marine officer said who frequently expressed his very aristocratic regret that such a captain as we had should have to put up with such a man. His proper place was running some minor golf club, he implied. I had another analogy. He was the kind of man supported by the Conservative Central Office whom the constituency party, in their wisdom, refused to accept. Nobody liked him, although he had his cronies, and my first instinct was to keep well away from him. There was something about that wide and fleshy mouth, those groomed greying hairs and that picture-postcard Beatty stance – I frequently observed him looking at himself in the wardroom mirror – that spelt danger to me and my kind. At the same time, the risks involved drew me closer to him. There is something about those you detest that becomes fascinating, especially at a young age, as if you remain incredulous and want to be convinced that a man is as awful as you first think he is. This was especially true when I had been drinking which I frequently had, since this was a hard-drinking ship and I fell in too readily with the others – a slow learner in all things.

But that night on the jetty at Portland, I still had much to learn. Standing in the shelter of the watchman's hut, I'd had but one glimpse of those lazy flickering eyes at close quarters, standing stiffly to attention when I was introduced some weeks before. Hearing my accent which went before my essential self like a banner, or a club held with hostile intent, he made the usual observations.

'Doubtless you'll make the rugger team?'

'Afraid not, sir.'

'Oh?'

I explained about the wound certificate I'd already collected. With a wound certificate, sick leave was mandatory and I'd had much more than my share. It was a mistake to explain. Such vulnerability let the side down, his favourite expression and later reserved exclusively for me.

'No doubt you'll make yourself useful in some way.'

Just as I did not like the look of him, so he did not like the look of me. But when I later came across him standing alone at the wardroom bar, I socially offered him a drink.

'Horse's neck,' he said. He was a man of code words. I did not know what it was. It was another black, but later, playing with fire, I came to drink it myself, the mixture of brandy and ginger ale as dangerous to me as it was to him. There came a time when we disliked each other so much that we were mutually fascinated.

166

I should, of course, never have waited in the watchman's hut, but the time passed pleasantly enough although the weather was getting up all the time, gusts of wind surging violently across the roof. It was also raining heavily at intervals, gouts of water eddying down the drainpipes. For that reason I stayed inside the hut and did not see the commander's car coming; but when it did, it approached at speed, stopping and skidding with a squeal of brakes hard up against the wall opposite, its headlights blazing. As the watchman and I looked out startled, we were the involuntary witnesses of the Commander's concluding act before the commencement of my first voyage. There was a woman in the front seat of the car with him, and the moment the car stopped, he was across the front seat and half on top of her so that we were greeted with a frenzy of arms and silk-stockinged legs as if the two of them were both struggling to get into the front legs of a pantomime horse. He was fervent, vigorous but inaccurate in his lusts and the sleeve of a white gown extended, fingers clutching upwards, finally to seize him by the scruff of the neck. The car window was open. We had picture and sound for the watchman had also opened his window.

'Ronnie – you're being a pig!'

'Come on, Daphne!'

'No, darling.'

'Poppet . . .'

'No, Ronnie!'

'He've left it a bit late,' the watchman said. He might have been watching a fly-half trying a last-minute break at Rodney Parade, the Newport Rugby Club Ground.

Daphne got out of the car minus a shoe and stepped straight into a puddle.

'Oh, fuck!' she said in the Roedean tones that were to fascinate me whenever I heard them.

The Commander slumped in the front seat, sulking.

'Now, be good, Ronnie,' Daphne said.

He hauled his raincoat sulkily from the back seat, removed himself, put it on, looked moodily at Daphne and the car, then wandered off into the darkness without another word.

Daphne stared after him, shrugged her shoulders, found

167

her shoe, then, after sitting still for a moment, eased across into the driving seat and reversed the car wildly, careering past us so that I caught a glimpse of a vivid slash of scarlet mouth as wide as his and then she was off, her own greying hair awry and expression petulant. As she passed, I ducked guiltily below the level of the watchman's window.

It was hardly the time to ask for a lift in the Commander's boat. The watchman, sensing my unease, said nothing and presently I left the hut and wandered down the steps to the jetty. The Commander stood there, a hunched figure staring at the sea which was now wild, waves surging angrily up the wall and receding at a rush. Dimly, out to sea, the lights of the oncoming pinnace were visible as it rose and fell, disappearing at intervals, the wind whipping up the swell which smacked lumpily against the stone wall below me. It was a gale-force wind and a dangerous short-falling sea, but the commander just stood there, lost in his problems and without – I was shocked to notice – the obligatory trilby. My own fading green trilby was now jammed on my head but I was forced to hold it on.

'Good evening, sir?'

At first, he did not hear me. I shouted, "Scuse, me!"

When he turned, his smile was automatic and it was suddenly a key to his character, that automatic smile. It greeted every problem, every untoward event.

I still had to shout.

'I was wondering if you'd mind . . .'

'Yes – yes – yes! By all means.'

It was too windy to talk and the sea kept rising dangerously below us. He was well-oiled I could see, whereas I had sobered up, thanks to the watchman's cheese-and-jibbon sandwiches; but before we could say anything, the car returned above us, its lights flashing, and presently Daphne reappeared clutching a headscarf with one hand and his missing brown trilby hat in the other. He looked up at her, then away. The hat nearly blew away in her hand, the wind lifting her coat and skirt so that she was silhouetted above us in the car lights – an attractive, slim, long-legged woman of forty, she was still in a temper. Clearly he wasn't going to go up the steps to get the hat, and in all that wind the danger of it blowing away was constant. So I went up the steps. I did not know what to say.

She looked past me at him, then thrust it into my hands.

'Thank you so much,' I said.

She turned around to the car, got in, and reversed away once more.

I took the hat down to him. He looked at it sombrely, then held it moodily behind his back with a curt nod of thanks.

It was, I remember distinctly, the night Ernest Bevin died. The watchman had told me in the hut. The Docker's KC, the watchman said, but I did not mention it now although I felt the need to say something completely unconnected with the events I had witnessed.

Presently the pinnace came nearer and you could see they were making way with difficulty and I had a sudden glimpse of the cox'n's inflamed face, reddened with temper as he looked at us. The pinnace should never have been sent on such a night as this and even in the shelter of the harbour wall, the pitching was constant. Water cascaded from the cox'n's face and he said later that all other boats had been cancelled an hour before. He was in such a rage, he could hardly speak when they came alongside, the fender boy just holding her off. We got aboard hastily, myself first following the rule of junior officers in the boat first, but it was not a night for ceremony. We pulled away at once, the cox'n without a word. The Commander led the way into the little cabin and lit a cigarette.

By now it must have dawned on him that I had been witness of his arrival at the jetty and he looked at me venomously, but before he could say anything, I said obligingly, 'Have you heard the news, sir?'

'News?'

'Ernest Bevin's dead.'

He stared at me as at a lunatic.

'The Docker's KC,' I said. I might have said, 'A bald eagle has been sighted over the River Taff!' He looked at me as at one possessed.

Immediately the motion of the pinnace became so violent that we were forced to hang on to the guardrails and, standing, I looked aft to see the seas piling up. It was lifeboat weather, the little pinnace taking water all along the deck, and when we reached the ship, there was such a rise and fall of sea that we circled several times, each time surfing, first above, then well below, the gangway platform so that it was too dangerous for us to jump. Through all this the Commander said nothing and was impervious to the weather, the cox'n and me. On the quarterdeck, the officer of the watch stood looking down on us anxiously and detailed the quartermaster to descend the gangway. After two or three runs I took my cue from the cox'n and the two of us jumped together, landing in the nick of time on the platform while the pinnace shot away and was, in fact, sent back to Portland that night as it was too rough to bring it aboard.

On the quarterdeck, I thanked the Commander for the lift.

'I hope you don't think it was an impertinence,' I said. I always tried hard in the beginning.

'Not at all,' the Commander said. 'We naval officers are not like that.'

It was a statement he was to repeat many times, usually the high mark on the barometer of his distaste. 'We naval officers can hold our liquor. We naval officers have certain standards, you know, Richards?' And once, leaning on a walking stick and pawing the ground in a brothel where a crowd of us had gone drunkenly ashore across the Gibraltar border to La Linea, he demanded an exhibition between two women.

'We naval officers expect the thing to be done properly!'

As I grew to hate his voice, so he began to hate mine and either of us had but to speak for the other to wince. But, inevitably, we seemed to be enjoined which was quite extraordinary since I was such a junior officer, although the fault was probably mine since my immediate colleagues were newly married men and I alone got drawn into the late-night excursions ashore which occurred all too frequently. If ever there was a late-night jaunt from the wardroom, I was among the party. And so was he.

There now followed a time in my life over which a veil should properly be drawn, but if I did not exactly follow the way of all flesh, I sampled enough of it and made my way with others to the bawdy houses when drunk as if attracted by a magnet. It was as if the Methodist in me was saying, 'We've had enough of virtue, let us now investigate sin.' Although I had a will of my own, it was not often present when it should have been, but I was no different from many of my shipmates as we rollicked along the unpaved dirt streets getting drunker and drunker until finally the whores' cries, '*Muy limpio!*' – 'Very clean!', and the inevitable sight of a desirable physical presence drew me, as I knew it always would, behind the bead curtain. I am ashamed to say that there were virtually children on offer in those brothels and although, acting on advice, I went for the Madame who remotely resembled the peppery figure of Carmen Miranda and she was kind to me, her soft and skilful mouth performing wonders with my taut body, it took me years to realise the full horrors of that filthy street and the abject, poverty-stricken slavery of its denizens. I should like to say that, covered in self-disgust and guilt, I learned my lesson but I was there the next night, and the night after – 'Hello Taffy, you come back?', and later in Paris joined the medical officer in an orgy that lasted the weekend. He was no comfort as a companion or an adviser, for when I got a mild case of footrot (no more!), I went to see him, whereupon he bent below his desk, removed his own sock and shoe to show me an even worse case of footrot than my own.

'Take a look at this if you're worried!'

Ashore, I escaped infection. I was careful and there were no after-effects for me, unlike the simple Welsh boy I knew who returned from a similar expedition and dosed himself with ship's Lysol in a frenzy of self-disgust. However, no matter how worldly I became, there remained a constant feeling that I had sunk low in my own estimation. There was within me a profound capacity for unhappiness and unless I was working and involved with some task I could perform efficiently, I drifted aimlessly in the company of others who were quite disposed to drink the nights away. It was in Gibraltar that I began to write again. I had earlier edited magazines in college and elsewhere and now, after a trip with a party of skiers up in the Sierra Nevada, I made an acquaintance with Spain that began quite ludicrously. We had to travel in our civilian clothes and these were completely inadequate against the cold weather. So we drew issue duffel coats – then a novelty in Spain – and once we got to Granada, they created a minor sensation since the film *The Third Man* (*El Tercedo Hombre*) was currently showing and Trevor Howard's distinctive duffel coat was much admired. The immediate consequence was that we were followed everywhere by gypsy guitarists who struck up the theme music whenever we appeared. It was in Granada that I declined to ski and made the acquaintance of a waitress, and later wrote to her, producing her letter in a pub at home to be told by my only Oxford acquaintance that the letter was written by an illiterate. But she was tall, slender and graceful, the sole supporter of two tubercular brothers, and when she took her hair down, it covered my face. Her name was Segunda, another indication of her lowly social status, I was told. No matter, I recited my school certificate Spanish poem in the dark.

Later we went to Le Havre, lining the flight deck and standing to attention while the Royal Marine Band played the *Marseillaise*, our entrance to the dock marred by the behaviour of striking dockyard workers who rattled tin cans as we came alongside unaided. In Le Havre we stayed a week and I visited my uncle's solitary grave at Honfleur once more, his companions unidentified save for the cryptic words *Soldat Allemand*. He was the only member of his bomber crew to be washed ashore after being shot down, and the fourth of my family to be buried in France, and my grandmother kept the sombre photograph of my placing flowers upon that grave until she died. That night I got very drunk, seized the six-foot English governess to the British Ambassador's children who had come to Le Havre for a Chamber of Trade Ball in our honour, and fell flat on my back during a spirited veleta, getting myself talked about once more. There were clouds gathering but I was unaware of them.

When we returned to Portland, a drinking session began in the wardroom which looked as if it was going to last all day, but as soon as the shore telephone cables had been connected up, there was a pipe for me, made publicly over the tannoy. An RAF group captain, a padre, wanted to talk to me. He was in the office of the C-in-C, Portland, and was planning to come on board at the C-in-C's suggestion. It was another long-forgotten uncle, once a minister of our chapel in Pontypridd who had made a career in the RAF. He was keeping tabs on me at my grandmother's request and had picked the Commander in Chief's office to do it!

172

I looked around the wardroom. One of our Commander's bright ideas had been to decorate the bar with straw for a South Sea Island party some days before and now only the debris remained uncleared. The Commander was, as usual, well away, seated in the corner with his cronies, exercising his voice on one of his favourite topics. A month before, he had objected to an officer's wish to bring the landlord of the Black Dog Hotel in Weymouth aboard as a dinner guest.

'I'm not at all sure whether we can have a publican in here. I mean, a man who serves the sailors?'

The publican was an ex-RAF officer and decorated.

'He was an officer, sir?'

'*Officer?*'

'In the RAF.'

'Ah, but you know what the RAF was!'

The guest was discouraged.

Now I heard my uncle's voice on the telephone. He was a pious man who had once shared a railway compartment with Aneurin Bevan and complained ever after about the amount of obscene language used. I made some hasty calculations. As a group captain he would outrank the Commander and his arrival on board with the ship in such a state was bound to reflect on me. 'Now the wretch is bringing the RAF brass here!'

'The C-in-C will arrange a boat. I'm speaking from his office now,' my uncle said.

'Best if I come ashore,' I said.

'Are you sure?'

I was sure. We had scarcely tied up and memories of the cruise were all about us, including its souvenirs. It must have been the booziest cruise in the *Indescribable*'s history. The VD rate was high on the lower deck. The Captain was leaving, the future of many was in doubt and morale was low. In Le Havre, the Commander had made a fool of himself from the outset by insisting on addressing the sailors before the first watch went ashore. His speech to nearly two thousand men was classic.

'I want to talk to you, not as your Commander, but as an old sailor. Next to the captain I am one of the oldest men on board and I want to say, first of all, that this is not a naval port but a commercial one and although I am not going to put any establishment out of bounds, I am going to give you certain advice. My advice is that you stay away from two bars . . .'

Here he paused and we listened with rapt attention while he named them. The first had a French name and was virtually unpronounceable, but the second was quite clear, the Arizona Bar. Its name there and then became emblazoned on every mind as if burnt in wood by a poker. There was further advice so incredible it too remains indelible in the memory.

'Remember that each man amongst you is an ambassador for your country. Treat every woman as you would your sister . . .'

The watch ashore, as it happened, was sisterless. There must have been a thousand men who tried to get into the Arizona Bar. There were fights, violence, riot squads, a massive police turnout with blood wagons arriving back at the ship at ten-minute intervals and a taxi driver got beaten up and thrown into the dock quite near us. We left under a cloud and when we reached our buoy in Portland, there were still five days to go before those of us who had indulged could be certain we were free from infection.

So I slunk ashore, hastily putting a sports coat over my uniform trousers, and soon sat with my beribboned uncle in a tea room, idly slicing a tea cake with a slight tremor. He was a North Walian, of another world and destined to march bemedalled on the Coronation Parade down the Mall to the intense pride of the family. At the time, there were still bite marks on my neck and I felt my foreskin itching. I had not even had time to bath and looked, I supposed, like an off-duty policeman with a considerable hangover.

When he spoke, it was deliberately, as from the pulpit.

'You should think very seriously about signing on,' he said. 'Your qualifications are very ordinary. You won't get much of a job in teaching without a degree.'

It was clear he had thought about the matter.

The woman who ran the tea shop was a divorcée who pursued naval officers and liked nothing better than to be invited on board for Sunday guest nights. She knew me and some of my friends. About to close she was nodding at me from behind the till to which my uncle had his back, indicating that I should stay, her invitation unmistakeable. My uncle was in uniform, the gold lace of his cap omnipresent. He had kept his nose to his particular grindstone all his life. A Welsh hockey international, he left his chapel to be an Air Force padre and there was a photograph of him at home sitting on a stone wall in Jerusalem which my grandmother kept highly polished in the front room. His was the way of piety and careful endeavour. Mine, it now seemed, was where it was ever destined to be – on the slide, as we said; and I remember distinctly thinking of an acquaintance of mine whom we called Shaky Jones, last seen heading for a beach with his blonde girlfriend, carrying a mattress between them. People said he was 'beyond', using the word in its dark Welsh sense, and now it could very appropriately be applied to me.

'The Navy's not quite my cup of tea,' I said euphemistically.

'You always were very difficult,' my uncle said. 'But I told your grandmother, I would reach you.'

He had, but soon he reached for his hat and gloves. I paid, winked at the proprietress, and saw him into his taxi. I did not raise my hat.

I saw Alun as promised, he wrote home; *he was looking rather pale, and I do not think he has the right attitude to make a career of the services.*

It was a view now openly expressed by the Commander who had dropped strong hints in the right quarter so that I soon found myself on draft, proceeding ashore once more to barracks.

When I was finally demobilised, I left my uniform jacket on the back of a chair, having sold or given away every other item of uniform I possessed. The jacket was threadbare but I had declined to buy a new one, brazening it out to the end. I sometimes dreamt of it and wondered what had become of it, and of all those nights spent yarning the night away. I had lived out my fantasies only to be disillusioned. I had gone through the bead curtain and it made not the slightest difference. Although I did not relish my time in the Navy and gave it precious little, alas, except to the bio-gardeners of the lower deck, I was somehow or other always grateful to it for my perspectives were broadened and ever after I was drawn to the company of others like myself who had been through its particular hoop. I had learned to survive in most circumstances, eventually to stop squealing – to shake down, as we said. There were many other incidents which I was to recall, eerie glimpses into other worlds, even that of espionage, of men under punishment shifting sand on the barrack square and once, temporarly posted to a fleet air arm base, I found myself flying upside down in the instructor's seat of a Sea Fury trainer in a practice low-level bombing run over the Needles. I later persuaded the pilot to fly over the Rhondda Valley, then a unique experience, but I had no ambitions other than to put it all behind me. I was not a man of action.

In the months before my demobilisation, I sat down and wrote my first acceptable short story. I was not to know it was acceptable for some years, but it seemed to me to be the only avenue of escape, not only from the Navy but from the purposeless act of being the self I then was.

TEN

After the second haemorrhage inside my eye, I endured a week when I hardly spoke. The opthalmic specialist was contacted but declined to come and I was not taken to see him again. It was one of those moments when you begin to realise that nothing is certain, and when doctors fall out or disagree, they are conspicuous by their absence. It was no use my asking any questions. No one could answer them, and since I was still taking reduced amounts of streptomycin and falling asleep for inordinate amounts of time, I welcomed oblivion in the way that I had earlier welcomed being drunk when things became intolerable in faraway places. But I could never lose consciousness for long enough, and although I growled inside myself and privately raged at intervals, it seemed there was no way out of that bed. Then the chest physician came to tell me that they were going to transfer me to another hospital. My first reaction was not optimistic. I thought they wanted to get rid of me – that I was, as ever, a problem best shelved.

At this time it was natural to transfer certain cases to a chest hospital near the coast where surgery was undertaken to remove the infected portions of diseased lungs, but this was never attempted with those who suffered from silicosis and I had perhaps taken an unduly pessimistic view of my plight since most of the men in our ward had been colliers and their stoical dismay had passed on to me. Others in the neighbouring ward were regularly transferred and when I joined the list due for transfer, it was at first thought to be a step in the right direction and I was congratulated as if I had achieved something. Our days were so devoid of incident that an extra bowel movement was newsworthy. Transfer-out was call for a special edition. Still suspicious I thought that the deteriorating eye condition was a burden the local hospital authorities did not want to keep. I had not yet fully understood what an allergy meant and although I was now taking more streptomycin then ever before and had put on weight, I had no sense of making progress and the second haemorrhage was proof to me of the finality of it all. I still felt weak and low, and existed in a dreamlike state for most of the day, although I could still manage to laugh at some of the most savage wisecracks. The harsher they were, the more they penetrated our particular gloom.

When the time came for me to leave the little ward, I well knew I was leaving men I would never see again. In a strange way that tiny eight-bed ward with its little routines, the regular filling and topping-up of the coke stove, the daily betting, the odd Saturday night flagon of ale, the handyman's bandy gait and cheery whistle, his grave attention in the early morning to the betting slips, together with the general excellence of the food, made it in all a homely place. If it was also full of horrors, these were palliated by our easy-going relationships, above all by the nurses who were strong and capable, ever attentive even when they were overworked and busy, usually displaying that intense, loving, and gentle care that comes more easily in long-term hospitals. It was not a clinical place. There were jokes and anecdotes and, very sensibly, the staff for the most part turned a blind eye to the rum in the HP Sauce bottle and such irregularities. It was a world on its own in there, grim and grey in its import, but nevertheless there was a warmth and a camaraderie that was essentially South Walian – open and classless, a host of kindnesses being daily and regularly performed in the most trying of circumstances. We had our upsets, and I was part of them, but eventually an even tenor prevailed. We shook down, as we said. Sometimes we heard screaming from the women's ward adjacent to ours, and there was constant friction there, we were told – some patients discharging themselves and preferring to die rather than endure the physical indignities of being so cooped up. The nurses told us they would all prefer to be on our male ward, no matter how serious or terminal our illnesses. More than anything the colliery jokes, the sardonic humour, the helping hand of patient for patient kept us together so that ever after I used to claim that I had an honorary five per cent 'dust', or silicosis – enough colliers had coughed over me! I felt myself lucky to have been in that milieu which provided me with an invaluable insight into the collective Welsh past and which I often recalled later in life when I was ensconced in some affluent circumstance – particularly, of all places, in the elegant and spacious Edwardian gents' lavatory of the Ritz Hotel in London. There I sometimes made it my business to make lingering and lengthy calls. Sitting composed in my own private Remembrance Day silence for the men I had known, I would recall their faces and the hardship of their lives as I reflected on my own. They would, I am sure, have appreciated the irony.

When I wrapped myself in my dressing gown and went around the beds to shake hands, very little was said.

'See you, Dai!'

'All the best, Al' . . .'

'So long, Emrys . . .'

'All you wishes yourself, our kid.'

There was optimism everywhere.

'They're not equipped to deal with bloody eyes in here, mun. Dust is all they bloody know.'

'And they can't do nothing about that!'

'What I'm saying is, the boy is better away from here.'

It was true and I knew it, but never have I left anywhere with such a strange feeling of having belonged. It was irrational. It did not make sense. There was hardly a man in there with whom I had a thing in common, except for a tenuous and very local membership of the human race. I was separated by age and experience and yet in the kingdom of the helpless, I was in some way the most helpless and no doubt I worried most since, after all, with the arrogance of youth I presumed on a future and most of them did not.

I went out through the door with the nurse to the ambulance and I did not look back. As I lay on the stretcher, the floaters reappeared inside my eye and the blood swirled, activated by the slightest movement – all melodramatic and ominous against the stark daylight and the gaunt shapes of bare winter trees. I remained a problem to everyone I knew.

It had not always been so. When I left the Navy, the part-solution to my own problems turned out to be an intimate acquaintanceship with other people's which to begin with, incredibly enough, I found through matrimonial guidance – one of my first tasks as a young probation officer.

'What I want to say, Mrs T., is that there are usually faults on both sides in these matters. It takes two to make a quarrel, you know?' (All this accompanied by an expansive twenty-year-old smile – mine!)

'It's his hands, Mister.'

'Pardon?'

'Everywhere!'

'What are?'

'His bleedin' 'ands! There's things I could tell you, you wouldn't believe!'

'You must tell me what you think I ought to know. If I can help?'

'He can't keep 'em off me. If he's not up me, he's in me and at me, front and behind, out of doors an' all – and *money*? I never see it. Terrible with money he is. I've warned him – half a chance, I'd make him pay for it!'

'Perhaps he's demonstrating his feelings for you, Mrs T.?'

The look on Mrs T.'s bird-like face now resembled that of a wizened sparrow at the onset of winter. She was an incessant complainer and trilled her complaints at whatever probation officer she could find to listen to her. Older officers passed her on to me and matrimonial guidance became one of my first tasks as a newly appointed probation officer attached to Clerkenwell Magistrate's Court in the Metropolitan Probation District where I was first posted. I travelled daily to the office in Camden Town and each evening, after court days, I would find myself increasingly dealing with those matrimonial cases referred by the magistrate for a preliminary interview which always took place when either party applied for a separation order. Soon I found a technique for listening to both parties separately, then bringing them together for a joint discussion. If the application were no more than a demonstration, the public token of a private rift, I would finally – much to the amusement of my colleagues – physically join the hands of the dissenting couple and lead them gently to the door while they stared at me mystified. I might have been a vicar at the altar for I kept hold of their enjoined hands until the last minute when they passed, often in a daze, through the door and on to the pavement outside.

'I've listened to both of you. There are faults on both sides, but, d'you know? – I believe you're no good without each other. Good luck!' Sometimes, unused to the sound of a Welsh voice, they would find themselves in a trance and the quarrelling did not begin again until they reached the street outside. It was a tactic of little therapeutic value, like that enacted by a New York Police commissioner whom I once met. As a young desk officer in the Bronx, he completely charmed a young woman who complained that she was being given lethal doses of electricity by a dead lover. He listened gravely, then began making a chain of paper clips which he finally attached to her belt. 'Madam, you are now earthed!' he said, and she went away delighted, never to return.

I was at the very beginning of a career to which, after the Navy, my three years of training had led me in the confident belief I could succeed. At last I had found what I wanted to do. One thing the Navy had taught me to do was to communicate, to be clear, and in the large caseload of Borstal and other male delinquents on licence, there were plenty whose experience of life was not wholly unlike my own. Their difficulties were legion, their rejection often total, and the inevitable and sometimes enforced recruitment into institutional life had given them an attitude which I found myself beginning to understand. Being so obviously Welsh, I was free of the class associations which at first so often bedevilled those new 'officers who came from a more privileged section of English society. It seemed to me that I had found my métier in mean streets, and somewhere along the line I became more and more aware of how fortunate I was, principally by being continually exposed to the incredible truths of other people's lives. The result was that I had lost any idea of myself as a person who could not cope. Those who are born and remain in one stratified section of society do not have any real sense of their place in the world, only of where they stand in their particular part of it and while they may prosper, they are less equipped to face difficulties when difficulties come. Imagination is no substitute for experience, and there is nothing more painful than the puncturing of a false confidence by the brute facts of experience. The childlike don, the temper tantrums of the rich man or the heartbreak of the deceived, are all the consequence of an unawareness of possibilities. In my own case, I had been confused and despairing enough, but at least I had a knowledge of the great injustices of life – a sense which made me hesitate to count my chickens even well after they were hatched. It was just as well.

It was also time for some good luck. When I applied to join the Social Science Diploma Course at the University College of Swansea, I was considered as a mature student – I still did not have my matriculation – and facing me in the interview panel was the woman professor of biology who had gravely inspected my gardening plot three years before. At first my heart sank, but I determined to relate the story and did so. I left nothing out, including my criticisms of the course.

'Blight, I remember!' she said, and smiled. It was a turning point in my fortunes. I made friends with my tutor, Robin Huws Jones, who made the lives of so many people easier by his inexhaustible fund of kindnesses, his meticulous attention to detail – later an inspiration to thousands. In my life, he was a saint in saint's clothing. It is hard to praise a methodical and good man who forgets nothing, whose appetite for work is omnivorous and who yet always finds the time for the slightest problem, an aptitude sorely challenged since much of his academic career was spent dealing with students from almost every country in the world. My own course was the first to be sponsored by the United Nations and I soon found myself to be the only white man in a year group made up of Arabs and Israelis, Malays, Pakistanis and Africans. As it happened, it was an exciting time to be in university and I entered a convivial society made up of many different nationalities whose intelligence was an eye-opener. We mixed well, there were romances, we learned as much from each other as from our tutors – many of whom were youthful and enthusiastic and responded to our maturity – so that if we tended to be separated from the main body of the student population by our difference in age and experience, it hardly mattered. So much of formal education in my experience was drab and uninspiring, a grey meaningless procession from lecture room to lecture room that characterised much of my training college experience, a good deal of which was the senseless accumulation of information – material passing, as the old joke says, from the notebook of the lecturer to the notebook of the student without going through the minds of either!

But my course at Swansea University was different, perhaps because I found I could succeed. Previously I had done no more than just hold my own, and when the time came for us to spend substantial periods of time with the social work agencies to which we were regularly allotted, I found that my doubts about myself had ended. It occupied two years of my life, that course, and although I kept a diary, much of it is uninteresting since for most of the time I worked, fearful of the consequences of failure as I was financing myself out of my naval gratuity with a little help from my grandmother. Now it was my turn to be the ex-serviceman, and like those I met at training college, I was for the most part conscientious, concerned to get a qualification and be off. Outside of classes I debated in the first of the *Observer* debating championships and was even invited to join the Principal at dinner when VIPs came – among them Hugh Gaitskell and Lady Megan Lloyd George, whom I greatly offended since she was then pushing a nationalist ticket and advocating a parliament for Wales but I, sharing the experience of most of my fellow students, had seen too much of Tammany Hall politics to want more Welsh government. Both were a disappointment, patronising and bored with us and the Principal's laughable jug of cider on the dining table. Students were still treated as schoolboys by the older academics, some of whom objected to the very presence of a social science course at the university. We should, they said, have been in a technical college. The English dons I met occasionally were often supercilious towards those not admitted to their courses, and I tired of hearing them disparaging those Welsh writers whom I was now reading avidly. When Dylan Thomas died, they could not wait – they said – *not* to read his obituaries, and for Welsh poets like Vernon Watkins and John Ormond they often had nothing but disdain. It was a time of debunking, although I lived long enough to see some of them, white-haired and greying, solemnly proceeding in flowing gowns to memorial services or summer schools held in honour of local poets by a university now intent on capitalising on them.

For the most part, I kept my enthusiasms private, a part of my unexposed life which remained secret for a good while yet. I was usually a model student and had, for a reason I now forget, the Principal's private telephone number which I was able to produce to good effect during a solitary lapse when I found myself involved in another scrape which began in the most innocent of ways.

After working hard on a seminar paper on the subject of alcoholism – 'In Wales, all alcoholics are anonymous!' – I found myself selected to lead the Christmas Debate, opposing the motion 'That This House Does Not Believe in Father Christmas'. In the course of the debate, a gang of rebellious students overturned the platform with the result that I added to my long list of curious injuries. For I dislocated a thumb in the fall and was taken by solicitous friends on the back of a potato lorry to the old Swansea General Hospital, the students assembling in a large group in the hospital corridor where they began to sing 'Abide With Me' until ejected by the police, while I remained nursing the projecting organ in out-patients. The casualty officer, later to be the subject of an unsuccessful divorce petition on the grounds of his persistent drunkenness, took a very puritanical view of me. He said that I'd had too much to drink to use a local anaesthetic and that I would have to stay overnight to receive a general anaesthetic. This would make it impossible for me to see the forthcoming Swansea *v* New Zealand match on the following day, but he would be pleased to relieve me of my ticket!

I refused, was later operated upon and spent the night in hospital, waited in vain for the casualty officer and discharged myself shortly before the match – the whole an event of little consequence except that I later found that during the course of the previous day, I and my friends had somehow offended a policeman on point duty with the result that two police officers called at my lodgings to complain about my behaviour. On being informed that the chief superintendent wanted to see me, my landlady announced that after the match 'I was going straight to Borstal!' I was, in fact, going to spend six weeks in such an institution as part of my course. This induced the police sergeant, whom I had never seen, to say, 'The proper place for him too!', a statement to which I clung when I eventually visited the chief superintendent who informed me that a number of us marching to the debate had given a military 'Eyes right!' to the traffic policeman, saluting him and thereby bringing the Force into disrepute by ridiculing him. I had no recollection of the occurrence, although it was probably true. However I pointed out that the sergeant, who was not present, had exceeded himself by intimidating my landlady – he'd demanded entrance of the backstreet terraced house and passed his comment on my suitability for Borstal-training. The police had also found out that I'd dislocated my thumb and been admitted to the hospital overnight. The chief superintendent now pompously enquired if this was evidence of my condition and if such injuries were in the normal course of university debates. It was clear that no charge was going to be preferred. Had it been left to the offended constable and myself, he would have had an apology and a pint; but I suddenly found myself dealing with a bully who revealed himself when he told me that he was in two minds whether or not he should telephone the Principal at the university. It was a threat softly uttered in that large office, its meaning clear. I took out my diary and gave him the Principal's home number in case the registrar reported him unavailable. Fortunately there was nothing concrete to complain about but it was a salutary reminder of what others, less articulate than myself, could expect, and when later I heard similar stories of intimidation from Borstal boys on licence, I was more sympathetic than I might otherwise have been with my service experience of hardened offenders and their evasions. Ever after, I had a memory of that uncomfortable half-hour when I learned more than was intended.

But very soon, aided once again by my tutor, I was accepted for the Home Office Probation-Training Scheme. I went to the Rhondda, to Derby and to East Anglia, and now, like any other trainee, I began to get the feel of the caseload – the name collectively given to the persons who pass via the courts into the probation officer's orbit. I met more people than at any other time in my life: a daily procession of faces which often returned to me in my reveries, as did the homes and lodging houses – so often with the stink of poverty omnipresent, but sometimes ostensibly genteel and nice. Once I even took a glass of dry sherry in the Hampstead garden of the head waiter at one of the best-known London hotels, while I listened patiently to the problems of his wayward son who had been deported from Germany after impersonating an American soldier, later embarking on a career of fraud. But more often than not, I was faced with the problems of poor people who were barely scratching a living and at the extremity of experience – their inability to cope, like their threadbare possessions, all creating a wan tide of dismay which ebbed daily as I made my way amongst them.

I did not have the problem of overidentifying with the unfortunate, since there were so many of them – an army of the inadequate whose dullness had brought them before the courts, usually for crimes which were bound to be detected. No one had prepared me for the low intelligence which is by far the greatest common factor of the non-professional criminals of the delinquent population, or the evasions, the lack of insight, the simple and uncomplex collective inability to cope which soon became apparent. I had little to do with professional criminals, but I had a sense of the other England which exists on the wrong side of the national blanket where the quality of life, even in those days of comparative affluence, seemed to be perpetually declining – an impression which was to continue, especially as I grew older and travelled more frequently. If I saw an actual book in a house then, it was an exception and most of the people I met were inarticulate and painfully so, save for the odd convicted homosexual or drug addict whose appearance before the courts led them into shabby waiting-rooms where they took their turn in the queue for whatever ministrations were forthcoming. I visited every kind of home, lodging and tenement and I found myself both liked and disliked, a salutary experience. Once in Derby, finding a family suddenly bereft of a mother who was sent to recuperate in a charity home after a long illness, I moved in and looked after four children for a lengthy period; but at another time, in a university town, I found myself in deep water, victim once more of a stratified society and a comic series of misunderstandings which led me eventually to head for the anonymity of London. Then, as had happened before and would happen again in my life, I seemed to move from one section of society to another with a bewildering rapidity, closing one door and opening another to find a different set of values, habits and mores – voices ascending and descending in the social range while I remained obstinately the same, as if my limp self was all I had as a marker. But in the intervals of travelling, I kept a firm base at home.

My grandmother took a keen interest in my probation-training. I would appear for weekends, renew old acquaintanceships, particularly at holiday times when my contemporaries were likely to be home since most of them – like me – were destined to leave our home town for ever.

'Where is it this time?' my grandmother would say.

Once I named a university town but I was merely to lodge there. I had no connection with the university.

'Oxbridge,' I said.

She was impressed. Her health was failing now and she was heavily dependent upon her neighbours who did her daily shopping. She liked to think of me being involved in a job which was free of the taint of profit, which had a social connection, but at the same time she had a sense of the wear and tear of persistent exposure to other people's difficulties. Perhaps she thought I would be too conscientious and, as ever, she had a mortal fear of the evils of the demon drink. If, as I frequently did, I visited the hostelries of the town, I would either return in the early hours of the morning when she had gone to bed or, together with others who still remained under the burden of the temperance yoke, I would munch animal chlorophyl tablets which sometimes had the effect of making you more drunk. It was the last nonsensical tribute we paid to the cloying hand of Welsh Nonconformity. At any rate I tried not to offend her; but in those days there was a magnificent Victorian hostelry facing Pontypridd's Memorial Park where the long bar was built of oak and was overlooked on one side by a large leaded-glass window in the shape of a Dutch mural, and in this corner on a bank holiday weekend you could be sure to find your contemporaries. This was the Queen's Hotel, long since destroyed by planners, and it was here that

187

impromptu eisteddfods were held on high days and holidays when the exiles came home. Going to the gents lavatory before stop-tap was often a lengthy business since you might be trapped by soloists, and Welsh airs came forth loud and clear – choruses of songs like 'Myfanwy' sometimes going on for so long that they interfered dangerously with your original purpose, especially when the acoustics provided by the handsome china tiles glorified male voices raised in a paean of longing, and raised perhaps for the last time in months. These were nights of succour before we wended our separate ways to alien England which alone could give us employment. Here, in the gents as well as at the long bar, you would see someone who had sat next to you at school appearing unexpectedly after an interval of years. Often it would turn out they were in one of the services, but some were in the most surprising of jobs. Ponty' boys, as I was to discover, did everything anywhere.

'What are you up to then, Dai?'

'Doing a bit with the old divorce.'

'You're getting divorced?'

'No, enquiry agent.'

Others were in the Metropolitan Police or the professions; most were teachers, eagerly recruited by Midlands education authorities, and many played rugby for small obscure clubs, meeting each other by chance in remote places. Of these, almost all had given up any thought of ever obtaining jobs at home and took for granted the inevitable fact of exile. It was not just that there were not enough jobs for us, but that few would submit to the councillor's fiefdom and we took it for granted that those without 'influence' would have little chance of success – especially if they would not make the well-worn canvasser's rounds of the local Labour nabobs who traded off favours with each other. Those who would not leave, particularly those who were married, often found themselves to be especially vulnerable and had to make do with inferior jobs for which they were overqualified.

It was my grandmother's proud boast that she had never had a councillor in the house, and since most of her own family had been forced to seek jobs elsewhere, she took my leave-taking for granted. It was a fact of life and in my mind there was a conviction that I would leave Wales for ever. If the emotional attachments were strong, the labyrinthine ways of local nepotists were distasteful, to me as to others. It was the beginning of a process of alienation shared by my contemporaries and which was to be repeated many years later when the Welsh language spoken by few in Glamorgan, came to be a requisite for many jobs, creating a new linguistic nepotism. Wales has always known how to rid herself of her ablest children.

But this was before and later. My posting to my final probation training area was, I thought, the last temporary move I would make and my grandmother waved me goodbye from the front door – the last time I was to see her standing on her feet. She was in her seventies then, her greying hair so thin that she constantly wore it in a hair net, her mouth still permanently drawn to one side as a result of her first stroke, her figure bent, legs and hands misshapen as she suffered severely from varicose veins and also, for most of her adult life, from a cruel rheumatism which disfigured her hands so much that she could not always wear a wedding ring. She wore a mauve cardigan, her favourite colour, the ever present black velvet neckband – a bent old woman, small and frail, whose fierce spirit and directness has remained with me always, and even today I cannot think of her without marvelling at my luck. She was not a perfect woman. Perhaps she had more understanding of me than of some of her own children, but she had an intimate grasp of essential things, a hatred of evasion and more courage than I have ever witnessed in a human being. If she did not understand the modern world, nor the complexities of life, only its savage pains, she had a confident sense of herself, of her own roles and her own part in life – all of which gave me a precious branch to clutch when I needed one most. Walking down the path that day, my heart was full, my mind echoing the things I never said to her. For in her presence I was often inarticulate, although I am sure she never expected me to be demonstrative and, perhaps with the diffidence of age, she seldom touched me – nor I her – although the feeling between us was beyond doubt. I gave no real thought then to the possibility of her dying although I must have been aware of it, and in my mind she has never died, although I have often been glad that she was not witness of my scamp's progress in the days when my own despair and unhappiness led me – as it so often did – into wild extremes of behaviour. I did not understand the modern world either.

'I don't know what I must look like? she said that day. 'Like the old woman who lived in the shoe, I daresay!'

Then she bade me make sure that the sheets on my bed in my new and as yet unseen lodgings were aired, an injunction born of her mortal fear of landladies. She spoiled me, of course, and where I was concerned she felt she always knew best. Now that I saw her so infrequently, I could never leave her without a flood of memories and that day I thought of my own dismal progress home from school after I had been told that I had completely failed my school certificate examination. My headmaster had, in fact, just grinned and shaken his head disparagingly as if my very arrival at his study even to enquire, was a massive impertinence. And he was right. On that day also, perhaps significantly, my grandmother told me of her own arrival as a young woman at Pontypridd Station just after the First World War, summoned home by news of her father's grave illness, and how from the railway carriage she could look up Graigwen Hill – then largely undeveloped – and see her old home with its window blinds drawn, a confirmation of what she already felt. This same prescience followed by confirmation was to repeat itself in my eighteenth year when I went to visit my first cousin, Michael, who was also eighteen and who died in my arms of a tumour of the brain; when I telephoned her, she caught her breath as soon as I spoke, knowing at once that I was the bearer of bad news. He had grasped my neck in an extremity of pain and his fingers had to be prised from my skin, a fact which I never told anyone but she knew the full horror of what I had witnessed, I am sure. Equally, though, I am hopeful that she had no idea of the problems along my tortuous way in the greater world or, indeed, that aspects of her character had passed on to me, creating their own special difficulties, especially when confronted by evasions.

I gave a final wave that day, shouldered my bag and went cheerfully to my last period of probation-training. I did not know then that I was leaving home for ever, and it was unthinkable that I could ever walk down the main street and not meet a dozen people I knew. It was just as well for I soon entered into a bizarre set of experiences which put me at odds with the world once more.

A letter had come from the senior probation officer who was to be my tutor, charged with reporting upon my capabilities to the Home Office. He had also found me lodgings so that when I arrived, I took a taxi to the house which had been recommended. It was the corner house of a terrace of semi-detached houses situated closely together – a narrow street of identical shapes containing a landscape of lace curtains, some of which quivered when my taxi pulled up alongside the house where my landlady was waiting for me up on the front step. She wore an apron and was wringing her hands on the newly washed step, one of the most agitated women I have ever seen. She wore her hair in curlers under a headscarf and her sharp visor of nose and mouth moved continuously, even before I got out of the taxi, although I noted we were being observed from the windows of the house next door. She had sharp staring eyes and she could not keep her hands still, and at once began a barrage of incessant chatter – words and phrases spraying out in a high-pitched montone which was largely incomprehensible.

'Gotcha-gotcha-gotcha-gotcha-gotcha-bag, I see! Bags-bags-bags-bags-heavy. Come this way-way-way, up the stairs, very dark-dark-dark here, room is ready, got-you-got-you-got-you, got you-got your letter. Don't want no more police-police-policemen, come in all-all-all-all hours of the night-night-night!'

She was like a frenetic bird, hopping from one foot to another. It was clear she was obsessively clean, and she followed me hastily up the narrow stairs and into the little bedroom where I had to duck under the eaves. She knelt hastily on to the floor to slide a sheet of cardboard over the carpet before I could put my suitcase down, immediately gesticulating through the open door across the landing to show me the bathroom. By the way she pointed, she indicated that I might need a wash. She also talked all the while, repeating words with a staccato machine-gun rapidity as if she was being pressed by an inner trigger until they seemed to be frothing from her tight little mouth, now giving a list of the names of her previous lodgers, then the presents they had brought for their children, next her preference for married men and the fact that no dogs were allowed, nor dripping raincoats in the hall – all in a quickening hiss of words that was once punctuated by a banging on the wall from a neighbour, an occurrence that was not commentated upon. It was like being in the same cage as a vociferous and drunken parrot!

'Mr Vicari-train sets, Mr Bone liked a nice lawn, offered to do it, Mr Goldhawk smoked a pipe but I told him and told him and told him and told him-told him so. No, I said. Mr O'Connor – the only Irish but you wouldn't know it, know it – know it, charm the birds-birds-birds off the trees-trees-trees-you'll be regular hours-hours-hours will you, not like the police-police police?'

She did not give me time to reply, planted herself in the corner of the little bedroom and it soon appeared that there was no way in which I was going to get rid of her. From the moment I set foot inside the brightly polished little hallway, it was as if she had perched on my shoulder, talking incessantly so that after twenty minutes it was as if a beak was hammering inside my ear. I set my suitcase down carefully, went pointedly to the bathroom but she followed me there, and while I peed behind the half-closed door, the chatter continued and when I came back and began to unpack, she continued talking, eyeing but not seeming to mind my meagre possessions. She stood all the while leaning forward, her eyes flashing, the head nodding in a permanent nervous tic while the words sprayed over me. They went on and on, pinioning me in a wall of sound as irritating as fluff.

I brought out my one suit, my naval shorts, the naval stiff collars I used for court days, some books over which she cast a perfunctory eye, then my underclothes and socks and these she seized from me, whisking open a drawer in which the lining paper was clean newspaper. Some of the socks she examined, frisking open my underpants and holding them up to her nose, then folding them and putting them away, talking all the while.

'I don't do-do-do-any washing only for specials. Stiff collars have to go to the laundry, there isn't a laundry for miles-miles-miles, you'll have to do those-those-those yourself-self-self. You can put your books-books downstairs, if you've a mind-mind-mind to. There is a book-book-bookcase!'

Once I had unpacked, she seized a duster and dusted the suitcase, laying some more cardboard under the bed where it fortunately just fitted.

I was slow to realise that she was completely mad. Although she offered to cook me a meal, after thirty minutes my ears were ringing with that incessant chatter and obtaining a key, I took myself off, hurtling down the street in any direction, but not without noticing the telltale net curtains shivering in the next-door window. I was lodging in a house that was constantly watched, it seemed. As I left, she stood in the front doorway still talking incessantly to the cold night air, the watchers once more about their business on all sides of the street.

I stayed out in a seedy public house as long as I could but she was waiting up for me, had even made a sandwich and, in fact, she brought it upstairs and hovered outside the bathroom door while I peed again, re-entering my bedroom and even when I began to undress, she hesitated and had to force herself to leave, her eyes gleaming. But somehow or other I could see she was friendly, friendly when she left, friendly when she trilled, 'Good night, good night, good nightie-ee-ee!' Then I heard her bedroom door close with the feeling that only a zoo keeper was missing, making his nightly rounds. 'Bit of trouble this evening in the birdhouse!'

In the morning she was up with the dawn and the knocking at my door was gentle, slow and insistent, again like the tapping of a beak. Tap-tap-tap! 'Hello-hello-hello! Morning. Didn't want you to be latie!'

She had prepared a decent breakfast but the chatter continued, over the gas stove, at the table, as I went hastily out into the hallway and down the garden path, the curtains once more moving on either side of the street as the unseen eyes stared at her. I made my way to the office and, introducing myself to the senior probation officer, I did not mention her, but when I returned that night, one of the neighbours was hovering in the porch – a little, bent, bald old man in carpet slippers, obviously one of the watchers. My arrival must have triggered something off for she had been found barefooted walking down the street in her underclothes, a doctor had been called and she had been committed to a mental hospital several hours after I had left the house. My belongings had been packed by the neighbour and I noticed that several copper lustre ornaments were missing from the hallway. I had to leave instantly and spent the night in a hotel, and all night I could hear her voice pecking at my eardrums. 'I'm gone-gone-gone-gone!'

The following morning, the senior probation officer was all apologies when I told him. Her name had been taken from the approved list of police lodgings. Now he would personally find new lodgings for me and in a much more select neighbourhood where, I was told, the chief constable lived himself. It was a step up from semi-detached country; there were chiming doorbells and rookery nooks with gnomes in the gardens, and I soon found myself in a comfortable house owned by an ex-Army officer's widow. She already had one lodger – a young economist who was an Olympic high-jump contender, a tall gangling young man, well over six foot with a fierce crew cut and a comedian's plastic face which could slip at will into a dozen grotesque expressions. He was also a superb mimic, a man of many voices – one to charm the youthful landlady, Mrs Madison, the other to send me into fits of uncontrollable laughter which turned out to be a cruel gift because it soon got me into trouble. When I came down to breakfast a few days later, he sat in the breakfast room, his enormous legs coiled under the table, his mobile face twisted into an expression of obscene ugliness as he leered at the open breakfast hatch, his right hand performing a masturbating movement under the table. In the same breath, he then gave out two voices – one audible, one barely heard (but heard by me): 'Good morning, Mr R, and how are the Welsh this a.m.?' and under his breath, 'Wanking their bloody selves to death!' When Mrs Madison entered bearing my breakfast, I was grinning involuntarily, but he had soon assumed one of his other faces – that of the disapproving visiting clergyman – so that this performance, and many that followed, resulted in my facial expressions being slightly out of key when the landlady addressed me, as she at first did, with the politest of early morning pleasantries. I was, of course, stifling a smile as she entered the room and was perpetually put on the wrong foot. I soon found that Mrs Madison insisted on joining us at breakfast, sometimes presiding over the tea pot in an expensive white bathrobe which parted at the crotch at inopportune moments when I would get a discreet dig in the ribs from my fellow lodger who had cultivated these obscene gestures to a fine art. She, of course, never suspected them, but from that first morning she viewed me with a perceptible distaste. He charmed her, putting on a tinny little rinky-dinky-do voice to tease her about her passion for flowers, her attachment to the snapping Pekinese called Chuckles who also disliked me since I had shoved him pointedly to one side with my foot during one breakfast. She was a precise, neat little woman who read books recommended by the librarian at Boots private library when she was not telling you that she did not need to take in lodgers, but only did so as a favour to the chief constable. She would air her prejudices, once telling me that Chuckles knew a good deal about people and she'd noted he didn't take to me. This was but the start. On top of the black marks I earned through those off-key facial expressions provoked by the economist and his sotto voce obscenities, I further endeared myself by producing a pair of naval boots. The weather was worsening, my job entailed a good deal of walking and I was anxious to save my only other pair of shoes. But the boots were the penultimate straw. Although they were highly polished – I once told her that my Royal Marine batman had boned them and brought them to such a highly polished state by holding them over a candle: 'Banks of swank!', he used to say – she was unimpressed and could not keep her eyes away from them, following them as if hypnotised. Also, Chuckles began to growl whenever he saw them. This pantomime was followed by her uncanny prediction of my visits to the bathroom when she would appear like a wraith, duster in hand, to clean out the bath or bowl after me. This habit of hers much amused my fellow lodger who commented in a cockney voice when she was safely out of earshot, 'That's wot comes of keepin' coal in the barf all yer life, Taff, my boy. People talks, see?'

If he sounds repulsive, he was not. He simply gave a variety of performances every day. He found her as laughable as I did, and privately responded to her as you would expect of a butcher's son from Gillingham. But, cleverer than myself, he set out to charm her and would engage in ridiculous conversations about the merits of Winnie the Pooh, Anthony Eden – 'A gentleman to his fingertips, you can tell by the hat!' – all in front of me in his false, posh voice. It was a completely spurious performance, one cliché following another at which Mrs Madison simpered her agreement; while later, in a nearby public house, he would revert to his normal witty and intelligent self. It must have been an age of mimics, pre-eminent among them Tony Hancock whom I once sat next to after a naval concert. His superb skills were author to a generation of imitators and I was to meet plenty of these, but none so devastating as my athletic friend whose height and ugly pinhead under his crew cut made him the image of the person I later imagined as the hero of J. D. Salinger's *The Catcher in the Rye*. Gawky, awkward and perpetually adolescent away from the university where he probably assumed another self, he was a catcher with a difference, however; for he unwittingly laid the ground for a farcical experience which finished me forever with suburban England.

From the start I was so busy that I was seldom in the house, leaving early in the morning and returning late at night, my boots treading country lanes at the end of the sugar beet season which was accompanied by a rise in the number of reported cases of incest. I soon declined my landlady's offer of an evening meal because I could never predict what time I would return, which was usually so late that all I wanted was to sleep. That, too, was a mark against me. I could not win. Daily I went about the countryside under the supervision of the senior probation officer, making home visits and eventually court reports on offenders which were duly presented to the magistrates. I soon found that there was friction in the office between the probation officers. Two were university graduates, the senior was not. An ex-chief petty officer in the Royal Navy, he was at first markedly disposed to favour me and the office rebounded with naval slang. One of the other officers, a calm and gentle intellectual who was a graduate of the university, had been a conscientious objector and had, I was told, many left-wing connections. In fact, as I once overheard a CID inspector say, his friends left much to be desired. It was a piece of information I should not have received but which was given to me because, for once, my acceptability as an ex-naval man was beyond question. But I promptly saw I would be similarly disapproved of, were my true feelings to become known. It was at this time that I was told a permanent position would shortly be on offer and that I should apply for it. I was flattered but ill at ease. If there were sides to be taken in an argument in the office, I was not as predictable in my opinions as I was thought to be and I did not much care for CID opinions on the political beliefs of my colleagues. There is also something precious about the atmosphere of a university town, often the cloying gentility which comes with a predominant social grouping and I never liked pecking orders. Then again, the job was in a probation area which was predominantly rural and I felt my métier was in mean streets. I did not think I would apply, but said nothing. I had my training to finish first.

Then the assizes came and it was my lowly task to see that the female probation officer's lavatory was made available to the presiding judge since it was the nearest available. Scandalous stories were spread by the young policemen about him. Three times divorced with the cyanosed face of a hardened whisky drinker, he was said to sit up late in the Judge's Lodging House, playing the fiddle, and had once been known to send out for women! I did not know him, but he terrified me although I noted his mischievous habit of calling for the police superintendent in the court at five minutes to bank closing time and coolly asking him if he could get a large cheque cashed, the sum involved being so large that the police superintendent himself had to sprint to a nearby bank to comply. Later I hovered about the corridor after checking the toilet paper so that His Lordship would be amply catered for and, although I was not supposed to be seen, he once passed me with a grateful nod while I pinioned myself, head bowed, to the wall. I sat in court daily, marvelling at the assurance of counsel. One of them had built up a lucrative practice defending American servicemen on drink-driving charges. A large imposing man with an Old Bailey ring to his voice, to my astonishment he turned out to be another mimic – especially with the presiding judge who was known to be partially deaf.

He would also conduct two conversations almost simul-
taneously like my fellow lodger. 'My lord may well feel,' he
would say in a loud stentorian voice, then lower his chin to add
under his breath, 'If my lord has any bloody feelings at all!' –
an aside which caused the young solicitor sitting behind him to
collapse with laughter whereupon the judge woke up and
ordered him out of court, no stare being as disapproving as
that of the barrister who had caused his mirth! All these were
rich comic pickings and included policemen, bored of
deposition-taking in the lower courts, passing around horror
photographs of mutilated bodies; one of a finger in a tin once
caused an elderly female probation officer to shriek aloud.
These savage jokes, like colliery humour, were but a defence
against the depravities of life. I enjoyed the jokes and was on
good terms with the working policemen who often displayed a
robust kindliness and whose humour matched my own –
when, that is, they were not themselves threatened, as they
sometimes were, by counsel out to make a name for
themselves.

The social event of the year was the Police Ball, and
although only a student still, I invited the female probation
officer who was at loggerheads with my senior. But their
enmity was no affair of mine and she and I enjoyed each
other's company – so much so that halfway through the
proceedings we tired of the jollity and decided to take a drive
out to the countryside. I had a slight cold and asked her to stop
off at my lodgings so that I could pick up a sweater, and there
now began a chapter of accidents which eventually sent me
packing with a vow never to return.

It was just after midnight when the car drew up near the
house. Although we'd had a drink or two and prudently
displayed the Police Ball tickets in the driving window, I made
sure the car was parked at the corner of the street so as not to
wake the malevolent Chuckles who slept with one ear open
listening for me in the kitchen. Relations had already reached
such a state with my landlady that I had declined her offer of
assistance with my washing, preferring to do my own on
Saturday afternoons and consequently I stowed my dirty
washing, together with my sweaters, in the space at the top of
the wardrobe where they stayed throughout the week. Now,

opening the front door as quietly as a thief, I tiptoed upstairs taking care not to switch on the electric light, glided into my bedroom, opened the wardrobe door, seized a sweater and backed down the stairs and was out of the house like a shadow without, so I thought, a movement from Chuckles. Since I had worn my only suit to the Police Ball and the following day was court day, I did not need to return there and did not do so, reporting straight to the office in the morning and from there to court. I was actually sitting in the probation officer's box when a policeman came tiptoeing in, bent double as a case was proceeding, to tell me that the senior probation officer wanted to see me urgently. All eyes turned to me as I bowed my way out, the judge looking up irritated, counsel flashing a stare as his cross-examination was interrupted, my hand involuntarily creeping to my dirty shirt. But I was allowed to leave without comment, and hastened to the office. There the typist averted her eyes, plainly disapproving of me. I had the unmistakeable feeling that I was in the cart again, the first time in years as it happened since I was busy most days and had no alternative but to lead a blameless life.

The senior probation officer had gone out of his way to welcome me and no matter what his disputes with his colleagues were, clearly thought of me as one of his own kind – a partner for his bluff, no-nonsense, northcountryman's ways. I was to be his ally against the incomprehensible perfidy of the jargon-loving psychiatric social workers then in their official infancy. We'd got on. But now he looked at me like the judge himself and came straight to the point.

'I understand that you had a woman of the streets in your lodgings last night?'

I stared at him, gulping. In the first place, whoever I had in my lodgings was no business of his; in the second, the suggestion was ludicrous and positively untrue. For once, I was stuck for words. I said nothing, blinked. But I was offended.

'Your landlady has just come in here to tell me.'

'My landlady?'

He nodded gravely, suddenly overwhelmingly pompous.

'She found a pair of your soiled underpants on the stairs and brought them in to show me. She said she heard you leaving the house at about one-thirty?'

In collecting the sweater in the darkness, I must have collected my dirty washing as well and dropped a pair of underpants on the stairs without noticing in my efforts not to disturb Chuckles. That bloody Pekinese! I suddenly saw him lying on his back, kicking his legs in the air – laughing. He could laugh. The whole thing was ludicrous.

'I was with Jean,' I said. I mentioned the name of his colleague with whom he must have seen me at the dance. I knew that because she positively did not want to join his group and drew me away from them.

'I've already been into that,' he said. 'She said she left you at midnight.'

I realised at once that she had denied being with me, perhaps because I was a mere student, younger than her, but more likely because there were also clouds gathering for her and her associate. She wouldn't want the senior to know that she had spent the night with me.

Suddenly, I began to laugh. The thought of the demure Mrs Madison wrapping my underpants in tissue, putting them into her handbag and demanding an appointment with the senior probation officer who would have been forced to listen gravely was compounded by the memory of that first landlady who had been certified within hours of my arrival. I imagined the senior dealing with the matter.

'Leave it with me, Mrs Madison. You may rest assured that the matter will be attended to! I can tell you in confidence that they took his first landlady away in a straightjacket. Please give my best regards to Chuckles!'

But the man in front of me said, 'It's not a laughing matter!'

'Why not?' I said. I was beginning to dislike him, his too easy affability, his assumption that I was always on his side, his vision of me as a younger version of himself – a Taff out of much the same stable, as he had once said. It was to take me some time to realise that he was a friendless man.

He reminded me that he would have to write a report on me at the end of my training, but I wasn't going to be blackmailed and I was beginning to dislike him more and more.

'Why don't you send the underpants to Forensic?' I said. I gave him no explanation except a flat denial. The whole affair was ludicrous, the accusation unfounded, and he could take it or leave it. My intransigence was reinforced by another inconsequential incident that happened to surface from the back of my mind. In the first week of my time there, I had come in late after a home visit to an attempted suicide and, again not wanting to put the lights on to disturb the malevolent Chuckles, I had unwittingly opened the landlady's bedroom door, realised the mistake – she was reading in bed – apologised and backed out, then forgotten about it. But she had mentioned it again as if it were a sinister threat with the likelihood of a repeat performance, perhaps as assault or worse. She must have lived on the edge of her nerves as far as I was concerned and I suddenly felt sorry for her. She belonged in Tudor tea rooms, clutching her library book, arranging the flowers in church, returning safe to Chuckles undisturbed by the likes of me. Then I thought about her journey carrying my underpants that morning and began to laugh once more.

The senior probation officer did not know what to do. I'm sure he believed me eventually because he made a special journey to London later to ask me to apply for the job he'd mentioned. He was sorry, he said then, 'for our little misunderstanding'. He should have realised the woman was neurotic. 'A poor widow,' I said. But it was an awkward morning.

When I got back that day to my lodgings, the underpants had been washed and were neatly folded in the centre of my bed. I did not speak to her for a day. The consequences of her action could have been serious for me, and if she wanted me to leave, I would have done so without her informing my employer. But I was already beyond the pale. I had about a fortnight left of my training to complete, so I asked her bluntly if she wanted me to find other lodgings. She did not. It was such a fag to move that I stayed on, but was seldom in the house. She did not apologise but she said I had upset her. I ignored her. When the time came for me to leave, she presented me with a pair of lemon-yellow woollen gloves which she said she had knitted especially for me. I was tempted to leave them wrapped in the underpants behind me when I left, but I did not do so. There had been another upset since my athletic friend had suddenly vanished without explanation to her, although he told me that there was a girl threatening him with a paternity order. My landlady was suddenly alone. When I left, she stood with Chuckles in her arms in the window. Both waved goodbye as she moved his paw in unison with her hand. Many years later when I was writing episodes for the first series of 'The Onedin Line', I had letters and comments from people I had known at this time who had recognised my name on the credits, some of whom said they always knew I would make good one day! I was disappointed not to receive one from her. She would have been delighted with the romantic atmosphere of the silliest episodes. Unwittingly I had become the personification of everything that threatened her in what I now recognise as her widow's genteel penury. I am sure she could not afford to keep up that cosy house, or the gardener, and that her days as the chief constable's neighbour, like those of her beloved Boots library, were numbered. But at the time, I closed the garden gate firmly and did not look back.

In the chest hospital, there were forms to be filled in, all kinds of details to be attended to before I even left the wheelchair after the ambulance had deposited me from the isolation hospital, and I sat in the sister's office awaiting my new bed, new ward and new companions. It was a more impersonal and clinical place. If you used the telephone, the sister disinfected it after you and the staff nurse, who bent on one knee to take my particulars beside me, was impatient.

'Were you in the Navy?'

'Does it matter?' The floaters had been shaken up by the journey and were once again active inside my eye, thrown into sharp relief by the whiter walls of this new hospital.

'Very important. You'll find out!'

'Well, yes, I was.'

'Royal or Merchant?'

'Done a bit of both,' I said, embellishing a little.

She made two ticks in the appropriate columns.

'I'll put it down. Did you have a rank?'

'I did actually, but . . .'

'Look, good boy, just let me fill these in now, and you can ask your questions when Doctor comes on rounds – that's if you can hear him.'

'Hear him?'

'He speaks very quietly and so fast you can hardly get a word in, but now I just want to get this form done, all nice and tidy for him.'

I answered all the questions. Something twigged. She lifted her lovely fresh young face and scratched her ear with the Biro.

'Oh, yes, you're the one with the Eye, aren't you? We've heard all about you!'

So I entered another ward, another world. There were no colliers in it. The patients were younger, more my own age. This hospital was situated on the coast and you could see the sea from every window; now I had but to listen and my thoughts were given wings once more so that everything that had happened to me was stirred again in my mind, but this time with a more healthy accompaniment as the Bristol Channel tides paid their twice-daily visit to the bleak shoreline beyond the window. Sometimes, you could just hear the surf rumbling on the rocky shore in the distance and I was glad of it. For a good while to come, the past was still to be infinitely preferable to the present in no matter which bed the present happened to be.

ELEVEN

The sister was brisk and efficient. She wore a starched cap and a red distinguishing belt, a mark of rank. There were staff nurses, nurses, probationers, orderlies and a precise daily routine. If before I had been spoiled because of my youth, now I was firmly put in my place. I was weighed, inspected, allotted a bed in a large ward and told to await the chest physician's examination when my questions would doubtless be answered. There was an air of confidence and matter-of-fact efficiency. The effect of entering such a large hospital with its polished corridors, gleaming windows and long spacious side wards from the previous tiny ward with its smoking coke stove and permanently closed windows was that of joining a warship from an old tug boat whose homely interior and easy-going ways were soon left behind me. I felt, perhaps for the first time, that I was really in hospital. Now there were a dozen or so men in the ward, most of them under forty. The beds were more widely spaced and at last I was free of that dreadful wheezing, the early morning orchestration of sounds from the silicotic symphony which began the colliers' day.

Immediately, my first hope was in the new registrar; later, it was vested in the chest physician whose expertise was somehow more assured than the casual manner of the local physicians whom I had met before. This was a place of well-established order and routine; surgical operations took place nearly every day and the floor below ours was nothing to do with tuberculosis but reserved for patients with heart diseases. 'The staff *run* down there!' a patient told me, as if to say that we were in some way relegated to the position of second-class emergencies and indeed on summer nights when the windows were open, you could hear the heart patients groaning after surgery and often the scampering accompaniment of the nurses' rubber-shod feet, whereas we lived in an atmosphere of comparative calm. Down below was where the action was, my informant implied, whereas all we had to do was wait while we fattened like ripe marrows on our daily injections. From him and other patients, always the first and most graphic diagnosticians, I learned that tubercular patients were only moved to this hospital if they were eligible for surgery. This implied a hopeful prognosis for the surgeon's knife was considered the most effective means of cure for infected lungs, the accompanying chemotherapy then being in its early stages. My informants then turned to questioning and attempted to place me in the ward's pecking order. Was I a double-sider?

'A double-sider?'

'Both lungs poxed?'

No, I was spared that, I said. But my eye was a distinguishing mark – even if none of the other patients seemed much interested in its condition. They couldn't see anything untoward and that was that. I quickly realised that now there was to be more privacy since medical examinations and interviews with the doctors took place in an office at the end of the corridor, out of earshot of other patients, and the whole régime was somehow more professional because of this. The facility was granted only to those who could be moved, of course, but since most of us were mobile, I felt myself to have taken a step upwards and waited eagerly for my first consultation. A few days were to pass before I met the consultant chest physician, but first I had a stroke of luck. I found that I had known the young houseman, 'Pip' Revington, as a medical student and that we had many friends in common. Suddenly, after months of adjusting myself to a sog of bedridden servility, I was freed of constrictions and able to talk on equal terms once more – in particular, to express my anxieties – an enfranchisement which was repeated when I met the consultant, Dr Len West, and his registrar, Hugh Fleming. All three sat down with me in the privacy of the examining room, so that for the first time in months I felt myself to have rejoined the human race. It was not that I had much criticism of the physicians I had seen previously, apart from the grunting uncommunicative rudeness of the German ophthalmic specialist, but now there was time to talk, a heady atmosphere of calm. The fact that neither Len West nor his registrar sprang from the British 'professional' classes – the one an Australian, the other a New Zealander who had received re-section surgery himself – undoubtedly helped diminish the traditional gap between doctor and serf. I was positively encouraged to ask questions and treated in an altogether more adult way, uniquely so in my experience of the medical profession at that time. Since I also had a friend who was the houseman, it was as if I had been removed bodily from the dungeons of ignorance and brought up free of manacles into the light, although like almost everyone else, they'd had no experience of the eye condition. When after several weeks they had received no satisfactory response to their enquiries from the ophthalmic specialist whom I had already visited, Len West slotted my file on the table and gave a typical sardonic grunt, his Australian accent a delight.

'Fuck him!' he said. 'We'll send you back to London for an opinion.'

I grinned. I felt at home. I was among friends. There was a future.

Dr Len West was fifty, forthright, sardonic, sometimes biting and sarcastic and, as I was to discover, a man of surprises for he was the only man I ever met who had read the whole of Gibbon's *Decline and Fall of the Roman Empire*. He was also a man of decisions, direct and forthright, and together with his soft-spoken registrar who was gentleness itself, a man of inexhaustible patience and kindness, he formed a team which saved my sanity after black introspective months. I was not to worry about the tubercle, they said. Now that I was taking streptomycin without ill effect, it was controllable. Normally, I would be ready for surgery in about six months. They would continue the daily chemotherapy but they wanted another opinion on my eye condition. Eventually they would send me back to Moorfields in London for an opinion about the advisability of surgery and its likely consequence upon my eye condition, but the target now was to be the infected lung.

'We'll attack it that way,' Len West said.

I was aware for the first time of a plan. I came away from the interview on my own two feet, slopping in slippers, but light of heart. Previously I had been too ill to have any sense of myself as a man with a future, the comas had precluded that as had, of course, the daily swirling of blood which obscured my vision every time I awoke. But now I was able to sleep normally, staying on my feet for much of the day, and later they discontinued the morphine eye drops so that I was once again able to read for a time. I felt some kind of normality beginning to return, especially when I was allowed on my feet for long periods. It was only at nights when I laid my head upon the pillow that the floaters came back. At last I had whole days in which to be normal, in which eventually to make my own rounds of the wards on the second floor, a process which drew me inevitably into the company of those who amused me the most. It was during this time that I met two men whose varied and picaresque lives were to be unfolded to me like the pages of a book, the like of which I had never read. They took the sting out of boredom, and remained alive in my mind for years, like a book I could never put down.

But all this was still in the future on the day of my first consultation with the medical firm, Messrs West, Fleming and Revington. That day brought an elation which was long overdue. It was to disappear again, but I returned to my bed in the long ward a man with a chance.

Somehow this ward was more impersonal than others I had been in, partly because of the greater distance between beds, partly because the patients were less communicative. There were more of them, though – some signalling at night to a wing of the women's wards which could just be seen from a side window. From my own bed I could see the dim contours of a small promontory as the light faded and, out at sea, the occasional lights of ships in passage down the Bristol Channel. When the winter fogs came, you could hear a lighthouse siren, sometimes the foghorns of vessels standing off and once, with the aid of binoculars, I made out the name of a pilot cutter, but the effect of this kind of concentration on my diseased eye was so disturbing that I did not do it again. However, in the bed near the window it was like being in a watch tower and when the fog came you would think sometimes that the ships were heading straight for you. Later, as my optimism waned and I settled in for the inevitable procession of days and months and the interminable injections of streptomycin, I began to retreat once more into memory. Now I had the backcloth for it, especially in the fog when the mist hung over the windows.

A long-term patient told me that in the previous winter a Spanish tramp steamer had gone aground nearby and the patients were provided with a daily entertainment as the whole complicated business of refloating her on falling spring tides took place under their very noses. As might be imagined, nothing is more pleasurable to long-term hospital patients than a disaster under the window. Every nautical expert in the hospital was consulted, bets were laid, a tide table produced, and arguments broke out as to the procedures being adopted, even as to why the stranding took place in the first place – as it did – on Christmas Day.

My informant had no doubts.

'Dagoes, what else?' he said. It was a familiar term of abuse for all foreigners. I could well understand the scene on that tramp steamer. Leaving the Navy to enter university, I eventually left university to board just such a tramp steamer, placing my pen on the desk after the final examination paper, leaving it there forever while I hurried to my lodgings to pick up a sea bag. I did not even allow myself time to celebrate and several hours later I stood on the bunkering jetty near the old King's Dock in Swansea, hunched in my six- year-old ex-naval raincoat, the rain coming down in a drizzle as an old Panamanian Flag tramp steamer slowly drew alongside. She was an ex-American Liberty ship, just over two thousand tons with a cargo of coal for Antwerp, her decks filthy, her ugly shape and ancient stove-pipe funnel soon to be as deeply etched in my memory as her chequered history. This was another tale created in my mind, too precious to be written for years.

That night, the elderly, grey-haired, uncertificated third mate appeared from the galley, swaying in drink, his eyes bloodshot and staring, a week's growth of beard evident. His hands shook as I jumped aboard and surveyed him rocking on his feet, blinking at me, at once fearful.

'Who the hell are you?'

'Harbour defence officer,' I said. 'We're putting guns on her and we're going to Guatemala in the morning!'

He was a grizzled man. He had been, like the boyish heroes of my youth, 'all over'. But his false teeth lifted and rattled. The smell of rum was overpowering.

'Bloody hell!' he said enraged. 'They never tell me anything!'

It was another of my jokes that went wrong. I had signed on as supernumary the previous day, but he had not been told and evidently I had arrived at an inopportune moment for twenty minutes later he punched the Captain in the throat and, a bigger crime still, knocked off the Captain's best trilby and was promptly discharged there and then on the bunkering dock together with his gear in two large metal buckets and a brown-paper parcel. But no sooner had the Captain stamped CONDUCT–VERY GOOD on his seaman's book than the rum began to speak again and once he was over the side, he stood on the jetty bawling up at us and shouting abuse from the dock.

'I always knew you was a dago bastard!'

'I verra sorry Meestaire Reecardo,' the Greek Captain said to me, rubbing his throat. 'We have theese leetle hupsets from time to time.'

That ship became my own private *Flying Dutchman*, a ghost ship whose voyages I tracked in hearsay until I could see her shuttling around the world's ports, her crew motley, her past captains a scream, all jocose and ruined men, herself a hooligan boat as her crew described her or, more graphically, a ship to sign off, not on, were it not for the fact that she flew the seductive flag of Panama which meant 'Money in pocket, no tax!' She was a rusty three-island tramp, a ship of many owners, and in her last years she kept a natural complement of men on the run – the cook had three maintenance warrants awaiting him from three estranged Liverpool wives, and there were other men with more past than future like the German third engineer. A haunted and shell-shocked man, he had a terrible nervous tremor and a pocket full of seaman's books, blotched and swollen from exposure to sea water and falling apart at their bindings. I saw them as he had clutched them in his hands after numerous shipwrecks and sinkings and, indeed, once put my arm around his shaking shoulders as he wept uncontrollably at the ship's rail when he saw a smart German liner make her way handsomely from a Belgian dock. 'One time I belong Hanza Line,' he said, and later produced the tattered discharge certificates to prove it. Now bad luck and incomprehension haunted him. The Yugoslav chief engineer was more phlegmatic although, in broken English and with a huge toothy smile, he once solemnly and seriously informed me that a portion of his penis was missing: he had seen it disappear in a Portsmouth shop doorway, a consequence – he said – of failing to obtain treatment for his seaman's 'cold' during passage on the worst convoy ever to leave Sydney when he lost three ships on three successive days. This was a tall story, but told over a Sunday treat of lunch – egg and chips – with operatic expressions, much gesticulation, a melancholy expression on his swarthy spaniel's face, his voice a falling aria of dismay, it commanded respect and we nodded solemnly. 'I seen him go on the pavement – a leetle bit of heem!' 'Yes, Chief,' we said. There was an expression of such sadness upon his face that it would have been impolite and inhuman to have raised the slightest query and, indeed, he added a telling detail: 'Down by the suspenders he fell.' It was enough. The most chaotic lives and the tallest stories belonged among the afterguard, the strange collection of nationalities who took their places in the saloon. Up for'ard the sailors were young Germans, clean in the khaki drill they had purchased in preference to the ship's kit, aloof in their youth and very sensibly keeping themselves to themselves while the down-below crowd were Somali Arabs whose king, the senior greaser, owned property and went ashore immaculate in a banker's suit, a silk shirt and sporting a green fez, once to be met by a tawny-haired blonde in Antwerp who whisked him off in a sports car. A man of impenetrable mystery, he was the Aga Khan of all greasers, deferred to even by the wounded chief engineer who put clean newspaper on his saloon chair every day, his dungerees being the oldest and filthiest I have ever seen. He picked his teeth and sometimes stabbed at his food with a clasp knife, causing eyebrows to rise, but he was the only chief engineer available and so he stayed – branded, I was to learn, with the mark of cowardice during a near-catastrophic mishap in the North Sea which had cost the real heroes their jobs. He had actually packed a battered suitcase and placed it by the lifeboat in preparation for abandonment only to have it thrown bodily into the sea by a previous mate who objected to this lack of confidence in his command – the Captain having been confined, talking to himself, in his cabin for three days with a bottle and his private horrors. There was this story and that story and I could take my choice, as indeed I did years later.

But it was never the same, never quite as it was when revealed in the half light, sitting on deck upon an upturned bucket beside a crate of beer, taking pot shots with an old air rifle at thin and stealthy rats who appeared furtively out of the open hatches once we had discharged our cargo. It was then that the newly promoted first mate – a young Cardiff man and one of the best storytellers I have ever heard – filled me in on the murky past of a ship that figures somewhere in the CIA records. She was a down-and-out old charlady of the sea who had poked her bluff and ugly nose into the rock-bottom tramping trades, so old, ugly and inefficient as to attract little attention when she went limping behind the Iron Curtain. Her masters were hard put to get crews and, until our present captain became part-owner and sometimes went over the side to chip paint himself, having got them couldn't keep them – their successive drink problems creating and recreating a maritime comedy of errors that I began to piece together until I could see them and hear them. Years later these stories were to alter my life when I wrote down a little of what I had visualised, but never as well as I should have nor, indeed, as well as I had told it myself in convivial company across the world when nights were free for yarning.

I see now that my life style was being formed in subtle ways. If I had left my pen on the examination table, never to sit another examination, my footsteps had led me into the company of natural storytellers; just as, when my body failed, so hospital became one more enclave where I was hunched in a corner, listening to men, always men, who now felt perhaps that their stories were all that would remain of themselves. Part memorial and part entertainment, these were accounts of lives recreated and suggested by incidents that long practice in the telling made come alive. All my friends were talkers, and good talk is very often the artistry of people forcibly confined without any other entertainment, in ships, hospitals and barracks. It is also unliterary and haphazard, but pointed so as to hold the attention. 'This is how I was, this is what happened!' says the victim – it usually is the victim since victims are more engaging heroes, and the man who slips on his own banana skin provided my favourite theme – the biter bit.

Of this brief period of my life I have made much since it provided me with a storehouse of memories and years later when I came to edit several volumes of Penguin sea stories, the faces of the sailors I met then returned to haunt me, as did some of the ships which they had told me about. Sometimes the faces of these men returned to me in dreams and I would remember their nicknames and the most important details about them.

There was One-Way Rogers, one of the oddest characters I ever met and who had the smallest forehead I had ever seen on a human being – so small in comparison with the rest of his body, an inch strip topped with black spiky hair that stood up like an inverted fringe, that it was as if some Neanderthal man had appeared through the doorway of the Seaman's Union. His face was pale, pinched and rat-like, and sharp, beady eyes scrutinised you like an animal's in search of food, lingering while he categorised you as friend or foe. He was an old ship's fireman, long expelled from the National Union of Seamen who continued to do him favours, however. He'd got his nickname 'One-Way' from the pre-war days of the banana boats which sailed in ballast out to the West Indies, an easy job for a fireman; but in pre-refrigeration days they shipped the fruit home green and sailed at top speed – a different story in the stokehold, and not to One-Way's liking. He'd made five outward-bound voyages but had jumped ship every time, coming home in a deck chair as a 'distressed British seaman' with the consul's help. Eventually, disbarred by the Seaman's Union, he still hovered about the Union office, hopeful of some employment on a foreign tramp which wanted a fireman in a hurry. One day I offered him a cigarette from a case. He took five. The next day a Portuguese freighter brought in a seaman with a broken leg. A whistle produced One-Way from a nearby archway where he sometimes slept and, seizing an abandoned sea bag which had been returned from the railway station, he made his way cheerfully to the jetty and the ends of the earth. Three fingers of his left hand were shrivelled and deformed, as small and useless as a baby's. The hand also bore an ugly scar as if it had been caught in machinery.

'A winch?'

'No, marlinspike.'

There was a touch of Robin Hood about One-Way. Attempting to free a prostitute from the clutches of her pimp in Marseilles, he had been taught a violent local lesson, his hand pinioned to a table. He was lucky to get away with his life.

Above all, there was my friend the Mate who was short, wiry and muscular with a crop of tousled black hair and an imp's grin. Described by his peers as 'real hard Cardiff', he was the most capable seaman for there was no task he could not himself turn a hand to, no situation in which he was not himself, the man in charge. He was about thirty then, six years older than myself. As a young apprentice he had been carried soaked and shivering in a blanket into a lifeboat from a sinking ship mined in the Bristol Channel and now he had a natural authority with a sharp turn of phrase that could, and did, stop fights among men three times his size. He was a man with standards in a ship with few of them, a little outpost of dependability, capable to his fingertips; a man in a lost line of such men whose calling had a nobility long since gone. He could handle men, any kind of man, any nationality in any shipboard situation. Hire him, you got your money's worth. Discharge him, you felt his loss. When he and the captain doubled up the watches and shared the vanished third mate's pay, it was on the first mate's shoulders that the extra burden fell; but they were broad shoulders for he was a man who seemed always to be going forward, that wagging finger poking at 'holidays' in the paintwork, his grin cheery when the dirty jobs fell twice in one day. He rolled his shirtsleeves up in the morning and rolled them down at the end of the afternoon, a gesture as predictable as bugle at sunrise and sunset. And in any weather, he was just the same. Seas rose and fell behind him, skies darkened and the wind whipped about him in angry gusts, but his grin remained. He was a natural leader, a man to be followed, and even the captain deferred to him.

He regarded me with interest but at first kept his distance because, he told me later, he had a strong suspicion that I was an intelligence agent. Why? I asked him. Because I didn't fit in on a ship like his, although he couldn't understand my presence on this voyage when we weren't sailing behind the Iron Curtain. But maybe next trip? Maybe I was making the first of several voyages?

If I was incredulous, he had the experience to back his suspicions and many stories of men recruited in the unexpected absence of regular officers when there were 'jobs' to be done behind the Curtain. Two voyages previously they had recruited a Belgian third engineer at the last minute – another like me with 'books in his kit', the mate said. When the Polish police at Stettin suspected that a stowaway had got aboard, the crew were shepherded on to the bridge by young soldiers using their rifle butts, and then brought down one by one into the saloon for interrogation. The Belgian engineer was overqualified. What was a man with a chief engineer's ticket doing as a third engineer on a dirty little tramp? The answers were plausible but while he was giving them, his cabin was being gutted. Another policeman brought in a bottle of Polish vodka and placed it upon the saloon table. The interrogating officer looked at it, then at the third engineer's discharge book.

'When did you buy this vodka?'

The Belgian gave a date corresponding to his last visit to Poland. It was all verifiable.

The interrogating officer smiled, spun the bottle around with his fingers and revealed a date stamp on the bottle's label. It had been bought several days before. This was the first lie and the beginning of the end of the third engineer. Tearing his cabin bunk from the wall, the police found a large sum of money and a false passport. Then they took him out into the companionway. Shortly afterwards, a stowaway was led out from the bilges. The Mate saw the third engineer handcuffed in the gangway. He was still cool – battered, but cool. But when he winked, he got a rifle butt in the stomach.

It was not the end, however. Months later, the mate found rolls of film hidden under the bridge lights. The ship was by now back in Antwerp. On the package was the address of a café near the docks. A visit to the café produced an American 'salesman' who eventually handed over a hundred dollars in exchange for the package. The third engineer had remained in Stettin.

In Antwerp, I was very curious to see the café and eventually we went there. It was situated conveniently near the docks in a red light area. There was a brothel to one side of it and in the window sat a huge naked girl with voluptuous thighs, but she was knitting demurely, a red light playing upon her and on the clicking needles. She beckoned us in but we declined. In the café, we ordered a brandy. There were off-duty tarts in the corner and a cat asleep on the counter. The woman behind the bar recognised the mate who enquired after the third engineer.

'He has given up the sporting life,' she said in broken English. But she ran her eyes enquiringly over me. The Third was serving a prison term, that was all she knew. There had been nothing in the papers, she said, but she had heard from his mother.

The café was drab and ordinary. The working girls were obviously tired and showed no interest in us. In one corner the red glow from the lights of the adjacent brothel reflected over a table where a slight man in a beret and a dirty raincoat sat staring into an empty cup. He did not look up when we entered. He bore an uncanny resemblance to the actor Kenneth Griffith in a character part and the whole place resembled the set of every spy film you ever saw.

But the moment we ourselves got to Belgium everything went wrong on board. On the way up the Schelde to Antwerp, the Belgian pilot who was young and immaculate in a naval uniform could not stand the fusty smell in the wheelhouse and asked for the bridge window to be lowered. He attempted this himself but it was stuck and would not open. The Captain removed his trilby and used it to shield his hand as he beat at the window with his fist. Suddenly the whole frame including the window fell outwards and smashed upon the deck below, and the wind and rain blew in for the rest of the passage.

Every morning you would go out and walk along the deck and find clumps of washers or rusty bolts which had appeared in the night as if, the Mate said, the ship was beginning to moult. As soon as we got alongside, there was bad news. No cargo had been found for us and the Captain began to worry. He was an excitable man of instant enthusiasms. During this period he found an ancient American Army spray gun which fired cartridges of DDT, and decided on a cockroach shoot; charging into the galley, he decimated everything in sight, huge clouds of spray emerging, while cockroaches fell dead in hundreds. He stood back breathlessly, an expression of complete satisfaction on his face until, to his shocked amazement, he saw one cockroach still alive and immediately began to clip on another cartridge; but the cook, who had not been consulted, sulkily killed the last survivor with a ladle. They both stood there staring at each other. I think the Captain was trying to take his mind off his immediate worries but as he had forgotten to inform the cook, all the cutlery and cooking pans were still in the galley and for weeks everything we ate was tainted with DDT. This, too, was a sign of the impending end.

When we had discharged our cargo, thick clouds of coal dust hanging like a pall over the ship, there was a problem with payment and the ship's money ran out. There was little to drink on board but the Mate and I 'won' a crate of Dutch beer from a big Esso tanker whose storekeeper I met by chance – a Welshman who had played rugby football for Cilfynydd. It was the first of many deals and during the long night the Mate and I shot rats, helping ourselves to the beer from our marksman's positions by the well deck while he told stories one after the other. There had been an alcoholic captain from Cardigan on a previous voyage who once, sailing from Swansea for Cardiff in a fog, had ended up in the Bristol Roads. The Mate called him Vasco da Gama Jones.

On Saturdays we used to go to a little bistro where there was a toothless old man who played the accordion for a glass of wine. There were two resident girls there, both huge and both five months pregnant, who had been abandoned by their lovers. We had very little money but the ship had no money at all and was soon moved to a pariah's berth where we ran out of fresh water with the result that it was almost impossible to keep clean. On Saturdays the Mate and I would do our best, but since we had been carrying coal and dust still lay everywhere, it was difficult to escape tidemarks and our fingernails and hands remained begrimed for weeks no matter how much we scrubbed them. The girls took pity on us and mine, Else, seeing the state of my hands, thought I would make a good husband because I obviously worked so hard! The girls were grateful for our attention for the bistro too, it seemed, was on the verge of bankruptcy and few other sailors ever came there. Sometimes we danced on the sawdust floor while the accordion played, the two girls resting their stomachs against us and crooning away.

'You want to look after the twins!' I would say.

'Plis? You tink I have twins?'

'He knows!' the mate would say. 'Medical man.'

'No, you kid me?'

'Yes, I kid you.'

'Tank God!'

And the arms around my neck would grow tighter, the huge bulk press forward, and once I thought I felt the baby kicking.

'I don't want "*Auf Wiedersehen*" time to come,' Else often said.

Neither did I. It was a real love affair, however temporary and bizarre; all the more so since I would sometimes look at my hand as I held hers and it was always ingrained with dirt, but she did not mind. She yearned for a regular man who would work for her, who would 'built house', she told me; whereupon I tried to look like the original Mr Do-it-yourself! The Mate and myself were well-content. The more we drank the more gentlemanly we became and it was strangely peaceful and domestic – the two of us like considerate husbands, sometimes bringing flowers we picked on the dockside and other small gifts. The little game we were acting out ended when the crew were finally sent home and the ship closed down, no cargo having been found. 'Auf Wiedersehen' time came all too soon.

I had a reunion with the Mate later in life but a mutual acquaintance told me that his wife, with whom he had been reconciled after a long estrangement, did not allow him to see any of his former acquaintances now that he had found himself a shore job. I never met his wife but she had once, he told me, broken seven pieces of a thirty-two-piece tea set over his head – a large and expensive gift which he had carried all the way from Yokohama by way of reconciliation. When I suggested that she might have had a reason, he gave that impish grin and told me that he did not have 'a chopper that stretched twenty thousand miles!'

I never saw him again, but I often used to think of him as I watched the ships move up and down the Channel from my hospital bed, recalling the lazy days in the bistro most – that accordion playing, the huge dreamy-eyed girls, and his fund of stories.

'We were in Takoradi once, tying up to tree stumps, prickly heat and brass bed knobs for currency, you know?'

It was Conradian, if a little less polished. 'We were sitting around a mahogany table that reflected the bottle . . . You fellows know?' Like Marlowe's companions, I too was invited to nod my agreement. I liked to pretend that I did know; but whether I did or not, there was no denying the pleasure. Later, however, disaster dogged me when I was persuaded to translate some of these experiences into television plays. I could never resist Vasco da Gama Jones as a character, but when he was transferred to the screen, I had the misfortune to have a famous alcoholic actor play the alcoholic captain of my creation. He, like the character he played, was a man of good intentions and for the whole of the rehearsal period, he gave a superb performance. But, shortly before transmission, extra time was required to dry out the shipboard television sets which had been hosed down to simulate bad weather. In the unexpected waiting period the actor himself took to the bottle and gave a performance so strange and full of inaudible mutterings that it was a travesty of my intentions, although a critic, later to become a leader of his profession, viewed it most favourably: 'The giant hand of Conrad lay over this tale!'

Once I found that I could read in bed, everything would change, I thought; but I soon found that I could not concentrate for long periods and had to ration myself.

Boredom set in. Then one day the probationer nurse who had been so concerned about my naval experience came excitedly to my bed.

'They're coming!' she said. She was very excited.

'Who?'

'The Watch Ashore!'

'Lucky sod!' a nearby patient called over.

It was a week before they actually came, their footsteps delicate, their tread deliberate, their lisle stockings rustling, their voices discretely lowered, their eyes compassionate but still gleaming at their find – a sailor! The Watch Ashore seemed to have a vanguard: two sixty-year-old ladies with anchor brooches in their lapels, both of whom had been on weekly visits to the hospital since the middle of the war.

'We are the Watch Ashore,' they said. 'It is an organisation that we formed and we are the mainstay of it. We comfort sailors. It is not for the Air Force or the Army, they can look after themselves. We are for sailors. Sailors! The Royal Navy and the Merchant . . . We understand you qualify on both counts?'

They were the widows of seamen, the representatives of a dwindling body of kindly housewives who came every Wednesday whatever the weather and they never came empty-handed. But they had a problem. Sailors were in short supply. In the whole hospital there were now only two: myself and a Polish seaman without a word of English who had collapsed with a lung haemorrhage in Barry Dock and remained when his ship left. We were all they had, that smiling, fair-haired boy and myself. As he could not communicate with them at all, I got the maximum attention, but we were neither of us ever without gifts.

I had cigarettes, an orange, an apple, a weekly *Reveille* and ten shillings for Christmas. For some reason he seemed to prefer *Woman's Own* and, I found out later, put it to good use. He seemed to find all women's magazines obscene and would hold them upside down, chuckling at the advertisements, particularly at the pictures of instruments for removing superfluous hair from various part of the body. I came to envy him his lack of English for, as the weeks went by, I had – alas – less and less to say to the visitors and once, to my shame, feigned sleep when the Watch Ashore came for the ump-teenth time. I heard them coming. They paused, hesitated, bent low over my bed, clucking with concern, peppermint breath wafting by my closed eyelids.

'There is something wrong with his eye,' a patient whispered.

They left on tiptoe, but the following week they brought me a magnifying glass and I felt more ashamed than ever. Then I grew jealous when the Polish seaman passed on his women's magazines to a frizzy-haired and slightly scatty Lithuanian orderly who began to visit him surreptitiously at night and sometimes obligingly slipped her hand skilfully under his bedclothes when the night staff were occupied elsewhere, and I could hear the springs of his bed rattling as she gently relieved him until – his hands frantic about her uniform blouse – he fell back gasping and cooed at the back of his throat like a contented dove. *Reveille*, alas, was not similarly negotiable.

So I settled down for another winter – at times, a winter that never seemed to end. I had by now reached what seemed the impossible weight of fourteen stone and never after lost it. I was a thin man no longer. The blood remained swirling evilly inside my eye but boredom took the place of anxiety, especially with the sound of complaining voices, some of which were querulous in the sharp, clipped accents of the docks – a taut mixture of Irish, West Country and Welsh intonations. They struck a harsh contrast with the soft valley voices of the isolation hospital. The worst were the self-styled experts.

'I've seen hundreds die with this complaint, mostly artificial pneumothoraxes, but perfectly normal people as well.'

The collective voice of the half-informed was like an insistent propaganda machine and, although you may pretend not to listen, you do listen and half-truths accumulate and coil at the back of your mind like grey snakes waiting their chance to rise again when new problems present themselves. It was best to lie low and I did so, and there followed days of absence in my mind – absence from the living who were all around me, and absence from the dead, for occasionally I received news of the old colliers I had left behind me. And they died one by one.

I seemed at times to be in limbo, a feeling that was heightened when a cubicle became vacant and I was moved into it. Now, for the first time, I was on my own, but I still tired easily and one problem was replaced by another. A man I had known in the previous hospital came to see me. A collier working on the coal face until the week before he entered hospital, he had never believed that he had tuberculosis, although doctors had found what they belived to be scars on his lung during a routine X-ray examination. He exhibited no other symptoms and was vain of his immense physical strength, even when admitted to hospital where he was given a three-month course of chemotherapy. But it made no difference to his X-ray picture. He was transferred to the surgical hospital where it was decided to perform an exploratory operation so as to examine these scars more closely. When first admitted to hospital, he had expected everything to take a few weeks; but when I saw him after an interval of several months, he was a changed man. He had lost weight, his physical strength had deteriorated. Worse, his nerve had gone and he had lost all his previous confidence, the absolute conviction that he was not tubercular.

'My grip has gone,' he said hoarsely.

He had been a well-built, swarthy and handsome man with massive forearms and a great breadth of shoulder, but now another man looked at me, a hunched and haunted figure, his face pale, his eyes staring.

I said the sensible things, expressed my confidence in the registrar, but he had passed beyond such urbane reassurances.

'I can feel myself going,' he said.

He was in a ward near my cubicle and I told him to come and see me whenever he felt like it, especially if he wanted to get away from the complainers, and he left, walking away like a sick man with a tired tread and bowed shoulders.

That evening I had a sixth sense that something was amiss. I looked for him in his ward. He was not there. I looked in the washrooms and I could not see him, although one lavatory door was seemingly permanently locked. I looked underneath it, stooping hurriedly and causing the blood to whirl in my eye once more. I was not supposed to stoop. But then I saw his slippers through a haze of blood and swirling black matter that never left me.

'Come on, you bugger!' I said. 'Out!'

Eventually, he unlocked the door. He had two Swan Vesta matchboxes full of sodium amphytol tablets, about thirty in all, and a glass of water. He had hoarded the tablets. He could not face the idea that he had tuberculosis like everyone else. I took the tablets from him and dropped them down the lavatory. They did not disappear when I flushed the lavatory. I had to open every one of them, before they disappeared. I told him I would tell no one and I did not, but he had to face things, I said. He was letting the boys down, I said, for he had told me that his shift mates made voluntary deductions from their own pay and every week made a substantial contribution to his wife and family. He was soon operated upon. His fears proved groundless. He was free of disease, the X-ray showed the scars of some colliery accident. They were not lesions. When he came to say goodbye, there were tears in his eyes; but my own condition had not improved one iota. The Conservative MP for the constituency had just made a VIP visit, hurtling around the wards, his breath hoary with old port. He was a kindly man, well-meaning, but he took one look at me, at my baleful stare, and did not stay long. I did not like being inspected. Then came my collier friend whose tears I abhorred.

'I've just had half the Cabinet here,' I told him. 'Now it's the working class drooling over the bed! What next!'

I still slept for inordinate amounts of time and I thought I had finally mastered the difficult art of remaining asleep when my pulse and temperature were taken in the early mornings. But one morning I bit the end off the thermometer, swallowed it and induced a general panic, having to eat half a load of bread as a palliative. Nothing serious happened but it added to my mood. Days followed days, an endless procession; then, travelling like a bug under escort, I was sent in a locked railway compartment to Moorfields Eye Hospital where I was once again scrutinised under a barrage of ophthalmic lights as doctor after doctor examined me. They were asked for an opinion on the likely effect of resection surgery upon my diseased eye, but once more they could not say. Nobody knew. I was returned like a parcel, but the medical team decided that I should be operated upon and the diseased segment of my lung removed – eventually. But there were months to go yet, and the days of absence continued.

I watched the seasons change, patients come and go. Once a Cardiff probation officer came to see me, alerted by the National Association of Probation Officers of which I was still a member. I was very conscious of his embarrassment. What could he do? There was nothing to be done.

'Is there anything you need?'

It was all I could do not to give a facetious reply. It was as if I had crossed over from officer to client, exchanging roles, and had become coarsened in the process. I thanked him, watched him leave, amused myself by composing the letter he would write. Somehow I knew that my probation days were over. It was not just the all-pervasive lack of strength which had lasted for over a year now, but that other, subtler things were happening to me; and, immediately, I did not see how I was going to get through the next months in hospital. I felt more isolated than ever and suddenly I had an untimely reminder of my own past which was also to lie heavily upon me in these, the worst months.

One night I looked curiously through the window of the next cubicle to mine after a new arrival was reported and was surprised to see the wan face of a schoolmate, an exact contemporary who had been crippled since infancy with a tubercular hip. I did not even know he was in the hospital and immediately remembered him as a boy, his pronounced limp, his self-effacing manner. He had been a cripple all his life and I remembered his days as a silent onlooker to all our doings in school, in the billiard hall, in the dances which he sometimes attended though he never danced. He was always pale, his face thin and sensitive, unchanged now in his early twenties. When I went in to see him, his eyes filled with tears in front of me. He had heard I was in the hospital, he said, but he had been in a different ward and nobody had passed on his messages. A section of his lung had recently been removed, but he was diabetic and the surgical wound had opened when he was roughly handled by one of the orderlies who was bringing him in a wheelchair to another floor. Now he was growing weaker. The wound would not heal and the strength was ebbing out of his body as he began to decline. I went in and sat with him, at first chatting in a desultory way, when he suddenly blurted out:

'I wanted to see a Ponty' boy.'

I did not know him well although we had been in the same classes and, of course, shared the same teachers. Now we reminisced and once again my old headmaster's voice came forth as I recreated him, my party piece; but I soon saw it was dangerous to continue as my friend's laughter only increased his pain. I stopped.

'Go on,' he said.

'No, Dennis.'

He had no stamina and no luck. He died the next night. I went in to see him once more. He held my hand shyly. He knew he was dying. His lips were moving inaudibly, murmuring my name, asking me to go on with the story I had abandoned the previous day, but I could not. I pressed the bell as he began to go into a coma and when the staff came, I slipped my hand away, feeling his fingers tighten then relax. I was the last person he saw in his life and he was glad of me, I knew. He was so quiet, innocuous, gentle, accepting. He was grateful for each day and that in a life in which each day was a struggle, for he was precluded from many things. I thought and thought about him and felt ashamed of my own demands upon life and people.

It was the lowest point of my time in hospital, worse than the night of my haemorrhage because now I had more time to think. Then it seemed to rain for a month and I lay in bed listening to the rain beating down. The cubicle had a glass wall on the seaward side and since the main door had a circular window, the impression of a ship was strong. But it was a ship without a destination and I lay like a prisoner on one side – I could never lay flat on my back since that seemed to activate the floaters – and I was more depressed than ever.

One night the male nurse was near, saw my light, my hunched figure sitting crouched on the bed, and came in anxiously.

'Are you all right?'

I shrugged my shoulders. There are days when you cannot be cheerful or give the automatic response.

'Shall I ask for sleeping tablets?'

That was a cop-out, I thought then, although later I was to demand – and steal – painkillers.

'No, thank you.'

'Would you like a cup of tea?'

'You're a prince!'

Had a restless night, he would write in his report; but I usually settled down again. Sometimes I would invent phrases, the awfulness of awful, but describing a condition does not alter it. However, it was during this time that I must have grown a little stronger and, as the old salts would say, took a grip of myself. I began to investigate other areas of the hospital, my footsteps taking me down unexplored corridors into other wards and cubicles, one of which I infiltrated like a secret agent.

And very soon my salvation occurred and I felt as if I had entered the pages of a living book where, on some days, it was as if its principal characters were writing me.

TWELVE

Adjacent to the main ward there were small side wards, some with only two or three beds, where the most seriously ill patients were confined. Their doors were always open, but the entrance would be blocked by screens if visitors were not permitted. I was carrying magazines back to the recreation room one day when I received a wink from the doorway of one of the small two-bedded wards. I had previously walked past it and often heard groans from within. I knew that the doctors hurried there frequently, but now the screen was pulled back and a man I knew greeted me, jerked his head and winked to indicate that I should enter.

The wink was Sparkie's wink and Sparkie, a short, stooped, often enraged, ginger, Cardiff man, I had seen before since he had recently become mobile and often helped out wheeling trays of cocoa about the wards, generally busying himself – especially when these little tasks gave him access to the kitchens or the sister's office. He was, he told me, 'a double-sider' and had already received resection surgery to remove diseased segments from one lung and was now awaiting a similar operation on the other. Hence the slight stoop, the careful walk with an elbow often held up protectively around his ribs, but somehow you never thought of him as vulnerable. Sparkie had a wide fleshy mouth which often twisted caustically as he expressed his disapproval of whatever was currently bothering him. Like his spiky ginger hair, he also had a wiry and resilient street-corner toughness which went back a long way for he was a graduate in institutional survival. He alone had obtained one of the maroon, US Navy, corduroy dressing gowns, now a rare hospital issue for the penniless and which still survived the war, and he very frequently carried

226

concealed parcels – little tins of food, goodies he had bartered or 'won' as he made his way busily about the hospital as soon as he could walk. He was a wheeler and dealer, took around the tea trolley like a street-corner vendor, with his cheeky cry, 'Tea's up!', his head bending inquisitively as yours did if you happened to open your private locker, his grin as he inspected your possessions as infectious as a clown's. He alone could get notes through to the women's wards, lay a bet or rustle up the odd bottle of the flat hospital stout and he was always first with the gossip about the orderlies, the nurses or any upset that occurred down the length of the wing. He had an engaging laugh which began at the back of his throat, a coarse worldly cackle that went with the wink, and he was the kind of man whose life story falls from his lips within minutes of meeting him – rare and priceless details like fine pearls scattering rapidly in quick succession as if from the broken thread of an old necklace. He had been, he gave you to understand, 'around', and he'd already proudly described himself to me as 'one of the Cardiff lags' in the bland way a man might describe his lifelong association with Rotary or some estimable charitable organisation. He had served four years in Wormwood Scrubs prison for his part in a night-time robbery on a bank safe and had once, as an acetylene burner operator, borrowed the Welsh Gas Board's equipment and placed himself in reserve at the Epsom home of a notorious London criminal waiting for a safe to materialise, all on a handsome retainer. The gang boss, as he told me with relish, had twenty suits and 'more pairs of shoes than you could get on a centipede!' He knew, for risking the wrath of some armed minder he'd crept upstairs and opened a sliding wardrobe in an elegantly carpeted bedroom, his eyes glistening as he surveyed the spoils including a camel-hair overcoat and a wide range of two-tone shoes. The promised safe did not materialise, 'grassers' or informers had done their work on that particular job, but he was handsomely paid nevertheless and returned home jauntily, well-pleased after a weekend 'on standby', whistling down the old drover's road to Wales in the Gas Board's van, clinging to a precious insight into the life of the other, criminal half that caused his surly mouth to relax and a sentimental glow to come to his eyes when he described it.

As a crook off and on since childhood, he only regretted his failures. Prison was the occupational hazard, 'college', as he referred to it unrepentantly.

His own career was spotty and chequered. He had, in the war, once cleaned out the headquarters of the Women's Land Army in Cardiff of all their clothing coupons and as many green woollen jumpers as he could carry, but he was now satisfied with the brief glimpse of real success in recall, the suits, the shoes, 'all the Scotch you could drink'. He was, of course, a Tory and would say, 'The working man will have the shirt off your back!', a favourite expression which he often uttered with the air of a man a cut above the mumbling bedridden socialists in the main ward who did not know how to reply to him for he overawed them. He was in his late thirties then and spoke with a rich Cardiff dockland accent, sometimes affectedly sticking out his little finger when he would deliberately flick cigarette ash over the hospital floor in one of his High Tory moods. The bond between us was a fine one. He'd found out that I played contract bridge using Ely Culbertson's system of honour tricks and not, as he put it, 'the bastard points system', then regarded as inferior. He had attended bridge lessons regularly in prison and played boldly with a photographic memory for cards already dealt, although he sat all the time with one eye wandering shiftily below that frizzy basin haircut like a Sunday afternoon street gambler ever alert for the sound of uniformed feet. He was also not averse to asking for a light for his cigarette when he would lean over you (and your cards) with a disarming grin and a throaty chuckle that seemed to say, 'Takes all sorts!'

It was his philosophy (and mine) but on the day when he bade me enter his little side ward, I saw him in a new role, that of factotum for his wardmate who lay flat upon his back without a pillow on a low bed.

'Come in and meet His Nibs!' Sparkie said. He inverted his palm, winked once more, this time proprietarily. He might have been a society hostess. He also liked being a Man Friday as I soon saw.

His Nibs was then about seven stone, thin, gaunt, emaciated, his face lined, occasionally wracked with pain, his thick black curly hair sitting limply like a mat upon his

228

pinched egg-white features, only his dark glittering eyes rueful and amused as he looked up at me. The bed sheets were drawn up to his chin and from his side, stretching below the sheets, a rubber tube extended to an electric pump and a large glass jar on the floor below the bed, the mechanism of the pump ticking away sinisterly as fluid was withdrawn from his lung via a wound kept deliberately open in his side. He had, save for those eyes which were sharp and intelligent, an exhausted look on his face that I had seen before and I thought at once that he was dying, for you could smell the sickly odour of disinfectant and worse – the wound had its own foetid smell of pus. At first there was no strength to his voice, just the laconic interest of those bright animated eyes. He was so frail then that you had no idea of the man, nor his spirit, nor indeed any hint of the laughter he could induce, just that attractive curly black hair tousled against the bed sheets. Every movement caused him to wince and everything that was said was accompanied by the sinister ticking of the pump. Swirls of blood like coloured thread twisted lazily in the liquid in the glass bottle below the bed. It was difficult to keep your eyes away from it. In an uncanny way it reminded me of Broncho's jar of preserved worms which I had seen by the light of naptha flares in the market stalls of my youth, a grim and unexpected reminder of the full circle we all must complete.

'Monty,' Sparkie said impressively. 'Montague Rice-Lewis Hesquire!'

I should have known that Sparkie would not have appointed himself factotum to anyone. A man like Sparkie was hardened to institutional life, the kind of man whose eyes flickered over you, sensing threat or gain, only rarely – if ever – giving himself over to worship. But His Nibs, Sparkie's own title, was the prince of victims with a certain farouche air and an insouciant arrogance which remained despite his predicament. One glimpse of that pale face resting weakly on the pillow was enough to tell you that he had once been a handsome man and those swarthy good looks and black glittering eyes made him the kind of man who is always attractive to a certain kind of woman; nor could you be in his company long without discovering, even in this extremity, that here was a man of parts. Later I was to discover a bar-room charm, a way of talking that spelt fast cars and easy money, the kind of placeless man that is nevertheless associated with racy talk and risk-taking, perhaps a racecourse man, certainly a car sales-man. But at the same time he had an engaging way of depreciating himself as well as everyone else, a raffishness that was as welcome in the despondent atmosphere of hospital as was Sparkie's belligerent and aggrieved air. They were neither of them proper men. About them both, there was always 'talk'; none of it was as engaging as their own.

When I first entered the cubicle, I thought Monty was dying and would naturally want me to back out; but he had no such intention.

'What have we got here?' he said weakly, in barely more than a whisper.

Sparkie knew about me, or at least as much as my record cards told him. He had his sources of information, even of extra food. For he once raided the refrigerator in the sister's office which kept such titbits as pineapple chunks and cream for the 'Special Diets' or those in particular need ('Nothing more fucking special than me!' was his unashamed motto). His language, invariably obscene, was a bizarre comfort to me now that I had recently been companion to so many proper men.

'A probation officer,' Sparkie said to Monty. 'Thought you might need one. You've had everything else!'

'I do declare!' Monty said.

'Sit down' said Sparkie, and added a perennial enquiry. 'How are we off for fags?' In Sparkie's company, your property became collective. It was his signature tune. 'How are we off for fags, matches? Got any stamps, have we?' And then that self-depreciating throaty chuckle.

I sat down, produced a cigarette for Sparkie. We all smoked all the time we were in hospital. It helps you bring up the phlegm, we said knowledgeably. We never thought of giving up the habit. Neither did the doctors encourage us to. Most of them smoked heavily themselves.

'Try him with a Welsh cake?' Monty said.

'His old lady brings them Wednesdays,' Sparkie said.

'Inedible but, as they say, the thought is there,' said Monty ironically.

Sparkie got out the tin box. 'Go on, fill yer boots!'

I took one. It was tasty.

It wasn't long before Sparkie, who had heard about my eye condition, volunteered his own cheerful diagnosis: syphilis! Monty looked at me interestedly. They were both disappointed when I told them about Eale and his mysterious disease. Neither I nor anybody else seemed to know very much about it and the only definitive sentence I have ever heard on the subject was many years later: 'There's a lot of it in Katmandu!' – this from a consultant who could not, or would not, enlighten me further. But that afternoon, and on many subsequent afternoons as Monty grew stronger and finally began to put on weight in leaps and bounds, eventually recovering his own arrogant self, we began what was to become an irreverent threesome.

'Monty's been in the mob,' Sparkie said. 'See his chest? Still shrapnel in there! Long-Range Desert Reconnaissance. You ought to see his back!'

'No, thank you,' I said.

Monty had been in recent dire straits. An operation to remove infected ribs had nearly been disastrous and for days his life had hung by a thread. Artificial respiration had eventually produced the foulest language in the post-operative ward and worse abuse than was usual even in that place. He had attacked the physiotherapist as soon as he found words, and strength:

'Keep your virginal hands off me!'

'He bloody told them!' Sparkie said with admiration. When the crunch came Sparkie, vociferous in private, was publicly inclined to hang back. There was what he was going to tell them, and what he actually said. In any group of men, he was the man who prepared bullets for others to fire. But he was also a witness, and an eager commentator on Monty's story and Monty's doings, especially when Monty's bouts of weakness came in waves and sometimes he could not finish a sentence. When Sparkie set up Monty's bed tray at meal times, propping him up with his own extra pillow, he was gentleness itself. But then Monty would take hold of a fork and push food aside like a wealthy client in an inferior restaurant – and then Sparkie would eat it, wolfing it down when the nurses were out of sight.

Sometimes Monty's bouts of coughing were painful to see, his thin body heaving, spittle forming on his lips, often blood-flecked, that tousled hair falling over his emaciated features, his eyes bright and staring. But he would recover and push aside the sputum pot as if it was some priceless piece of antique silver. Then he would ease himself to a sitting position when he could compose himself, shaking his head like a swimmer emerging from the water. Sparkie would gauge his moods, egg him on when the moment was right.

Information came at different times; in Monty's hearing, and out of it. There was, as ever in hospital, very little privacy.

'Come from a very good family,' Sparkie said once with a coarse cackle. 'Up your way somewhere, the valleys. Old man a colliery manager. There's two Sirs in the family.'

'Sirs?'

'Yeah, you know, Sirs.'

'Knights, you mean?'

'Uh?'

'Knights of the realm. They used to call Cardiff the City of Dreadful Knights!'

'No, no, his lot are all very Welshic, Doctors an' the Bank an' that. Big Bugs, all of 'em.' Sparkie was clearly impressed and two of Monty's relatives, if not household names, were well-known enough – the kind of men prevailed upon to address St David's Day banquets, one a public servant.

But Monty's own father had died when he was a small boy and when he came to talk of this period in his life, it was in a mocking and offensive way.

'Father died and mother married again – absolute bastard, a nose picker!' Monty said with a grin. His step-father was a Methodist minister and this set Sparkie off.

'You knows the sort, Al'?'

'Well . . .'

'Washed his hands of our Monty early on,' Sparkie said; 'so our Monty had to go away to school, dint you, Mont'?'

Sparkie was presenting Monty to me on a plate like a proud impresario. It was as if he had discovered him. 'Tell him!'

'Mother, fair play, didn't want me mixing locally, not in the valleys – no offence to you, old man! – but, Christ, that bloody council school was full of nose pickers too!'

'So off he goes, away to school with his tuck box!' Sparkie said, chortling. It was a story he had heard before and one which he never tired of hearing. Now his carrot head bobbed with pleasure, the thick lips drooling with anticipation. 'Go on, tell him!'

Monty had been an unhappy public schoolboy. Later I filled in the details from a most unexpected source, his mother. She had been hard-pressed to pay the school fees, using up precious insurance money, but he had gone in neat blazer, a purple cap and gartered stockings – and indeed, the tuck box. But as the years went by he'd made dismal progress, survived, run away, returned, survived again, then – as Monty himself said – he'd run into a little local difficulty.

'Tell him! Tell him!' Sparkie urged. He could never wait for the end.

'A little local difficulty with one of the maids,' Monty said.

'In the airing cupboard!' Sparkie added with relish. By now he was part of an act, a second narrator: 'Matron caught him after Footer! *At it!*' Sparkie said in that rasping superior accent. What Sparkie liked about Monty was, he told me, that Monty spoke 'like a real Gent!' He had himself been away to 'Collidge' at an early age, but the story which he privately called 'Our Monty on the job in the airing cupboard', was like a bedtime treat to him, a private confidence that became a public entertainment.

This was my introduction to His Nibs and very soon in the little side ward at the end of the corridor we three began to recreate our collective pasts, enumerating the footsteps we had taken – above all, the naiveties of our very different expectations. Monty, the senior member, was fifteen years older than myself, but that was the least of what divided us. For Monty's life was unique in its pretensions; representing, as it did, a kind of flawed progress which began with a conscious and encouraged denial of his roots, it was ultimately a warning against all effort. It was also a crowded life into which the world's events had intruded, ill winds often arriving as if from an angry holocaust, blowing down upon him and singling him out. Twists of fate like angry bees had stung where it hurt, and in the first weeks of our acquaintanceship, I began to piece them together.

233

At first it was like clothing a skeleton for he lay immobile for months, often gasping like a fish on a slab and cursing with pain when that rubber tube was removed – his language foul and temper abominable at times, but his will to survive magnificent. His tongue was the only part of his body which he could control and his offensiveness was somehow necessary. Whatever he was, I thought, he was a survivor, a card, a man who would emerge eventually, albeit in tatters, but still holding trumps, his mocking restless spirit cloaking a courageous refusal to die. I had reservations early on, but he had guts if nothing else. It was the rarest of commodities.

But all these things I came to know slowly and what was at first so interesting was that everyone who knew Monty spoke of him as a kind of celebrity. He fascinated Sparkie and it was not until my visits became more frequent and we formed a kind of club that I understood why. Monty's life, as revealed by Monty to Sparkie, was like a book the pages of which Sparkie could not wait to turn. There was – as revealed – disaster and surprise on every page and the editing imposed by Monty's long periods of exhaustion or pain only served to whet Sparkie's appetite: the pages were enough of a rarity to provide a treat.

Sister, I knew, treated him with kid gloves and kept her distance, but she did that with others. What surprised me was that Monty's mother, whom I also came to know slightly, also spoke of Monty as a celebrity and appeared to have done so all his life. Here, perhaps, was the key, I thought. His Nibs had always been His Nibs. But no matter what I thought, Monty, even in that emaciated condition, seemed to give off an aura, a sense of difference, and it fascinated me. If I read more into the pages than Sparkie did, it did not matter. For both of us, in our condition, he was a bestseller in months when there was nothing else on the library shelves. I knew, and I had already had enough of the well-thumbed book of myself.

Sparkie had taken over Monty, lock, stock and barrel and one of the main reasons, I discovered, was Monty's mother, to whom he was very attentive. He it was who anticipated her coming when he would hurry down to the visitors' entrance to meet her like a consultant who was taking advantage of the temporary benefit of having a royal patient. First he would examine Monty's watch to check the time, bundle on the maroon dressing gown, slick down that spiky ginger hair and then he would be off, hurtling down the corridor, his ankles visible above the slopping slippers, an elbow protecting his damaged ribs, his whole frame bent over like an injured hockey player's, all the time licking his lips with anticipation.

Mrs Rice-Lewis had come to depend upon him, she told me, and she seldom came empty-handed, perhaps sensing that Sparkie would not allow it. Monty, left behind and flat upon his back near that constantly ticking pump, took little trouble with his own appearance, although Sparkie shaved him on visiting days. But even flat on his back, Monty retained a certain aura. When free of pain and amused, he would reach for a sputum pot, shooting the cuff of his pyjama top as he might when stretching for a large gin and tonic. He was a man of many such mannerisms.

The real conundrum, however, was Monty's mother. She was everything which you associate with the stereotype of the Welsh Mam: a short, stout, dowdy little woman in black astrakhan, her homely bespectacled face under the inevitable nondescript hat as plain as a currant bun. She had his dark eyes, but they had long lost their spark. In her seventies, her speech was slow and simple and she made masterly under-statements. You could just see her as a Methodist minister's wife, a benign support and prop. Respectability might have been her middle name, in strange contrast to her only son. I could imagine her saying of Sparkie, 'He's a bit of a rough diamond, but he is very kind to our Montague.' It was true. She was a woman who thought the best of people, often waving back from the visitors' bus to which Sparkie returned her, while he called hoarsely with that crooked grin, 'Don't forget the old Park Drives, Mrs L! Must have our fags!' And she seldom forgot them.

When he met her, Sparkie would seize her shopping basket and sometimes take her by the arm. Sometimes he gave his consultant's report on the week.

'Bin having a few restless nights. Off his food too. Can't get him to touch nuthin!' This with a look into her shopping bag.

'Oh, dear . . .'

Once I heard him warning her.

'He's not looking a bit too clever. You'll have a little bit of a shock.'

She was never upset, just concerned, often replying with one of her masterly understatements.

'Montague has always been very difficult. He has not looked after himself.'

And Sparkie would nod gravely, hoarding these statements for repetition when Monty described one of his escapades. Sparkie also questioned her at times. He had a habit of tucking his thumbs into the folds of that maroon dressing gown, nodding gravely like counsel addressed by a judge.

Monty's step-father was still alive but he'd had enough, she implied, adding, 'We've done everything we can for him.'

Counsel would nod his head sagely. It was a pantomime, but a necessary one, and it took me a long time to realise that Mrs Rice-Lewis was as much a part of it as Sparkie. She too, I came to suspect, was a woman of disguises, not the blank innocent she appeared.

In time I came to see her often myself, but Sparkie was unwilling to share her and I have a suspicion that he had told her my eye condition was infectious, if not worse. That way he hedged his bets as a precaution against my taking over his role, and she once pointedly said that she was very glad that Monty had Mr Sparks to help him. Sparkie preened himself.

'Oh, we've got to help each other out. I just does my little bit!'

When we expressed an interest in Monty's school career, half-encouraged by Monty who was glad of anything to break the long painful silences between them, she brought in various memorabilia of his childhood which she had kept. They included some of his school reports, various photographs, and a War Office telegram informing her that he was 'missing presumed killed'. We all looked at it but she had a strange absence of feeling, as when she produced other such souvenirs. It was very puzzling. She seldom sat alone with Monty; Sparkie was always there and later myself, and our presence was encouraged by both of them. If Monty grew bored, Sparkie would assume his consultant's role again and get to his feet, inspecting his patient with a proprietary air as if to say, 'I think he's a little overtired.' She very seldom went to the

236

sister's office to receive or request information. She left it to Sparkie, and Sparkie never failed her. There were times, especially when Monty said very little, when you felt she had come to see Sparkie as much as Monty and that she depended on him. It was touching, but it was also very funny as Monty and I both knew. We also knew Sparkie in all his moods.

Sometimes before visitors came, he would croon an obscene version of a popular song to annoy one of the foreign-born cleaners:

'"Wimmin do get weary . . . wearin' the same fuckin' dress . . .

So . . . try a lil tender-ness!"

How are you today, Fifi, my darlin'?'

Like us all, the consultant in his maroon robes had another side; but he was a constant and predictable tonic, and Monty's mother felt this too.

It was Monty that remained the enigma. If it is hard to describe the effect of that slight man laying prone on the low bed, it is harder still to remember the sequence of events when there were really no events, apart from his slow recovery. Days passed, then weeks, and I became a constant visitor, taking away precious details of both their lives which I hugged to myself, turning them over and over in my mind when I returned to my own cubicle until I saw, or thought I saw, the high and low moments of Monty's life as if illuminated by a bright light. I did not realise then quite why I was attracted or had fallen under a spell, but I had little else to occupy me.

Our group sessions became an irreverent court of enquiry into the most bizarre strokes of fate which had fallen upon us and, as club members, we reserved the right to exaggerate and bend the truth for the sake of a smile as we relieved the weight of the leaden hours. There was this story, and that. Monty kept mentioning his influential relatives. Severely wounded in the desert campaign in North Africa, he had eventually found his way to a base hospital where a relative of his mother's operated upon him, performing a marathon operation whose scars remained. But he soon contracted tuberculosis, was returned to an army hospital in England where he befriended an ex-jockey and lived on his wits, profiting by inside information until he was finally invalided home. His life thereafter was a chapter of accidents since, as his mother said, he refused to accept the fact that he was an invalid. Now he went cheerfully and recklessly to the dogs. Once, following his arrest by the police after a bad car smash when drunk, his mother advised him to see yet another relative – the chairman of the magistrates' bench in a town near my home. Monty did so and after an amiable luncheon when he exaggerated his war experiences, he was heavily fined and disqualified for seven years.

'Seven years?' Sparkie said. 'Lucky you had that bite to eat then! Otherwise, it would've been the rope!'

It reminded Sparkie of the story of the old lag bemused by the new Preventive Detention Act when a man could be sentenced, not for a single crime, but for his entire criminal record. Custodial sentences were regarded as an offence against natural justice since they not only took note of the present crime, but others for which sentences had already been served. But Sparkie put it his way.

'Heard about Alfie?'

'What did he get?'

'Twelve years.'

'*Twelve years for nicking a shirt?*'

'Yeah, but it had two collars!'

Sparkie preferred to listen than to talk and he would sit absolutely still, nodding gravely, and occasionally he would put one hand at the back of his neck as he scratched it, holding the elbow with the other hand, rather like chimpanzees do at the zoo. There were times when Monty's eye caught mine and we would look at Sparkie and collapse laughing, especially when there were matters which Sparkie did not fully understand. But he would respond with relish.

'Think I'm bent? Take a look at yourselves, especially Squinty boy here!' he would say, referring to me; and it was true, I was often forced to squint.

But never in my life have I seen such an appreciative audience as Sparkie. He was the kind of man of whom playwrights dream, responding instantly as if to a physical action aimed at his body, his laughter instinctive, erupting in spontaneous flow, his reduced lung capacity compensated by the fact that his whole frame shook, rumblings and wheezings coming from his shrunken chest like notes from an organ on whose keyboard something heavy had fallen. And his eyes literally lit up, the pupils sharpening to a fine point, that puckering mouth relaxing its normal surly pout and opening wide so that his broken teeth were fully exposed as he literally dribbled his appreciation. He gave himself mind and body to the performer.

Although Sparkie was an enthusiast, it was Monty I thought about most when I returned to my cubicle, going over the day's takings, as it were. It was the little boy in the sailor's suit who had stood so solemnly outside the colliery manager's detached house that interested me. I had been like that too. It was that persona that would never be the same again. His was, I supposed, a childhood like any other until his father's death which was followed by the slow deterioration of his conduct in the local council school. 'He couldn't seem to concentrate,' his mother said. Monty put it differently when she was not there, and although they had high hopes for him when he went away to school, they did not materialise. Monty was miserable, but in those years he must have acquired the first of the layers which we carry with us and which was to last ever after, colouring his speech and many of his attitudes. Even when unhappy, he always regarded himself as a cut above the others and although he found some place for himself, there were dissatisfactions early on. Mrs Rice-Lewis had kept some of his school reports: 'Montague is a natural rugby player and an asset to the Second XV.' This was familiar enough to me and now and again I liked to think that there was always a chance of things going right in Monty's life. Later when he was on his feet and able to move around, I could imagine him as a natural rugby player – one of those lean and dashing three-quarters whose confident movements made them so elusive, their intentions ever hard to predict. He had the aggression and the cheek to succeed. Young and fit, his confidence would have made him a very dangerous player. But he was untypical in everything. He did not really enjoy playing rugby, and used his prowess only when it suited him: 'He is not a team man and did not pull his weight in the School Sports.' I could imagine it. By this time in my life I was not a team man either, and neither was Sparkie. He had never played any game in his

239

life, except card games. Sport was for mugs. Nothing in it for him.

Having been hurt at a young age, Monty also learned to hurt and he was, even in that prone and desperate posture when attached to his pump, hated by some. The public school had given him a certain manner, the way he sometimes had of addressing people as if from an impenetrable distance which infuriated the nursing staff. It was the kind of voice which created menials on the spot. He spoke down to people but when he wanted to ingratiate himself, his voice was subtly different and confidential, as if he were letting you into secrets. At the same time he was ever the car salesman who is kept for the wealthier clients or the most seductive model with the concealed defects. Ordinary people saw something superior in him. It was what repelled them and yet they were attracted when that voice softened. This is what had happened to Sparkie. But there were deeper things which bound them together: their humour and a joint conviction of the malevolence of fate.

The weeks went by. Monty had his tube removed but he was still in such pain and so weak that there was no cause for celebration, which was just as well for the tube was reinserted again as the lung did not clear of fluid; having been long-damaged, it was constantly prone to infection. Now Mrs Rice-Lewis came more regularly but her visits palled. Sparkie, who had no visitors himself, had found another source of supplies and was not as attentive as usual. Sometimes Monty's mother came twice a week and now I sat with her, but I did not have Sparkie's charm and, with Monty so weak, I began to feel that she was strangely insensitive for he was unsuccessful in trying to persuade her not to visit so often. Monty was long-estranged from his mother and there were moments, as she sat by his bed when he lay with his eyes closed, that produced the uncharitable feeling that her visits were not a simple act of goodwill, but a wish to be in on the last act. It was a suspicion sharpened by watching her sitting there mutely with that blank face when he was wracked with pain during a relapse – and he had several. I felt that she had always predicted this kind of end for Monty and had only come to confirm it. No doubt she had suffered much because

240

of him – he had been near death on many occasions – but it seemed to me, now more than ever, that there was an absence of any real feeling between them. On her part the rote movements, the gifts he did not want, the cakes he would not eat, were all a token. She was surely more intelligent than she appeared but perhaps, sitting there in silence, her hands composed, her face blank, concealing herself behind those quaint sayings, she too was exhausted. If it appears uncharitable now, it did not then. We had all been in hospital for over a year and, like all long-term patients, we had formed a world of our own and she was an intruder.

Then Monty began to recover again, but as he grew stronger he grew more bored. He began to fill out, washed and shaved himself, even managed a cigarette – a real sign of health! But then he had words with Sparkie. On the really bad days Monty was sometimes incontinent, especially if some upset had occurred when the tubes were removed or the bottle changed. If the staff were overworked and Sparkie was out of the cubicle, Monty would be alone for long periods and when Sparkie returned, he would complain, 'The niff I've got to put up with in here!' He was not always good-humoured and, like two scarecrows, they would come to the verge of a quarrel, only drawing back because Monty tired rapidly when he would relapse into himself, leaving Sparkie to make the conciliatory gesture. In recall, we tend to think of all days in hospital as being the same, but each day there was a new annoyance. Monty was growing stronger, though, and he was a man who took things into his own hands. One day during one of the long periods of silence between them, Monty picked up a newspaper and feigned surprise.

'Good God!'

'What's up?' said Sparkie, the carrot head lifting above a comic.

'You wouldn't believe it!'

'What?'

'Mother's up again.' Then he named the Cardiff stipendiary magistrate. 'Shoplifting. It's the third time. She'll go down!'

'Get away?' said Sparkie, disbelieving.

Monty became strangely silent.

'You're not bloody serious?'

Monty made no reply, relapsing into himself. When Sparkie came to look at the newspaper, Monty had torn out the column. He didn't want everyone in the ward to know.

Sparkie pondered over it. It seems incredible that he believed it for a moment, but Monty refused to answer questions, affected a deep hurt. As Sparkie sometimes said, 'He's gone on the moody again.'

When Monty's mother came, Sparkie skirted around the subject delicately.

'Them store detectives makes a lotta mistakes, Mrs L?'

'Mrs Rice-Lewis looked at him blankly.

'Pardon?'

'They're worse than the police, I knows!'

Mrs Rice-Lewis gave a baffled wooden smile, one of her favourite expressions. Behind her back Monty tapped his forehead significantly with one finger to indicate a diminution of her mental processes and, at last, Sparkie caught on. For him it became the joke of the week, and their rapport began again.

'I pisses myself every time he opens his mouth!' Sparkie said, reporting the matter.

It was a vile joke. Perhaps we laughed because we were in such a vile condition. The story spread around the ward. Sister complained to me. 'I don't know what you're doing in there with those two!' But I put on a face. I too was a man of disguises. The incident marked a turning point in Monty's fortunes. He continued to grow stronger. Now he could talk for a whole afternoon. There were riches to come and back I went to that grim little outpost of failure, drawn there for relief, for entertainment, for Sparkie's coarse cackle, for the ironic lift of Monty's eyebrows, as well as for reasons which I did not fully understand. There I did not have to put on any kind of front.

'How are you today?' Sister said every day.

She was so efficient, concerned and kindly that I would not have answered her with the slightest irony and so daily I mouthed platitudes. Later we argued over Suez, but she very sensibly retired and kept her distance once more while I arranged my day so that I could go to the Club after lunch. Membership had also improved my status elsewhere. When

Sparkie called in my cubicle wheeling the morning tea trolley, I automatically got the pickings, the newspapers I had not managed to obtain, the cleaner's gossip, the casualty reports, sometimes the surgical lists, the all-important news of who was to be operated upon and what their form was – in particular, the months they'd had to wait.

Once Sparkie called unexpectedly when my friend the houseman was sitting on my bed. Sparkie's expression was caustic and he withdrew immediately.

'I dint know you had company,' he said with the disapproving air of an English officer who had found me mixing socially with a native.

It was his disapproval which I feared most since the medical staff did not help the days pass more quickly.

'We'll review the position in another month,' the chest physican said – every month.

THIRTEEN

And, apart from my membership of the Club, nothing changed. Boredom got into my skull. I would count drops of rain falling down the window panes, the footsteps of the nurses hurrying down the corridor, all pointless exercises in futility. Reading in fits and starts, I discovered it was the age of the angry young men. Lucky them, I thought. I also had nightmares, some of them more horrible than the conscious mind could conceive, including one in which my gentle and slender mother who never expressed anything but her wan and timid love for me, appeared in the role of witch and jumped on me, attempting to scratch out my eyes – an action of such horror that I can only conceive it to be some projection of my own mind's efforts to understand the pains caused her by my birth – separation from my father amongst them. I never succeeded in putting a face to my ever absent father although, according to a public house tale, I am supposed when very drunk to have met him in a bar while on leave from the Navy. But the evening immediately vanished from my mind beyond recall, and he was not identified at the time. In hospital I did not think of him and my reveries were the only escape, soon to be fed by my new friends who began increasingly to occupy my days.

In particular, there was Monty. We were all interested in his first job. If he was not expelled from school, he came close to it, leaving by mutal agreement, and there now began the long process of total estrangement from everything he had known and the first of his mother's intercessions with the most influential of her relatives. To them she wrote the first of what was to be a long series of letters which she would go on writing all her life. There was a perennial phrase which made me rock

244

with laughter. 'We are having a little difficulty with Montague.' This was in 1936. At sixteen Monty was beginning life under a cloud, his references the best the family could muster, his educational attainments the poorest. His mother had remarried and it was thought best that he should leave home. What was to be done with him? A new start was generally agreed upon. The family influence was powerful. 'Perhaps he will settle down in the Bank?' his mother said. And so it was arranged, and he found himself getting off the train at Richmond wearing a bowler hat.

''king bowler hat!' Sparkie said, chortling and rolling his eyes, the spittle standing out on his lips. Once the pages of his favourite book began turning, all was forgiven.

Monty had been taken to an outfitters with a list of clothing recommended, including underclothes, suits, a hair brush, shoe trees, and a bowler hat. Then his step-father had found him suitable lodgings through chapel connections. The well-established members of Mrs Rice-Lewis's family had made their recommendations, so had his step-father, and it was as if the two most important influences in the old Wales had conspired to provide the thrust to eject him on to a new stage. The job in the bank was procured by an uncle, a man of influence in London; the lodging and much advice were obtained and given by the chapel. He also had his father's old trunk and a reserve of gold sovereigns sewn into the lining and contained in a black leather bag. I could imagine his mother saying, 'We've done everything we can for him!' I could see them seeing him off at the railway station, the guard tipped, the trunk secure. Somewhere at the back of my mind there now occurs a warning against what was, perhaps, a contemporary hazard; for it occurs in Dylan Thomas's unfinished novel, *Adventures in the Skin Trade*. There was, it seems, a general Welsh caution as to the avarice of Irish landladies and Monty was aware of it. But within six weeks of installing himself as little more than a messenger boy – the bowler had soon been discarded – he had changed lodgings. He had met an Irish girl crying on the street because she had lost her pay packet, and had taken her home. Within a month he was in new lodgings, sharing her mother's welcoming Irish bed.

245

'Montague did not settle in his lodgings,' his mother said innocently; that was the start.

It was the first part of his life as a dark horse, for one rearrangement led to another and he found a niche for himself in the bank, and eventually rediscovered his prowess as a rugby player. He was well-fed and filled out, undeniably prosperous. There was also a bank rugby team, then the United Banks Fifteen – a representative side, a cut above the others. He distinguished himself in both, was sought after, and found friends – in those days, he was the good chap of good chaps. He had, he said expansively, discovered what *It* was for. He did not go home for two years. He cut off his roots completely. But as a rugby player, he shone. Physical fitness did not take much effort. They were mostly knockabout games without the ferocious competitiveness of Welsh club football. They, and the social life which followed, introduced him, he said, to the better class of girl. The only bother was that the rugby season ended and, with it, the extended clubroom jollity. So he took the advice of his team mates and, following the popular trend, joined the Territorial Army with the express intention of converting winter bonhomie into lazy and gregarious summer evenings, carrying on the social season at the Army's expense in convivial summer camps. Summer camps were notorious, he was told. Girls flocked to the vicinity. Sport was at a premium in the Army. If he could play rugby he could surely play cricket? And he was a public-school man. If there was a storm gathering in Europe, trouble coming and conscription a possibility, best to be in it from the start. There was a London regiment looking for officer material. The arguments were persuasive. But, Monty told us, he delayed for a long time. He already had a sixth sense for official snags. There had been problems in the bank, he once indicated in an airy way, problems over the irritating discipline of signing for things – nothing serious when you were a rugby blue-eyed boy, but he was now wary of putting his signature to anything, especially a form that was binding. He gave no more details than that.

'You wouldn't nob it!' Sparkie said. The idea of joining anything was an anathema to him. 'Sign once, you sign your bleeding life away!'

246

So Montague, with the same feelings, delayed and delayed until at last he was made to feel the odd man out and, more important, his manager applied a little pressure. There was just the hint of other money difficulties. So he signed on, joined the Territorial Army. It was the summer of 1939.

'Didn't you read the papers?' Sparkie said.

'Only the racing pages!'

'Serves you bloody right, then.'

At first, the summer of 1939 was eventful. 1940 proved different. The news of the war had even affected the racing pages of the newspapers. Very soon the British Expeditionary Force in France was on the retreat and Monty was with it, facing the penalty of that unwise signature. The London regiment to which he had attached himself had joined the regulars, following them to France and then Belgium, and stood poised to make its presence felt after weeks of rumour and an irritating lack of orders or real intelligence. At least that was how I imagined the military picture, but Monty did not put it quite like that. He knew his audience. Sparkie was not interested in military strategy and neither was I. What interested me was that Monty, under fire, was soon to change his allegiance to his origins for he now formed a sudden and necessary friendship which was the fruit of bizarre circumstances, an affair as choice and necessary as his relationship with Sparkie. Monty had soon become disenchanted with khaki as a colour. The Army was not quite what he had been led to expect. His vision of himself as officer material had not been shared. There had been upsets, uncouth voices, stamping feet. The Army in wartime was a place where people of no consequence took themselves very seriously and there was a sudden lack of interest in good rugby players, so that Montague had learned what Sparkie could have told him at the outset, what everybody told me in more peaceful times, 'Lay low! Keep your head down. Don't get yourself noticed.'

He had finally adapted this philosophy when, as Rifleman Rice-Lewis, he awoke early one morning in the thick mist of a Belgian dawn, his regiment dug in along the banks of the Royal Albert Canal. They were defending a small bridge over the canal, a task made difficult by certain limitations: the shortage of rifles meant that one rifle had to be shared by three men, only three rounds of ammunition being issued per man. The bridge in front of them had been packed with explosives but there were no detonators. They had been dive-bombed for days, vomiting with fear, bile in their mouths as they buried their faces in the earth as Stukkas softened up the path of the advancing German Army. There had been many casualties and now considerable shortages in the matter of equipment, even of orders, for they had been constantly on the move, hurtled backwards and forwards as a relief holding company without being quite certain as to exactly what they were required to hold. It was, Montague implied, a time of confusion, in the whole and in the particular, and there was an added complication in the matter of his personal disillusion with the Army in general. But there was one bright note, as there usually is. Rifleman Rice-Lewis awoke first in the slit trench he shared with his new intimate, one Hughsie, an acting, temporarily made-up lance sergeant – a veteran of years of service in the Indian Army who, wise in army ways, was singularly handicapped. He could not read or write which implied the need of a sympathetic friend and Montague, who knew how to be discreet, was eager to help. There was also a taproot to the past which was to save Monty's life and give the lie to the War Office telegram informing his mother of his death. Hughsie was from the same mining valley as Montague and indeed had begun life as a collier boy in the pit of which Monty's long-dead father had been manager. It gave Hughsie a proprietary interest in his protégé that was to last. Hughsie, too, was ginger, Monty said and Sparkie smiled delightedly. But Hughsie was tatooed which Sparkie much disapproved of since tatoos made police identification all too easy. Hughsie was also an old soldier. 'An old, old soldier!' Monty said with a wink. Sparkie nodded. He knew. 'North West Frontier, all that,' Monty said.

In my childhood I had seen such veterans with Frontier medals and burnished silver-topped swagger sticks, some of them with waxed moustaches, outside the recruiting office in my home town. But Hughsie was a recently made-up sergeant, the business of not being able to read or write circumvented only because of immediate need and the overwhelming presence of barely trained riflemen who had joined for the summer camp, the girls, the extended rugby season. Hughsie was also a dab hand with an entrenching tool, his particular expertise, and Monty, his great admirer, contrived to praise and watch when Hughsie, exasperated at Monty's lack of expertise, lost patience and took the tool from him. The result was that they shared the deepest and most expertly made trench, its sides firmed, the protective cover the best – always with Monty's warmest congratulations.

'I knows you!' Sparkie said when this detail was mentioned. 'I knows you, what you was up to. Foot on the shovel, get the Gaffer to do it!'

'Well, he was trained as a collier,' Monty replied haughtily, and it was true.

On that particular morning, Monty woke up first and he saw the mist was so thick that it would be impenetrable for an hour or two. Damply, he perceived that it lay in thick patches on the ground and of course it soaked through their winter greatcoats, the still-blancoed webbing, and moistened the barrel of the rifle they shared. He remembered an unnatural silence. They were dug in at intervals of about forty yards, the other men in groups of three, with a sentry near the bridge – or supposed to be near the bridge. He stretched himself, moving his stiffened joints, stood up. Hughsie snored nearby, the brass cap badges of his previous three regiments glistening on his trouser belt, the history of his long Army past revealed. Then Monty thought he heard a peculiar chatter as ephemeral as a snatch of song in the far distance, a few notes travelling over the water of the nearby canal. He heard it, then he did not hear it. He thought he must have been dreaming, then he heard it again. Somewhere in the mist someone was speaking in German, a light voice fading and returning, but all in the distance and so insubstantial as if it might be part of memory rather than reality.

Though they were very close to the canal, he could not even see the near bank and the voice was far enough away to be on the other side, but indistinct enough to be illusory. Monty stood up, peered through the mist but he could see nothing. Then he heard an engine revving up and falling silent, still without seeing anything. So he awoke Hughsie gently, crouching to one side. There was a skill to waking Hughsie up. If Hughsie had been on the beer, he was inclined to sleep the sleep of the dead but if shaken roughly, he would wake like a dervish, coming instantly alive and lashing out with his fists – the automatic reaction of a man who has slept in the open in distant climes where thieving tribesmen had been known to infiltrate the lines in the night. He had once broken a lance corporal's jaw with a punch that came from sleep, an instant reflex movement, his dangerous reflexes well-known. He was also a one-time regimental middle-weight champion, another valley boy with educated fists. 'You had to be very careful with Hughsie,' Montague said. 'He had these little habits.'

Sparkie had known old lags on the prison wing in the Scrubs with the same propensity. It was the storyteller's detail which drew forth an appreciative nod from the informed audience. Hughsie was one to be watched, as well as his little peculiarities.

So Monty always woke Hughsie gently, crouching to one side, stretching out an arm to his shoulder, watching consciousness creep over his square face until he stirred himself and sat up, 'scratching that ginger barnet!' Monty said.

'What's up?'

'Something moving.'

'Where?'

'Over there?'

'What's that bloody sentry doing then?'

'Listen . . .'

They listened. Then they both heard the voice, then another and then the clanking of tin cups and a conversation – all a considerable distance away. They had no doubt the voices were German. Then came the first of the two most important sentences of Monty's war.

'Bloody hell! They're 'ere!' Hughsie said. He put on his boots, a sign of the importance he attached to the matter, and spoke in a hoarse whisper, bidding Monty stay where he was, not to move an inch, and went to investigate. He took the rifle and sloped off in a crouch, jamming his forage cup on his head as he went. (Their tin hats had also been mislaid.) Their officers were quartered in a bivouac tent about four hundred yards away on a slight incline with a better view of the distant bridge. A runner had been despatched the previous night to obtain detonators in order to blow up the bridge should an emergency arise, but he had not returned. Hughsie had threatened 'to chase the bugger up', but had not done so. Monty watched him disappearing into the mist, shivering and feeling the cold as he did so. It was an eerie experience and he noticed Hughsie controlling his cough, the permanent trace of malaria.

'Very thin blood, Hughsie,' Monty said. 'Very yellow he got in the mornings.'

In the minutes that followed, Monty thoughtfully packed his haversack with such rations as were to be had. He put on his own boots and surveyed the kit which lay about him. The voices had fallen silent and the mist remained thick, but now there were different areas of density and soon it would slowly begin to clear. The voices had begun again when Hughsie came hurrying back, bent double, hurtling along, crouching down in the little trench beside Monty and lowering his voice as he spoke. He had something in his free hand which Monty could not at first identify. Then there was the second most important sentence of the war so far.

'Hey, Mont', Hughsie said hoarsely. 'Can you read a map?'

He spread an Army map of the terrain on the grass. He had removed it from the officers' quarters where it had been dropped on the floor. The officers' quarters were empty.

'Empty? What's up?'

'Time we got out of this little lot, you and me!' Hughsie said.

Their officers had deserted in the night, Monty said.

Hughsie looked at the map, its unfamiliar signs and shapes and held it forth to Monty, his eyes appealing. Monty nodded. Yes, he could read a map. They had come to the same conclusion without a word spoken. Silently they scrambled out of the trench, their backs to the canal and later, as they made their way stealthily towards a wood, they began to hear the unmistakeable sounds of an army on the move. A panzer division faced them on the other side of the canal, but it was cautious at the sight of the only bridge remaining to them and still left standing, and suspected a trap. Hughsie and Monty got away alone, clearing first one field, then another, then scrambling down to a subsidiary of the canal where they found a barge on the move and jumped aboard it, making further progress until a savage blitzkrieg obliterated what was left of their regiment ten minutes later. Having made one step on the run, there was no option but to take others and they began a full-scale desertion through France, aiming always for the coast. Hughsie had a secret plan and a ready explanation in the event of them being challenged. He had retained his rifle and maintained his regimental appearance at all times, shaving daily but allowing Monty to grow more and more scruffy. If confronted with any known authority, he was going to tie Monty's hands behind his back and pass him off as a prisoner awaiting court martial for rape which then carried a sentence of death. It was a bold and extravagant lie, unusual enough to make enquirers uneasy. They would not want the responsibility of dealing with the two of them, Hughsie reckoned. He knew the Army. But as it happened, they did not need the pretence, finding themselves unexpectedly aboard an Air Force lorry unchallenged and then, avoiding big towns, they took off again on their own. Very shortly, the whole of France seemed to be on the move. They made their way cross-country through abandoned châteaux, helping themselves to such delicacies as they fancied; they even passed close by a French Army Officers' school where uniformed cadets were still being given instructions in sword drill, their poise immaculate. Finally, Hughsie marched Monty up the gangway of a British destroyer just before Dunkirk became a household name. But when they landed at Dover, their good luck deserted them. They had a quantity of brandy with them from which they had drunk freely on the voyage and it had given them a false confidence which caused Hughsie to relax. Beside the dock there were a fleet of Greenline coaches drawn up, one of them bearing the name of their depot. Before them, the local ladies of the WVS had set up tables and were issuing cups of tea to exhausted soldiers, many of them scattered and long-separated from their regiments.

'A cup o' char,' said Hughsie jauntily, 'then we'll be back in barracks in time to go the dogs!' He meant racing greyhounds which were his passion.

As they supped their tea, a Guards officer approached. Hughsie drew himself up, saluted with precision.

'Are you men fit?'

'Yessah! Fought our way outa France, sah!'

In Monty's view, this was going too far. It was an unnecessary flourish, the one lapse in the old soldier's code of survival – the embellishment that trips the embellisher.

'Jolly good!' said the Guards officer. 'Get aboard those coaches over there.'

They hurried towards them like little children going on a treat. Everything had worked. They were undetected and alive. They had also made a profit on the side. Their haversacks still contained brandy, and Hughsie had 'wrist-watches up to the elbow!' But when they boarded the coach, they were driven all night to Liverpool, marched aboard a destroyer and shipped back to France for the defence of St Nazaire. That was a bloody business and, once again, they just escaped with their lives. This time, though, they went by the book – honourably discharging themselves when shifting amunition in an exploding dump, for which Hughsie got a 'Mention in Despatches'. An officer even cleared a way for them with a drawn pistol among a rabble of drunken soldiery, many of whom were left behind. There was shooting, panic, disgrace – but they were not of it.

For me, the story was both a revelation and a confirmation of long-held suspicions. Every film I had seen about the war until that time was a propagandist's weapon, and there were clearly defined codes of conduct which usually resolved themselves into stereotypes of courage and cowardice. Perhaps Monty's was the first war story I had ever heard in which the characters were identifiable as known human beings, and did not behave in expected ways. Listening to Monty, you saw things differently. It was not just the number of things that went wrong but, in the telling, there was a sense of reality that once more accorded to my own perceptions of things as they really are. I could just see the two of them on that long chaotic journey through France and, once more, the dénouement at Dover was a case of the biters bit. Monty, of course, elaborated on their evasions of duty, not on their approved and courageous actions under supervision when there was no alternative. It was as if, in recalling, he was reaching for those aspects of experience which reflected the chaotic nature of life, the shocks in store, the other side of the official history, the dangerous farce behind the documented drama. Other people gave the public handouts. Close to the ground, the troops knew better. As in my own life, there was education, and there was bio-gardening.

And Sparkie followed it all with appropriate wheezes and nods, occasionally hissing his approval at the tactics adopted like a staff officer well-qualified to pass comment. So far as general policy went, there was only one road to follow, and it was crooked. But there were still skills required. As it was, the extravagance of Hughsie's braggadocio at Dover stayed in Sparkie's mind. 'Fought our way out of France' indeed!

'You should've limped, or something,' Sparkie said. His face showed his disappointment with Hughsie. It was a bad slip-up.

But then Monty made many slip-ups and there were, of course, more to come. Monty, however, stuck to Hughsie and Hughsie, reverting to his lowly corporal's rank, stuck to Monty. It was the kind of relationship which was duplicated with Sparkie, the one complementing the other. Hughsie continued to keep a low profile and encouraged Monty to do the same, but the memory of their initial success must have lasted. A year later they found themselves driving a Bren gun carrier towards Newport docks, chance homing pigeons bound ultimately for the Middle East and the desert war. Hughsie had thought up a system and reckoned that by continually flicking the linked tracks of the carrier against kerb stones at every possible opportunity, it shouldn't be too difficult to contrive a breakdown when they would be removed from the convoy in which they were travelling, thus securing a further withdrawal from the military operations which had gone so badly for them. It meant a bumpy ride and Monty was dubious, but as the convoy of vehicles travelled slowly at night, Hughsie was able to take every chance that offered to weaken the links. He bumped them heartily and at speed whenever he saw no possibility of detection, taking care to avoid the eyes of passing military policemen and the observation of others in the vehicles behind – all of which meant that they would suddenly accelerate around corners, the whole business bone-shattering and scarcely alleviated by Hughsie's cunning grin, his tuneless humming and muttered asides.

'That was a good 'un! That must've cooked something good and proper! Listen, man, it's bloody rattling!'

By the time they approached the ancient border town of Chepstow, Hughsie had grown reckless. Familiar terrain beckoned. There was a barmaid he knew there in a public house called The Green Man. His idea was to break down in Chepstow, if not actually under the historic archway and outside the public house, then nearby and at least he could spend the night there, if they did not miss the troopship altogether.

'We'll have our feet under the table,' Hughsie said. 'You stick with me, Monty boy, I'll see you right.'

It was a carefully thought-out plan, but it backfired in Chepstow.

'He went too far,' Monty said again.

Revving up, Hughsie hurled himself, Monty and the Bren gun carrier at an ancient whitewashed staging post, one of those wayfarer's signs that had been in position since Dick Whittington's time. The carrier mounted it, hesitated, then suddenly turned over on its side with the result that Hughsie fell out and broke a leg. The Bren gun carrier was righted and rejoined the convoy and while Monty went with it, to be shot through the chest with tracer bullets in Libya, he survived. Hughsie, recovered and reposted, was killed on his second trip to France. There was a bullet waiting for him, and it was as if he had always known.

'Bought it!' Monty said. 'RIP Hughsie.'

I can remember Sparkie's silence in the little ward. At the time I could see Hughsie, but now I only see Sparkie, his aggrieved pockmarked face, his staring eyes, that fleshy mouth ever open and glistening, the audible sniff with which he greeted the dénouement. He was listening to the demise of one of his own kind, unknown, unsung, one of the faceless warriors of whom we only knew the fewest of details, a collier boy turned soldier whose life, like most of our lives, goes unrecorded. It seemed without point or purpose save to capture our imaginations for a brief afternoon. Sparkie's death would be like that too, he knew, I am sure. There were few who would mourn him and perhaps for a moment in the little ward we had a sense of the transience of life, all as inconsequential as the fluttering of a butterfly's wings. It was upsetting. But only for a moment.

Sparkie cleared his throat, produced a sizeable globule of phlegm and deposited it noisily into his sputum pot where he examined it with clinical interest.

'Poor old Hughsie!' he said.

But I doubt if he ever thought of him again.

Monty's story had an unusual effect upon me, an effect that lasted. The whole story actually came in dribs and drabs on separate days. There were other details which I have now forgotten, but not the all-important ones and, listening to him during the long afternoons, it was perhaps the first time that I began to see one human life as a whole. I did not believe Monty would live long, but I saw his progress to the little hospital ward from the cradle and I saw him, of course, as hero; but that was what he wanted me to think. For months I sought his company but later I was to think that I had invented him in a way that Sparkie was not invented. Monty had a way of telling stories, reassembling surface happenings – the brightly etched pictures of heroes and villains sketched in profile only, himself included. It was as if he was replaying excerpts from the film of the book, but took care not to get down to the substance of the book itself. Perhaps the prose was too dense, the paragraphs too numerous, the plot still uncertain. Sparkie, on the other hand, was aggrieved and resentful and did not have Monty's detachment, although I froze with him as he described the effect of a mousetrap going off unexpectedly in someone's kitchen when he was about his burglarious enterprises. It was difficult to identify with Sparkie. His lack of intelligence prevented it although, between us, Sparkie and myself, there grew a lasting bond.

There were also other things happening. Apart from my immediate relief from boredom, there was a fascination for me in that little ward which I did not then fully understand. I think now that I was drawn into the Club because I qualified for membership in several ways and there were aspects of myself, especially of some of my feelings, which were daily reflected there. We are all of us unique but we are less separated from each other than many of us would like to believe and we three, Monty, Sparkie and myself, were all fatherless children. We had all ended up in the same tubercular boat, and if my instability was marginal by their standards and other codes more binding, we still shared a sense of hurt that we could not articulate. Perhaps I was lucky in that I was better able to control my feelings, but I felt them just the same and I was not in any way different in that sense of loss which comes from a childhood where one parent is missing, or reviled. We were deficient people and no matter how we might have attempted to adjust or cover up, the sense remained – in my case, carrying on into maturity – constituting in many ways an unbridgeable gap, a wound that is covered over but never completely heals.

We shy away from the thought of the incurable condition. It is an offence to optimism, a brake on reason, the very idea of it an abrasive check to the smooth persuasiveness of other voices, including our own when we decide on courses of action involving children which do not fully take into account the hurt we may cause. Victims propagate victims. Monty had a child, long-abandoned, whom he never spoke about. Sparkie was not sure of his own paternities, but violence and bad luck were never to desert him and, a year after we met, his common-law wife was to be involved in an attempted murder case as victim. Perhaps, as the lids of the sputum pots rattled and Sparkie's after-lunch expectorations and coarse cackles mingled with Monty's wheezing and the sinister ticking of that electric pump under the bed – perhaps in all this, which I viewed hazily through my one good eye, perhaps I learned something about the consequence of childhood deprivation and the course of the next twenty-five years of my life was in some ways determined then. If I had children, I would never abandon them. I did not expect another twenty-five years of life then, and these were not my thoughts at the time, but I suspect now that there was a mysterious attraction to my two friends – an attraction that impelled me to move closer to them, perhaps unconsciously seeking all the time to understand the paths of behaviour that must have wound their way through my own missing father's life. I do not know, nor was I ever to know, but I attended daily like a conscientious member bent on his curious research. Why me? Why them? Why us?

I also, as Sparkie would say, laughed like a drain very frequently, and that was my immediate debt.

Then everything changed. First, Monty grew stronger, the tubes were removed, the wound healed and he began to put on weight rapidly, especially when he was allowed on to his feet. Within weeks, he was a different man. His face filled out, he looked more swarthy, jowls appeared and his lips were perpetually drawn into an irritated, impatient scowl. Now his tone was sarcastic, his manner unpleasant, those glittering black eyes flashed malevolently. He suddenly seemed, as someone said, 'a nasty bit of work'. He grew irritated with the hospital, with me, Sparkie, and everyone else. He was no longer dependent on Sparkie and shed him like a winter coat. Sparkie had also got himself into trouble with the sister for redistributing food delicacies intended for 'Special Diets' once more, and was moved back to the main ward where his movements were more easily observed. Like myself, he was waiting for surgery but Monty was finished with surgery. He would never subject himself to it again, he said. He'd had enough of doctors, the constant waiting and total dependence on others. It gave him the bird, he said. He demanded clothes which his mother brought in, and then she abruptly stopped visiting and never came again.

It was the clothes that made me think I had invented Monty. Whereas before I had imagined him as a cross between Basil Seal and the Good Soldier Schweik, now he was himself unedited, undirected, free of the script, and a total disappointment. Pyjamas, like dinner jackets, have a certain anonymity. When Monty dressed in a loud sports jacket, there was a flashiness that belied his earlier aristocratic manner and took away from the exuberance of his speech. Now he was seen as a man of tiepins, shoddy cigarette cases, glittering cufflinks. When his mother stopped coming, old cronies made their first appearance and they would be seen with him walking in the hospital grounds, their heads bent together in earnest discussion. Monty was also frequently seen doing sums on pieces of paper, monopolising the telephone when he could, eagerly waiting his mail – all new phenomena to us. He attempted to sell one of the doctors a new car, was unsuccessful, then offered a second-hand bargain and this failing, suggested a rental scheme. But now he did not confide in us and when Sparkie was moved back to the main ward, the Club broke up. The dissolution had been coming for a long time. We had long exhausted our fund of stories and once Monty recovered his strength, thoughts of the future came between us like barriers put up overnight. We had shared the past but the future, like a crime uncommitted, was not to be discussed. One day a woman came to see Monty. I saw her briefly out of the corner of my good eye. She was shapely and attractive, a sweater girl with vivid blonde hair in a pageboy style. She was heavily made-up, her face drawn with worry. Monty hustled her by the arm into the corner of the recreation room and when she left, tears stained that thick pancake make-up. The visit was brief and ended abruptly. We did not ask the relationship, Monty did not explain. For days he wore a savage frown, brooded, grew moody and spent more and more time on the telephone.

'That was his bit,' Sparkie said evilly. 'Now she knows he's not going to croak, she's after the bunce!' He rubbed his forefinger and thumb together pointedly.

Indeed, money now seemed to be Monty's obsession. He was now entirely independent, did not need Sparkie and spent his afternoons on his own. I soon became preoccupied with my own concerns. One day I was told Monty had had a stand-up row with the surgeon, and then discharged himself prematurely. One of his cronies came to collect him, parking a large Jaguar car on the physician superintendent's reserved parking space. Monty did not say goodbye either to Sparkie or myself. When he left unseen – we only heard that he had gone – it was as if he had never been. I remembered the day the surgical registrar looked at the swirling matter in the bottle under his bed.

'Is that blood, or debris?'

Neither Sparkie nor I brooded over Monty's sudden departure and Sparkie's attitude soon softened as he spoke of him.

'Not the same without our Mont',' he said one day as he came round with the tea trolley. 'A boy and a half, he was!'

Then the chest physician told me that I was ready for surgery. I was to be 'done' on the same day as Sparkie which for some reason cheered us both immensely.

'Perhaps we'll both end up in the same bucket!' Sparkie said. 'Let's hope they got the knife sharpener in this week. We don't want no old Gillettes hackin' away on us, kid!'

Sparkie and I grew closer and as we did so, he reverted to his consultant's role – only now it was for my benefit, rather than for Mrs Rice-Lewis. I still lay nightly upon my bed, the evil swirl of blood inside my eye continuing as the floaters moved every time I suddenly raised my head. My eye condition had not changed in fourteen months, save to grow worse with the second haemorrhage. There was simply no progress and while the medical opinion was in favour of surgery, and the tones of the doctors, calm, reasonable and assured, it was Sparkie's voice which implanted itself upon my consciousness.

'You wait!' Sparkie said before we went up to the next floor for our ordeal in the operating theatre. 'I'm not telling you nuthin, but you just bloody wait!'

'What d'you mean?'

'Well, ask your bloody-self! They're operating on the lung, in they? And the lung don't never stop movin', get it? Even under the 'fluence? So, it's a hit or miss job, in it? Like puttin' a French letter on the spoke of a wheel while it's movin'!'

'You're a treasure, Sparkie!'

'You wait, mate! You can't tell me, I've had it done on the one side, remember! I knows, I bin through it.'

It was true. So he had.

'Charming,' I said. 'Nice talking to you, Spark'!'

'Give you a tip, mate. They offer you any Veganin, painkillers, anything like that, take the bloody box! Grab all you can. Fly, you gotta be in here. Fly, I'm telling you. Real fly!'

His advice was constant and covered every contingency.

'If you gotta watch, valuables, anything like that, send the lot home, 'cos you're out cold for two days. That's if you're not gonna leave anything to me!'

Had he been near me, I would have held his hand when I was wheeled down the corridor on a trolley, but as it was, a nurse held mine.

'There's nothing to it, boy,' she said, her voice soft and Welsh. I remembered other nurses saying, 'Expectorate, my prince! Come along, lovely!' They would say anything.

I trusted no one. I was more afraid than I had ever been, so afraid as to exhaust the capacity for fear about myself ever after.

'You'll look great with a white stick,' Sparkie once told me when we talked about the worst thing that could ever happen to us, if we stayed alone. He articulated all my fears, and went on and on. 'Tap-tap-tap!' he said. 'Ex-serviceman too. Up the British Legion! I can see it. Watch them collectin' boxes though. Easy to open, they are, a tin-opener'll do the trick a treat. I knows, I done a few. Never mind, they'll give you a dog! You'll look great with a Rin-Tin-Tin!'

On the day, you feel your mouth dry, you are aware of the noiseless opening of doors, the gentle whirring of the trolley's rubber tyres, then the bright bright lights of the operating theatre which appears cavernous, as high as a cathedral.

Unfamiliar faces, white masks, the hard brightness of those lights which I saw through a swirl of red, always that evil bright arterial blood.

'We've got to be careful to keep his head level – mustn't let it drop below the level of the body,' a voice said. I was aware of losing consciousness. Very soon I was no longer a part of anything I knew about.

FOURTEEN

I have had the experience of being suspended upside down in limbo on only one occasion and then with an accompanying feeling of not quite belonging to my own body. This was after acrobatic flying when strapped to the instructor's seat in a naval Sea Fury training aircraft. I was once plunged downwards on a mock bombing attack on the Needles lighthouse, one of three aircraft flying in close formation, wingtip to wingtip, finally climbing out of the dive at the last moment to gain altitude once more and then to do a victory roll – a procedure repeated several times. It is the kind of manoeuvre you see performed in films, but like the firing of handguns, the actuality of the experience is very different from anything you imagine. In that unpressurised piston-engined fighter aircraft as it hurtled down through the clouds, the wind tearing through the struts and the parachute upon which I was sitting seeming to push me upwards in the cockpit, I experienced a complete reversal of normal sensations. My eyes bulged, my stomach turned around, pain seared in my eardrums as if there was some fiend active and alive inside them. The whole sensation was enough to cause me to believe we were climbing when we were actually diving, the white-capped sea below us suddenly as high as the clouds themselves, which actually appeared to be under us as we left them behind. I had gone for a trip, a sudden impromptu lark as a passenger with a pilot friend and it was my first experience of total disorientation before my body adjusted. There were seconds when I did not think it would adjust and the agony in my ears reminded me of a boy I had seen once who suddenly and unaccountably began screaming in the dressing room after a rugby match, his pain uncontrollable. No one could identify it. He had not been kicked or apparently injured and it was not until he was rushed to hospital that an earwig was found in his eardrum. It was the kind of freakish torture that I shall ever associate with that most boring of subjects, other people's operations.

When I came to in what seemed the half-light of the post-operative ward, nurses were by my side in an instant.

Was I sitting up? I cannot remember. Disembodied, I still seemed to be suspended in a crouched position. I was not aware of the bed. I was crouched as an animal crouches in a trap, tasting blood, a rime of it about my lips. I was gasping-gasping-gasping, crouched there in that blue haze and it was as if, there and then, with a marked and leisurely slowness, I was being run over by a double-decker bus, a bus moreover driven by someone like Sparkie, reading a comic as he reversed, his attention elsewhere as he absent-mindedly kept his foot on the pedal. You can only make a joke of it, but all my life I shall remember that helplessness, my own incontinence and complete inability to utter a single intelligent syllable for an hour or so. I might have been suspended in a sea of pain, held in the trough of a wave, held buoyant and motionless in a skein of tiny threads which pulled at me, folding and unfolding, each lapping movement passing over me and through me, a series of ripples and jerks, each one more subtle and more devastating than the last. My chest, my ribs, the top half of my body seemed to flap like sheet metal flaps when held in a steelworker's tongs, but barely held, and searingly hot from the furnace. I could not speak at all. But then I heard the familiar ticking of an electric pump, the sound tiny and far distant in the eddying sea of pain. If it was attached to me, I did not know where or how.

A nurse said, 'He's coming round.'

I was unsure of the faces. They'd removed their masks. They were peering at me as if I was a transparent object dimly obscured by the wave that held me. Then the surgeon came, greying and distinguished. He held my head, a new movement, a fresh application of the tongs, and more pain. I could not push him away. I could not protest. I gasped and gasped and gasped. My feelings must have been violent. I wanted to hurt him, to protest. I would have hurt anybody.

I remember distinctly what he said.

'We were very worried about your eye.'

The nurses' faces appeared beside his, then the sister from my own ward who had come up to the theatre especially to see me. She bent over me. I was aware of faces trying to hold me in their sights as from a distance. I saw them all and wanted to lash out.

Writing about it in fictional terms, I made it funny.

I couldn't speak. My back was open. I had this drip set up and they'd made a mess of this last one so that there was blood all over the smock which I still wore. A pair of tubes wound out of my side down to a bottle on the floor. There was a clock or something in the bottle. It kept ticking. Tick-tock . . .

'Well?' the surgeon said again.

I thought he meant, 'How did I feel?' Like one of those women who've been violated by a Congolese regiment, I thought. Speak? I couldn't get a word out. There was still stuff at the back of my throat, my lips were dry and my throat scraped, substances clogging it. Perhaps it was a rubber solution back there? I couldn't feel pain in one place, it came in waves like a double-decker bus coming forward slowly every minute, inching over me, soft tyres, hard bus. It was like being held in a vice, slow pain, an ache in my eyes, hard balls of pain behind them, and in my side, jagged holes where the tubes entered into me. Consciousness, what was that? Being aware of pain. After the waves, stab wounds: jabs.

The theatre sister came in with a grin.

'He's being a baby!'

I tried to frame some terrible sentence. Where did they get her from?

Oh, the pain! Inch by inch, it crept along again, slow, buckling rubber truncheons expanding as they came, beating up my body. I knew there'd been a big cut. Forty-nine stitches. They didn't mention the muscles. Another con. If I had muscles, they felt like they'd fallen out of bed and left me behind, hanging on nerve ends. My arms . . . I was like a man lying on stumps.

I couldn't get a word out. I groaned.

'Aaaargh . . .'

'There he goes again,' the theatre sister said plaintively. 'All the time!'*

But the reality was more bizarre. I was aware of the surgeon's face pressed close to mine, then the nurses' faces behind him, all as large as crowd faces blown up on a cinema poster. I felt offended at being spied upon, as if they were intruders with no business to be there, these cruelly imported witnesses of my uncontrollable bowels, my incontinence, my continual involuntary gasping.

'Your eye?' the surgeon said urgently, awaiting a reply. He shook me.

I do not think I realised even then that I saw them with absolute clarity with both eyes. I wanted them to go away. But the evil swirl of blood which had been my constant companion for months and months and those streaky black floaters that washed lazily backwards and forwards like tiny rushes in a slow-moving stream had gone completely. My sight had returned and was absolutely normal.

'Your eye?' he said again. I could tell he was anxious and concerned, but I hated him.

I began to cry, to moan, then a snarl of exhaustion and pain.

'My back!' I said. 'Oh, my back, the pain . . .'

'You must expect some pain,' the sister said.

There was no harm which I would not have done to her either.

'Can you see?'

'Yes, yes, yes, but oh, oh, the pain . . .'

'Men are babies where pain is concerned,' a nurse said disparagingly later. 'Goodness gracious me! How would they manage in childbirth?'

It was the voice of the WVS, I thought, gently chiding and refreshingly normal. Whereas for months I had lived with the constant repetition of bad language, the forcefully expressed opinions of the ignorant, now the shock of surgery was to induce a new reality. I did not value my sight. I was not relieved, I just wanted to escape from that pain. I lay there for days trying to stop breathing. Once I knocked over a blood transfusion with the result that my white smock became

Home to an Empty House (1973)

drenched with blood. A friend, not realising I had been operated upon, came unexpectedly to see me, and not finding me in the downstairs ward, made his way unaccompanied to the post-operative ward, walked in unannounced and saw me drenched in blood and gasping. He stopped appalled, his eyes filling with tears before he was hustled out. It was the architect friend who had illustrated my bio-gardening thesis years before, my only presentable manuscript, and he thought I was dying. I saw him clearly but, still, I did not feel the relief that you would have thought would accompany the return of my full sight. It would be a week before I did, but even then my preoccupation was with avoiding any movement because movement meant more pain. For years I would suffer nightmares of being held as in a vice in that cramped position, as if the surgical assault upon my body had left wounds upon my unconsciousness marking me just as permanently as by the long scar across my back. That the diseased segments of my lung had been removed, that my sight had returned to normal and that the operation was in every way successful did not register for days. It was a miracle but it did not seem like one. I was ungrateful. I wanted to be left alone. The cheerful smiles of the sister seemed not to take cognisance of the way I felt, or of what I had suffered. There were so many hurdles to overcome: the journey down the corridor and into the lift to reach the cubicles below, the two physical acts which required lifting my bulky fourteen stone in and out of the wheelchair, and finally I would have to be manoeuvred into an ordinary bed. These were major acts, fraught, it seemed to me, with danger. I took each hurdle as it came, following Sparkie's advice and hoarding Veganin, the simple and largely ineffective painkilling tablets that I unreasonably expected to keep me in lengthy sleep. It was as if my worries about my sight had never been, and by the time the stitches were removed – painlessly, the sister neatly snipping them one by one: 'There now, that didn't hurt, did it?' – I had been, it seemed, a man without a functioning memory for a long time.

The shock of surgery was more than I had ever expected and no one had warned me. I had listened to scores of men who had received the same operation, but they had never described it in terms that were anything like the reality and the effect on me was to induce an unreasonable resentment which in turn had the beneficial effect of driving away the nagging doubts and fears that I would lose my sight – the dull ache of worry which had haunted me since I trod wearily from that London eye hospital nearly two years before. On that day the shadows lengthened in the dim afternoon sunlight, the oncoming buses seemed blurred as I looked at them and I put one foot in front of the other with leaden steps, my career ended, my future in tatters, so I thought.

And now I was ungrateful! Like Monty, who was also ungrateful, there was a residual feeling that it had all been too much and more than a man should be required to bear. I also thought foolishly that I was out of the wood, and immediately began impatiently to consider the future. Then, for the second time, I had a great desire for expensive things and began to gaze at the magazine advertisements for cardigans, clothes, suits, shirts and ties when, apart from uniforms, I had never owned more than one presentable suit of my own in my life. I wanted to be on my feet, dressed and clothed, elegant and normal, in no way associated with illness. But I was fourteen stone, three stone heavier than when I had entered hospital. Nothing fitted me. My dressing gown was in tatters. I was tired of it. I was tired of hospital, of hospital food, of institutional jokes and the whole routine of shaving in a mirror above a bowl beside the bed. It was several days before I could shave myself, but I forgot my helplessness as I forgot my worries. And my impatience was total.

It was a week before I saw Sparkie. His operation had been delayed for some reason and when I saw him, I was able to walk down the corridor but he was still hunched in the crouched position in bed, his stitches still inserted, his pain recurring as mine had done.

I was unsympathetic.

'You bastard!' I said. 'You didn't tell me what it was like.'

'I bloody did!'

'You bloody didn't!'

'Oh, well,' he said; 'if I'd told you you'd have scarpered.'

He was right, I thought. It was the reason why other men only described the operation in the most vague and ambiguous of terms. And perhaps they forgot more quickly because of the intensity of the pain, the loss of control of the bowels, the physical degradation and the trauma of the experience as a whole. They forgot because they wanted to forget. Perhaps if we could remember everything life would be unbearable. Now trying to explain my immediate ingratitude to myself, I realise that I was no different from other men, particularly Monty and Sparkie who felt the same in the aftermath of pain. It was too much to bear and now, over thirty years later, I doubt if I would face a similar operation voluntarily. Perhaps this is cowardice, but if it is, I am unrepentant. Few surgeons understand the totality of the experience. That the operation was wholly successful in my case, that I have a life about which to write, is not the only factor. Something happened to me in that period which I have never been fully able to articulate, and perhaps it is simply the sense of a lost physical innocence. I did not want to believe that such an extremity of pain existed.

But the experience also changed me in subtle ways. I ceased to be naive. I widened my conception of reality. Before, like the suburban housewife who sees the general horror of war suddenly become clear in the shape of a fleeting glimpse of a dismembered limb on a television, the inclination was to turn away. My life, so enclosed and lived for the most part in a small place, was but one life among many and my understanding of pain deepened because I could not turn away. I had been trapped, and whatever I had thought of myself, whatever vanities I possessed, they vanished when I learned I was just like other men in my immediate reaction to that traumatic experience. I was not so special after all.

But then as I gained strength, the fact I was able to look directly at the sunlight, to read without strain once more, to greet each day without fear, all meant that at last I was beginning to recover. It was as if I shed each separate fear like a succession of petals and I slowly began to lose some of that unhealthy obsession with the self which had lain within me like an unhealthy core despite my attempts to involve myself with the lives of others. And then, imperceptibly as each day became more crowded, then I realised how lucky I was and my thanks became voluminous and were given without reserve. I have never written anything that gave me more pleasure than the letters of thanks which I wrote ultimately to the medical staff; but first there were more surprises and setbacks, echoes and reminders of that mocking fate which I allowed myself to forget completely. Having been ungrateful, I became embarrassingly profuse in my thanks. I was unwary in that too.

I remained in the cubicle for the rest of my time in hospital whereas Sparkie, once he could walk, was returned to his ward like damaged goods to the general sorting office. But he came back to see me every day, and very soon, there was a special request.

Like Monty, once he had turned the corner, visitors also began to arrive in his life like birds returned after migration. One of them was a girl, his 'special', he said, and there was further information given in that hoarse confidential voice. He was required to demonstrate his affections. Could he borrow my cubicle one afternoon?

'Half-hour, like? On the QT?' He winked, stuck his tongue out and waggled it, cackled. 'We won't mess the sheets or nothing! You knows how it is, Al'?'

He joked, but he was in earnest. It required an effort of intense concentration for him to meet your eyes with his own, but now he did so and stared at me intently, his cheek muscles twitching. 'Come on! Favour?'

It was the last favour I did for Sparkie, drawing the screens across the little porthole of a window on the corridor door – later, they widened them into larger squares which could not be obscured! In my role, first as hotelier, then as corridor patrolman as I hovered in the vicinity in case anyone should want to enter, I was uneasy. Had anyone enquired, I do not know what I would have said. But fortunately there was a steady stream of visitors' traffic down the corridor, few hospital uniforms and, in the event, my presence was unnecessary. Sparkie's 'special' was tall, rangy and long-striding in a black flowery dress with high-heeled shoes of a bright metallic purple hue exactly matched by her eye shadow. Her hair was negroid, her long nose haughty with flared nostrils, her eyes dreamy and vacant – a tall, stringy creature of swirling movements with a mincing step and wide vacuous smile. He did not introduce me. Indeed, he was already sweating with the effort of keeping up with her, but they nodded to me like patrons at the cinema to an usherette as I held the door open for them. I had made the bed, pulled the far curtains, left two glasses beside the water carafe and put the Watch Ashore's bowl of fruit far to one side. I also lowered my eyes discreetly and although Sparkie nodded appreciatively, he declined to speak. His face was strangely wooden as he passed me. He had slicked down his hair with water and soap and his face shone but now there was a peculiar glazed expression upon it, no trace of a smile, nor any evidence of our previous intimacy. There was something almost professional about his unusual solemnity. He might have been an undertaker entering a room to measure a corpse. She entered with a whirl of skirts and I caught a whiff of a strong perfume. As the door closed, I heard him shove a chair purposely against it.

The door would not lock and clearly I was not to be trusted absolutely. Afterwards, he did not escort her down the corridor and she passed me as aloofly as she had entered, her composure unruffled, her eyes still dreamy, her steps long, those purple heels clacking. She disappeared like a sexy stork, all legs and craning neck.

I entered.

He lay back against my pillow, a packet of my cigarettes removed from the locker drawer, the sweat caked upon his reddened forehead, his face an alarming blue, a shade darker than the colour of her shoes. He inhaled and coughed violently.

'Bloody hell!' he said. 'Bloody hell!'

'You found the fags?'

He went into a paroxysm of coughing, wiped the sweat away.

Finally, he managed a grin. 'I don't care if I do go blind!'

He never spoke of his domestic life, then, or later. I had the impression that this had always been a tenuous relationship. She had come in 'to decide'. I gather she had decided and he was well-content. He thanked me, borrowed my cardigan, removed himself from the bed delicately, still coughing and wheezing. The spiky hair, having dried in points, now seemed to sprout, pinnacles of it pointing in different directions like the antennae of a sea mine. He remained flushed, wheezed again, took another cigarette 'for after', nodded his thanks once more and made his way out and down the corridor, slopping in his slippers. With his rounded shoulders and shuffling gait, he looked like an old man. This was not the Sparkie who did his rounds with the tea trolley, eyes 'sussing out' the contents of your locker, his grin wide and throaty chuckle infectious. It was the domestic Sparkie, head bowed and shoulders bent with the weight of his resumed responsibilities. He walked as if he had a mortgage on his back. Perhaps he already had a dismal view of the problems which would face him in the future. Of sex, he had once said, 'I'd rather have a chicken sandwich any day!' Now his pensioner's gait showed his weariness and he shook his head sorrowfully from side to side.

I did not see much of him afterwards. I was now up and about myself, hardening my soft feet by walking as much as I could in the hospital grounds. It was spring. I began to give my mind to plans. Another month went by but I remember little of it. In my mind, I had begun to rejoin the world. Unknown to Sparkie, I even kept a bottle of sherry hidden in my wardrobe and entertained the houseman on his rounds once more. It was time to be normal again. If I had believed playtime was over, now it was to begin again – or so I thought – and very soon I would be discharged.

When I eventually left hospital, it was without any sense of relief. For a week I was in a state of constant irritation. Most of my friends had left before me, there was hardly anyone I knew. Walking down the wards for the last time, it was like quitting a train full of strangers. I was also going to a strange place. My mother, profiting by my grandmother's small estate, had taken a mortgage on a small café and the spacious flat above it in the seaside town of Penarth; but I knew no one there. For the first time in her life she was able to provide a home for me and since the furniture was from our old home in Pontypridd, we sat beside the ancient Welsh dresser, the brass candlesticks and silver collier's lamp like a pair of exiles beside trappings from another land. But my mother was happy. She had her own place at last. She was brisk and cheerful, busy with the café, constantly coming upstairs to see how I was and bidding me to eat heartily. I discovered she was a good cook but I soon found I had no appetite.

Most of my clothes had been burnt. The few I had did not fit me. I walked a few streets to buy a blazer and flannels, several shirts. The trousers chafed my legs, the shirt collars were uncomfortable, the blazer felt like a suit of armour. I was still a pyjama person. For three days I did not go out again and when I did, it was to buy a thermometer. Within a week I found that if I walked up a hill, I had to sit down at the end of it. I disliked crowds, put off travelling on buses. I was morose and silent, and knowing no one I sat in parks watching children playing, solitary and alone. I seemed to be sweating continuously. Every time I went out, I had to change my underclothes.

My mother began to worry. There were long awkward silences. She had only just moved to Penarth and we had not registered with a doctor but she decided that my problems were psychological. There were jobs to be done in the café but I was so weak, I could not hammer in a nail. I joined the local library but there was nowhere to sit down, so I often returned without a book. I remained in a constant state of irritation. I felt I could never earn a living.

My mother said, 'You'll have to change your ideas like I've had to,' her eyes filling when she spoke.

I think she saw me as a permanent invalid.

'It's up to you to make the best of things,' she said.

This was the first of many admonitions which I would receive. When I returned to the hospital for a check-up, the physician scoffed at me when I mentioned my constant lassitude.

'It's the old story. You've got an institutionalised mentality. You've got to shrug it off. You're free!'

I had decided to give up probation and return to teaching, but the problems were enormous. First I had to satisfy the Ministry of Education that I was physically fit, but each day I grew wearier. I would begin to write a letter but the pen would trail off the page and I would end up doodling, the letter unfinished. I would open a book, read one page, change to another book and repeat the process, a trail of unread books lying beside my chair as I stared into space. I would look at myself in the mirror, seeing the tiredness in my own face; then I would sit for hours in a chair without moving, only to stand

272

up exhausted. My mother's worry increased. I went out of the flat more to relieve her of the burden of myself than anything else. One day I met the nursing sister from my ward quite by chance and asked her out for a drink. She had contracted tuberculosis herself when younger. She said she understood.

'It's an old problem,' she told me. 'You've simply got to pull yourself together.'

It seemed that all my life people had been telling me just that. But she offered concrete advice.

'You must exercise,' she said. 'Plan a routine.'

So I walked again, walked and walked. I pounded the seashore, mounted cliffs where I could see the hospital in the distance and stood there watching the ward lights come on as the daylight faded. It was not true that I was unconsciously wishing that I was back inside, safe within its protective custody. I hated hospital. I hated the enforced confinement, the exclusivity of the immensely unattractive world of men. I had spent most of my adult life in institutions, and they had no attraction for me. So I turned my back on the hospital, chose other routes. Once I went home to Pontypridd to stay with friends and now I walked measured paths and distances which I had known as a child and they also proved too much for me, depressing me even more. I would not accept the fact that I was an invalid, but now I grew weary in public houses even in the company of friends. I began to hate noise. I could not stand being jollied. I would arrange meetings with friends but I arrived late and left early, and seemed more and more to be on my own. I met one or two old patients. I asked them to tell me of their experiences. We have been through it, their smiles said; we know.

'What is it?'

'You've got to pull yourself together!' they said.

It was like a chorus.

Soon I found that I could not concentrate on anything for long; my mind would wander and I would begin to daydream, even to fall asleep with a book open upon my lap. I began to drink water in large quantities, a habit I suddenly developed. I grew irritable with myself. Fingers seemed continually to be pointing at me. My headmaster's voice returned with his constant admonitions.

'It's up to you now. The hospital has done its best.'

By chance, I met the registrar whose calm assurance had so comforted me over a year before. He had come to live nearby. He asked me to a party at his home. I did not mention my problems, but I suspect he knew them. I had grown to look anxious. I had been out of hospital for two months. This was the first social occasion I had attended in two years. I bought a new shirt, a new tie, and a new pair of shoes with an extravagance that was quite unlike me although I have known men and women who will spend their way out of a depression. I had no logical reason for being depressed, but I was depressed. The more I exercised, the worse I felt. I seemed to be continually filling glasses with tap water and everybody I consulted about my lethargy, general practitioner, physician, nursing sister, ex-patients, all told me the same thing. One man spoke seriously of the 'cage mentality' of returned prisoners of war, nodding gravely as if I shared the problem. I did not have Sparkie with me to hoot sardonically. The implication was unmistakeable. My problem sprang from an attitude of mind, my mind, and only I could solve it. The accusation was even in my mother's eyes as well as everybody else's, as if I were in some way lacking in moral fibre.

I spruced up for the party. I had spent so much time on my back that the soles of my feet had become as soft as a child's and all the walking served only to blister them. Then I had lent my head against a bedrail for so long that my hair began to thin imperceptibly where my head had lain. I seemed incapable of making correct judgements about the size of shirt collars or shoes. I walked with an ungainly lope, tugging at my neck, continually buttoning and unbuttoning jackets; but I would show them.

I can remember making an entrance at the party. The house was a converted farmhouse, one of the walls had been replaced with a large window making the room exceptionally light as if it were a painter's studio. There were women there in summer dresses, all strangers. There was no one there I knew, except the amiable registrar. His wife had answered the door. Now he left a group to come towards me, staring.

'What will you have to drink?' his wife said.

I did not have time to answer the question. Her husband led

274

me to the window, pulled down my eyelid, exclaimed, 'My God!'

My eyeballs were yellow, were to get yellower, like my entire body.

I had a severe infective hepatitis – yellow jaundice – the result of a defective blood transfusion during surgery.

I left the party at once and returned to hospital the same night. I never had that drink.

Of the next three months, incarcerated once more in a cubicle, I remember little that is worth recording. Put on a diet, I lost weight so rapidly that my flesh sagged. Later, so did my new blazer, while the flannel trousers flapped as if they had always belonged to someone else. My appetite disappeared completely and I had to be prevented from scratching myself and my lurid yellow body, but in case I should feel sorry for myself (just in case!), there was a man next door with the same condition together with some even more unwholesome complications whose hands were permanently bandaged and sometimes tied to the bed for the same reason. At night he was often led out naked on to the balcony to cool off, his condition incurable, and he died before I left the hospital. Strangely enough, once a diagnosis of my own condition had been made, I felt immensely relieved and no one was more expert at settling down to the familiar routine.

Once more I lay flat on my back but now the smell of my own urine was odious, my body completely yellow, the sight of me a challenge to any romantic novelist. I did not want any visitors at all, but I received one – an old face in a new role who came hurtling down the corridor to see me, his fleshy lips parting, that carrot top weaving and bobbing, his sardonic face now rank with health and his breath redolent of best bitter beer which he breathed delightedly over me. He soon began to wolf grapes, apples, all the fruit that I was allowed, before he dived knowledgeably into my locker.

'We've got fags, have we?'

It was Sparkie.

'How are you feelin' *in yourself*, my ole cocker?'

He had come to the hospital for a regular check-up and he had heard the news of my return from an orderly, whereupon he had come at once, on the run!

There was no one I would rather have seen that day. He wore tattered dungarees under a grey jacket and a red sports shirt several sizes too large for him. He also carried a carpenter's rule in his pocket. He was, he said, 'back on the tools', but what the tools were, I never knew, and he had clearly forgotten that he had once told me he invariably carried a rule or some identifiable tradesman's tools when burgling in case he should be required to explain his presence to some unworldly householder. He was in good spirits, and he was 'back with the bird, shacked up a treat'. He mentioned a public house on the edge of Tiger Bay long since pulled down where I might see him, and where there was always going to be a welcome for me. There, it went without saying, he would fix me up with a bit of skirt if I was short, as between old friends. He was one hundred per cent fit and all his worries were over, except – would you believe it? – he'd come with a mate in a van and the mate had left his wallet on the kitchen table, and they weren't quite sure if they had enough petrol. But, he wasn't asking me. There was an orderly down the ward who owed him a ten spot. The important thing was, I'd had a little upset and not to let the bastards grind me down!

He hadn't seen Monty, but he'd seen so-and-so, and his wife had left him, and he wasn't the only one, and did I know there was a big bust-up going on between the surgeons and the physicians and – worse – only the previous evening someone had whipped a young probationer nurse up to the doctors' quarters and Matron was playing hell?

It was as if, I thought, the hospital was waiting for Sparkie to feed it with all the gossip that lay dormant when he was not there. He attracted bad news and scandal, stirred up the muddy waters of the pool and flitted by like a dragonfly bearing the seeds of dismay which he scattered with delight the moment he had alighted. He stayed an hour, ignored the visitors' final bell, finished the fruit, the cigarettes, borrowed a thriller with a lurid cover – 'Your tastes have declined!' – and then he was gone.

But not before he had made a final diagnosis.

'Jaundice,' he said knowledgeably. 'You won't be able to have a good drink for a year, will you?'

And he was right again.

But now there was a difference. Within a month, I began to recover. My steps were firmer. I was lighter on my feet. I found the energy which I had lacked for so long. I still walked as we all did with that slight stoop, the protective elbow raised as if fearing a further assault upon my ribs. The days went by with a speed that was new to me. Very shortly I was about the hospital grounds every day, sunning myself. When I was finally discharged, I could have run down the long drive of the hospital and I soon lost my aversion to crowds. I could see. I could breathe. I could walk. I was free of pain. One day I even did a tap dance in the park.

Threads from the immediate past persisted. I was to see both Sparkie and Monty again, and for a time Sparkie appeared and reappeared in my life like a shadow, his hunched figure emerging from shop doorways, appearing mysteriously at bus stops or in the dark recesses of arcades. Once he jumped off a Cardiff tram as he saw me about to enter a timber store, immediately making himself ready to undercut both retailer and wholesaler.

'Bit of floor-boarding? I'll get you a lorry load any time, any size, and half the price!'

There was usually a snag, like delivery after dark.

I met Monty once in the bar of a large hotel where my orange juice caused his eyebrows to rise. He had no time to waste and was clearly involved in a deal. He looked altogether more elegant. He wore a natty suit of houndstooth check, a curly-brimmed brown trilby and kept shovelling a yellow silk handkerchief up his sleeve. He was sweating slightly and kept casting glances over his shoulder, like Sparkie did. I asked what he was doing. Perhaps I did not hear him correctly, or perhaps I misunderstood, or perhaps he was having me on.

'Got a bit of a deal on – Carmarthen.'

'Carmarthen?' It seemed such a sleepy old town, and not his style at all.

'Flogging a fire engine actually!' he said.

I watched him go. In the lobby he was joined by an older, more elegant woman than the one I had seen previously but he clearly did not want us to meet. I noticed his slight stoop which, like Sparkie's, had become more pronounced, and then he was gone from my life for ever. I heard later that he had refused to attend the hospital for check-ups and died in a 'flu epidemic. I last saw Sparkie in a white jacket pushing a hot-dog stand away from the crowds outside the Cardiff Arms Park on an international match day. He was moving away from me across the street and obviously down on his luck. I was close enough to see that his eyes were streaming, a cough causing him to bend double before he straightened himself. He was gone before I could cross the road to pursue him. When I turned into the gates of the rugby ground in the convivial company of old friends, it was as if I was moving into the future whereas he was heading inevitably for the past. I never saw him again and I heard that he too had died.

Earlier, a short story I had written years before was broadcast and, again quite by chance, I came across my old headmaster making his way through the Memorial Park in my home town. He was by then an invalid, heavily mufflered, his vocal chords much affected by cancer. He was an old, dying man. But he had heard the broadcast, and after pleasantries, he found his inevitable remark – that joshing humour that always succeeded in taking you down a peg or two.

'Scribbling now?' he said. 'Can't you earn a living any other way!'

High above us on the hillside stood the tall stone memorial to the dead of two world wars, the names of the regiments and battles of my long-dead relatives inscribed in stone; further away, just behind another mountain, lay the tombs of other ancestors, long overgrown. I had left them all and was never to return save as a visitor, an event that would once have seemed as extraordinary to me as does my survival now.

It was time to make another life for myself and I now began to practice as a writer, stealthily and by night. By and large, so much had – and, in a sense, had not – happened to me, it seemed the natural thing to do.